Six m
Six more
One UNIFO

Don't miss a sto
bestselling miniseries, featuring irresistible soldiers
from all branches of the armed forces.

Check out

FULL SURRENDER
by Joanne Rock
ebook November 2012

and

DISTINGUISHED SERVICE
by Tori Carrington
February 2013

UNIFORMLY HOT!

The Few. The Proud. The Sexy as Hell.

Dear Reader,

What happens when you take one sexy diner waitress, put her directly in the path of a hot Marine on leave, create a phosphorus-burning chemistry and then tell them they can't have sex? Well, read on...

In *Distinguished Service,* active duty Marine Mace Harrison is back in Colorado Springs for two purposes: to be awarded the Navy Star for courageous deeds he views as only doing his job, and to feel out old friend Darius Folsom's new security firm Lazarus, where he hopes to work in six months when he retires his uniform. What he doesn't bank on is meeting irresistible beauty Geneva Davis. They click on every level from the moment they meet. Problem is, Geneva is in no condition to get involved with anyone, and he is in no position to take on anyone in that condition. So they strike a bargain: pretend to date for the duration of his leave to clear out unwanted emotional clutter from their lives. A platonic arrangement that finds them exactly where they shouldn't be—setting fire to the bedroom sheets...

We hope you enjoy Mace and Geneva's blazing-hot, emotional journey toward sexily-ever-after. Curious about upcoming Tori titles? Visit www.facebook.com/toricarrington.

Here's wishing you love, romance and *hot* reading.

Lori Schlachter Karayianni and Tony Karayianni aka *Tori Carrington*

DISTINGUISHED SERVICE

BY
TORI CARRINGTON

First published in Great Britain 2013
by Mills & Boon, an imprint of Harlequin (UK) Limited,
Eton House, 18-24 Paradise Road, Richmond, Surrey TW9 1SR

© Lori and Tony Karayianni 2012

ISBN: 978 0 263 90295 2
ebook ISBN: 978 1 408 99656 0

14-0213

Harlequin (UK) policy is to use papers that are natural, renewable and recyclable products and made from wood grown in sustainable forests. The logging and manufacturing processes conform to the legal environmental regulations of the country of origin.

Printed and bound in Spain
by Blackprint CPI, Barcelona

RT Book Reviews Career Achievement Award-winning, bestselling duo Lori and Tony Karayianni are the power behind the pen name **Tori Carrington**. Their more than fifty novels include numerous Mills & Boon Blaze miniseries, as well as the ongoing Sofie Metropolis, P.I. comedic mystery series with another publisher. Visit www.toricarrington.net and www.sofiemetro.com for more information on the couple and their titles.

This book is dedicated to dear friends
Cris Gaytan Beck and Deb Leahy Dunphy, whom I
think of fondly every time I see my right foot:
You both are tattooed on my heart.

1

LAZARUS SECURITY WAS EXACTLY the type of well-oiled engine he could see himself willing to get his hands dirty with.

Mace Harrison squinted into the watery early November sunlight where he stood near the back of the training center strategically located behind the building. Everything at the company was top of the line, including personnel. Situated on several acres just outside Colorado Springs, Lazarus was an extraordinary operation that in a short time was already gaining notable momentum within the private security industry.

It was one of the reasons why he was there.

The other was Lazarus partner Darius Folsom.

He nodded at his old friend now.

How far did they go back? Fifteen years, at least. To the first time Mace's parents had shipped him and his older brother Marcus off to live with his paternal grandfather for the summer? Their military family had moved to yet another house in yet another city and he'd been young enough to need supervision, and old enough to cause trouble because he'd hated moving. And then there was his need to escape the shadow his brother cast that threatened to suffocate him. Dari and his family had lived around the block from his grandfather and he and Mace had become fast friends.

They'd enlisted in the Marines at around the same time—by that point Mace choosing to live at his grandfather's house, which offered him greater independence—but they hadn't been stationed together until the past year.

Darius Folsom had recently completed his second tour, but Mace still had a six-month stretch ahead of him. He was back home for a brief week break, investigating job opportunities, Lazarus at the top of the list.

Of course, it was also possible he'd take on that counterterrorism desk job he'd been offered in Washington, D.C.

And he was purposely ignoring the fact that he was also there to accept an award he didn't deserve and didn't want.

The Navy Cross…

A small bit of metal that might as well be the size of a Humvee as far as he was concerned.

Of course, some brave men and women went their entire lives without receiving such an honor.

He supposed he should feel guilty for not wanting it. But considering everything…well, many had made the ultimate sacrifice and received nothing more than a military burial.

How would his brother feel about the medal? He imagined Marcus would give him one of his trademark smirks and slap him hard on the back. "Still running after me, little bro? Think you'll catch up? You might want to pick up the pace."

Of course, Mace could only guess at what he'd say. Because Marcus wasn't there. Not anymore.

But Mace still felt shadow hands choking him from behind, a sensation that was even stronger when he was within a hundred miles of his parents.

A time like now.

"So what do you think?" Dari said hesitantly, after having given him the nickel tour of Lazarus Security, apparently having noticed the darkening of his expression.

"Impressive," Mace said, shaking off his thoughts although he knew better than to try to rid himself of the shadow; that would be there forever. "Very impressive."

Darius's grin was his response.

"Good job, old pal." Mace squeezed his shoulder. "This is really something. You can tell you've put a lot of work into it."

"Thanks."

It still amazed him that Dari drew such words close to heart. Oh, not from anyone. The big, tough Marine wasn't easily flattered. But when it came to his friends... Amazing. "Don't let the success go to your head," he teased now.

Dari laughed. "Don't worry. This is a joint endeavor and I had very little to do with the start-up. I was too busy overseas getting my ass shot and saved by someone we both know."

Mace grimaced as he glanced at his friend's leg. "You'd have made it out on your own."

"Maybe. Maybe not."

What went unsaid was that several of their team hadn't made it out.

And it was that incident that not only still gave Mace—and very likely Dari—nightmares, it was what had ultimately earned him that damn medal he'd be accepting at some sort of bigwig event that Saturday.

He wondered if it wasn't too late to hop onto the first transport out. He'd take full-on assault from enemy forces over what he was facing in days.

"That's how you earned it," Dari said.

"I was just doing my job."

"No, Mace, you always do more than your job."

"You'd have done the same."

"Would I have? I'd like to think I would. But I don't know. While I would have ultimately done what was needed, I would have likely hesitated that split second to assess the situation before diving in. You…" Dari fell silent, undoubtedly reflecting on that late afternoon in the mountains of Waziristan when they'd been lied to by villagers and surrounded by enemy forces the instant they were outside town. "You charged straight in, to hell with the consequences."

"Some would say that's stupid."

Dari squinted at him. "If you had hesitated, a leg wound would have been the least of my worries. And you'd have returned home to attend a very different event."

Mace didn't even want to consider that possibility. Not then, not now.

"What's done is done," he said. "I'd prefer it if everyone looked forward rather than back."

Dari half-smiled. "Yeah." He nodded. "Yeah."

Mace shifted his weight from one foot to the other, wishing the subject done.

"Come on," Dari said, seeming to pick up on his mindset. "Let's go into town and grab some grub. I've got a favor to ask. Oh, and I hope you don't mind, I told Megan we'd meet up with her at The Barracks afterward for a drink."

Mace nearly sighed audibly in relief. "Fine with me." He'd known Dari's wife since she was little more than the reason his friend bought acne cream when the occasional zit popped up on his face. He'd only been in town for a few days and he'd enjoy the chance to catch up with her, find out what both of them had been up to outside their working at Lazarus together.

"She'll be alone, right?" he asked, a thought occurring to him.

"What?"

Damn.

His friend had never been any good at lying. "Hell, Dari, I'm not in town for that long. I'd like to spend some time with my friends before heading back."

"Surely there's a little room for some friendly company."

"No. There isn't."

"Aw. She's a real sweetheart. I promise you'll like her."

That was the problem, he thought.

He didn't want to like anyone. Not right now. Not without knowing where he was going to land in six months, if, in fact, he landed at all.

Not after what had happened the last time he'd tried to make a long-distance relationship work.

"Sorry," Dari said. "I know you asked me not to do it. And I really haven't. It's Megan's idea. I know how you feel about people knowing your business, so while I made your feelings on the matter known to Meg, I didn't tell her why you felt that way. Without that…"

Without that, she couldn't understand why he was adamant about not dating while on this leave.

"You'll understand if I pass on that drink then," he said.

Dari looked disappointed, but finally he nodded.

They walked back to the main structure, passing armed recruits making their way out to the state-of-the-art shooting range along the way. He shared his friend's disappointment. He truly would have enjoyed having a beer with him and Megan tonight. But to be placed next to a woman hoping to be swept off her feet, one who looked at him with big doe eyes, who promised forever and then moved on to someone else while he was overseas…

No.

And that meant a long night stretched out in front of him with nothing to do but stare at his motel room walls.

He could go over to see his grandfather again, but he'd gotten into hot water with the nursing home attendants for having stayed past regular visiting hours once already. He didn't want to risk having his visitation privileges revoked.

His grandfather...

Mace grinned even as he shook his head. The old man had one foot in the grave and still somehow managed to chase around anything female like a spry twenty-year-old.

Well, okay, maybe a spry twenty-year-old with a walker.

He remembered their last conversation. "Give me something, kid," Dwayne Harrison had requested that morning. "Good-looking stud like you? Them skirts gotta be falling all over you. Surely you could send some sweet stuff my way."

Mace had merely smiled.

Oh, he planned to date again. Hopefully soon. Once he was able to get rid of the bad taste Janine had left in his mouth.

Of course, he could always go over and visit his parents. They'd settled back in his father's hometown five years or so ago when his dad finally retired.

Still, somehow, he didn't look at their house as home.

And the shadow hands tightened at the thought.

Dari cleared his throat. "I don't think I've had a chance to say it yet, but...well, I was sorry to hear about Janine. You deserve better than what she did to you."

Mace turned his head so quickly to stare at Dari, his neck cracked. It wasn't like his friend to mention something so personal in such a casual setting. At least, not without downing a few beers first.

"What?" Dari asked.

Of course, his friend couldn't know that Mace had no sooner switched his cell phone on after his flight than he'd received a voice mail from the woman in question. He'd stopped dead in the middle of the airport terminal, staring at the notification. He hadn't heard from her in nearly eight months. What could she possibly want now?

He'd found out soon enough. Her words still reverberated through his mind.

"Welcome home, Mace. I know I'm probably the last person you expected to hear from, but... Well, I just wanted to say I'm sorry...again. And to tell you I'd love to see you while you're in town. Call me...please."

Curiously, hearing her voice hadn't moved him in the least. But her apology and her request to see him again had elicited a very specific response: Hell no.

He opened the door and stepped aside so his friend could precede him inside. "Something tells me you're getting a bit soft around the middle."

Dari rubbed a rock-hard six-pack.

"Not that middle."

They chuckled and walked back to Dari's office in the front of the building.

While Mace could make light of his relationship woes when the situation called for it, there was nothing but heaviness in his heart at the memory of Janine's betrayal.

"So, Rocky's Diner after I close up shop here."

He nodded. "Rocky's Diner. Meet you there in an hour."

They shook hands and gave each other a bro hug. Then Mace headed out to the parking lot where his rental car waited, trying not to think about Janine...or the phone call he'd gotten from her that morning.

He failed.

GENEVA DAVIS TOOK three meat loaves out of the industrial oven, swiping the back of one of the oven mitts across her brow after placing the last on the stainless-steel counter. Two of the kitchen staff had called in sick this afternoon, leaving her and one of the other waitresses to pick up the slack at Rocky's Diner. Monday's Meat Loaf Mania was one of their busiest nights when all staff was present. Handling it with two people short was going to make the evening hell on earth.

Trudy Grant, the mercurial owner who was a combination of Betty White witty cuteness and Bea Arthur brashness, hung up the phone on the wall near the door. "Cindy just called in." She shook her head. "This damn flu is going to put me out of business."

Make that three people short.

Of course, Trudy's proclamation was an exaggeration; something or other was going to put her out of business at least three times a day. Still, somehow she'd managed to keep the diner's heart beating for the past twenty years when she'd bought the previous owner out.

Tiffany, the other waitress, breezed by with warm pies to stock the counter displays in the other room. "Cindy ain't sick. Cindy has a blind date tonight."

Geneva shared a smile with Mel, the main cook, but didn't say anything as she slid off the mitts and gave the large pot of homemade mashed potatoes a stir. As expected, Trudy went off like a bomb, filling the kitchen with inventive curse words. Everyone moved around her, giving her the wide berth she required. They all knew the steam would dissipate and Trudy would be operating on full throttle again soon without risk of being scalded.

Geneva moved around Mel, where he tossed burgers, to turn off the alarm for the French fries. She took the basket out of the oil and hung it on the rungs above to drain.

"Oh, and Gen?" Tiffany poked her head back inside the kitchen. "Your Baby Daddy Dustin just took up residence in his usual place at the counter,"

Geneva stood perfectly still for a moment, staring unseeingly at the golden potatoes, battling back a sudden surge of nausea.

"You okay?"

She glanced at where Mel had leaned in to quietly ask the question.

"Yeah. Fine." She smiled. "Thanks."

She removed her hand from where it lay against her stomach, a spot she often found it resting lately, and then tipped the fries out onto two plates and salted them.

Lately, it was getting harder and harder to face Dustin. She didn't know how to explain in a way that would register with him that just because she was pregnant, it didn't mean they were a couple. And that she didn't expect anything more from him but to be a good dad. But he seemed determined to make something out of nothing. And his unwanted attention was eroding what had once been a great friendship.

A friendship that had accidentally become more for five whole minutes a little over two months ago.

It wasn't that the sex had been bad…

Okay, maybe it had been.

But that wasn't the reason she didn't want to be anything more than a joint parent with him. They were friends—period.

And the one-nighter had happened on the day she'd buried her mother in the ground and her sadness in a bottle of tequila.

"I remember my wife couldn't even keep crackers down during her first try," Mel said, putting two cheeseburgers onto buns and then handing the plates to her.

"Thankfully I haven't been sick once." She smiled as she dressed both burgers and then balanced all four plates on her arms. "I only feel like I'm going to be."

All…the…time.

Trudy gathered her wits. "With my luck, your first time will be all over one of the tables. A full one."

"Knock wood," Geneva said, edging through the swinging doors to deliver the burgers to Table 6, passing Tiffany as she went.

"Trade you Table 7 for 3," the too-pretty nineteen-year-old said.

That meant there was someone male and attractive at Table 7, one grouped in her regular station. She didn't even glance that way. Instead she took in Table 3. A crowd of rowdy teenagers.

"Pass."

"I'll share the tip with you. Fifty-fifty."

Geneva kept walking.

"And you can keep the other tip."

She let her silence speak for her.

She genuinely didn't have it in her to deal with the other table just then. Not after pulling a double shift and working all last night to get in a rush job to design a last-minute sales flyer for Johnny's Jalopies car dealership.

She said hello to Dustin as she passed without stopping to hear what he might have to say, then waited with a smile for the couple at Table 6 to move their joined hands before placing the burgers and fries down in front of them.

"Anything else I can get you for now?" she asked.

"Ketchup," the girl asked.

"On the table."

"Oh. Thanks."

"Are the pies fresh?"

"Always. Today there's blueberry, apple and, of course, Trudy's chocolate marshmallow."

"I'll take a piece of the blueberry," the girl said.

"And I'll have Trudy's," the guy added.

"Very good. You want them now or after you've finished?"

"Now."

"After."

"I can do both," Geneva said.

She got the coffeepot, which unfortunately happened to be near where Dustin sat, and the blueberry pie. After delivering the pie, she moved on to Table 7, filling the two cups that had been turned up to indicate coffee would be appreciated.

"Welcome...gentlemen."

Wow.

Okay, so she didn't normally agree with Tiffany's taste in men, which seemed to run from blond kids with mohawks to tattooed motorcyclists. But this time, the fickle teen was spot on.

She recognized Darius Folsom. He came in to the diner often enough and was a great guy along with a great-looking one.

But his tablemate was new.

And he was hotter than a July Colorado Springs day.

She silently cleared her throat. Not that she was interested. After all, she was an expectant mother. But she did still have a pulse.

And, apparently, a sex drive. Something she hadn't anticipated, given her condition. Which probably explained her unusual, spellbound response.

Just looking at this guy made her think of sweaty sighs and hungry kisses.

"Hi, Geneva," Dari said with a smile. "It's crazy in here tonight."

She made an effort to ignore her curiously overwhelming chemical reaction to his friend. "It always is. What can I get for you today?"

"Meat loaf, of course."

She looked at his guest...and nearly lost her breath.

God, did eyes come any browner?

And the way he was looking at her...

"Well, if he's game, so am I. Meat loaf."

She smiled, probably bigger than the situation called for.

"Meat loaf it is, then. Are you sticking with the coffee? Or would you like to add something else?"

"Milk," Dari said. "A nice, big cold glass."

"Make that two."

"You got it."

She turned from the table feeling something other than nausea stir her stomach. It was a welcome change. Not overly so—while she wasn't and had never really been involved with Dustin, she wasn't shopping either—but nice nonetheless. It had been a long time while since she'd felt anything other than expecting.

"I hate you," Tiffany said as they passed again.

"I love you," she said back and then disappeared into the kitchen.

She leaned briefly against the wall inside, savoring the very female feelings while she could. She knew better than anyone that she'd soon have to nip them in the bud.

"You all right?" Mel asked after seeing her face. "You look a little flushed."

"What? Oh, yes. I'm fine. It's just hot in here."

How long had it been since she'd experienced that unmistakable spark of attraction? Long enough for her to have forgotten what it felt like. Even though she knew exactly how long: since before her mother fell ill a year and a half ago.

She briefly closed her eyes, willing the sudden cold away.

How alive it made her feel, that spark of shared attraction. Hot summer sunshine seemed to course through her veins even though it was a chilly and rainy November day. And twenty pounds at least had been lifted from her feet.

"It's not like you to waste time daydreaming," Trudy said as she passed with a mop.

Geneva blinked.

No, it wasn't like her.

And like that, the moment to nip the sexy sensations had arrived. Time to return to the real world where sexy strangers didn't exist.

Damn.

2

"I KNOW YOU SAID you don't plan to be in town long, but about that favor I wanted to ask…" Dari said.

Mace found himself following the pretty waitress with his eyes. She was all curly light brown hair, tanned skin and long legs, even in the unattractive white orthopedic shoes she wore.

He bet her thighs were toned and strong and could grip his hips like nobody's business.

And that mouth…

"Hmm?"

He looked to find Dari grinning at him.

"Thought you weren't interested in dating," his friend said, indicating the waitress.

"I'm not." He sipped his coffee, which was surprisingly good for diner fare. "I might, however, be interested in getting laid."

Dari howled with laughter. "I stand corrected."

"You're sitting, but I get your point." He put his cup down. His words were meant as a joke, but just barely. The waitress did stir something in him he hadn't felt in a while. And while it was physical, there was more to it. There was a genuine quality to her smile, a kindness. "Are you really asking for a favor already? I've been in town, what?" He looked at his watch. "Five minutes?"

"I meant to ask you the first minute."

Dari's expression, more than his words, got Mace's attention. It wasn't like his friend to exaggerate. Whatever he was going to ask was important.

In his career in the military, Mace had come to understand how important it was to immediately recognize who he could count on...and, more importantly, who he couldn't.

Going back to their teenage years, he'd always been able to depend on Dari.

He grimaced, wishing his friendship skills extended to relationships. Maybe he would have had better luck.

His hand instantly went to his cell phone where another voice mail waited from Janine. He didn't expect it to be much different from the first one.

"Shoot," he encouraged now.

"Okay. I've given you a brief rundown on how quickly Lazarus has grown in such a short time. And with that, comes growing pains. Most notably, we're attracting some high-profile contracts I'm sometimes afraid we're not prepared for yet. This one falls solidly into that category." He paused. "There's an ex-general, now a political radio pundit, coming into town the day after tomorrow for a three-day stay, including two public rallies. We've been hired to handle security for the public end of his schedule—transportation, et cetera—in cooperation with his personnel and local law enforcement. While I'm sure we can handle it, well, it would be stupid not to utilize our assets. And I see you as a definite asset in this case, what with your background and your connections."

He nodded. "Go on."

"Well, in a nutshell, I was wondering if you would consider sitting in as co-lead on this one?"

Mace sat back, carefully considering what Dari was saying...and not saying. His friend went on to share some additional details, such as the name of the dignitary. He was familiar with the guy. Hell, nearly everyone in the western hemisphere was familiar with him, if only because of his skill at gaining attention, usually by exhibiting offensive behavior.

"Okay, I get the military connections and the growing pains. But this job sounds pretty run-of-the-mill, tooling around with a political celebrity. What is it you're not telling me?" Mace asked.

"There have been threats."

"Threats."

"Yes. Specific to his visit here."

For the past few years, Mace's military career focus had been counter-terrorism, so this was right up his alley. But...

"And...?" he led.

Dari chuckled and pointed a finger at him. "Never could get anything by you. Truth is, these threats are serious enough to concern his security personnel and serious enough to concern me." He checked the cell phone he had on the table next to his wrist. "And...well, if I'm hoping that by pulling you in on this job, it'll convince you to sign on with us when your tour's over in six months... that's between me and the wall."

Mace considered him.

Dari grinned. "Did I mention that it won't hurt business to have a Navy Cross recipient on board with us? No? Well, then there's that."

He grimaced at the reminder.

"By the way, Megan and I are looking forward to attending the ceremony Saturday."

"You're going?"

"Of course, I'm going. My ass is part of the reason you're getting the sucker. What makes you think I wouldn't be there?"

He took a deep breath.

"I plan to sit up front and center."

"Refill, gentlemen?" a knockout blonde smiled at him suggestively as she held up a coffeepot.

Mace found himself looking for the pretty brunette even as he and Dari held up their cups. The waitress topped them off then hovered for a moment before finally moving away.

"You didn't even look at her," Dari said.

"Sure I did. She's too young and too…"

"Eager?"

"That, too."

They shared a laugh.

"Okay," he said.

"Okay what?"

"Okay, I'll do it. Where do you want me when?" He laughed and looked around the diner again.

There she was.

He found himself relaxing in to the booth as the waitress who'd garnered his attention came through the kitchen door looking even more attractive.

She brought their meals quickly despite the busyness of the place. They ate while Dari outlined the specifics of the assignment.

This beat the hell out of staring at the cracks in his motel room ceiling, feeling guilty about not spending more time at his parents' any day.

And it made him forget about those shadow hands pressing against his neck for a much-needed while.

Mace's gaze followed their waitress where she bussed the table next to theirs, even as another couple moved to occupy it. She was calmly efficient and attentive, smiling warmly despite the obvious crowdedness of the diner as she took their drink orders.

He couldn't help noticing that there was a guy about his age seated at the counter who kept trying to get her attention for more than a second at a time...and that she did everything politely possible to avoid giving it to him.

She briefly glanced in his direction and their gazes met, inspiring something a little more than respect in his response to her.

He smiled and she returned it before she moved on to another table then went back into the kitchen.

Oh, he'd bet she was the type who'd be up for anything, any time. A challenge, a new experience, a new restaurant, it wouldn't matter; she'd be in...and make it doubly worth it just by being there.

"Okay, I'd better get moving," Dari said, edging from the booth. "Megan's already at The Barracks." He stood, pocketing his cell phone. "Thanks for agreeing to come in on this job for me, Mace. You have no idea how much of a relief it will be having you aboard."

"You haven't seen what I charge for babysitting a political big mouth yet."

"Whatever it is, I'm sure you'll be more than worth it." He peeled off a couple bills to pay for his half of the meal. "Sure you won't change your mind and join us for a drink?"

"I'd rather step directly into enemy fire."

"I believe you would." They shook hands and agreed to meet at Lazarus the following morning, then Dari left.

Mace sipped on his coffee and watched his friend through the front window of the diner, even as more customers approached.

He glanced around. The place was more than busy, it bordered on chaotic. At different times, he was aware of a woman swearing in the kitchen, a couple of tables complaining about the lateness of their meals and from what he could tell, there wasn't a busboy to be found.

His cell phone vibrated in his pocket. He fished it out to find Janine's name highlighted again. He sat and watched the screen blink until her call finally rolled over to voice mail.

Why was she being so persistent?

He couldn't even begin to guess. So he didn't try.

He slid the cell back into his pocket without checking the message.

"Dessert?" the pretty waitress asked.

He looked up at her. Despite everything, she managed to treat him as if he was her only customer, where the other waitress practically shooed people from the tables the instant they took their last bite.

"Trudy's chocolate marshmallow pie is the house specialty."

He took her in, noticing how the world seemed to rush around her in a blur while she stood perfectly still.

Of course, that could be just him.

The vintage jukebox in the corner. Definitely the jukebox. He'd play a song—an old one—pull her into his arms...lean her against the machine and work his hand up her skirt to find out just how sweet those thighs and what lay between them were...watch her smile melt into a sexy sigh.

"Maybe later," he said.

He didn't detect any flicker of disappointment that he wasn't leaving to free up the table for another diner.

"And only if you promise to have a piece with me. It'll be my price for having leant a hand…"

THREE HOURS LATER, Geneva was even more impressed with Mace Harrison than when he had first slid from the booth, introduced himself, then asked for an apron and bussing tub.

What guy did that?

None that she knew of.

And certainly not a complete stranger. She'd verified he was new in town since none of the staff nor Trudy could remember seeing him in there before, much less knew him.

And certainly not a completely hot stranger who made her feel like a wanted woman instead of the host of other titles to which she'd grown accustomed lately.

Refusing his generous offer hadn't even entered her mind. Truth was, they were busier than she could ever remember being and Trudy's usually easily dismissed sounds of dismay had begun turning into very real ones.

Mace had been as good as gold, a natural as Mel had noted, his sheer size and impressive presence not interfering with his assisting without being asked, and doing at least two of the jobs for which they were short staffed, lightening the load for the rest of them.

Was he military? She guessed yes. And that normally would have counted as a strike against him in her personal notebook, considering her experience with members of the armed forces.

But what had happened tonight was anything but normal.

And what was happening to her fell solidly into the same category.

Finally, one by one, satisfied customers began to ease to a workable trickle, and then the staff began to leave, including Trudy herself, who begged off with a migraine. Thankfully, Dustin had given up trying to corner her an hour ago and left, as well. Only Mel remained. But seeing as closing time was in ten minutes, he had only one order to finish up and she knew he'd be leaving, too, as he always did to get home quickly to his wife and family.

Now, as Mace stood spraying dishes to go into the washer, she couldn't help staring at his hands. He'd rolled up the sleeves of his crisp white shirt while the full-body white apron covered the front from his chest down to his knees. If his feet hurt in his dress shoes, she couldn't tell, even though he'd been on his feet all night.

Her own dogs were barking loudly and she wore the equivalent of gym shoes.

Geneva absently wrapped up the little that remained of the meat loaf and mashed potatoes, not realizing she was still staring at Mace until he asked, "Did I spill something?"

She met his gaze, reading the telltale grin there, then smiled herself. "Sorry. It's been a long day."

Tiffany had left in a huff about the same time Dustin had, apparently disappointed that her obvious flirting wasn't gaining her any more attention from the unhired help than Mel got.

Actually, Geneva was pretty sure she'd gotten less.

Interesting. Not many men were capable of refusing the pretty blonde's charms at normal speed, much less when she amped them up. And she'd definitely set her sights on Mace.

A few minutes later, Mel removed his apron and grabbed his jacket. "Well, it's that time again, kids."

Geneva held up the paper bag she'd readied for him and he took it, giving her a loud kiss on the cheek.

"Thanks, doll. See you on the morrow."

"Tell Alice hi."

"Will do. 'Night."

"'Night."

And just like that it was only her and Mace.

Well, and three people at two tables in the other room.

He finished up the dishes while she closed the last of the garbage bags then washed her hands.

"How about that pie?" he asked.

"How about it? Take a seat at the counter. I'll join you in a minute."

"Deal."

She watched as he did as suggested, trying hard not to stare at his tight rear end and failing.

All right, she could be forgiven this once, right? For being selfish? For being needy?

For being a woman?

She went about wrapping up and putting away a few other items. It had been a long day. Still, strangely she didn't feel tired.

She peeked around the window that opened up into the dining area, catching Mace's gaze.

"Be right there," she said.

"Take your time."

She ducked back away and caught her breath.

Okay, she could do this. All she had to do was serve him pie and coffee and tell him she was pregnant. That was sure to douse whatever spark had ignited between them but quick.

Only she was hoping it wouldn't...

3

MACE CLEANED UP after the last of the customers, then fed change into the vintage jukebox that had remained pretty much silent all night, selecting a few '50s classics before sitting back down at the counter. He glanced at his watch. Twenty minutes had passed since Geneva had said she'd be right there. He'd noticed an employees' locker room off the kitchen and guessed she'd taken advantage of it. He realized he was still wearing the borrowed apron and took it off, laying it on the stool next to him.

The past few hours had passed in a welcome flurry of activity. The best decision he'd made was to trade his night of motel sitting for lending a hand at the busy diner. He'd never done very well left with too much time on his hands. And even he could jog only so long before his muscles protested.

Bussing tables and doing dishes and occasionally filling coffee cups had given him something productive to do. And feeling like a part of a team hadn't hurt.

If Geneva's gratefully surprised and sinfully sexy smile every now and again had anything to do with his sense of satisfaction, he wasn't copping to it.

"Sorry," she said, finally coming out of the kitchen. "I just wanted to finish a few things up."

He blinked. She still wore the same gray uniform and ruffled white apron, but she looked…different somehow. Refreshed. And hotter than hell.

She put down something in a bag and then moved to the pie case while he rounded the other side of the counter.

"Coffee?" he asked, holding up a pot.

"I'd love a cup of decaf."

"One decaf coming up."

He poured two cups and placed them on the counter while she took not one, but four different pie plates out of the display case. Each held at least two pieces. She reached into the fridge and pulled out a can of whipped cream, placing it next to them.

He sat down and she took the stool beside him.

He was abnormally taken with the can of whipped cream; the thought of licking a line of it off her skin from collarbone to toes, stopping for longer stays along the way that seemed particularly tempting.

He wondered what she'd say if he suggested it…

"I figured since you wouldn't let Trudy pay you, you're entitled to as much pie as you want." She handed him a fork.

"Part of the deal was that you join me."

She held up her own fork.

He chuckled, watching as she dug into what he guessed was the chocolate marshmallow one. Damn, but she had a sexy mouth. What made it even sexier still was that she didn't appear the least bit aware of the effect she was having on him.

"So, tell me," she said around a bite, "are you from around these parts, soldier?"

He chose the blueberry. "In a manner of speaking, yes."

"Dubious answer to a yes or no question."

To his surprise, he found himself explaining his being a military brat and staying with his grandfather as a teen. Even more surprising was the casual way in which he did so. He wasn't usually given to sharing information with anyone. But she made it easy, her face open, her interest unselfish.

There was something strangely…intimate about sitting, just the two of them, in an empty retro diner, '50s music playing on a jukebox, the street beyond the front windows quiet and dark.

Even as they talked, he watched her eat, something he found strangely erotic. He couldn't remember enjoying watching a woman eat. Then again, he could barely recall a woman eating in his presence, unless she was a colleague or a friend.

But watching Geneva savor the blueberry pie didn't qualify as either.

"Which branch?" she asked after he'd fallen silent for a moment, reflecting on what he'd said; reflecting on her.

"What?"

"Which branch did you choose?"

"Marines."

"Same as your father?"

He paused. "No."

Curious, he'd forgotten having chosen a different path than his parent.

Funny how things worked out.

"I can relate." She got up. "I could go for a glass of milk. How about you?"

Surprisingly, the idea appealed to him. "Sure."

She poured them two large glasses then sat down again.

"I take it that means you're from around here in a manner of speaking, as well?" he asked.

She nodded, then licked a milk mustache from her upper lip. Mace felt his pants tighten at the innocent move.

"I followed...someone here five years ago. I've been looking for a way out ever since."

"He still around?"

She smiled. "Who said it was a guy?"

"I did."

Her smile widened. "No, he was history two months in."

For reasons he couldn't be sure of, he was glad that not only was the guy part of her past, but she didn't seem to have a problem with leaving him there. "Where are you from originally?"

"Ohio. Toledo. Whipped cream?"

She shook the can and then held it above the pies.

Mace felt the urge to reposition the tip above her lips so he might kiss it from them.

"Sure," he said instead.

"Tell me when..."

She began spraying...

And spraying...

Covering what remained in all of the pie pans.

"When?" she asked.

"Huh?"

She stopped spraying and laughed. The sound was deep and husky...and made him want to kiss her all the more.

"I was waiting for you tell me when."

He chuckled and switched his attention to the cherry pie, taking an extra-big bite to assuage the growing desire to run his fingers up her knee, which was left nicely bare by her skirt.

"So tell me about the other guy," he said.

She held a hand under her cream-dripping fork as she moved it toward his mouth. "What guy?"

He began to refuse the bite of chocolate marshmallow

pie, or rather her offering of it, then did the opposite by opening his mouth instead.

"The one at the counter panting after you all night," he said with his mouth half full.

"Dustin? Dustin doesn't pant. He moons." The smile eased from her face and she suddenly avoided his gaze.

Then she appeared to make her mind up about something and her expression opened up again.

She brushed her hands together then went to the register, taking out a handful of change. The jukebox had gone silent while they talked.

"Any requests?"

"B-17."

She laughed.

He liked that she got the reference.

"Who sang that song?" she asked. "No, wait…don't tell me. I'll get it."

"I'd tell you if I knew. Female, I know that."

"Olivia Newton-John."

"Yeah…yeah. I think you're right."

She made her selections then came to sit down again. "I know I'm right. B-17 is the song."

They shared a laugh as she picked up her fork again.

God, but he couldn't remember a time he'd enjoyed an evening more. Her easygoing demeanor, sexy smile and revitalizing openness made Geneva great company.

And, he hoped, great in bed.

"So, does it always get that insane in this place?" he asked.

"You'd be surprised by how popular Meat loaf Mondays are." She smiled and licked her fork. "It's usually pretty busy all the time, but right now the flu is knocking down a few more staff than usual." She sipped her milk, reminding him of a kitten lapping cream. "Well, that and blind dates."

"Excuse me?"

"One of the missing waitresses had a blind date, I guess. At least that's the rumor." She toyed with a bit of crust. "I hope it's not true or Trudy might fire her."

"Can she afford to?"

"Afford to or not, she will. Trudy's funny that way. You could break every glass in the place, but if you're honest and here on time, she'll keep you on."

"I'm thinking honesty is important in a business of this nature."

"Yeah." The song changed from an upbeat to a slow tune on the jukebox. "So how long are you in town?"

"A week."

The reminder of why he was back here was enough to loosen the fit of his pants a bit, but not much.

"You staying with family?"

He shook his head. "Nah. Bunking at the motel on University. You?"

"I live here."

He chuckled. "Right. Sorry."

"My mom and I did live together for a while, though..."

Something in her voice captured his attention.

She cleared her throat. "She passed a little over two months ago."

"I'm sorry to hear it." Damn. Talk about a pants-loosening change in conversation.

"Thanks. She was sick for a long time. Lymphoma. She was diagnosed shortly after she moved here."

He didn't know what to say, so he said nothing.

They ate in silence for a while.

Then she leaned back and groaned. "God, I can't believe I ate so much of this. I feel like I'm going to burst."

Mace looked at where they'd nearly polished off all four

pies. "I can't believe it, either. Although I think I have a ways to go before I reach bursting stage."

She smiled. "I may have room for a bite or two more."

Geneva Davis was unlike any woman he'd met in a good long while. By now, most of the women he usually dated would have checked their lipstick at least twice and made one run to the ladies' room to check on the rest of their appearance.

Of course, he allowed that this wasn't much like a date, either.

Still…

"Are you career?" she asked.

"Military? Nah. Six months to go."

He found it interesting he'd answered in the negative. When had he made the decision not to sign up for another tour?

Just then, he realized. No matter what happened at Lazarus this week, he knew he didn't want to exchange active duty for a desk job in Washington.

"Thank you," he said.

"For what?"

"For asking me that. I didn't know what my answer would be until you did."

"You were considering staying longer?"

"I was."

"But not anymore."

He took in her pretty face. "Not anymore."

His cell phone vibrated at the same time hers rang.

They laughed. Mace took his out of his pocket even as she consulted hers.

Janine.

Damn.

He refused the late-hour call and put the cell back into his pocket, watching as she pretty much did the same thing.

Then she began toying with the crust again.

"Someone you don't want to hear from?" he asked.

She nodded. "You?"

"Yeah."

Then, surprisingly, he found himself telling her all about Janine and what had gone down eight months earlier.

He couldn't be sure how long he'd talked, or exactly how much he'd revealed, but she'd patiently listened, nodding when the situation called for it, making encouraging sounds when he needed them.

"So...just to be sure I'm following you," she said once he finally stopped talking and teetered on the verge of regret for having said too much. "She not only left you for someone else because you were gone too long... She was messing around with him while you were still a couple, even introducing him as a friend to you during your last leave and including him in things you did together.... And now that you're back, she wants to see you again?"

He grimaced. "That would be the long and the short of it, yes."

"How do you feel about that?"

He raised his brows and leaned back. "I don't know."

And he didn't. Not really.

He did know he didn't want to get involved with her again.

She fell silent.

"And your phone call?" he asked.

She blinked up at him. "Huh?"

He repeated the question.

"Oh. Dustin."

"Ah. The panter."

"The mooner." She rested her chin in her hand, her elbow propped against the counter. "Or, as the rest of the diner staff like to call him, my baby daddy."

She tilted her head slightly to look at him as if waiting for his response.

"Oh. You have a child together."

"No. Not yet."

He squinted at her. "Now I'm not sure I'm following you."

She looked away as if weighing whether or not to continue, then met his gaze fully, her chin coming up a tad higher than before. "I'm pregnant...and he's the father...."

4

THERE. SHE'D said it.

Geneva paid an inordinate amount of attention to the crust she was pushing in and out of the whipped cream that remained in the chocolate marshmallow pie pan. By rights, she should have said something much sooner. The minute they'd sat down at the counter. Maybe even found a way to casually mention it early on. Something along the lines of, "Gee, I can't remember my feet ever hurting this badly when I wasn't pregnant," or "Boy, if I wasn't pregnant, I'd take you back to my place and do all the naughty things I see playing out behind your sexy eyes."

She couldn't be sure why she'd been hesitant to say anything.

Yes, she could; she knew exactly why she hadn't shared the news: because for that short time, she'd enjoyed being just her. Just a single woman enjoying flirting with a hot, single man.

"You're...pregnant?"

The two words broke through her reverie. She tried to decide whether the emotion behind them was more of shock or regret, but all she seemed capable of concentrating on was now that the proverbial cat was out of the bag, there was no getting it back in. You couldn't exactly retract something like that. Pretend you were joking.

And why would she? For a frivolous, albeit surely hot night between the sheets with a handsome stranger?

Wasn't that how she'd ended up as a single, expectant mother in the first place?

She grimaced and found herself eating the crust, even though she hadn't intended to.

Comparing what had happened between her and Dustin two months ago and...well, tonight, was like saying the satin of a wedding dress and the satin that lined a coffin were the same.

She drank the rest of her milk to help wash the crumbs down.

"Yes," she said simply.

Mace sat back as if stepping out of the path of a speeding truck. Not that she could blame him. Essentially, that's what she was, wasn't she?

Not that she viewed her baby in that light. While unexpected, she'd instantly grown attached to the idea of having a child growing within her. Her son or daughter. And meeting him or her topped the list of things she most looked forward to.

When it came to the opposite sex seeing her as dating material, however...well, she could understand how that would come as a major deterrent.

Was there such a thing as a pregnant-woman fetish?

She nearly laughed at the ridiculous thought.

What man in his right mind would want to make love to a woman already pregnant with another man's child.

"So, you two were...are a couple?"

She blinked to look at him. "Dustin and I? No. We've always been just friends."

He nodded slowly but she could tell he was not only not

following her, he was so far behind he couldn't make her out in the distance.

She propped her chin in her hand and tried to explain. Not that the confusing story was all that clear to her.

Taking care of her mother while her illness had slowly ultimately robbed her of the tiniest breath had hollowed Geneva out until sometimes it seemed only her beating, hurting heart remained. Her friends and everyone at the diner had been a tremendous source of support, but only she knew how deep her pain went. How watching her mom die by millimeters had profoundly impacted her.

Yes, she could have put her mom in a hospice. But she'd wanted to spend every moment with her that she could. And the only way she could work out how to do that was by having Hospice come to them at her apartment.

Then, suddenly, her mother was gone.

It still seemed…strange, somehow. The shock she'd felt at not having her mother there anymore. She'd been moving toward that end agonizing moment by agonizing moment, yet the moment she was finally released, Geneva hadn't wanted to let her go.

And Dustin had been there to hold on to instead.

"We met when I first started taking graphic design years ago at University of Colorado, Colorado Springs," she offered. "We'd always been friends and had never even considered dating," she said quietly. "And I know he doesn't want anything more now. Not really. He's projecting what he thinks traditionally should happen on to our untraditional circumstances. Trying to do what's right."

She looked to find Mace still nodding…and still somewhat behind her.

Finally, he smiled awkwardly and shook his head. "I'm sorry. My response probably falls just shy of rude…or is maybe full-out rude. It's just that I'm having a hard time wrapping my head around the fact that you're pregnant."

She smiled. "Stick around. It won't be hard in a month or so when I start showing."

She caught herself. Of course, he wouldn't be around in a month or so. He'd be off somewhere on his final six-month deployment. And even if he wasn't, there was no chance he'd stick around anyway.

She squinted at him. Was there?

Behind him, the jukebox clicked on B-17.

They both laughed.

"Okay," he said. "Time for me to stop acting like an idiot and accept the fact that I misread the signs."

"Signs?"

His gaze moved over her face and she felt herself blush. "Yes. The regular girl-guy stuff."

She smiled. "You didn't misread anything. I'm pregnant, not dead, Mace."

He wore that "speeding truck coming toward him" look again.

She reached over and touched his arm. "Sorry. You're obviously having a hard time with this. So why don't we just keep this simple." She held out her hand. "Hi, I'm Geneva Davis and I'm pregnant. Would you like to be friends?"

He stared at her hand, then her face, then her hand again. He slowly took it. "I'd love to be friends, Geneva Davis."

FRIENDS…

A good ten hours had passed since his late-night conversation with Geneva in the deserted diner, the jukebox playing in the background, whipped cream, pie plates and glasses of milk littering the counter in front of them, and all he could think of was, despite everything she told him, he wanted to be much more than friends.

"Sir?"

Mace looked at Jonathon Reece, one of Lazarus's personnel.

"Darius would like to speak with you." He held out a cell.

He took the phone. "Thanks."

He stepped away from the table in the downtown Denver hotel conference room. He'd been in there for an hour going over the sketchy schedule of the visiting dignitary with Lazarus reps and sheriff's deputies, waiting for Darius to arrive.

"Hey," he said into the phone.

"Hey, yourself. Look, I got called in on an urgent matter back at the office. Would you mind taking the lead?"

Mace glanced at the ten Lazarus reps, nine men and one woman, who were looking expectantly at him.

"I'm afraid it looks like it would be for the duration. I've got a kidnapping/ransom case out of L.A. that just came in...." Darius continued.

Mace grimaced. Not because he wasn't up for the job. But because he would only have today to build up a rapport with the personnel he would be overseeing.

He took in Reece standing military tall a short ways away.

"I'd rather not. Isn't there someone else you trust? How about Reece?"

"He's good, but I need someone with more experience. And I'm not talking security. One of Norman's reps will be there in an hour. He'll give you a full rundown of what we're looking at threat-wise. And the sheriff's office already has several routes mapped out."

"I've seen them."

"Good." Dari said something to someone on his end of the line. "I really wouldn't ask this of you unless it was absolutely necessary, Mace. I'd owe you big-time."

"Last check, your debt is already considerable."

Dari chuckled. "Got me there. Tell you what, I'll name my firstborn after you..."

Mace held the phone to his ear even after he'd signed off, the mention of children bringing Geneva back to mind.

Why, oh why, did she have to be pregnant?

He handed Reece his cell, took out his own and told the crew to take fifteen.

He'd gotten her number last night, but honestly hadn't intended to use it.

Why then was he running his thumb over the cell pad, the mere thought of hearing her voice making his pulse run faster?

The room emptied out and he sat on the edge of the conference table. He pressed the button to illuminate the cell screen only to find another voice-mail message from Janine.

He sighed and rubbed his face. At his motel, he'd finally retrieved her messages. Five all told. The first two had been quietly nice. The next two longer narratives—the last one, she'd simply said she really needed to talk to him.

He didn't like the sound of that. And, yes, he admitted, a part of him was afraid of how he'd react when he finally saw her, even though he knew, with everything he was, that he wanted nothing to do with her.

"Frank and I broke up... Well, I broke up with him... Almost immediately after you left for your last tour... Look, Mace, I know I have no right to ask you this, but it's important I talk to you... In person... Apologize..."

But it wasn't that message so much as the next one that proved the cause for concern:

"I've missed you..." A small, nervous laugh. "You know how hard that is for me to say, don't you? Me? Who's never wrong about anything." A pause then, "But I was wrong about this. Wrong about you. I should never have done what I had. You didn't deserve it. We didn't deserve it. I really need to see you. Please..."

It had been damn near impossible to get to sleep after that one. He hadn't heard a word from her in months. Then the minute he gets back into town, he's bombarded with calls.

He honestly didn't know what to do.

He caught himself running his thumb over the cell pad again, Geneva's name and number highlighted in his address book.

He smiled.

Yes, he did. He knew exactly what to do...

5

"BE MY GIRLFRIEND for a week…"

Geneva couldn't believe her ears. She was washing up her few dishes, trying to ignore how it would usually be double, but not now that her mother was gone.

She dropped a glass and it broke in two at the sink bottom. She hadn't realized she cut herself until she saw a perfect dot of blood on the tip of her left ring finger. She braced her cell phone against her shoulder, then ran the small wound under cold running water, wrapping a paper towel around her finger.

"Hello? Geneva? Are you still there?"

"Who is this?" she asked.

Silence.

She laughed. "Sorry. I know it's Mace."

She knew it was Mace because his name came up. She'd entered him into her address book the instant he'd given her his number before leaving the diner the night before.

Only she hadn't expected to hear from him.

Ever.

"So…" she said. "I'm still here." She turned and leaned her hips against the counter. "I'm sorry. I'm thinking it might have been better to begin that sentence with something like 'Are you sitting down?'"

Mace chuckled. "Are you?"

"No."

"Then maybe you should."

"Maybe I should." She didn't budge from the counter, although she did look at the small table and two chairs set against the wall she hadn't used in over two months. "I'm sorry? Could you repeat what you just said?"

"I asked if you might consider being my girlfriend for a week."

His request made no more sense now than it had the first time he made it.

"Wait, I think I'm missing an important word there," he added.

"And that would be?"

"Pretend."

She squinted hard. "I'd like to say that helps, but… well, it doesn't."

He laughed again. "I'm working so I can't go into detail right now, but let me just say this. You want…what's his name? Dustin? To stop pursuing you. And I want my ex to stop her useless efforts. So, if we date, or pretend to, it should go a long ways toward helping us to that end."

"Ah," she said.

Okay. Now his meaning was beginning to sink in.

"What time do you get off tonight?" he asked.

"Seven."

"Okay. I'll pick you up at 7:15 at the diner for our first date."

"Okay. Sure. Date?"

"Pretend date. I'll take you somewhere I'm sure to run into Janine. And, I'm guessing, Dustin will be at the diner when I pick you up?"

"Probably." Most likely.

"Well, then…a win-win all the way around."

She heard voices on his side of the phone.

"Look, I've got to run. I hate to rush you, but, well… what do you say?"

She found herself incapable of saying anything.

The idea of spending time with Mace? For any reason? Phenomenal.

"By the way," he said, "if this is to work, we can't say anything to anybody about it. The fake part, that is."

"Of course." Funny he should say that. She'd been considering asking for a little time so she could call Trudy and ask her advice. But he was right. If this was to work, they couldn't tell anybody. If Trudy knew, well, then so would Mel, then Tiffany…and within five minutes the news would reach Dustin's ears.

"So, is that a yes?" Mace asked.

She found herself smiling, imagining the possibilities. "Yes. I guess it is."

She swore she could hear him smiling. And her body reacted the same way it would have if he'd been standing in front of her—with a rush of heat.

"Good," he said. "See you tonight then."

He ended the call, leaving Geneva to remain standing at the counter, smiling stupidly at the opposite wall without complete comprehension of where she was or what she was doing.

"Oh, stop it," she told herself. "It's just a game." She pushed from the counter to get a bandage from the bathroom. "He needs to scare off his ex and I…"

Her hand went to her still-flat belly.

And she needed to convince Dustin that while he was welcome in her life as a friend and as the father of her child, the door was firmly shut when it came to anything else.

She passed her home office, which was essentially what would have been the dining room, got what she needed from the bathroom, then heard her active computer chime, indicating she had email.

She fastened the bandage to her cut and clicked to access the message. It was from Johnny's Jalopies. She'd sent them the copy they'd requested last night.

"Love it! But..." she read.

More changes.

She sighed and sat down in her swivel chair. Whoever invented the word "but" should be taken out back and shot. Multiple times. With a large-gauge shotgun.

She read over her client's suggestions—the fifth round—and wondered how an auto repair shop owner had gotten so picky. It was a Black Friday sales flyer, not a family crest.

Family...

She caught herself rubbing her belly again and smiled. If she needed a reminder of why tonight would only be for show, she had only to remember her condition. Of course, Mace wouldn't be interested in dating her otherwise. Why would he?

So she'd go out with him and help scare off her ex. Do what he wanted. Enjoy his company. Have fun. And he'd do what she needed. Which was...

She caught sight of the Harvest Dance flyer she'd helped design pinned to her corkboard then took it down. The event was this Sunday night. Perfect. She and Mace, dancing, obviously a couple, should be enough to persuade Dustin she wasn't interested.

She called the number listed on the flyer, arranged to pick up two tickets, then began writing Mace a text with the info.

She hesitated pressing Send, rereading the message five times.

Should she be friendlier? Perhaps act like a girlfriend? Maybe even ask him before arranging for the tickets.

She gave an eye roll and pressed Send.

Then she sat back, ordering herself not to check for a response every two minutes.

She tilted the cell phone so she could see the display then laughed at herself even as she got down to the business of responding to Johnny, trying to ignore the zing of electricity that seemed to course through her body...

DAMN, HE WAS LATE.

Mace checked his watch for the third time in as many minutes as he got out of the rental car he'd parked outside the diner. The meetings in Denver with the sheriff's deputies and General Norman's men had taken much longer than he'd anticipated. Simply, this assignment wasn't going to be quite the run-of-the-mill one he'd first thought.

Norman was receiving death threats, very plausible ones, in connection to his Denver visit.

It seemed the controversial radio show host, who was rumored to be considering a run for political office, was not only popular with his supporters, but with his haters, as well.

And more than a few wanted to see him dead.

His visit to the Mile High City was for four days and his schedule was jam-packed.

"What's being done to find the suspect?" he'd asked three hours into the meetings.

Everyone had stared at him as if he'd grown an eyeball in the middle of his forehead.

He held his hands, palms up, on the reams of documents in front of him. "It's just common sense to me. I mean, we're spending all this time arranging to protect Robin from an unknown threat when, maybe, we should be getting to know the threat better." "Robin" was Norman's agreed-upon security name, as in bird dropping in for a brief visit before heading south again.

That's when the meeting took a turn that had ended up extending it. And he'd still had the forty-minute commute back to Colorado Springs and a stop at his motel for a shower and change of clothes.

He glanced as his watch as he opened the diner door for exiting customers. It was just before eight. Geneva was going to be pissed. If she was even still there…

He stopped inside the door.

She was.

She sat at the end of the counter looking better than any one woman had the right to.

Certainly any one pregnant woman.

He swallowed hard. She wore what to anyone else might look like a simple fall flowered dress. But to him, it might as well have been a fire-engine-red teddy and garters. She sat on the stool with her long legs crossed and was half turned away from him, talking to the diner owner, her dark hair a sexy cloud around her face.

He felt the urge to loosen his tie, only he wasn't wearing one.

Then she saw him.

Oh, boy.

Maybe this hadn't been the brightest idea he'd ever had. Damn if he didn't feel like walking up and kissing her breathless.

She didn't get up. She merely swiveled her stool until she was facing him more fully. He noticed the V of the neck of her dress that revealed soft, tanned skin and full breasts.

He realized he hadn't moved since entering and forced himself to walk toward her.

"Hi," he said, holding out the simple red rose he held. "Sorry I'm late."

Her smile seemed to take up the whole of her face. "Forgiven."

He barely registered that the room had gone quiet. Everyone was watching them, a few customers at tables but mostly staff gathered around the counter...and Dustin, who sat closer to her now, but had likely occupied the same end stool he had the night before.

"Hi," he said, extending his hand to the guy. "I'm Mace."

The other man hesitated, then accepted his shake. "Dustin."

"Dustin? Nice to meet you. Geneva's told me a lot about you. Congratulations on the baby."

He appeared surprised, then wary. "Thanks."

For a moment, Mace felt sorry for the poor guy. He couldn't say he blamed him for wanting more. But it was Geneva's call and he had no cause to question the line she'd drawn.

"Ready?" he asked her.

"Ready."

She got up and he helped her with the light, fall raincoat she took off a neighboring stool. He caught a whiff of her perfume—the scent of something fresh and sexy—and was helpless to stop himself from humming as his fingers brushed her hair back over the collar.

"You smell good," he said.

"Better than meat loaf?"

"Better than meat loaf."

Her smile widened. "You smell pretty good yourself."

He was aware of the jukebox playing and wondered if

she'd made the selection. No, he didn't wonder. He knew she had. Because the song playing was B-17.

He offered his arm and she took it.

"Good night, everyone," he said as he opened the door for her.

"Have fun" was one of the many returns.

Fun. Yes.

Somehow Mace didn't think the word came near covering it.

6

GENEVA COULDN'T REMEMBER a time when she'd felt so... tongue-tied. She didn't have a clue what to say as Mace drove her to their destination. And where were they going again?

She found herself burying her nose in the bloom of the rose he'd given her, breathing deeply then smiling. There had been a minute or two when she'd been afraid he was going to be a no-show. And she hadn't quite known how to feel about that. Had it been a real date, she would have been upset. But because it was a pretend one...?

Then he'd stood looking at her in that way from the door. And all thought of real or pretend had faded away like the morning fog, leaving her happy he'd come.

Thankfully, the ride wasn't long. He pulled into the parking lot of a place called The Barracks, which appeared to be a pub she'd passed often but had never been to.

"Thank you," she said as he switched off the car.

He looked at her. "You're welcome. I think. What are you thanking me for?"

She held up the rose. "For this. For saying what you did to Dustin. For suggesting we go out."

His gaze caught and held hers for long moments, making it all too easy to forget this wasn't real at all.

"I'm thinking I'm the one who's going to come out ahead in our little arrangement. Stay where you are. I'll open the door for you."

He got out before she could ponder his words. Then he got her door, allowing her to climb out. Then he closed it behind her and offered her his arm again.

She took it and shivered.

"Are you warm enough?"

"Enough. Yes."

Truth was, her shiver had nothing to do with the chilly evening.

"I was hoping we'd have a little time before Janine arrived," he said as they walked inside the pub. "But I'm afraid my lateness isn't going to allow for it. I'm thinking she might already be inside."

"Have you told her anything?" she asked as he helped her with her coat.

"No."

"Mace!"

A man called out to him from a nearby table packed with other guys. Geneva stood smiling politely as he greeted each of them. It was easy to see they were longtime friends he hadn't seen in a while. That he took time to introduce them to her touched her in a way she was unprepared to acknowledge.

"Sorry about that," he said after he'd spoken to them for a few minutes, promising that they'd get together for a beer before he left town again.

"It's okay."

He led her to a free table and pulled out a chair for her. She sat down and thanked him.

"Have you eaten yet?" he asked.

"No. But that's okay. I had a big lunch."

Truth was, the heavy smell of all things fried was doing interesting and not welcoming things to her stomach.

"You sure?"

She nodded.

A waitress appeared. He placed an order for a beer and asked what she wanted.

"Tomato juice with Bloody Mary mix on the side, hold the vodka."

She looked to find Mace smiling at her.

"What?"

He shook his head. "Nothing."

She shifted in her chair, trying but failing to look casual. In all honesty, she felt anything but in Mace's presence.

"I have to admit, I feel a little sorry for the guy," he said.

"Who? Dustin?"

He nodded. "Yeah. I mean, I can't blame him for wanting more."

She felt herself blush. Which was stupid. "He just thinks he wants more. He feels he has to man up or some sort of thing."

He held her gaze for a long moment then shook his head. "No, Geneva. It's not something he thinks he wants. It's something he wants…"

She fussed with her skirt and recrossed her legs, readying an objection, but somehow couldn't find the words.

Then she caught sight of a knockout blonde at the end of the bar. The woman seemed intently focused on their table.

"Um, what does Janine look like?" she asked.

"Why?"

"Because I think she's already here."

His grimace spoke volumes. "I was afraid of that."

Geneva looked at him. "She's beautiful."

"Yeah. I guess she is. I just wish it went beyond skin deep."

"How long did you guys date?"

"A year."

"Well...it must have gone deeper than what you're saying to have lasted that long."

"Nah. I just hoped it did."

The blonde got up. "Don't look now, but she's heading in our direction," Geneva added.

She watched as he stiffened.

"Mace?"

He looked up and smiled. Only it wasn't the type of smile she'd seen him wear before. "Janine. Hi."

He got up and gave her a brief hug then turned. "I'd like you to meet Geneva. Geneva, this is Janine."

"Hi," Geneva said. "Nice to meet you, finally."

One of the blonde's perfectly penciled brows arched at the last word. Geneva couldn't help noticing the way Mace's smile broadened.

"Nice to meet...you, too. Geneva, wasn't it?"

"Yes."

"I'd like to say Mace mentioned you..."

"Well, we haven't exactly talked," he said.

"No. But I was hoping to talk to you tonight," Janine said pointedly. "Alone."

"Sorry," he said. "But if you'd like to join Geneva and I...?"

Geneva's stomach tightened at the thought of sharing their table with the pretty blonde, despite Mace's obvious coolness toward her.

"No, no. Go on ahead. I'll catch up with you another time."

"Okay."

"Have a nice night," she said.

"Thank you. I'm sure we will," Geneva said. "We always do."

Mace waited until Janine walked away then sat back down, his shoulders still stiff, his face tight.

"What's she doing?" he asked.

Geneva looked casually over his shoulder. "She appears to be…yes, she's leaving."

Finally, he seemed to relax. "Good."

She couldn't help relaxing a bit herself.

"Sorry to tell you this, but that's not the last you're going to hear from her, I'm afraid."

He reached across and covered her hands with his. "Why do you think I asked for a week of your time?"

His grin was all too warm…and far too sexy.

"Five minutes," he said.

"I'm not following you."

"Oh yes, you will. In five minutes. Through that door. I'm going to take you somewhere to get something proper to eat."

"Really, that's not necessary."

"It's completely necessary. No arguing."

Their drinks arrived, but neither of them touched them. She watched as Mace peeled off a few bills, placed them under his beer bottle, then got up to help her back on with her coat.

She was glad it was just going to be the two of them again. And their…friendship.

LATER THAT NIGHT, Geneva opened the door to her apartment. She didn't think twice about leaving it open for him to follow her inside. This wasn't a date and they'd spent the past two hours laughing and talking at a nice Italian restaurant up the street from The Barracks. She'd had minestrone soup and garlic breadsticks—something she'd never dare order on a real date—and accepted a couple of bites of his seafood linguine.

"Coffee?" she asked, shrugging out of her coat and stepping out of her shoes, leaving both by the door.

"I'd love some. Nice place."

"Thanks."

Her mom would have loved Mace, she couldn't help thinking. Besides the fact that he was hotter than any guy she'd ever dated, he was kind and smart and knew how to make a woman feel like a lady.

She put the coffee on, then got cookies out of the cupboard.

"Thank you."

Mace's quiet words caught her off guard.

At the restaurant, both of them had laughed over how successful their first night out as a "couple" had gone, joking about where they could take it from there. He'd agreed to attend the dance, so long as she went to some event or other with him on Saturday afternoon.

"You're welcome. Thank you back."

"You're welcome. But that's not what I meant."

She took mugs out of the cupboard. "Oh?"

"I really enjoy spending time with you."

She couldn't help a goofy grin. "Ditto."

She busied herself getting out the cream and sugar and arranging them on a tray with the cookies.

"Why don't you find something on the stereo while I get this ready?"

"What? Sure."

The moment he left the room, she exhaled, unaware she'd been holding her breath. The way he sometimes looked at her... She gave a tiny shiver. It was all too easy to think this—what was happening—had little to do with a fake relationship and everything to do with a real one.

She heard the soft strains of Harry Chapin and caught her breath. Moments later, she placed the tray on the coffee table in the living room.

"Is this okay?" he asked, turning from the stereo.

"Yes. More than okay. One of my favorites. One of Mom's, too."

"Are you sure? If it makes you uncomfortable…"

She shook her head. "No, it's perfect."

A week ago she might have burst into tears at the selection. Even now, her eyes moistened. But the rough edges of her grief were slowly beginning to soften and she was beginning to be able to appreciate things connected to her mother.

He joined her on the sofa and accepted his coffee cup.

"So, tell me…" she said carefully after handing him a cup. "Why do I get the feeling you're not over Janine?"

7

THE WAY MACE SAW IT, she could have dumped the contents of his coffee cup down the front of his slacks and she couldn't have surprised him more.

"I'm sorry. What?"

She sat back on the flowery sofa that boasted a ton of pillows and tucked her legs under her, looking sexier now than she had earlier. Which, considering what she'd just said, was a bit of a feat.

She picked up her coffee cup and shrugged lightly, although he got the impression there was nothing light about the question she'd just thrown at him.

"I don't know. The way I see it, if you're not truly interested in someone, then you feel indifferent toward them. And I think indifference is the furthest thing you feel when it comes to Janine."

Mace rested his forearms on his knees, cupping his coffee in his hands, carefully considering her words.

"Does that make sense?" she asked.

"To a certain extent, yes." But that wasn't all of it. "I suppose what you're saying is true in some ways. But not in the way you mean."

"Then in what way?"

He looked at her, hating the idea that she believed he still might be harboring emotions for his ex. "What remains in my feelings for Janine is hurt. And maybe confusion." He shook his head. "No, definitely confusion. A lot of it…"

He sat back as well so he partially faced her.

The apartment was feminine, but not overpoweringly so. While the sofa they sat on boasted a chintzy flowery upholstery, the rest of the furniture was almost mission style, and there wasn't another flower in the place. He'd noticed the dining room didn't boast the traditional table, but was rather an office…and a working one at that. He recalled her telling him she was also a graphics designer and that she had nearly built her client list up to the point where she could permanently quit working Rocky's. But she said she liked the routine, and could see herself still working part-time for some while yet, if just to make sure she got out of her apartment regularly.

Besides, she'd told him, some of her best ideas came while she was watching a customer's face as he or she tried to decide between the open-faced roast beef sandwich or the closed.

Of course, he could have done without that particular comparison; it made him think of edging something else open…

"It's complicated," he said, continuing his thread of thought. "I mean, I loved her. God knows I loved her. I would never think of doing to her what she did to me. It just wasn't a consideration. My parents…well, they've been married for over thirty years and to my knowledge, neither of them have ever looked at anyone else, much less been unfaithful."

Geneva nodded. "I understand. When you love somebody, well…"

She left her sentence unfinished.

So, he tried to put a period on both. "What I'm trying to say, I guess, is that yes, in some ways, you're right. I'm not over it. But the emphasis is on the 'it.' Not Janine herself, but what happened between us at the end of our relationship." He sipped his coffee. "I thought I was over it, had moved on. Until..."

"Until she called."

He held her gaze. "Yeah. Until she called."

"So I'm guessing you just tucked those feelings away into a neat little box—or tried to, anyway—and now, well, now the lid's off and they're tumbling back out at you again."

"More like a lasso around my ankles."

Her expression was so soft, so understanding, he felt something shift inside him merely looking at her.

"I wish it wasn't that way. I mean, who in their right mind would want to feel this way? But..."

"But it is what it is."

"Yeah. In a nutshell."

He watched the way she smoothed her hand over her tucked legs, back and forth, forth and back.

"Have you ever been in love?" he found himself asking.

Her hand stopped midcalf. "Pardon me?"

He smiled, knowing by her reaction that she'd heard him.

She looked down into the contents of her cup. He wanted to tell her she wasn't going to find the answers there. Then again, who was he to say? Maybe that's where they'd be. And he might be better served looking into his own cup before asking stupid questions like the one he just did.

"Yeah," she said. "Or at least I thought so at the time. The guy I followed here..."

The chirp of his cell phone didn't so much as cut her

off—he guessed she hadn't intended to go any further—as it did give him the reprieve he was looking for.

"I'm sorry," he said.

He took the phone out: Jonathon Reece.

"I have to take this."

"Go ahead. No need to apologize."

He got up. "Harrison," he said simply.

Upon leaving the Denver hotel earlier, he'd appointed Jon as contact. So he wasn't surprised now to hear that tomorrow morning's pre-event route run-through had been moved up a half hour by Norman's people.

"See you fifteen minutes before then."

"I'll be there. Oh, and look for the changes you suggested in your email box by day's end."

"Thanks."

He disconnected and turned to find Geneva staring off at something he couldn't see. A result of his question? Her earlier comment? Or something else entirely?

He couldn't be sure.

What he was sure of was he wanted to know more about went on in her mind.

"Sorry about that," he apologized again.

"That's all right. Everything okay?"

"Yeah." He sat back down next to her. "A friend of mine—Darius? I think you know him from the diner—asked me to take over a security detail for a visiting personality in Denver while I'm here."

"Anyone exciting?"

He told her.

She made a face. "I was hoping for Taylor Swift."

He chuckled and picked up his coffee cup only to find it empty. When had that happened? He glanced at his watch to find the hour later than he thought.

"Wow."

"I know. I was just thinking the same thing."

"I never really understood the whole 'time flies' thing, but...well, I guess it's true." He put his cup back down. "Well, except for the past half hour or so. That part of the night I could have done without."

She laughed softly. "Oh, I don't know. It's something you need to think about maybe. I mean, if you are still holding even an ounce of love for Janine...well, you owe it to both of you to find out."

"And do what?"

She shrugged slowly. "That's for you two to decide." She rubbed her belly, which was flat and unfairly showed no signs of the baby growing within her. "Then again, we all make mistakes. Maybe yours is fixable."

He squinted at her, wondering if she was trying to fix him and Janine back up.

But that didn't make any sense. Why would she try to do that?

Either it was the most unselfish thing a woman had ever done...or the dumbest.

He decided the first one was the case because if anything was clear, it was that Geneva was no dummy.

"So, you're saying I should give her another shot, then?" he asked quietly.

She dropped her gaze and something flittered across her beautiful face.

That's what he was looking for. Disappointment.

She didn't want him to reconcile with Janine at all. Rather, she was trying to make sure it was not something he wanted.

And he knew beyond a shadow of a doubt that he didn't.

As for what either of them did with that information from there...

He firmly tugged his thoughts away from that particular trail.

"I should be going," he said, getting to his feet. "Dawn comes early and I've got to be awake to greet it."

"Me, too."

She walked with him toward the door. He turned to face her.

Without her shoes, the top of her head came to his nose. Perfect.

"So," he asked. "What's the next step in the dating game, other than that dance you told me about?"

"I don't know," she said. "Maybe you can stop by the diner tomorrow night, say around dinnertime, if you wanted to?"

"It would have to be late. I probably won't be getting back from Denver until after seven or so."

"Okay. I'll hold some pie for you."

"Deal."

He knew he should be reaching for that door handle, letting himself out, but, dammit, he was having a hard time convincing his feet to move.

"Thank you again," he said. "You know, for tonight."

"You're welcome again. And thank you."

They both laughed at the sweet ridiculousness of their exchange.

He took a deep breath. "Okay, I guess this is the part where I leave."

"Yes, I guess it is."

His gaze fastened on her face. "Can I kiss you goodnight?"

She was clearly amused by his question. "Is that something friends do?"

"It's definitely something friends do. You know, on the cheek."

"Okay."

He took her hands in his, the subtle scent of her perfume surrounding him as he leaned in. But somewhere between his genuine intentions and the actual act, right when he might have brushed his lips against her cheek, he rerouted and hit her full-on on the mouth instead...

8

Wow…

Geneva didn't quite know how to respond.

She'd be lying if she said she hadn't imagined this, what it might be like to experience Mace's kiss. She'd dreamed about it last night. Thought about it all day. Then each time, she'd told herself to stop because there was no chance it was going to happen.

Yet here he was…kissing her.

She stared straight into his open eyes as his lips pressed against hers. The meeting was soft…sweet…unexpected. Then something within her sighed and her eyelids drifted closed, allowing her to fully appreciate the sensations tingling outward from where they touched, however briefly.

He slowly pulled back and she nearly whimpered, only to feel him press against her again.

Geneva couldn't be sure how it happened… One moment they were saying good-night and he was joking about a friendly kiss on the cheek, the next their kiss pole vaulted into wickedly hot territory, with no mats around to cushion the fall.

Oh, wow. Just…wow.

He released his hold on her hands and she felt his fingertips on either side of her jaw. She skimmed her hands up the thickness of his forearms, heat unfolding deep in her belly like a long-forgotten love note. His tongue dipped out and she welcomed its wetness in her mouth, inviting him as far as he wanted even as she hesitantly explored his openness.

Had she ever been kissed like this? She felt breathless and so vividly alive she could barely stand it.

Then he touched her breast.

She was pretty sure the gasp she heard was her own. But she wasn't entirely clear. Somewhere over the past few minutes, she'd stopped being herself. Stopped being aware of anything but the thick pulsing of blood through her veins, the wetness between her thighs, the need for more—much more—building in her belly.

Yes...

Mace cupped her breast through the fabric of her bra and dress, seeking for and finding her stiff nipple. She bit her bottom lip briefly and continued kissing him. She was so very sensitive, so very aware of every nuance, every touch, in ways she hadn't been before.

He reached for the buttons that ran down the front of her dress and she shivered as his fingertips met with her bare skin. He found her breast again, tunneling underneath until her bra cup gave and her confined flesh popped free.

His barely audible groan fed the flames flicking over her, but paled by comparison when he ran his tongue over her nipple.

Geneva moved her hands to his shoulders for support, just in case her knees decided to give out under his slow, concentrated attention. His lips tugged at her, his tongue teased, his mouth tasted. By the time he moved back up to her mouth, leaving her fully damp and shivering, she was pretty sure she couldn't remember what her birthday was, never mind her name.

Then she felt the backs of his fingers against her stomach...

She sucked in air. She honestly didn't know if she could stand it anymore without...without...

His fingers touched the damp curls between her thighs through her panties.

She nearly passed out from sheer pleasure...

MACE COULD SMELL Geneva's scent, thick and musky, as fully as her perfume. And it was driving him beyond crazy with need.

No, he hadn't planned to kiss her.

No, he hadn't anticipated his hand moving to her breasts.

No, the thought of touching her womanhood hadn't been part of tonight's schedule.

But he'd be damned if he could stop himself.

Especially since she seemed to want to be touched as much as he wanted to touch her.

His fingers found the crotch of her panties and he groaned. She was soaked.

If he needed any more impetus to continue, that was it.

But as he worked his index finger inside the elastic to run the length of her, he knew a moment of pause.

He forced himself to drag his mouth from hers and pull his hand away. She made a small sound that nearly sent him straight back in.

Instead, he drew away to stare into her heavy-lidded eyes. "Is this...okay?"

"Okay? Yes. Oh, yes..."

He waited for her to register what he was asking.

"Oh." Her cheeks flushed even deeper as comprehension dawned. "Um, yes. I'm a fully functioning female for at least the next six months."

He couldn't help his grin. "Good."

He leaned back in and reclaimed her mouth.

God, she tasted, felt, smelled so good...

Of course, what he was avoiding was asking himself a very important question: whether or not he should be doing this.

He groaned inwardly, not wanting to stop. It had been a good long while since he'd wanted someone so intensely.

The touch of her hand against the front of his slacks chased the air from his lungs. He held it there, waiting, wondering. Her fingers lightly traced the outline of his erection and it was all he could do to keep his hips from bucking forward, seeking more.

He restlessly turned her, pressing her back against the door and reaching back between her thighs, his need surging to urgent within a blink. Geneva's return affections intensified his building need as she tucked her fingers into the waist of his slacks.

So hot, so wet...

Mace dipped his index finger inside her dripping channel, stroking back and forth before coming to rest at the delicious bit of flesh at the apex. He gave a gentle squeeze... and she made a sound deep in her throat and shuddered in a way that made him think she'd come.

Sweet heaven, he wasn't going to be able to stop himself.

He fingered her opening, then slid his index finger into her. Her tight muscles immediately contracted and she moaned, making his erection even harder.

If he had any doubt of her having achieved orgasm, he didn't now. He caressed and stroked her until her shudders began to subside and she melted against him, her beautiful face flushed, her lips trembling, her eyes huge pools of sated bliss.

He couldn't remember a time when a woman had been so easy to please. He didn't know if it was him...or her... or perhaps even them together, but whatever the reason, he decided he liked it.

Perhaps a little too much.

He slowly removed his hand from between her legs and kissed her deeply, leisurely tangling his tongue with hers, finding even that simple action almost painfully erotic.

His cell phone chimed once.

Geneva smiled at him. He smiled back.

"I have to get that," he whispered, kissing her again.

She nodded. "Okay."

He slowly removed his weight from her, making sure she could stand on her own before reaching into his pocket for his phone.

The text was from Reece: he had emailed him the promised travel routes for tomorrow.

"Important?"

He ran his hand over his face, the fog of desire slowly dissipating and reality returning. But not so much that he didn't register the scent of her on his fingers...or stop to appreciate it.

"Yeah," he said.

He searched her face, looking for what, he couldn't be sure. Something? Anything? Everything?

"I've got to go," he said quietly.

A brief flash of regret crossed her features then she smiled again. "Okay."

He lifted his hand and brushed her curls back from her face. She was still flushed, her lips plump and well-kissed, her eyes sleepy and sexy. "See you tomorrow?"

She nodded.

"Good."

She stepped away from the door and opened it for him, appearing to lean against it for support.

Damn, but she was beautiful. He'd give anything not to have to leave her.

"Good night," he said.

"Good night."

He forced himself to move through the open doorway, then down the hall, and the stairs, every step seeming to take superhuman strength to make until he reached the parking lot and his rental car. Before getting in, he glanced up to find her watching from her living room window. He raised a hand to wave. She waved back.

Then he climbed in and drove away, trying not to think about her going into her bedroom, stripping down and climbing into bed...alone.

Oh, boy. If this was what friendship was doing to him, he'd hate to think what would happen if they dated.

Then again, what passed between them felt absolutely nothing like friendship.

Oh, boy.

He lifted his fingers to his nose and breathed deeply.

Oh, boy, indeed.

He smiled and switched on the radio...

9

GENEVA LAY ON HER SIDE in bed, pressing her hot cheek against her pillowcase, cooling her skin as well as hiding her dorky grin. Which made her feel even sillier still since there was no one around to see it.

She sighed and rolled onto her back, her entire body seeming to vibrate.

Oh, how good it had felt to be kissed, touched, to the point where she no longer recognized herself. She liked, no loved, who she'd turned into. And she wanted to get to know her better.

Wanted to get to know Mace better. A lot better.

Of course, that was an improbability. But just having those few minutes with him earlier...

The power of her sigh seemed to bow the windows outward.

She found herself absently touching her belly in much the same way she had been in recent weeks, yet differently. There was life in her and life all around her. Rainbows bursting with color and light even in the dark of night. Bright passion reminding her she had needs beyond her usual day-to-day grind.

"Friends. We're just friends."

She grasped the extra pillow on her queen-size bed and hugged it close, breathing in deeply, imagining she could still smell his cologne, still smell him.

She rolled on to her side again and stared at the clock. It was after midnight. She needed to be up early to work the breakfast shift. Then she needed to finish the Johnson account, follow up on two important quotes and work on a new logo for Ames Green Technology.

Why did she have the feeling she wasn't going to be able to sleep?

And why didn't she care?

She moved the pillow to rest between her thighs.

Wow.

She restlessly licked her lips and then replaced the pillows with her hands.

Oh, yes. That was much more like it…

She imagined it was Mace's hand there still, stroking her, probing her, bringing her pleasure.

Her cell phone chimed once and her hands froze. Who would be texting her so late?

She rolled over to retrieve her cell from the nightstand.

Mace.

She held the bit of plastic and electronic wizardry against her chest and smiled that dorky smile again before even reading it.

"Really enjoyed tonight. Sweet dreams…"

She read and reread his words, taking notice of the ellipsis at the end, as if leading into something else.

"Stop it," she ordered herself.

She accessed the text again and responded.

"'Night night. Sleep tight."

She hesitated, then pressed Send.

She lay for long moments just holding the phone against

her chest, then forced herself to put it back on the nightstand.

This could be dangerous, a little voice whispered.

But it would be oh, so worth it…

MACE CHECKED HIS WATCH: one hour until transport.

The route from Norman's hotel to the hall where he was scheduled to address a political rally was exactly 1.354 miles, and he was walking it one last time before being picked up and driven to the hotel.

Having spent a great deal of time in Colorado Springs, he'd always viewed Denver as the city's older, bolder sister. Buildings were bigger, streets were wider and the citizens more nervy.

Having spent the majority of his career specializing in counter-terrorism, he knew a view from the street would help him note aspects he wouldn't otherwise see; side entryways into commercial courtyards, parking garages that couldn't be blocked, public buildings and private residences he couldn't hope to cover. He'd walked it the day before; he was walking it again.

He'd gone over the intelligence the Lazarus team had gathered on possible suspects behind the threats made on General Stan "The Man" Norman's life. The detail—including sheriff's deputies and Norman's private security—all had photos of the nine most likely, with special emphasis on the fact the threat could originate with more than one of them…or none.

The day was clear and seasonal for November, with temps around fifty degrees. Mace's plain black suit, white shirt and nondescript tie were enough to identify him to fellow team members, but weren't obvious enough that he stood out in the crowd. Of course, if someone looked close enough, his reflective sunglasses and earpiece could give him away.

He listened as final pre-event checks were made on those premises deemed the most vulnerable and okays issued, even as he noted additional weaknesses in the route and considered options to protect them.

He was seriously considering rerouting the rally drive, even though Norman himself had made it very clear this was the one he wanted to take, since there were at least two "support" gatherings along the way scheduled to watch his car go by. While Mace had never overseen nor participated in a similar occasion, he'd educated himself over the past two days enough to where he felt semi-comfortable.

And he didn't care for the changing variables.

In addition to the support gatherings, he was assured there would also be anti-Norman assemblies, as well.

Midmorning pedestrians walked the streets alongside him, commuters drove on the streets, bike riders zoomed by and delivery trucks came and went. Nothing looked out of the ordinary and he had every reason to expect everything to go smoothly.

Still, he couldn't help feeling he was missing something.

He acknowledged the sensation could stem from caution honed over his years in the service, time he'd spent stationed where anyone and everyone was a possible suspect, including women and children, in innocuous locations that appeared peaceful but could turn into hell within a blink.

Combine all that with natural instincts that had rarely steered him wrong and he wouldn't be comfortable until this assignment was over.

He reached into his pocket for his cell phone. He didn't realize what he was looking for until he didn't see it: namely, any calls or texts from Geneva.

Merely thinking her name made him hot for her all over again.

He slid the cell back into his pocket and ordered himself to get back on point.

The memory of her mouth, her soft cries, were enough to keep him up longer than he'd have liked.

If only Reece had texted him a little later, he would have taken her back to her bedroom and found out just how far her responsiveness went.

"Sir, check complete." Jonathon Reece's voice came through his earpiece.

He moved to press the button to allow him to respond when a man wearing a gray hoodie walked from one of those courtyards that caused such concern and cut in front of him, catching his shoulder.

Mace stopped, watching as the man unapologetically continued walking across the street with barely a look at traffic.

Awareness ran through Mace as he tried to match the man to any of the nine guys they'd identified as threats and came away with a negative.

Which meant little. Yet it could mean everything.

"Sir?" Jon's voice sounded again.

Mace pressed the button that was part of the earpiece. "Very good, Reece. Have everyone walk it again, this time from the opposite direction."

Silence. Then, "Roger that."

He released the button. He knew Reece disagreed with his orders. But he would do as requested, no questions asked.

The hooded man disappeared from view into another courtyard across the way.

Mace remained watching after him, then crossed the street to follow…

"So…"

Geneva wiped down the counter after the lunch crowd had mostly dissipated and the instant she reached the end where Trudy was taking her usual, post rush coffee, her friend and employer decided some conversation was in order.

"So, what?" she asked.

Trudy stared at her over her reading glasses where she read the daily paper, words unneeded.

The diner had mostly emptied out aside from a couple of lingering regulars and the help, including her and Trudy, the day cook and a part-time busboy who even now cleared the last of the tables and was preparing to mop before the dinner shift took over.

"Sit," Trudy ordered more than requested.

"I just wanted to finish—"

"Now."

Geneva poured herself a cup of decaf and sat.

In the time she'd worked there, Trudy had proven to be just as much of a second mother as she was an employer to Geneva. She had her own family, but everyone who worked the diner was an extended family of sorts…unconditional until someone violated the terms.

Like Cindy, whom Trudy had fired the next time the blind-date opting brunette had showed up for her next shift and had forgotten to feign the illness from which she'd claimed to be suffering that had kept her from work. Unfortunately, that left them short another pair of hands every day until Trudy found a suitable replacement. Something experience told Geneva could be weeks.

"So, does he know?" Trudy asked.

Geneva pretended that adding sugar and creamer to her cup required her undivided attention. "Who?"

Another over-the-glasses look.

"About the baby? Yes. Yes, he does know."

Trudy made a quiet sound. "And do you think he might stick around for a while?"

Geneva nearly choked on her coffee.

Trudy sighed. "That's what I thought."

Geneva felt inexplicably irritated. "I know you're concerned about me, Trudy. Really…I do. But this…Mace…" Merely saying his name made the butterflies that had taken up residence in her stomach flutter faster. "He makes me feel good. The way he looks at me…makes me feel not like a waitress, or a friend, or an expectant mother, but like a…well, woman…I like it. What's wrong with enjoying it while I can?"

"The problem is your hormones are running in circles…and it's important you not forget you are an expectant mother."

"Trust me, that's not something I can exactly forget."

"Oh? Because the way I see it, you're trying pretty hard."

Talk about pins and balloons.

Of course, what Geneva was leaving out of the equation was that despite last night's unexpected turn of events, she and Mace weren't truly dating, they were only pretending to date.

Not that she'd tell Trudy that. Aside from agreeing with Mace that they couldn't tell anyone in order for this to fly, she knew the instant she breathed word one to the talkative diner owner, everyone would know. Then what value would their agreement have?

She shivered for reasons having nothing to do with the temperature.

"Uh-huh," Trudy said, rustling her paper.

Geneva took a sip of her coffee. "We're dating. Nothing more, nothing less."

"Pregnant women don't date."

"Why not? Last time I checked, we're still human."

"No, you're not. You're hormonal."

"I'll give you the hormonal part. At any rate, what does it matter? In a week he'll be gone and everything will return to normal."

"Depends on how you define normal."

How did she define normal? What happened last night? The mere thought...

She couldn't help smiling.

Which earned her another Trudy frown.

She pushed her cup to the other side of the counter where she could collect it when she walked around.

"Are we done?" she asked.

"I am," Trudy said. "I think I've made my point."

With a fine-honed carving knife, Geneva wanted to add, "And I hope I've made mine."

She rounded the counter, dumped the contents of her cup into the sink and put it in the bussing bin. She caught Trudy watching her and could have sworn she was hiding a grin behind the paper she pretended to read.

Geneva shook her head and grinned back, then hurried off into the kitchen.

10

MACE RODE in the trailing car in the passenger's seat, keeping an eye out and listening to route reports as Norman's limo drove under the speed limit ahead of them. That sense of wariness remained with him, even though everything was going like clockwork.

So far...

Ahead of the limo, Jonathon Reece rode in the lead sedan, and in the limo itself were two more security personnel, in addition to Norman's personal assistant and event organizer, who had met him at the hotel.

He resisted rubbing the back of his neck to smooth the prickling there.

General Stan "The Man" Norman had been presentable enough, direct and to the point, an extension of what had likely made him a successful general. More importantly now, he was content to let them decide what he needed to do...beyond his predetermined routes.

Mace didn't get it. While rumors surrounded the one-time general, now political talk show radio host's future political plans, he couldn't understand why the guy garnered so much attention.

"Have you listened to his show?" Dominic Falcone asked Mace from the driver's seat.

"No."

"If you had, then you'd know why. They don't come any more confrontational than the general. Name one group he hasn't manage to offend and I'll point how he managed to do it."

"Sticks and stones…"

"Yeah, well, we all know what words are capable of."

Indeed, they all did, as history and armed conflict bore out.

In Norman's case, it seemed many people were interested in stoning him simply for the words he chose.

Earlier that day, the man responsible for putting Mace in this position had called to consult with him. He'd reminded Darius of his mounting debt and assured him he had everything well under control. They'd talked a bit about the kidnapping case that had taken his friend away, and then Dari had asked about the girl he'd been spotted with at The Barracks.

If he didn't know better, he'd think that had been the true reason behind Dari's unnecessary call.

"Geneva?" His friend had sounded incredulous when he'd told him. "You do know…"

"Yes, I do."

Dari's silence had been louder than a car bomb. "Hey, far be it for me to suggest you don't know what you're doing, but, well, do you know what you're doing?"

"I'm enjoying her company."

Enjoying her company. Those words seemed to fall far short of the mark. Whatever he was doing, Geneva and her soft lips were there, along the fringes of his thoughts.

He'd texted her a short time ago to tell her he'd see her at the diner later.

She'd texted back with a smiley face and told him to be careful.

He'd nearly texted back saying he was always careful. But then he decided not to. Mainly because he wondered if careful entered anywhere into their situation.

Oh, he knew they were only pretending to date. That when she'd revealed her circumstances, a real relationship was out of the question.

But what had happened last night? There had been nothing fake about his actions...or her reaction.

He'd liked it.

More than liked it, he...

He set his teeth together.

He needed to keep his head in the game.

He and Dari had talked a little while longer, then his friend had signed off with a quiet, "If you need anything, call."

Mace suspected that Dari had been talking about more than his assignment.

They were nearing the point where he'd run into the hooded man on the street earlier. He went on alert, actively scanning the areas he'd seen the guy. Unfortunately, he'd lost him in the crowd. That meant one of two things: he lived in the area or he was the one they needed to watch out for.

"Damn."

"What is it?" Falcone asked.

He indicated the corner of the next block where a group of people with signs were gathered.

"Looks to be protesters," Falcone noted.

That's exactly what they were. Even at a distance, he could read the signs that ranged from, "Go Home and Be a Man, Norman!" to "Think Outside My Box!"

He'd allowed for the possibility of protestors. He just

didn't like that they were gathered so close to where he'd run into the suspicious character earlier.

"I'm getting out," he said.

"What?"

"Slow down."

He issued the command for the lead car to do the same, which would alert the limo driver to follow suit, allowing him to walk alongside the cars until he felt it was safe to move forward.

He climbed out, unfastened the protective strap of his shoulder holster and stepped up next to the limo, careful of traffic coming in the opposite direction.

He heard a woman's scream from his left, then a shot rang out.

Damn!

He watched as a bullet hit the limo's shockproof passenger's window and ricocheted off.

"Move, move, move!" he ordered through his earpiece.

The lead car took off and the limo followed, as did Falcone, protocol dictating the target be protected first, leaving him behind.

He ran in the direction the gunshot had been fired from…

GENEVA LOOKED at the wall clock that hung above the jukebox for the fifth time in as many minutes. Seven o'clock had come and gone, and other than the brief text that morning she'd received from Mace saying he'd see her later, she hadn't heard from him.

"What's the matter? He stand you up?"

The words came from Tiffany, who appeared a little too smug for her liking, and were loud enough for everyone—including Mel in the back—to hear.

She caught Trudy's gaze through the window from

where she worked in the kitchen and tried not to make a face.

She wasn't so much afraid of being stood up as she was worried about Mace's safety.

Word of the attempt on General Norman's life was all everyone was talking about. It dominated the news that played on the television in the upper corner of the diner that was usually set to a national news channel and muted so you had to read the scroll but it had been changed to a local station to keep up on developing reports on the event.

The goings-on had brought out more people than usual for a Wednesday night. Reactions ranged from "They shouldn't have missed," to "There are a lot of crazies out there."

All Geneva could think about was Mace's safety.

In the middle of refilling the coffee cups on Table 3, her cell phone vibrated in her pocket. She nearly spilled the hot liquid as she hurried to get it out.

"Sorry," she said, hurrying away.

Mace!

"Hey," he said simply when she answered.

"Hey, yourself. You okay?"

"Okay?"

"Yeah. What happened today is all over the news."

"Don't worry, I'm fine," he said, but she wasn't convinced. "Sorry, I'm late."

A thrill ran up her arms at the thought he was still coming. "It's okay. The diner's packed."

But she had reserved a booth in the corner after the last occupants had vacated it at six-thirty.

"Will you be long?" she asked.

"I'm here."

His words sounded both in her phone…and her free ear. She turned to see him behind her.

She was sure people around her thought her insane as she ran toward him and hugged him hard...

MACE HAD SEEN such welcomes over the years. At airports, on bases. He'd watched wives and girlfriends embrace their loved ones like they might never let them go.

But he had never been on the receiving end of one.

He couldn't help chuckling, breathing in the sweet scent of Geneva's hair. "If that's your reaction to my being late, I'll have to arrange to do it more often."

She drew back and smiled up at him. "I'd advise against it. Trust me."

Was it possible he missed her? Yes, it was. He'd missed her smile, her wit, her presence. It should have struck him as odd, but somehow it didn't.

"Sorry I'm late. Something came up at work."

She squinted. "I already figured that out." She indicated the television. He looked to see the scene from today being played out via someone's cell phone camera.

He frowned, watching the cars race off even as he ran after the gunman. But just as had happened earlier, he hadn't found him. Or her, as the case may be.

But he'd bet a year's salary the hooded man from earlier in the day was the one behind the shooting.

"Are you okay?" Geneva asked.

"What? Yeah. Yeah, I'm fine." At least he was now. Earlier, he'd been so worked up, he'd barely been able to speak without shouting. He couldn't help thinking they should have been able to prevent the incident.

He should have been able to prevent it.

"Come on. Let's sit down," Geneva said.

She led him to a corner booth and righted the coffee cup waiting there, filling it from the pot she'd put down before hugging him.

He watched the easy, fluid way she moved. Took in the concerned expression on her beautiful face. The way her hair curled around her head. The bow of her lips as she bit on the bottom one, caught herself, and then stopped.

"Hungry for anything in particular?" she asked.

You, he wanted to say.

He hadn't said it, but given the way her eyes darkened as she looked at him, he thought he might have.

"Surprise me," he said instead.

She twisted those lips he seemed inordinately fascinated with. "Anything you're allergic to? Dislike?"

"Nope."

"Okay. But no complaints allowed if I bring you something you don't like."

He thought she could bring him liver and he'd not only eat it, but enjoy it.

And he hated liver.

"Will you be joining me?"

She looked around, then back at him. "I'm already supposed to be off, but the place is packed…"

"That's okay. I understand."

"But I haven't eaten yet, so, yes, I will join you. At least for a meal."

"Good."

He sat back, watching as she filled a couple of coffee cups and delivered a check on her way toward the kitchen. She had the type of legs he'd love to run his hands over… but it was the memory of the tight wetness that lay between them that made him instantly hard.

He was glad he'd come to the diner. He'd seriously considered canceling, staying back at the motel to go over tomorrow's schedule, continue consulting with the team to find the man responsible…and devise ways to make sure the guy wouldn't get another chance to squeeze off a round.

As it was, he'd merely planned to drop by, do his part as Geneva's fake "boyfriend," then leave.

Now he hoped she'd let him come home with her.

Someone sat down in the booth opposite him. He blinked to find it was Geneva's friend, Dustin.

Damn.

11

"I CAN'T APOLOGIZE ENOUGH," Geneva said for the third time
as Mace followed her out to her car an hour later.

The diner had pretty much emptied out in the interim,
with the buzz of the day finally dying down like a caf-
feine high. One of the customers had recognized him as
the one in the footage and quietly approached him, but
he'd deflected the inquiry.

It had been Dustin he'd been more focused on.

"She's going to marry me," the other man had said.

Mace had stared at him as if Dustin had just told him
he had a vest of plastic explosives strapped to his chest
under his plaid shirt.

As far as guys went, Dustin didn't look too bad. A little
soft around the middle, maybe. The type that would run
from a fight instead of face it.

Well, except in this case, apparently. It appeared the
guy had decided to stand up for Geneva.

"I'm sorry?" he'd said in response to his statement.

"You do know she's pregnant with my child."

Mace had nodded, experiencing a pang he couldn't quite
identify but didn't like. "I do. I also know the circum-

stances surrounding the situation. And that she has no intention of marrying you."

The guy had looked so genuinely heartbroken, Mace had felt instantly bad.

"Look, no hard feelings, but she doesn't feel that way about you. And from what I understand, you don't feel that way about her, either. You two were friends, right?"

"Right."

"And that one night was an accident."

He didn't respond.

"I appreciate and respect that you want to do the right thing, Dustin. And I'm sure Geneva does, too. But I'd recommend you try to get the friendship back before you destroy even that. For the sake of the baby, at least."

Geneva had come up then, looking a little upset and worried that Dustin was sitting at his table. Then she asked what he was doing there.

Mace had raised his brow at the other man as if to provide a punctuation point. Then he extended his arm.

"Good seeing you again, Dustin," he'd said.

Dustin's jaw tightened, but he shook his hand and got up. But rather than taking his regular seat at the counter, he'd left.

"No need for apologies," he said to Geneva. "That's what all this was about, wasn't it? Getting a specific reaction?"

"What did he say?"

"Probably what you're thinking."

The night was chilly and he didn't think the light sweater she wore was protection enough, so after she unlocked the car, he opened the door for her.

"The chicken fried steak was great," he said. And it had been. Doubly so when he saw she'd had the same thing.

"Was."

He squinted at her. "Sorry?"

"You said that's what this was about. You know, Dustin's reaction." She hesitated getting inside the car. "Past tense."

He smiled. "Tell me why I'm not surprised you're one of those type of girls?"

"What type?"

"The type that easily reads people."

"So you're saying…"

He grinned at her. "That it's too cold to be standing out here. Get in the car, Geneva."

She made a face.

He chuckled and opened the door wider.

She climbed in and started the engine, but kept one foot outside so he couldn't close her inside. He couldn't help looking at the way her skirt hiked up, revealing a nicely shaped knee.

"Are you going back to your motel?" she asked.

He grinned. "I was thinking about it."

"Want some company?"

He didn't know quite how to respond.

If you had asked him what might come out of her delectable mouth next, her question wouldn't even have rated a spot on the list. In fact, he'd pretty much accepted he'd be spending the night alone.

She cleared her throat. "I have something I'd like to talk to you about."

"Okay."

"If you'd rather not…"

"No, no. Please, do come over."

She looked suddenly shy, sexily so. "I have to swing by my place, shower some of these food smells off me and change first."

"And I'll have to clean up the room."

She laughed. "See you in an hour?"

"An hour."

"Okay."

"All right."

She finally pulled her leg back inside and he closed the door for her then knocked on the window.

"Room 3," he said.

She looked so damn hot when she smiled he nearly kissed her. "See you there..."

He stepped aside as she put the car in Reverse and backed up before shifting into Drive and leaving the lot.

She wanted to talk to him about something.

He wondered what.

While they ate, he'd easily relayed what had happened that day in a way that didn't make him grind his teeth. Talking to her was so effortless. He couldn't imagine what she wanted to say. In private.

He blinked. Well, he'd find out soon enough, wouldn't he?

He walked over to where he'd parked a couple spaces up. He found himself hoping it was something that would find her lying in his bed.

He cursed under his breath.

First he needed to clear off the bed.

OKAY, MAYBE she was being too forward.

Geneva hesitated outside Room 3, her hand raised to knock. She curled and opened her fingers then dropped her hand back to her side, her courage abandoning her.

What was she thinking? Oh yeah, about last night...

She swallowed hard. Last night had been phenomenal. But had it been little more than aberration? A spur-of-the-moment thing not meant to be repeated?

Halfway through her shower, the anticipatory high she'd been running on had begun to dissipate, knocked back by

Trudy's words earlier, then Dustin's descent on Mace's table.

Was it possible Mace wanted to do more than fake their dating?

She closed her eyes and took a deep breath, releasing it slowly.

Oh, criminy, ask him already...

She lifted her hand and forced herself to knock.

The door opened so quickly, she nearly fell inside.

"Whoa," Mace said, steadying her.

She laughed. "That was fast."

"Yeah. I thought I heard something."

"My breathing?"

"That must be it."

She was running late, taking more than the hour she'd promised. Sixty minutes had been more than enough time to get ready and drive over. But then she'd started to wonder if she was doing the right thing.

Taking in the welcoming expression on Mace's handsome face, she felt instantly better.

"Come in," he said.

She did.

"I tried cleaning up, but..."

The place was pin neat. She'd bet he earned extra points in the service for his efforts.

"Okay, so it's clean."

And so was he, if his damp hair and fresh soap smell was any indication. Which explained why he'd changed. He wore a soft pair of jeans and a honey-brown T-shirt.

She walked in and he closed the door after her. The radio played on low—a local country station—but otherwise it was quiet.

She turned to say something to him at the same time he

stepped forward to say something to her and she bumped right into him.

But rather than apologize, Geneva did something she'd hoped they'd get around to, but certainly hadn't planned on doing now.

She kissed him.

And he kissed her back.

Wow!

If she thought last night had been something, well, now she was sure her skin was going to burn from the instant heat generated by the mere touch of his mouth against hers.

She made small hungry sounds she'd never in her life imagined she'd ever make, running her hands restlessly up his back then down over his hind end, then up again, tunneling under his T-shirt and the hotness beneath.

She'd changed into something as casual as what he was wearing. They plucked and tugged and pulled and kissed until they were half undressed and then fell onto the nearby king-size bed.

Geneva wrapped her legs around his hips, one of her jeans legs still half on, her T-shirt half off, one bra cup pushed up. He shook his leg to free himself from his own jeans, one hand cupping her exposed breast, the other reaching between her thighs.

Yes, yes, yes…

Had she said the words? She couldn't be sure. She was unaware of anything other than the thick pulsing of blood through her body and her white-hot need for the man even now sheathing himself with a condom.

She worked her hand between them, gently grasping his rock-hard erection and positioning it against her waiting flesh.

Her breath caught and held and she arched her back,

swimming in sensations that flowed over and through her like vivid colors.

Then he entered her...

She moaned so loud, the sound almost roused her from her dizzying state.

Almost.

He felt so good. So very good...

He withdrew, then slid in again, this time to the hilt.

Her back came off the mattress.

Had she ever wanted anything so much?

A hunger that surpassed anything she'd ever experienced rushed through her. She grasped his hips and tilted her own, taking him deeper still.

He thrust once, twice...

Then uttered a curse and went rigid.

12

"I'VE GOT TO...STOP for a minute..." Mace whispered into her ear. "Sorry..."

Geneva swallowed so hard she heard it. "It's okay."

She made a small sound as he rolled off her to lay flat on the mattress next to her.

She didn't know what she should do, so she did nothing.

She lay staring at the ceiling, wondering if what had just happened...well, had.

Had he really come that quickly?

Of course, last night she had nearly achieved orgasm by his merely blowing on her.

Well, a bit more than that, but still.

She fought to catch her breath and wondered if she should put her clothes back on, or take them the rest of the way off. She settled for a compromise as Mace pulled the covers over them both: she took off the jeans but left her bra and T-shirt on.

"Wow," he said so softly she nearly didn't hear him. "That's a first."

She laughed. She couldn't help herself.

At least he wasn't trying to pass off that he had intended to do that or that it hadn't actually happened.

They lay for long, quiet minutes. Geneva attempted to rein in her runaway emotions, but was having a hard time. She'd been a teenager when she'd last been left hanging this way.

Mace slid an arm around her shoulders and pulled her to him. She gladly went, laying her cheek against the warm granite of his chest.

"Just give me a minute."

"It's all right," she said.

And, she discovered, it was.

While she'd have preferred more, she really was okay with leaving things where they were. After all, there was always tomorrow.

At least she hoped there was.

Now that her breathing was returning to semi-normal, and her temperature cooling a bit, she found it was delicious just to lay this close to him.

He smelled so good.

"So," he said quietly, even as his hand smoothed up and down her back from her bare bottom to her neck. "What was it you wanted to talk to me about?"

She dragged her nose against his collarbone. "Huh?"

"Earlier, outside the diner—"

She struggled to clear the cobwebs crowding her brain. "Oh! Yes. Sorry."

She collected her thoughts and slowly rubbed her leg against his. But then he surprised her by touching her knee and then smoothing his hand to the back, pulling her leg over his and placing her sex in direct contact with his thigh...a thigh he maneuvered so it pressed against her.

She lost her breath briefly then bore down against his hard muscles.

"This," she rasped.

He moved his thigh. "This?"

"Uh-huh..." She bit on her bottom lip. "After last night, I was going to suggest that maybe we could add sex to our arrangement..."

He moved his leg back and forth against her clit.

"Sex?" he whispered.

"Mmm, yes." She arched into him, amazed by how wet he made her by doing something so simple. "We don't have to alter the agreement. We can still act like a dating couple. But we'll just be friends..."

"Friends who have sex?"

"Mmm-hmm..."

His hand took the place of his leg. She gasped at his touch as he ran his fingertip along her hungry opening then moved on, teasing her.

She reached to see if he might be ready to go again. He'd removed the condom and she happily saw he was mostly erect again.

And she was all too willing to get him the rest of the way there.

She wrapped her fingers around him and squeezed gently, then stroked him as confidently as he touched her.

Oh, yes...

She wanted to taste him so badly her mouth watered. His weight felt so good against her palm. She slid down the sheets until her mouth was at his waist level then slid her lips down over the tip of his erection, licking as she went. He tasted of desire. She took more of him in and his hips bucked involuntarily.

"Sweet hell," he muttered under his breath, tangling his hands in her hair.

Geneva licked him, stroked him until his breathing quickened and he appeared on the verge of coming again.

She hoped he would. She wanted to taste him fully...

Instead, he grasped her shoulders and pulled her up

until she was kissing him. She all too readily straddled him even as she focused on the talents of his tongue in her mouth, moving her wetness along the length of his erection then back again, holding off when he tried to enter. Finally, he'd had enough. He quickly donned a condom, then grasped her hips and thrust hungrily upward.

She gasped, her mouth opening against his, incapable of movement, incapable of words, incapable of doing anything but riding the delicious tsunami of sensation that rushed over her, through her, in her.

Yes…

Mace pressed his hand against her shoulder, gently moving her until she sat upright.

She rocked her hips, then again, leaning her right hand back against his thigh. He touched her breasts, lightly pinching her nipples, adding to the hot chaos swirling within.

She felt like she could do this forever, wanted to do it forever, feel his thick hardness filling her to capacity, ride him until they were both raw…

She wasn't sure how long she'd stayed like that, merely moving on top of him, but when she heard him groan and he grasped her hips, she braced herself…and welcomed him thrusting wildly up into her.

Oh, yes!

"Mmm…"

A while later Mace lay with Geneva curved against his side, enjoying the quiet, contented sounds she made.

"So," he whispered against her hair. "Is that an adequate answer to your question?"

Her giggle made him smile. "Mmm-hmm…"

Adequate didn't come near describing how he felt about the past hour. After a perfectly horrific start, he'd regained his momentum—with some hot help from Geneva—and the two of them had set the sheets on fire.

Her responsiveness? Mind-blowing.

Actually, he was coming to see everything about her was mind-blowing. For all intents and purposes, she was the perfect woman. Kind, sexy as hell, levelheaded, funny, wild in bed, smart, sexy as hell... Wait, he'd already said that.

Yes, well, it bore repeating.

How in the hell he ever thought he'd be able to keep his hands off her was a mystery.

Then he remembered...

He couldn't help gazing down at where she curved against him. More specifically, at her belly.

Flat and toned, it was impossible to believe a baby was growing within her. But there was.

He waited for some sort of feeling other than post-coital bliss to hit him...

Nothing. At least nothing associated with the guilt he expected.

He honestly couldn't say that outside his admiration for her for going ahead on her own, with no expectations, no grudges or regrets, that he felt anything but a growing physical need and fondness for her.

Which brought him to his next need for her appearance.

"I want you to meet my parents."

Her soft sounds stopped. So, it appeared, had her breathing.

Hell, at his poor choice in words, he found himself holding his breath.

"Wait...that didn't come out right," he said. "What I meant is that I'm having lunch with my parents tomorrow and I'd like you to come with me."

"Play the role of girlfriend? For your parents?"

She'd moved slightly away and propped her head up in her hand, her elbow planted on the bed. He missed her warmth and closeness instantly.

"Yeah," he said simply. "Oh, and you'll be meeting my grandfather, too."

She squinted at him. "Are you sure you want me to lie to them?" She shifted, appearing uncomfortable. "I mean, it's one thing to do this with friends, but..."

"Quite another with family?"

She had a point.

When he'd first considered asking her to go with him, he thought it was the perfect way to get his mother to stop hounding him about grandchildren. But now...

And, of course, there was always the situation surrounding his brother...

"I want you to come," he said. "We don't have to lie. We can just tell them the truth—that we're friends." He wished she'd bring her heat back. "They don't interact with any common acquaintances, so there's no risk of the truth getting back to anybody."

"The truth..."

He grinned. "We'd, of course, leave out the sex part."

"Of course."

He moved his fingers over her propped-up arm and encouraged her to come closer.

He sighed in gratitude when she did.

They lay like that in companionable silence for a while, her rubbing her leg against his, his hand caressing her bare back.

"I have to warn you, they'll probably talk about my brother the entire time," he said quietly. "And my grandfather will probably flirt outrageously with you." He chuckled. "No, no probably about it—he will."

"I didn't know you had a brother."

Mace winced, but didn't say anything immediately.

He was curious why he'd offered up the comment so easily. He hadn't mentioned Marcus until well into his relationship with Janine. And even then, she had found out via his parents...which is probably why he'd thrown up the warning now.

"I don't," he said quietly. "At least not anymore."

She tilted her head to look up at him, but didn't say anything.

"Actually, that sounds cold. And my feelings for my brother are anything but." He took a deep breath. "I don't know. It's complicated..."

"How did he die?" she asked quietly.

"9/11. He was one of the firefighters who'd gone into the Twin Towers...and never made it back out."

He could feel her shocked stare in the darkness.

"It's all right. You don't have to say anything. Everything's been said already." Over and over and over again...

He grimaced and ran his hand over his face.

How had his love for his older brother gone from something he cherished to a burden to be hauled around, forever a weight on his shoulders?

He realized it was somewhere around the time his parents had stopped living and had gone into a sort of prolonged mourning trance it took him a month to recover from whenever he visited.

He hadn't been aware he'd spoken the words aloud until Geneva said, "It must be very difficult for you."

He extracted his arm from around her and pushed to a sitting position on the side of the bed. "Yeah."

He didn't know why he'd said the things he did to her, shared emotions he'd never told anyone.

She gently touched his back.

"I'm going to go grab a shower. I have a long day ahead of me tomorrow."

He heard her gather the blankets around her. "Okay."

He switched on the bedside light, got up, grabbed his jeans and headed for the bathroom, not so much needing a shower as he did a moment to himself.

Marcus...

He turned in the doorway, taking in the somber expression on her beautiful face.

"I'd love to come with you," she said quietly. "You know, for lunch tomorrow."

He said nothing.

"If the offer still stands?"

"Thanks."

She smiled at him. "Sure."

"Don't go anywhere until I get out?" he said.

She nodded.

He quietly closed the door then silently banged his fist against the cheap wood.

What had he been thinking?

Obviously, he hadn't been.

He switched on the shower, hoping the hot water and few minutes to himself would give him back the balance he needed.

Yet, somehow he knew it wouldn't.

13

GENEVA SAT AT HER DESK the following morning, trying to finish up some work before Mace was scheduled to pick her up for lunch. But she wasn't having much luck.

Last night, well, last night was a mix of both the fantastic and the confusing. She and Mace...

Her mind broke off, veering from her attempt to control it, as it had so often since getting up that morning following minimal snatches of true sleep.

She released a bone-deep sigh, remembering the way Mace had kissed her, touched her, filled her, bringing her to climax again and then again. He'd moved her more than merely physically, touched something vast inside her that had everything and nothing to do with sensual pleasure. She'd felt somehow joined with him on every plane. Looked into his eyes while he was inside her and saw him, herself and everything in between, as if nothing separated them.

Then he'd shut her out as solidly as he'd closed the bathroom door.

She caught herself absently scratching her arm through her sweater and stopped.

The swing was extreme enough to leave her breathless.

She knew his emotional withdrawal was related to his brother. What had he said his name was? Marcus. Yes, that was it.

But after sharing so much with her, why had he moved away, more than just physically?

As he'd requested, she'd stayed in the room until he emerged from his shower. She'd dressed and semi-made the bed and was sitting in one of the two chairs near the window. But he'd looked the same when he came out as he had when he went in, puzzling her all the more.

She knew whatever he was going through had nothing to do with her. But she couldn't help thinking his distancing himself wasn't a good sign.

Baggage. Everyone carried around their fair share. She looked down at where she rubbed her belly. Would Mace open up and share his with her? Or would he move on, his psychological suitcase still securely locked?

Of course, she was assuming that they'd remain in contact when he returned to duty next week…

She squinted at the computer screen, finding the prospect of saying goodbye to him permanently somehow inconceivable.

Her cell phone rang. She fumbled to pick it up, almost desperately thankful for the distraction, reading the display screen. Not Mace.

She took a deep breath and accepted the call from her client. No doubt he wanted more changes.

Ah, well. At least it was the distraction from her thoughts she needed, if not wanted; perhaps it would spur her into action work-wise until Mace got there. Then she'd know more how to proceed with what was becoming an increasingly complicated situation.

Was it simply a speed bump? Or had the countdown to goodbye already begun?

She told herself it didn't matter, one way or the other.

But she hoped with everything that was in her it was the former and not the latter...

THE MORNING HAD GROANED by without a break, but the instant Mace saw Geneva coming out of her apartment building to meet him instead of waiting for him to come up, it was as if the rain parted, allowing for a sweet ray of sunshine to shine through.

He got out of the car to open the passenger's door for her.

"You look great," he said, appreciating her dress and heels, while trying not to stare at her sexy legs.

"Thanks."

She climbed inside and he closed the door after her.

In the little downtime he'd had since last night, he'd been dreading this lunch with his parents, as well as dreading what he might see in Geneva's eyes when he saw her.

Until now...

While he wasn't exactly looking forward to seeing his parents, the open and warm expression on Geneva's beautiful face served as an eraser to the morning's stresses. And his own worries.

After getting little sleep, due in part to the incredible woman seated in his rental car, he'd met up with Jonathon Reece at Lazarus to review footage of yesterday's events, trying to identify the gunman and apprehend him before Norman's next rally, which was later this afternoon. Neither the general's team, nor the Denver police department, had any clue who it might have been. Not even a bullet casing had been retrieved, indicating the gunman had either plucked it up after firing, or perhaps even shot through something in order to catch it, such as a Ziploc bag. And that meant they weren't dealing with a random nutcase as they had suspected, but a possible pro. Eyewitnesses hadn't been able to give any more description than he'd already discerned from his chance run-in with the suspect. The guy was a Caucasian male somewhere in his late twenties, early thirties, wearing a gray hoodie with the hood up and fastened tightly. They couldn't even say what color his hair had been, much less his eyes...and neither could he.

He climbed into the car.

"Are you sure you're up for this?" he asked Geneva.

She blinked at him. "I'm sorry?"

He smiled. "This lunch. It's not too late to back out."

She laughed. "Sounds like you're the one more likely to back out."

"That's because I know what awaits."

"It can't be that bad?"

"That's because you don't know what you're walking into."

She smiled back. "Well, then, it might be a good idea to put it behind us as quickly as possible."

He shifted the car into gear. "A good idea, indeed."

The restaurant where he'd arranged to meet was some five minutes away, making it an easy drive for him, yet far enough away from his parents' place that they couldn't press him into going home with them for an extended visit. The last time he'd gone, he'd barely been able to breathe. If it were possible, they'd turned the house into an even bigger shrine to Marcus's memory than it had been before, including photos he hadn't ever seen.

Within moments, he'd pulled into the restaurant parking lot. He wasn't surprised to see his parents' sedan already parked near the front in a handicapped spot since they'd picked up his grandfather en route.

His grandfather...

Now him, he was looking forward to seeing.

He didn't realize he'd turned off the car and was just sitting until Geneva lightly touched his arm.

"Ready?" he asked, taking the key out of the ignition.

"Yes."

And before he knew it, he was being led to his parents' table near the front of the restaurant where they'd undoubtedly watched him pull up. He introduced Geneva to them.

Sharon and Mike Harrison were a kind couple. Friendly to everyone with whom they crossed paths. And they openly welcomed Geneva now, as he expected they would. If they were surprised he'd brought someone along, they hid it well. But he noticed his mother, especially, smiled a little more widely.

But it was his grandfather who smiled the widest.

"Well, hello," he said in a way that would have been almost salacious had he been a younger man.

He watched Geneva for her response; her own eyes danced with the same playful light as his grandfather's. Which is what he'd hoped. Given her position as a waitress, he guessed she encountered more than her fair share of open attention. He was glad she wasn't insulted by his grandfather's.

Dwayne Harrison got up with a little difficulty, leaving his cane untouched as he pulled out the chair next to him with gallant flourish. "Please, if you could be kind enough to grace an old man with your pleasant company."

Geneva accepted while Mace returned his parents' curious glances with a smile.

"I didn't realize you would be bringing someone with you today," his mother said.

"Sorry, I invited Geneva late last night and didn't have a chance to tell you before now." The free seat put him between Geneva and his father.

He didn't miss his mother's expectant expression, indicating she was waiting for more.

He didn't deliver it.

His grandfather was busy charming Geneva who, indeed, appeared charmed.

"So, have you been dating long?" his mother asked.

Geneva nearly choked on her water. She quickly picked up a napkin and dabbed at her chin, giving him an amused glance under the thick fringe of her lashes even as his father suggested maybe the question was too forward.

"We're not," Mace said in answer to her question.

"I'm sorry?" Sharon said.

"Dating. We're not," Geneva provided. "We're just friends."

"Just friends…"

"Good," his grandfather spoke up. "That means the field's wide open for me. A man my age needs all the help he can get."

The men and Geneva laughed while his mother appeared appalled.

Menus were brought and orders placed, Mace silently counting the seconds when the meal would be over with and he could get out of there, even as he admired Geneva and the easy way she handled his grandfather and his parents. Things were going so well, in fact, he found himself relaxing, enjoying the company rather than suffering through it.

Sharon Harrison was still an attractive woman. A golf lover, she'd kept in great shape and could easily pass for a decade younger.

His father, on the other hand, looked his age. Dedicated career military, he'd seen his share of violent conflicts, both on the front line and commanding them.

Geneva easily conversed with his parents as if she'd known them for years instead of minutes.

His mother sighed deeply. "I wish you could have met our Marcus. You two would have gotten on famously."

And just like that the light mood fell through the floor…

14

GENEVA SLID A GAZE in Mace's direction at the mention of his brother. His body language couldn't have been any clearer: the smile vanished from his handsome face, his jaw clenched and his shoulders squared. And had he really just looked at his watch? Yes, he had.

The table fell silent at the mention of Marcus. But whether it was in deference or warning, she couldn't be sure.

"I'm sure I would have liked him, too," Geneva said quietly.

Sharon Harrison seemed to take that as some sort of cue and continued on Marcus, who instantly became not so much a memory but a palpable presence.

Even Mace's grandfather had gone quiet, pretending an interest in his soup.

Within a blink, everything had gone from light and happy to somber and heavy.

While Geneva genuinely wanted to know more about Mace's brother and his family, she had the feeling that the cloud descending on them all wouldn't help her in that endeavor.

"I thought you all should know... I'm pregnant."

The table fell silent.

Geneva supposed she should be appalled at her own forwardness. She usually wasn't the type to draw attention to herself. But the growing toxicity of the current environment was making her uncomfortable. More importantly, it was making Mace unhappy. And she'd do anything to prevent that. Even make a spectacle of herself.

Luckily, her words had the intended impact by distracting her tablemates from their dark thoughts.

Sharon coughed, apparently having trouble swallowing, while next to her, Mace's grandfather gave her a nudge even as he fixed a grin on Mace. "Harrison guns still firing straight, eh?"

Thankfully Mace laughed. Not the kind of polite, accommodating laugh but a full-out chuckle. "Wish I could take the credit, Gramps, but truth is Geneva and I met only a few days ago."

"The baby's not yours?" Sharon asked.

"The baby's not mine."

For reasons she wasn't entirely sure about, Sharon asked Mace to trade seats with her. A waitress appeared to help rearrange their plate settings.

"I hope you don't mind," the older woman said with a warm smile. "I've spent so much time around guys, well, it's just nice to enjoy female company. So tell me all about the baby..."

Geneva couldn't remember the last time she'd experienced such complete acceptance and excitement directed at her. Oh, Trudy and the girls were happy for her, but guardedly, realistically so.

On the plus side, Marcus's name disappeared from the conversation. On the minus, Mace's dad and grandfather seemed puzzled.

But it was Mace's reaction that mattered. Just as quickly

as he'd tensed up, he'd relaxed again. And when she looked to find him smiling at her, she swore she could feel it like a physical sweep of his hand against her bare back.

She wasn't sure what, exactly, she'd done…but she hoped that she did it again soon. Preferably the next time they were alone together…

"THAT WAS INCREDIBLE," Mace said quietly.

Geneva released her seatbelt after the nearly two-hour lunch with his family, trying not to feel too smug. She knew she'd saved the meal by offering herself and her pregnancy up as a willing distraction.

They'd ridden to her place in silence, but now Mace reached for her hand and held it fast in his.

Her heart hiccupped and she returned his grasp, reveling in the warm feel of his skin against hers.

"Thank you," he said.

"For what?" she asked as innocently as possible. "The way I see it, I should be thanking you."

"For what?"

"For a terrific meal. For a good time. For sharing your family with me."

He looked away and grimaced.

She got the distinct impression his reaction was a pre-programmed one. Because from where she sat, the only grimace material had been that brief period before she'd announced her pregnancy.

"Your family is wonderful, Mace," she said.

He looked at her, seeming to search her face for an answer she wasn't sure she had, but openly allowed him to search anyway. "I'd forgotten that," he said. "Thank you for the reminder."

"No problem."

They sat in silence for a few moments.

It was the middle of the day and they still held hands but there didn't seem to be a rush to leave.

But she knew he would be leaving. He needed to get back to work protecting that political bigwig.

But she'd be damned if she was going to remind him of that and miss out on sharing this closeness.

"I don't know how late I'll be tonight," he said.

She nodded.

"I'd ask you to wait up…"

She smiled at him. "If you did, I would."

He smiled back. "I'm thinking we could both do with a bit of sleep."

She looked down and nodded, trying to hide her disappointment.

He squeezed her hand and she squeezed back.

She didn't know how much time they had left together, but she wanted to enjoy every moment. Still, he was right: they did need some solid rest.

"Call you tomorrow?"

She nodded again. "Sure."

He leaned over to kiss her.

She was sure he'd meant to give her a brief goodbye peck, but the instant his lips met with hers, they lingered.

Geneva breathed deeply, taking in the sweet scent of him. How she was coming to look forward to his kiss, his smell, his touch.

He leaned back and she sighed.

"Let me walk you up."

She began to object but he'd already opened his door and was getting out.

She waited for him to open her door, feeling ridiculously touched that he liked to do these little things for her.

Before she knew it, they were standing outside her apartment door.

"Thank you again, Geneva." His eyes were earnest. "I can't tell you how long it's been since I've enjoyed my parents' company. Today, well, today isn't something I'm soon to forget."

"Good," she said.

She reached out and touched the side of his handsome face, smiling deep into his eyes. Then she leaned in to kiss him softly, communicating more than gratitude or sexual need or even friendship.

Long minutes later, he made a low sound in his throat and pulled away.

"If I don't go now, I'm afraid I won't."

"And your point is?"

He chuckled as he quickly kissed her one last time and slowly took his arms from around her. "Talk to you tomorrow?"

She nodded. "Talk to you tomorrow."

She watched him go, stopping every few steps to look back at her before continuing again. She didn't go inside until she heard the downstairs outer door close behind him. Then she closed her own and leaned against it, staring at nothing and everything. She told herself she should be concerned about her wistful state. But her heart was hearing none of it…

15

TOMORROW AFTERNOON'S RALLY was going to be far more dangerous.

Mace didn't like it. He didn't like it one bit. If his radar had been tweaked while walking the route on the first go-round, this time alarm bells were going off.

He told Darius about his concerns over the phone. His friend was still in Oregon working the kidnapping case.

"He refuses to cancel," Dari said finally.

"Well, then, we're just going to have to do the best we can to protect him. So long as you've outlined the risks and made your recommendations, that's the only course of action to take."

"We could pull out."

Silence.

Mace knew it was a radical solution that wasn't really a solution at all.

"Then we wouldn't get paid."

"I feel that strongly about this."

"I know you do."

He paced the length of the conference room then back again, the men around him giving him a wide berth.

Forget that the perpetrator from yesterday's rally had

yet to be caught; there were warning signs that tomorrow's event would leave Norman even more vulnerable.

First off, the venue was larger, harder to protect, not to mention the turnout was predicted to be quadruple, possibly more given the publicity received.

Second, well, the gunman had gotten a taste of fame himself. Who was to say he wouldn't make the next attempt bigger? Bolder?

A normal man might be scared off.

But they were dealing with someone who was far from normal here. Someone driven, someone insane enough to make the first attempt might be doubly motivated to make a second.

He took a deep breath and stopped pacing.

"Okay. I just needed to say the words," he said to Dari.

"Yeah, I know. And they would have been the same words I'd say if our roles were reversed."

"Yeah."

He doubted that, but he was grateful to his friend for saying it.

A few moments later they disconnected and Mace turned to face the guys. They had their work cut out for them.

But he had every confidence they could do it.

"Okay, let's get down to it…"

GENEVA'S CELL PHONE CHIMED. She rolled over in bed and squinted at the clock: it was just after five-thirty. Who would be texting her that early? Probably Trudy. She likely needed her to fill in again at the diner this morning.

She groaned and reached for her cell phone. She'd worked the dinner shift last night and with a football game running into overtime, they were kept busy until well into the night. She didn't get home until after eleven and while she'd made really good tips, she felt like she'd gotten maybe two hours of solid sleep.

She accessed the text and experienced an instant infusion of adrenaline.

It was Mace.

"I've got an hour to spare. Do you want coffee?"

Geneva tossed off the blankets even as she began texting back. "Where are you?"

"Outside your place."

She hurried to the window, instantly catching sight of him where he leaned against her car holding up two cups of extra-large coffee in white foam cups.

"I'll buzz you in."

She looked down at her faded flannels, grabbed jeans and a sweater, then hurried to press the buzzer to let him into the building. Then she opened the apartment door even as she dashed for the bathroom. She'd gotten on her jeans and was putting on her sweater when she heard, "Hello?"

She cracked the door. "Make yourself at home. I just need five."

She closed the door again then ran the water, washing up and upgrading herself to mildly presentable. Once finished, she stood staring at her reflection. What was she doing?

She found herself smiling. She didn't care. Right then, the only thing that mattered was that she had fifty-five minutes left to spend with Mace.

She emerged from the bathroom to find him standing in front of the living room window staring outside, sipping coffee. He looked so damned good in dark slacks and a crisp white shirt, his dark hair combed and neat. She, on the other hand, felt like a field mouse who'd just emerged from a dusty hole.

He sensed her presence and turned to face her, that grin of his lighting his face. "Hi."

"Hi yourself." She cleared her throat.

He put his coffee down and stepped closer, folding her into his arms. "I hope you don't mind my stopping by so early unannounced."

"No, no." She found she had a hard time breathing with him so close. "Not at all."

He smiled down at her then leaned in for a kiss. "Good, because I have another request to make."

Sleep still clung to the fringes of Geneva's consciousness, emphasizing her wholehearted response to his kiss. "Oh?" she somehow managed to say, even as her thighs vibrated as if he were licking them instead of her lips.

"I want to spend every moment possible of the next hour inside of you..."

MACE WASN'T SURE what had made him say the words. One minute he'd been on his way back to Denver following a long night and an even longer day ahead of him. The next he was pulling Geneva close and her sleep-enhanced scent made his need level surge.

She blinked liquid hazel eyes up to stare at him and he chuckled softly, trailing his fingertips over her jawline before leaning in to kiss her even more deeply.

She felt so good. Better than anyone had a right to. Holding her in his arms made him feel all-powerful yet grounded, hot as hell yet cool as could be.

And it made him want her with an intensity he was loathe to ignore.

He drew back and looked at her, waiting for her response.

He heard her swallow thickly. "I'm sorry. Was I supposed to say something?" she whispered.

He groaned and led her to her bedroom, drawing her close the instant they were inside. He kissed her then pulled off her sweater as she undid the first few buttons on his shirt and tugged it the rest of the way off. Within moments, they were stripped and breathless.

She turned, rubbing her bare bottom against him, then reached an arm back and positioned her head so she could kiss him over her shoulder.

Dear God, but she was sexier than any woman he'd ever known.

He curved his hands around and cupped her breasts.

She caught them in her hands. "Gently," she whispered.

He lightened his touch, kissing her more tenderly. Her quickening of breath told him she approved.

He snaked his right hand down lower, over her abdomen, lower still…until his fingers rested against the springy hair between her thighs.

Geneva made a small sound in the back of her throat then caught his hand. But rather than move it away as he was afraid she might, she budged it the rest of the way down until his fingers pressed against her dampness. Then she grasped his wrist as if to steady herself as he stroked her.

So hot, so wet…

He moved his fingertips back and forth and forth and back, lightly pinching her clit. At her gasp, he slid his middle finger between her silken folds, moving deep within her.

She went limp in his arms. He gently moved her toward the bed. She reached out until her left hand rested against the mattress, bending slightly, even as she continued kissing him over her shoulder. He increased the frequency of his thrusts, taking pleasure in the way she bore down against him. He lowered his other hand and stroked her outside even as he did inside.

"I...want...to...feel...you..." she rasped.

"You will, baby, you will." He thrust deeper. "Come for me now..."

She moaned, her hips rocking against him.

Geneva's mouth opened against his in a gasp. He breathed it in and kissed her deeply, feeling her slick muscles contract around his fingers. He continued stroking and caressing her, drawing out her crisis, supporting her weight as she surrendered to the sensations rolling through her.

"Please..." she whispered, kissing him languidly.

He didn't need any more encouragement. His penis was so erect it was nearly painful. Watching, bringing her to climax, had turned him on more than sex.

He sheathed himself then pressed against her soaked flesh. She kissed him, replacing his hand with hers, then took him in.

He nearly groaned aloud at the feel of her surrounding him, tight, still shivering. She reached her other hand out until she leaned completely against the bed. The sexy sight of her back, her hips, her rounded bottom made his erection pulse harder. He smoothed his hands down her spine then grasped her hips, holding her still as he surged into her. Her low moan echoed what he was feeling as he thrust again, then again.

"Yes, oh, yes..."

Each stroke brought him closer to her...closer to orgasm...closer to a euphoria that left him wondering with awe at its complexity and simplicity.

He slowed, afraid of coming too fast. Geneva bore back against him, shifting her hips hungrily. He reached around, finding her damp curls, and rubbed her lazily. She caught his wrist. Not to pull him away, it seemed, but to hold him there as her body stilled, her back arched.

Mace groaned and surged into her again, reaching for an unnamable something he needed more than he'd ever needed anything.

Then, suddenly, it was upon him...

His entire body stiffened, his blood roaring past his ears, through his body, making him feel totally, gloriously alive.

Geneva moaned.

Somehow, he found the will to thrust into her again, and again, harder, tilting his hips to change the angle of his stroke.

She went still and her breathing seemed to stop.

Mace grasped her hips tightly, moving in, pulling out...

Reaching out his hand and taking her with him as he toppled over the edge into sheer bliss...

16

GENEVA LAY BONELESS in bed, her hand resting against Mace's thigh next to her. They'd both ended up there, and somehow she'd managed to cover them both, but beyond that, she could do little more than marvel at the music pulsing through her body and focus on trying to breathe again.

She sighed and curved against Mace, who seemed to be wearing the same expression she probably did as he stared wide-eyed at the ceiling.

"You okay?" she whispered, kissing his shoulder.

"Hmm? Oh. Yeah." He grinned down at her then kissed the top of her head, rubbing his hand against her tangled hair. "I'm… I don't know how I feel…"

She sighed again and closed her eyes. "Yeah. Me, too."

They both chuckled then fell silent again.

She couldn't be sure if the spontaneous element of their lovemaking was behind her elevated reaction, but whatever it was, she wanted to do it again.

And again and again and again…

She guessed Mace would be in complete agreement.

"You need to be in Denver again?"

He nodded, his hand running lazy circles along her back. "Yeah."

"Oh, okay. By the way, I thought you should know, your mother called me last night…"

MACE WENT TOTALLY and utterly still in abject terror.

"What?"

He was incapable of any other verbal response. Only that one word.

Geneva gave a quiet laugh. "No worries. She just wanted to tell me how much she enjoyed meeting me."

Had his mom ever called Janine? He couldn't recall. In fact, in that one moment, he couldn't recall much of anything. His mind was frozen on the image of his mother calling Geneva…and Geneva picking up.

"I haven't even heard from my mother," he said.

Geneva shifted slightly. "Maybe because she thinks she's bothering you whenever she calls."

He tucked his chin against his chest so he could look down at her. "Is that what she said?"

"In so many words…yes. She did."

That was odd. He'd never considered that his mother might feel awkward about calling him.

"What else did she say?"

Geneva snuggled a little closer to him, putting her wet sex in direct contact with his thigh. He grew instantly hard.

What had they been talking about?

Oh, yeah. His mother.

"That's between me and your mother," she said in answer to his question.

He grimaced. "I can only imagine."

She shifted again, this time to prop herself up on one elbow so she could look at him. "Can you?"

"Mmm." The way she kept moving her sex against him was driving him to distraction.

"I'm not entirely sure you can."

"One word: Marcus."

She seemed to consider him for a long moment. "Not in the sense you're thinking."

He blinked.

"Let's just say I think there's a whole lot going unsaid between you two."

"Oh, I think everything's been said. And then some."

"Do you? Well, then I'm not sure which of you is more stubborn."

He raised his brows. "And you're an expert on my mother and me because...?"

She visibly winced then smiled. "I don't consider myself an expert on anything," she said quietly. "But I am a good listener."

"Most people hear what they want to."

Mace didn't particularly care for the words coming out of his mouth, but Geneva had touched on a sore spot... and refused to stop.

"Even if that's the case, I didn't have to listen to hear what she had to say."

Poke...poke...

"The day Marcus died..."

There it was.

"Your parents feel like they lost two sons, not one."

Mace experienced a sensation similar to a boulder being dropped onto his chest.

"I can see you're surprised."

"I'm also horny."

She nudged him with her closed fist against his chest. "That goes without saying."

He glanced at the clock then rolled her over so she was under him, her thighs spread wide. "I've got twenty minutes. Do you really want to spend them talking?"

He watched her gaze roll over his features then back up

to his eyes. She smiled and slid her feet around his calves and arched her back. "Oh, I think I've said all I need to. For now…"

Good.

He kissed her deeply even as he reached for another condom. This time when he made her come, he wanted it to be so hard she couldn't utter a word until sometime tomorrow…

GENEVA LAY BACK against the sheets, listening as her apartment door closed behind Mace. Every inch of her felt so vibrant, alive. She pressed her face into her pillow and breathed deeply, taking in his scent even as she ran her hands over her still-vibrating body.

What he did to her…

Her breasts trembled, her belly quaked and her thighs were saturated with the proof of her need for him.

Oh, how she would love for his semen to be there…

She shivered at the thought even as she lazily touched herself.

He'd loved her so thoroughly, you would think she'd be satisfied. Instead, she wanted more. Oh, so much more.

She couldn't remember ever feeling this…sexual before. Uninhibited. Needy.

She stroked her swollen flesh then inserted her fingertip inside, moaning as she recalled how he'd touched her just a short time ago.

Mmm…

Her cell phone rang.

She slowly reached for it.

It was Mace.

"What are you doing?" he asked.

She smiled. "Touching myself."

"Grr… That's my job."

"Yes, well, since you're not here to do it…"

There was silence for a few minutes while she continued stroking herself. Then he said, "I miss you already."

Geneva clutched the phone against her shoulder and closed her eyes before responding. "Miss you more."

She put the cell phone back on the night table then rolled over, bunching the sheets between her thighs and stretching languidly.

More…

She definitely wanted much, much more…

Was Mace ready, willing and able to give it to her?

She didn't know.

What was clear was how incredible things could be if he was.

Her cell phone chimed.

She saw a text message.

I Love You.

She blinked at the words. Then read them again.

Was it possible?

She was about to write back when another chimed in.

Sleep well. Talk to you later.

She responded with a smile then held the phone close to her again.

When she awakened a couple of hours later, she was still holding it there…

17

"ARE WE READY?"

Funny, was it really only yesterday he'd asked Geneva the same question prior to going to lunch with his parents?

Was it really that morning he'd said those other words he'd never uttered in his life?

I love you...

Not only had he said them, he'd typed them. They were in black and white, unmistakable, permanently evidenced.

Was it possible he'd never said them before? Not even to Janine? Not even to his parents? His grandfather? His brother?

Yet he'd texted them to Geneva.

And he'd meant them.

He scrubbed the back of his neck, trying to ease the tension there.

Love. He felt it. For his family. His friends. And he had felt it for Janine.

And now for Geneva.

But it wasn't something he'd thought about a great deal. It was an obvious statement that required action, not words, similar to his military lifestyle.

Then why had he been moved to say them this morning?

And were the words welcome?

He scrubbed his neck harder, fighting to review his checklist. Post-coital misstep. Yeah, that's what he could put it down to. The sex had been so incredible, he'd still been half out of his mind. Capable of saying anything.

Still, that didn't quite cut it. What was happening between them was different from the challenges he faced at work, even though they were no less intense. There were road signs posted all over the place. Unfortunately, he was spending so much time enjoying the ride, he wasn't really registering the signs until after he had passed them. And there were no U-turns to be had.

And if he could? He didn't know.

Reece came up. "Ready, willing and able, sir."

"Ready, willing and able."

And they were. At least as much as they could be.

When all was said and done, all they could do was their best.

"Good," he said. "Oh, and Reece? I want you to take the lead today."

The other man hesitated. "Sir?"

He grinned. "She's all yours."

"Are you leaving the premises?"

"No. But while I'll be listening in, I won't be in contact."

At least not unless there was an emergency.

He planned to move at will, no worries about calling shots and overseeing details: all those had been taken care of and Reece was more than capable of overseeing them.

He needed to be on the ground.

Alone.

"Very well, sir," Reece said.

"Good. There's an hour before departure. Do what you need to do to prepare your men."

Reece did as he was asked and Mace took the opportunity to slip from the room.

He ran into one of Norman's men outside the door. The guy had been looking for him.

He shook his head. "Sorry. The man to talk to is Reece."

He vaguely heard an objection but gave it little attention as he continued walking down the hall.

A TAKE ON the street hustler's shell game. Find the car, any car; which one held General Norman?

Except in this case the question wasn't which one, but rather did any of the five hold the man?

That was the tact Mace decided to take en route to today's lunchtime rally, scheduled to make the noon news coverage, not just locally, but nationally. He was coming to understand this was the way most of these rallies were done. Maximum exposure was the name of the game.

But with maximum exposure came maximum risk.

As he listened to the team communicate via his earpiece, he mentally reviewed the plans. The cars were due to pull out in five minutes. But that wasn't all that was on his mind; he'd been working hard to try to uncover the identity of the gunman from the last outing. While his sources had spat up a couple dozen likely suspects matching his physical description and MO, Mace had the feeling they were dealing with someone off the grid. For the guy to have felt comfortable enough to move so freely, he had to be relatively sure he wouldn't be easy to find.

Either that or he was psychopathic and was unconsciously looking to get caught.

It was a toss-up which was more dangerous...

He accessed his cell phone, checking for texts. He knew who he was hoping to hear from, but the queue was empty other than brief channel communications from Reece.

He rubbed his thumb pad over the keys then put the phone back into his pocket.

"We're rolling…"

Reece's announcement sent him into motion.

He'd changed from his security detail clothing into jeans, a green T-shirt, brown suede jacket and a Bronco's ball cap, going for as nondescript as possible in the hopes that the suspect wouldn't recognize him if their paths happened to cross again.

He stood across the street, half a block up from the hotel, which gave him a clear view of the parking lot entrance and all points in between. He'd just bought a paper from a corner kiosk and tucked it under his arm, looking everywhere but directly at the cars exiting onto the street one by one.

There were so many windows, both inside and outside the hotel. The suspect could be in any one of them.

He eyed pedestrian and automotive traffic, thinking everyone he saw could be the suspect…including the woman with blond hair and large glasses.

He headed in the same direction as the convoy and took out his cell phone, pretending to answer a call and consult his watch.

He made out the sound of a siren.

While the sheriff's office was involved in the detail, they weren't supplying an official escort. So that meant whatever was going on didn't involve them.

He watched as a fire truck pulled into the intersection a block up.

Or did it involve them?

Shit.

He contacted Reece. "Looks like we've got a problem."

And he didn't think it was by accident…

GENEVA SAT AT THE DINER counter, her fingers wrapped around a coffee cup although she couldn't have swallowed if she tried. She was in a lull between customers, waiting for the local news to come on at noon in the hopes that they'd be covering Norman's visit.

She checked her cell phone: nothing.

Not that she expected anything. She knew Mace was busy. Doubly so since the rally was due to begin in a few short minutes.

Still, she'd hoped for something.

Of course, she could always text him. But she didn't want to seem needy. And after falling back to sleep for a while earlier, she'd wondered if she should have said something in response to his proclamation. At the very least, she should have acknowledged it. Had she said those same words and he not responded...

She turned her coffee cup in circle. Of course, Mace wasn't like her. And she didn't think he'd obsess the way she probably would have.

Of course, she wouldn't have guessed Mace to be the type to say those words, either...

Trudy turned the television up, pretending it was something she always did, but Geneva knew she'd done it for her as much as to satisfy her own interest. Talk around the diner was still all about what had gone down the other day. And the fact that Trudy and the crew knew Mace...well, it only made it infinitely more interesting.

"We're breaking into regular programming a couple of minutes early for the noon news update. There appears to be something unusual going on surrounding General Norman's rally today. If you'll remember, it was only two days ago that..."

Geneva tuned out the newscaster's voice. Her gaze was glued to the live footage being run. There was a fire truck blocking an intersection in downtown Denver a couple of blocks up from where the reporter said Norman was staying, and a five-car procession stopped while traffic was backed up, bumper to bumper, behind them.

She felt like she'd swallowed her coffee cup and it was stuck in her throat as she tried to spot Mace.

"What's going on?" Tiffany asked, coming up beside her.

Trudy was the one who answered from the other side of the counter, quickly explaining what they'd heard so far before hushing the waitress and everyone else. She grabbed the remote to turn the volume up even further.

"The guy's a stationary target now," Mel said, peeking his head through the service window.

"Looks like it's just a fire or something," Trudy said.

"Right," another male customer said, leaving his table to stand closer to the TV in the corner. "Looks like a setup to me."

Geneva felt suddenly dizzy at the thought that Mace was in one of those cars, an unwitting target of the man threatening Norman's life.

She took out her cell phone: still nothing.

"You okay?" Trudy asked, taking the stool next to her.

She nodded, but couldn't say anything as she continued staring at the television screen. She didn't dare blink for fear she'd miss something.

The reporter filled them all in on the details from the other day and footage from the event was run.

"Wait, hold on a minute," the reporter's voice broke in during his explanation. "Looks like something is starting to happen…"

The footage continued to run even as he spoke, nearly driving Geneva straight out of her skin as she willed the camera to switch back to live action.

"It appears the police department is clearing the street behind the procession...yes, yes, they are. Officers are directing traffic to side streets. The last of the procession cars is backing up."

Then, just like that, there was a flash of light and the camera went dead, cutting off the feed.

"Trent? Trent, are you still with us?"

The female news anchor held her hand to her ear as if listening through an earpiece when an image finally came back on. She appeared to realize she was back on the air and removed hand, her expression one of shock.

Oh, God, no...

18

HOLY SHIT!

Mace watched as the second to last car exploded in a bright, yellow ball of flame. Broken glass and flying metal moldings hit surrounding buildings, taking out windows.

For a split second, he was back in Iraq and a convoy car had hit an IED.

Then he blinked and brought the current sight back into focus.

"Stay put!" he shouted into his mouthpiece. "Repeat, do *not* get out of the car!"

He suspected taking the last car out was an attempt to get everyone out and allow for an open shot on Norman.

All the cars were designed with just such a scenario in mind—essentially the vehicle portions housed safety pods engineered to withstand just such an attack. That meant the two security personnel in the subject car should be okay, with little more than a few cuts and bruises.

Norman himself wasn't in any of the cars. In fact, right about now he was arriving at the rally site in an unmarked, unrelated vehicle that had left the hotel ten minutes before the rest of them.

Had it been a car bomb? Seemed likely. Still, Mace

found himself eyeing the surrounding buildings. His gaze caught on a wisp of smoke coming from an open window some ten floors up. His first clue that this was the real deal was that the window was even open at all in a business structure where windows were required to be closed due to safety issues that had nothing to do with rally processions and controversial political figures.

Even as he listened to Reece ably direct the action on the ground, he rushed the door to the business building, mentally mapping out exits. He was going to get this guy, come hell or high water...

WHERE WAS HE?

Geneva didn't dare leave the support of the diner. Normally the lunch crowd was replaced by the dinner one, but today no one was leaving and the eatery was quickly filled to capacity by those watching the action being replayed on the local television station that had switched to live programming. It had been some time since Colorado Springs had seen this much activity and its residents were drawn together to experience it together.

Unfortunately, Geneva's connection was a little more direct.

Why didn't he call?

"Anything?" Trudy asked as she passed.

Geneva was standing in the middle of the diner floor, her arms filled with plates of burgers and fries even as she checked her cell phone. She shook her head, put her phone back in her apron pocket and continued on to Table Three.

Following the abrupt cut-off of live coverage earlier, the five-minute wait as a new connection was set up ranked up there as some of the longest of her life. The on-the-ground reporter and his cameraman were fine, it was explained, but their equipment had been taken out by the blast.

And what a blast it had been, too. At the first sight of the broken car sitting in the middle of a blackened circle on the downtown Denver street, Geneva had nearly projectile vomited, imagining Mace inside the vehicle.

That's when she began texting...

She told herself not to. That he was probably fine and that Mace had his hands full and the last thing on his mind would be her and her active imagination. But she hadn't been able to help herself.

Somewhere after the tenth panicked text, she'd forced herself to stop, even though her dread continued to grow.

It couldn't be good, his unresponsiveness.

So instead she'd watched coverage along with everyone else, both of the rally that the general had made it to safely even though all five cars in the procession remained at a standstill on a downtown street, blocked on one end by a fire truck that was now needed, and the disable vehicle. She'd gasped when firemen had gained access to the car, pulling out two men. Were either of them Mace? She'd run up to the television and stood directly underneath, not daring to blink as the reporter narrated events.

Ultimately, it was decided both men were fine...and neither of them was Mace.

At one point, she'd ordered herself to stop. Mace was a military pro and episodes of this nature were a regular part of his job.

But this wasn't Afghanistan: this was Colorado. And stuff like this wasn't supposed to happen.

After delivering the plates and refilling coffee cups, she caught herself standing in front of the television again, coffeepot in one hand, thumbnail of her other between her teeth. At this point, they were merely rehashing earlier events. There was no new information, no footage that included a shot of Mace.

It was just after five and while "Breaking News" was stamped in a special red icon in the upper right of the screen, the station had rolled into its usual pre-news hour.

She found it ironic that one of her basic reasons for never dating a man in the military had been because of the long separations that frequently found the object of a stateside lover's attention wandering. She'd never really considered the risk angle—the fact that the lover might wander off…permanently.

She'd turned her cell phone volume on high. It loudly chirped now.

Geneva fumbled to get it out of her apron pocket, nearly dropping it. Those aware of her connection to Mace stopped to stare at her.

A text.

From Mace.

Her relief was so complete, her knees nearly gave out.

She made it to the counter where she leaned against it for support as she accessed the text.

Running late. Meet you at the dance…

She stared, dumbfounded, reading it again.

He was okay.

The word swirled around and around her head.

He was okay.

"So?"

She looked to find Trudy hovering.

She blinked. "He says he'll meet me at the dance."

Dance?

She realized she'd completely forgotten about the dance.

"Girl, I need you here."

She nodded, then pressed the needed buttons to respond to Mace's text.

No way was she going to work overtime at the diner when she had a chance to see Mace.

She wrote, then rewrote the text. Finally, she settled on a simple Okay.

She sat for long moments, cell phone crushed in her hand, staring at the television screen, attempting to connect the surreal scene continuing to play out with the mind-blowingly normal one going on in her life.

"Running late. Meet you at the dance…"

His words as casual as if a meeting he was in was going long or he'd been caught in traffic.

Not that he'd been involved in a car-bombing incident that nearly took two men's lives.

"Table Five needs service," Trudy said, passing her.

Geneva looked at her blankly, her words taking a moment to register.

An hour. That's all she was going to give the diner. Then she was going home to stand in the shower until the water ran cold, or until her thoughts started to make sense. Whichever came first.

And then she was going to that dance.

19

HE SHOULD HAVE CANCELED.

Mace knew that.

Still, even though his mind was occupied with the day's event, he was late as hell and probably in hot water, the thought of seeing Geneva, even for a few minutes...well, it eclipsed everything else.

He straightened his Marine full-dress uniform jacket and scanned the good-sized crowd at the outdoor dance, his mind still going over the second attempt against Norman's life.

After pinpointing the position of the assailant, he'd rushed into the business building with backup on the way only to find the vacant office from which the rocket had been launched empty...although very recently occupied. The suspect had left behind items he probably hadn't intended to, which indicated Mace had just missed him. A scope bore a good fingerprint that Mace had immediately entered into the system. While nothing had come back yet, he had men out pulling samples from hotels and motels in the area hoping for a match and a further lead. He also had guys reviewing video from cameras in the area.

The two security men in the target car had suffered minor burns and concussions but thankfully, they were okay.

And General Norman had gone on to his rally as if nothing had happened, not learning the full extent of the second attempt until afterward.

It had been after seven before Mace realized what time it was…and remembered his promise to Geneva.

Now it was after nine.

The Harvest Dance was set on a farm outside Colorado Springs in a hulking old barn. A big band was set up in a corner among hay bales and there was a large dance area in front of the makeshift stage, while tables full of those taking advantage of the unseasonably warm night were set up both inside and outside the barn under large tents.

He didn't know how he was going to find Geneva. He hadn't heard anything from her after her simple "Okay."

Maybe he should call her.

Then he spotted her.

His stomach tightened in a way not all that different than it had in the wake of today's events, yet was entirely different. She was standing near the barn doors, a glass of what looked like wine in her hand though he guessed it was likely juice, her profile turned to him as she took in the scene. She had on a red high-waisted dress and heels, her hair swept back from her beautiful face, looking perfectly matched to the nostalgia-era setting.

He stood still, merely watching her when she seemed to sense his presence. Her chin went up and she turned her head, meeting his gaze.

Her smile erased everything that had happened that day. Nothing existed but her.

They met in the middle of the distance separating them and she hugged him. He happily hugged her back.

"Thank God you're okay," she whispered into his ear.

She smelled of gardenias and something spicy. It was all he could do not to press his lips against the long line of her neck. Damn, but she looked beautiful.

He hadn't thought about her worrying earlier. It wasn't until later he'd discovered the news about the car explosion had been pretty much broadcast live, which meant she'd probably seen it.

"I'm even better now," he whispered back, settling for brushing his lips against the shell of her ear as he pulled her slightly closer.

She smiled up at him.

As he smiled back, he couldn't help feeling as if he'd known her forever…yet as if they'd just met.

"You want something to drink?" she asked.

He watched her mouth say the words, but didn't immediately register them. The band had launched into a slow classic.

"What? Oh. No." He offered his arm. "But I would like to dance with you. Do me the honor?"

"The honor would be mine."

He took the glass from her hand, placed it on a nearby table, then walked her the short way to the dance floor. As he pulled her close, he couldn't help thinking there was nowhere else he'd rather be in that one moment. She fit just so against him, her soft sigh communicating she likely felt the same.

It had been a good long while since he'd danced with anyone. But Geneva wasn't just anyone. She was…she was…

He looked down at her.

She was beautiful. In every way.

"I was worried about you," she said softly.

"I know. I'm sorry. I should have called."

"I know you had more important matters to attend to."

Just then, he couldn't think what those could be. He was filled with the sweet scent of her, the feel...and wanted more. Oh, so much more.

"I was afraid you weren't going to make it tonight," she said.

"I was, too."

He smiled down at her and then held her closer still.

He closed his eyes, listening to the music, content to feel her heart beating against his, for now.

"About your text this morning..." she said so softly he nearly didn't hear her.

Had it really been only that morning since he'd texted those three words? Yes, he realized, it had been.

"Shh," he said into her ear. "Let's just enjoy the moment, okay?"

Her head nodded against his cheek.

He pressed his lips against her temple.

So much, so quickly. From one extreme to the next. Given the drastic swings, part of him wondered if his instincts and emotions could be trusted. But it was a small part, if only because this felt so right.

A tap on Mace's shoulder. "May I?"

He turned to look at Dustin.

He grimaced as he gazed into Geneva's surprised face. She looked back at him.

"Sorry. The lady's dance card is full," he said, experiencing a possessiveness with which he was unfamiliar.

Geneva gave Dustin an apologetic smile and then Mace danced her away from reality back into the dream...

A HALF HOUR LATER, Geneva reluctantly left Mace with some friends to go in search of Dustin. She'd much rather stick by Mace's side, get to know more about him and talk to his friends' dates and wives and girlfriends, but she needed to talk to the man who was making it his business to complicate her life in ways she didn't appreciate.

There. She found him talking to Tiffany from the diner near the open bar set up outside.

"May I speak to you for a moment?" she asked, after saying hello and telling Tiffany she looked great.

"Dance?" Dustin asked.

"Talk."

They both looked at Tiffany, who appeared curiously disappointed.

"Sure."

Geneva led the way and stopped on the fringe of the happy crowd.

"You've got to stop this, Dustin."

"Stop what?"

"You know what," she said. "You've got to stop acting like we're anything more than just friends."

His gaze dropped to her belly. "Oh? I'm thinking you need to stop acting like we're just friends."

"We're going to share parenting, but as for anything romantic…"

She watched as his expression darkened.

She touched his sleeve. "I'm sorry if this flies in the face of your basic instincts, Dustin. Really, I am. But…well, I just don't feel that way about you. And the days of marrying just for the sake of a baby have long since passed."

"But…"

"There really isn't a but."

Then it struck her. She suddenly realized because she spent so much of her time dodging his advances, she wasn't including him in a way that might allay some of his fears… and get him to accept a more fitting role.

"I have an ultrasound scheduled for next week," she said quietly.

His brows raised.

"Would you like to come with me?"

"Yes," he said. "I'd love to come with you."

She smiled at his quick answer.

"Will we learn the sex of the baby?"

She laughed. "No. Not yet. We're still a few weeks away from that, but you're welcome to be present then, as well."

He seemed to search her face long and hard.

"I'm not going to exclude you, Dustin. You are the baby's father. You're welcome to participate any way you'd like in that role."

"But nothing more."

"Friendship. You know, like what we shared before."

He nodded.

Thankfully, he appeared more thoughtful than genuinely hurt.

Had he really been afraid she'd cut him out?

"And Mace?" he asked.

"Mace?"

Then it struck her: Dustin wasn't only afraid of being cut out; he was concerned he might be replaced altogether.

"I don't know," she said truthfully.

While she hoped Mace might play a role in her future—and by extension in the future of her child—well...

"But whatever tomorrow holds," she said to Dustin, "you'll always be the baby's father."

He appeared satisfied with that. More than satisfied, he looked happy.

"Can I be there for the birth?"

Her eyes widened and she laughed. "How about we leave that decision for when we're closer to the birth?"

He grinned. "Fair enough."

She looked over his shoulder at the way Tiffany was watching them in a curious way.

She squinted.

Oh. Another light bulb moment.

Geneva cleared her throat. "Now that we've settled that, it looks like someone might like to dance with you."

"Who?"

She nodded in the other woman's direction.

"Tiffany?" he said incredulously. "We're just friends."

"So are Mace and I..." Geneva said. Then she smiled.

20

SHE DESERVED BETTER…

Mace hated parting ways with Geneva at the end of the dance, but he needed to hightail it back to Denver before the suspect trail grew cold. Now, hours later, all he could think about was her, all warm and sleeping in that big bed of hers, alone. And how much he'd like to crawl in behind her, draw her close, then lose himself in the touch, feel and taste of her.

He couldn't recall a time when a woman had captivated him to the degree where she was always on his mind. To where his every thought, every action, automatically extended to how it might affect her or them.

He'd never achieved that state of…consumption with Janine. In fact, every time he found a message waiting for him on his cell phone, which had thankfully trickled down to once a day instead of several, he was mildly surprised to find he'd forgotten about her.

"Match."

Reece's one word snapped his attention away from thoughts that might concern him if given further examination. He looked up from where the documentation on yesterday's reports from various team members was spread out on the conference room table before him.

Jon came over to where he sat. He placed a printout of the fingerprint found at the scene yesterday next to another. "Falcone lifted this from the front desk counter at a budget motel on the outskirts of town an hour ago."

They had their man.

Though if he was correct in that assumption, there was little chance their guy was still at the ratty motel on the edge of town. Especially if he'd spotted Dominic Falcone.

Still, it was a lead where previously there hadn't been one.

"Falcone still on the scene?"

"No. He's moved on."

With countless hotels and motels in the metro area to accommodate conventions, there was a lot of ground to cover, so it was anybody's guess where any of the men were at that given moment.

Mace pushed from his chair and grabbed his jacket. "Then let's go…"

GENEVA SAT AT THE DINER counter, the breakfast rush having slowed to a hushed trickle, proposals from her other job open before her in preparation for a meeting in an hour scheduled to take place at the eatery, since she wouldn't have time to go home and change and get back in time to meet her client.

Trudy plopped down on the stool next to her and sighed, slapping her morning paper onto the counter. "What a morning."

Geneva made a notation in the margin of the proposal. "Any luck replacing Cindy?"

Trudy made a sound that verified what Geneva had already suspected. "I haven't had time to interview much less hire anyone."

"You could always hire her back."

"I could..."

Geneva raised her brows. The usual Trudy response to such a suggestion would have been a snort and a dismissive scowl. Far be it from her to rehire someone who'd already proven herself unworthy. Her tolerance threshold was wide, but surpass it and there was no going back. Once you were out with her, you were out for good.

At least that had been the case before.

Although now...

Trudy opened the paper, pretending not to notice her open scrutiny although Geneva knew perfectly well she was aware of it; Trudy was aware of everything.

"Should I give her a call? You're going to be short-handed this weekend."

Trudy didn't respond, indicating the moment of Zen breakthrough had passed. At least for the time being.

Geneva returned to her proposal, figuring her suggestion was at least worth a shot. Truth was, considering how busy it had been lately, they needed an extra pair of hands. And while Cindy was known to call in sick once or twice a month without a hint of the sniffles, she was a good worker.

The idea of training someone new when there was already a well-trained waitress available was unthinkable.

And, according to Tiffany, Cindy was very much interested in having her old job back. Her new one at a nearby chain restaurant wasn't exactly working out the way she'd hoped.

"What are you doing next Tuesday?" Trudy asked.

Geneva glanced up from her proposal. Tuesday. Was it

really only four days from now? It seemed so far away... yet so soon.

She hadn't taken much note of the time lately. She'd been existing in an oddly enticing clockless bubble full of emotion and sighs. But now that she was being asked, she realized only two days remained of Mace's leave. Next Tuesday...

Next Tuesday, he would be long gone.

Her heart stopped pumping.

"Geneva?"

She looked at Trudy, but didn't really see her.

"Did you hear me?"

"What? Oh. Yes. I heard you."

"It's not a complicated question."

Maybe not. But it did involve a complicated response. Albeit one she would never dream of sharing with Trudy.

One she really didn't really care to explore her own response to, either.

"Why? What's going on?"

Trudy shrugged as if it was of no importance. "That new Julia Roberts movie is out. I thought maybe you and I could catch a matinee or something."

Geneva raised her brows.

While she considered her employer a dear friend, they'd never really socialized outside the diner.

"Sure. Let's go. It's been a while since I've been to a show."

"Me, too." Trudy stiffened. "I was thinking it was time to change that."

Geneva smiled then returned to her proposal. It seemed her friend was making a lot of changes lately.

It seemed both of them were.

Her hand went to her belly and she stared off into space. The thought of Mace not playing a role in any of those changes was so impossible to fathom, she couldn't bring herself to consider it. Not just now. Wherever she was, whatever she was doing, he was there, on the fringes of her thoughts, a presence that made her blood hum and her mouth smile. To consider otherwise…

No. She wasn't ready for that.

But she would have to be soon.

Whether she wanted to or not.

"Maybe we can do some shopping for baby clothes afterward," Trudy said.

Geneva's hand stopped and she smiled, grateful for the happy distraction. In just a few short months, the baby growing within her would be a separate human being with needs of his or her own. And as each day passed, that reality grew more and more. She couldn't wait to meet her child.

"Yes. Maybe we can," she said softly.

She glanced over at the stool of Dustin's choice, hopeful that after their conversation last night, he'd accept his role as father and let the rest fall aside.

"Wow!"

So seldom was it that Trudy was impressed with anything, it was worthy of note. Or, at the very least, her attention.

"What is it?"

Trudy turned the newspaper so Geneva could view the page she was reading. It took a moment to understand it wasn't a story her friend was sharing, but a photo. More specifically, a photo of her and Mace, taken last night.

Wow, was right.

With her in her retro forties dress and him in uniform, the big band behind them, the shot could have easily been taken decades ago. And the way Mace held her, looked at her…

She shivered.

"I hate to tell you this, sweetie, but he's going to break your heart."

She heard the words of warning, but paid them little mind as she caught on something under the caption. "Can I see that?"

"Sure."

Geneva opened the paper at the crease. "Local Hero to be Awarded Navy Cross."

Talk about wow…

When Mace had told her he wanted her to attend an awards ceremony with him, she'd had no idea he'd be the one getting the award. She'd assumed it was an event he was required to attend. And while the occasion certainly was that, well…

Wow!

"What?"

Trudy took the paper back and read the caption.

"That's our Mace, isn't it?"

She didn't miss the "our" as she nodded.

"Give that back."

Geneva did so blankly, unable to read the rest of the story.

"It says here that he rescued five of his fellow soldiers, carried one out on his shoulders. Holy cow. The one they're talking about is Darius Folsom." She showed her that page and Geneva barely registered the photo of Dari, the regular with whom Mace had been dining the night she met him, featured near the end of the story.

What kind of man didn't share something of that nature? Didn't tell her why they were attending a medals ceremony, what he had done?

She knew. The type of man who truly was a hero.

"I'm going to that."

"Going where? To Afghanistan?"

"No. To the ceremony."

"Tomorrow?"

She nodded again. "I'm his date."

She met Trudy's gaze, seeing in her eyes the same type of emotion ballooning in her: an acute mix of awe...and fear.

Awe that she had captured his attention.

Fear that Mace was undoubtedly going to break her heart...

21

LARGER THAN LIFE and twice as evasive.

Mace was beginning to really not like this guy. Not only had he made two attempts on General Norman's life, he was proving harder to find than a glass of water in the desert.

"Sorry. He checked out sometime before the maids hit the room at around noon yesterday," the motel owner said from behind the counter.

"Can we see the room?"

"There's another couple in there. They checked in late last night."

Mace pulled a hundred out of his wallet and placed it on the counter under his hand. "A call telling them the exterminator needs to get in there should help them decide to move to another room."

The owner didn't hesitate. He picked up the motel phone and dialed. A moment later he hung up.

"I'll have them moved in ten minutes."

Mace nodded then walked out of the office to join Reece where he stood under the entrance port.

"Anything?" he asked.

Reece shook his head and pocketed his cell phone. "The guy's off the grid."

The term meant the fingerprint hadn't turned up an ID. The guy they were after wasn't registered anywhere and had no arrest record that they knew of.

He watched the couple in Room 13 exit and the owner hurry out of the office to take them to another room on the other side of the complex.

But it was the sight of a baby carriage that caught his attention.

He stared at the simple blue fabric and then the baby within. The little guy couldn't be more than a couple of months old. And it was all too easy to imagine the pretty blonde pushing the stroller as Geneva.

His throat choked off air.

"They're clear," Reece remarked.

Mace coughed, forcing himself to look at the room and not the baby. "Okay, I'm going to go check it out. In the meantime, I want you to ask for access to the surveillance footage from the night before last when the owner gets back."

Reece nodded.

"See if you can get the names of the maids who cleaned the room and find out if they're on the premises, as well."

"Roger that. You want me to interview them."

He'd thought of doing it himself, but he was coming to trust Reece nearly as much. "Yeah. Go ahead. See if the guy said anything, or was carrying anything of note."

"Got it."

With that, he strode in the direction of Room 13. The owner met him at the entrance.

"I can give you ten minutes."

He didn't argue the point; he only needed five.

He stepped inside, blinking against the dimness after

being out in the bright daylight. He pulled the cord to open the curtains, careful to visually skim the floor under the window as he did so. The place smelled of baby powder. He tried to ignore it as he gave the room a walk through, then went around again, checking garbage pails. Baby wipes and empty formula bottles.

Damn.

He could have done without the reminder that Geneva was expecting…especially since he wasn't sure where he stood on the idea of children.

Simply, he hadn't given the idea much thought.

But to have the decision already made for you…

He dropped to one knee and checked under the first of two queen-size beds. He used the end of a pen to fish out a candy bar wrapper that was unnoteworthy along with a small slip of motel paper torn from a pad.

Now that was a little more interesting.

As he stared at the number written on it, he couldn't help thinking that he couldn't have gotten luckier had it said: "Answer here."

He pocketed the paper then sat down on the chair near the door, squinting at the room. But even as he tried to concentrate on his thoughts and where they were leading, his mind drifted back to Geneva and what the immediate future held for her.

What was he talking about? Long-term was more like it.

He ran his hands through his hair several times then drew in a deep breath.

What was he doing?

More accurately, what were they doing?

In two brief days, he shipped out…

He heard footsteps approach the door. He looked over his shoulder to meet Reece's gaze. If the other man found his sitting in the chair unusual, he didn't say anything.

"The owner's putting together a copy of the surveillance footage now," he said. "And the maid on duty yesterday is off today."

Mace got up. "Have him hold on to the footage for pickup later."

"You sure?"

"Yeah. We're heading to Lazarus."

Darius had gotten back into town that morning. He and his old friend needed to powwow…

"ASSIGNMENT IS DONE. Successful. We were even paid an unexpected bonus."

Mace walked through Lazarus headquarters with Darius, trading the offices for the outdoors. Recruits trained on the course but he paid them little heed. His attention was on his friend.

Dari looked at him when he didn't immediately respond. "The guy's still alive. That was our job. And we did it well."

"The suspect is still at large."

"It's not our problem."

Mace's footsteps slowed. It took Dari a moment to realize he wasn't keeping pace. Finally he stopped and turned back to him.

His friend grimaced. "Look, I understand how you feel about loose threads. But when we began Lazarus Security, I learned quickly that more often than not, it's best to cut them rather than follow them through to the end."

"Because there's no profit in it."

"Because there's no sense in it."

Mace stared out at the new recruits.

One of the biggest reasons he's signed up for the Corps was because it was the only thing that made sense to him in a world that made none. There was structure and discipline, a chain of command and a clear enemy. If working in the public sector meant the type of chaos Dari was suggesting, perhaps he'd be better off signing up for another stint, going pure career.

Dari slapped a hand onto his shoulder and gave a good squeeze. "You've got two days of leave left. Why not spend it doing something you'd enjoy doing?" He grinned. "Or someone?"

It was Mace's turn to grimace. Referencing Geneva that way was so off base, it was offensive.

"Aw, hell. Don't tell me you're still seeing that pregnant waitress?"

Now he was offended.

"Uh-oh. You are."

"And if I am?"

"If you are…"

Mace's cell phone rang.

He fished it out of his pocket even as his friend fished for words to complete his sentence.

Janine.

Damn.

He repocketed the phone, sending her to voice mail.

"That her?" Dari asked.

"No."

He began walking again and Dari followed suit. Silence reigned as they skirted the training area, the autumn sun beating down on them, the report of gunfire from the firing range cracking the only sounds.

"I've released Reece from his temporary contract," Dari said. "He's heading back to Arizona in a couple of hours."

Mace nodded. "Understood."

He felt Dari's visual scrutiny.

"Let it go, man," his friend finally said.

Mace squinted at him.

"Norman has moved on. Job is done."

He thought of the bit of paper he had in his pocket. The one that would sew everything up. He hadn't had the chance to tell Dari what he'd found because he'd been cut off at the pass before he had a chance to try.

Maybe Dari was right. Maybe he should just cut his losses and move on. Visit his parents. Take his grandfather out. It would be a good six months before he'd have the opportunity again.

"I'd also suggest you let Geneva go."

Mace stopped dead in his tracks.

Dari held his hands up. "Hey, I'm not saying anything any other friend wouldn't."

"You're out of line."

"Am I? Because I don't think so."

Mace turned and headed back toward the compound.

"Don't get me wrong. Geneva's a great girl."

Great didn't begin to cover it, but he kept his thoughts to himself.

"But…"

Dari drew in a deep breath. "But you're fresh out of one relationship, Mace. At a career crossroads. You don't know what's around the next corner much less five years from now. If you hook up with Geneva, your fate is sealed for the next eighteen years plus."

"That's a shitty way of looking at it."

"Maybe. And I sure don't like saying it. But Geneva's a package deal. You take her, you take her kid. Life and relationships are tough enough without that kind of baggage."

"She's not baggage."

"Yes, she is. Heavy baggage."

His back teeth locked together. Outside the choice of words, his friend wasn't saying anything that hadn't been hovering on the fringes of his thoughts for the past few days.

Still, hearing them come from Dari gave him a target to focus on.

"Continue seeing her and it'll only get more complicated."

He wanted to tell Dari about his and Geneva's temporary arrangement. Their ruse to pretend they were dating during the length of his leave. But somehow he felt doing so would be a betrayal.

Besides, they'd gone beyond pretend some time ago, hadn't they? What was developing between them now was very real, indeed.

"Look, I know what I'm talking about. Not that Megan's pregnant, I don't know if I'm ready to be a father. Frankly, the idea scares me spitless. And I went in with my eyes open."

Mace listened.

"Are you really prepared to take on the role with a woman you just met? Be a father to a child that isn't yours?"

His cell rang again, this time indicating a text.

Geneva.

Will I be seeing you tonight?

He put it back into his pocket without responding, feeling the slip of paper with the phone number on it as he did so.

"Just promise you'll think about it," Dari said as they continued walking back toward the main compound.

"Trust me, thinking is about all I'm capable of right now…"

22

THE SINKING SUN SET the autumn leaves of the trees opposite Geneva's living room window ablaze while a cold wind blew the ones that had fallen around the parking lot, signaling the change of seasons.

She wished she didn't fear the change of seasons wasn't the only thing the wind was blowing in.

She'd texted Mace hours ago asking if she might see him tonight. He had yet to respond.

He was probably busy.

He was probably avoiding her.

She attempted to warm herself with herbal tea and sorted through emotions as varied as the color of the leaves outside.

Even when Mace was busy, he managed to drop her a text, no matter how brief. And she knew General Norman had moved on. National news said the guy was now in Chicago. Which meant Lazarus Security was no longer needed.

So the only answer she had for his silence was that he was avoiding her.

Her chest ached in a way that made it difficult to breathe.

Heartache.

She didn't realize she'd come to expect so much from him in such a short amount of time.

She told herself it had been only a few hours since she'd heard anything. And she was likely allowing her imagination to run away with her. But given the limited amount of time they had left, well, every precious second counted.

She considered ways to distract herself. After all, it had only been a few hours. There was no need to think he wouldn't call or come over tonight.

Still, for reasons she was ill equipped to identity, she sensed that she wouldn't be seeing him before tomorrow.

Tomorrow...

Seeing how stirred up she was getting now, well, maybe she should cancel. After all, their original deal had outlived its purpose.

She closed her eyes. What an inappropriate way to refer to the bonds that had developed between them.

"I *love* you."

His words still filled her lungs like a breath full of sweet, autumn air.

Of course, he hadn't vocally said the words; he'd texted them. Still, in that one moment, he'd been experiencing the type of emotion that inspired the communication.

And she knew she loved him...

She was unsure when it had happened. She only understood that she did. Sometimes it seemed her body was incapable of containing the enormity of what she felt for him.

And the fear of losing him forever...

The battle raging within her stole her breath away as effectively as the wind.

She blinked to clear the moisture from her eyes. What did she know about battles? When compared to Mace...

The Navy Cross.

Wow.

The one word was still all she could manage when she thought of what he must have endured, what he'd done to earn the award. Not because she was surprised—far from it—but because he'd shared neither the importance of the award nor what acts had merited it.

Her cell phone chimed. She'd left it on her desktop to prevent herself from checking it every few seconds and now rushed to answer it.

"Hello?" she answered without checking the ID.

"Geneva?"

It was a woman. Not Mace.

She swallowed past the wad of sandpaper in her throat. "Yes."

"Hello, dear. I hope you don't mind my calling, but this is Mace's mom? Sharon?"

"Oh, yes, yes. How are you?"

While it wasn't Mace, she welcomed the distraction.

"I'm fine. How are you doing? And the baby?"

Geneva smiled, her hand automatically going to her belly. "We're both fine, thank you."

"Good. Good."

It dawned on her that she likely shouldn't welcome contact from Mace's mother. It would only make things more awkward when they parted ways.

Parted ways…

Her heart swelled painfully against her rib cage.

Not only the reality, but the inevitability of their parting after tomorrow hit her hard.

But she'd known the deal going in, hadn't she? She'd understood that what they had was only temporary.

Then what was she doing speaking to his mother? Surely she was only inviting disaster.

Especially since she didn't imagine Mace would appreciate her continuing any kind of connection with his family.

Then again, Sharon believed them only to be friends. So anything that did develop…well, would be between her and Sharon.

Right?

"I'm sorry if I'm interrupting something…"

"No, no." Geneva hadn't realized she'd gone silent until Sharon spoke again.

"I can try back again later if this is a bad time."

Geneva walked back to her spot in front of the window, telling herself it was to enjoy the fall foliage and had absolutely nothing to do with her hope she'd spot Mace pull up. "Now is just fine. How's Mike?"

"Oh, he's well. He's in the other room reading the paper. I just cleaned up the dinner dishes…"

And suddenly, the two of them settled into a pleasant conversation about nothing and everything.

Fifteen minutes in, Sharon circled back. "Anyway, the reason I called was to ask if you're attending the ceremony tomorrow?"

Geneva briefly bit her lip, wondering what her answer should be. While Mace hadn't retracted the invitation, his silence might be exactly that. She didn't know if it was a good idea to continue a ruse that had already snowballed into so much more.

"Yes," she said softly, unable to deny herself any chance of seeing him.

"Good! I was hoping you would be there. You see, I'd like very much for us to sit together…"

And just like that, Geneva found herself tumbling straight down the rabbit hole…

MACE SAT IN HIS RENTAL CAR outside Geneva's apartment building, staring up at her dark windows. It was after midnight and he'd spent the better half of an hour trying to figure out what he should do.

An hour? Try the past day.

His earlier conversation with Dari left a bad taste in his mouth.

Had he been irresponsible for getting involved with a mother-to-be?

Mother-to-be...

Such a narrow term to describe Geneva. She was so much more. But the fact that she would be a mother soon, very soon, should have played a larger role in his decision to see her. Strangely, it hadn't.

Then why was it such a big deal now?

He imagined her in the coming months growing plumper, rounder, softer, sexier. Saw her holding a tiny infant, smiling. But somehow he couldn't insert himself into that picture. When he envisioned her, her future, he saw only her.

He rubbed his face as if trying to rid himself of his skin.

Still, she deserved better than his silence.

He should have called her. He'd started to several times.

Tomorrow... Was it really his last day in Colorado Springs?

Yes. He left on the first transport out, first thing Sunday morning.

He knew such an acute sensation of...was it sadness? Yes, he suspected it was.

Never before had he not looked forward to heading out. Not because he wanted to escape anything, but because being a Marine was his job, what he did best. And that job required traveling to where he was needed.

And now?

Now the idea of stepping onto that plane left him feeling...reluctant.

Perhaps it was simply because he'd be leaving Geneva behind. There was so much change laying on her horizon that he wouldn't be a part of. Was that why he was feeling this way?

Whatever it was, he wanted to shake it off. Put on his sweats and run until he wasn't merely physically exhausted, but mentally, as well.

He should call her now.

He wanted to call her now.

What he really wanted to do was go up there, kiss her senseless then lose himself in a way no run would ever match.

But to do so would prolong the inevitable.

It would give her cause to hope there was going to be more.

Damn. When had something so simple grown so very complicated?

And what was he going to do about it?

His cell phone beeped.

He took it out of his pocket and stared at the text announcement, not realizing he was hoping it was Geneva maybe having spotted him, taking the decision out of his hands.

It wasn't.

It was Janine.

I'm at The Barracks. Meet me? We need to talk.

He sat for long moments after putting the phone back into pocket. Geneva's windows remained dark.

Janine.

Not a day went by since his return when she hadn't tried to contact him, talk to him. Their brief exchange at the bar the other night apparently hadn't been enough.

So much unfinished business.

He started the car and began backing out of the parking spot. Maybe Janine was just the distraction he needed right now. Meeting with her might help him decide one way or another where his path lay.

As he drove away, he looked up at Geneva's windows one last time. He couldn't be sure, but he thought he saw her bedroom light switch on, her silhouette against the glass.

He kept driving...

23

SHE STILL HADN'T HEARD from Mace.

Yet there she was, in a simple yellow dress and brown suede jacket and shoes, at the awards ceremony that had been his first "faux date" request.

The day was sunny and cool, frost on the grass at the site slowly melting off. Men and women in uniform wove easily through the crowd of civilians while those in higher command stayed closer to the stage. Geneva had never felt more out of place in her life.

She must have decided at least a dozen times not to come. Yet she ultimately had. If this was going to be the last time she saw Mace, well, she still wanted to see him. If only to say goodbye, congratulate him and wish him well.

"Geneva?"

It was a male voice.

She turned to find it wasn't the one she was hoping for. Instead, it was Darius Folsom and his wife, Megan, whom she had seen only a few times but knew on sight.

"Hi," she said. "I'm guessing you're here for the same reason I am?"

"In a manner of speaking," Dari replied. "I'm responsible for Mace getting that medal."

Megan elbowed him. "He's making it sound like he should be up there with him. What he means is that his is one of the many asses Mace saved." She smiled at her husband. "Something for which I am very grateful."

Geneva recognized several others she'd seen come into the diner with Dari, but couldn't ignore the fact that neither Dari nor Megan were inclined to introduce them, although she was certain they all had to also be Mace's friends.

Like she wasn't feeling awkward enough...

"Geneva!"

Once again, she found herself grateful for Mace's mom's interruption. She told the couple it was nice to see them, then turned to look for her.

Mrs. Harrison waved her hand, making her easily identifiable where she stood before a front row chair.

Front row.

Of course. Where else would she expect a medal honoree's family to sit?

Only she wasn't family. And her level of discomfort notched upward.

She considered merely waving back and choosing a seat closer to the back, but thought better of it. First of all, she wouldn't put it past Sharon to come get her. Second, the prospect of sitting near Dari and Mace's friends wasn't any more appealing.

Had Mace said something to them? Or had they said something to Mace?

She thought back to when she'd first discovered she was pregnant. She'd told Trudy, making it clear she had no intention of marrying the father, who she hadn't immediately revealed was Dustin. The salty diner owner had frowned at her and said, "You do know you're going to be the focus of gossip central for at least the next five years."

Geneva had laughed. "This isn't the fifties."

"Maybe not, but it might as well be. We women may have come a long way, baby, but in a lot of respects I'm afraid we'll never reach our destination."

Her next remark had helped erase a bit of the sting. "You're also never going to have your figure back."

Of course, Geneva had never really given Trudy's gossip warning any sort of weight. But as she made her way through the crowd with a weak smile, she couldn't help filing away Dari's expression as he'd spoken to her, which matched several of the other guys' in the group to which she hadn't been introduced. It had said: "Stay away from Mace. You have too much baggage."

She was somewhat relieved to note that Megan and the other women hadn't seemed to be wearing that same look.

She reached the front row and was enveloped in a hug by the sweet-smelling woman that was Mace's mom. She felt the breath she wasn't aware she was holding whoosh from her as a quiet sigh.

For a moment she was tempted to close her eyes, imagine the fear away and replace it with something much nicer. The embrace was so genuine, it would be all too easy.

Instead, she returned the hug then greeted Mace's father and grandfather, grateful that not a glimmer of the gossip shadow existed on either of their faces.

"You'll be sitting next to me, of course," Mace's grandfather said after kissing her cheek, his eyes sparkling suggestively.

For the first time, she felt slightly ill at ease, although at the lunch where she'd met them, she had been completely comfortable. The power of suggestion, she realized. If some people thought less of her, viewed her as unworthy, perhaps others might view her as loose and unfit for more than a romp.

She forced the thought away, refusing to allow anyone

to classify her as anything less than she was…including and especially herself.

"She most certainly will not," Sharon said. "You'll surely talk throughout the ceremony if she does. No, she'll be seated next to me."

Geneva found herself laughing at the light rebuke, happy to be rid of her concern, then turned to place her small purse on her chair…only to find herself staring straight into Mace's handsome face.

Mace.

Chills that had nothing to do with wind raised every tiny hair dotting her skin.

Mace…

DAMN. DAMN. Damn.

Geneva looked so incredible, everything else instantly faded away; she was a vividly clear figure against a blur of blurry colors.

Last night, he hadn't closed his eyes once. This morning, he'd felt every last minute of lost sleep, until now.

Now…

Now he felt like he could leap a tall building in a single bound.

"Hi," she said quietly.

He allowed his gaze to slide over her skin, taking in the sudden pinkness of her cheeks, the almost shy flash of her teeth, the curve of her long neck. The scent of her filled his every sense.

He'd missed her.

He told himself that was ridiculous. It had only been a day since he last saw her.

Still, he knew beyond anything that was tangible that he had missed her—on too many levels to count. He missed her laugh, her smell, her words, her body.

He'd missed her.

And if he could, in that one moment he'd take her hand and lead her away to someplace private where they could be alone. Make up for the lost time he'd so stupidly allowed to slip through his fingers.

Talk about stupid...

Against everything he knew was right, he'd gone to The Barracks last night and met up with Janine.

"Your mom called last night," Geneva said, hesitant in a way he'd never seen her before. "She invited me to sit with her."

He heard what she was saying but it took a moment for it to register. Did she think he needed an explanation? Obviously she did.

He berated himself for ever making her feel that way.

"Oh. Good." He looked to his mother whose own smile seemed a bit brighter than usual. But when he glanced back at Geneva, he could have sworn he glimpsed the same sadness he'd experienced last night in her eyes.

And his own sense of the dark emotion deepened.

The event organizer touched his elbow and quietly told him it was time to take his place with the others.

He nodded then met Geneva's gaze again. "I..."

He what?

He swallowed hard.

He had absolutely no idea what he was going to say, or where he went from here besides up on that stage to accept the award they insisted on giving him for simply doing what any other Marine would do.

"Good luck, honey," his mother said, stepping between them and kissing his cheek. "We're so very proud of you."

He blinked at her. He'd half expected her to say, "Marcus would be so very proud of you," as she'd said when he first shared the news.

His father followed suit along with his grandfather, no mention of his brother.

And then he and Geneva were alone in the gathering of others once again.

She smiled at him, but not in the way he'd come to look forward to. No, this one was tinged with melancholy and caution.

"You'd better go," she said quietly.

He looked over to find the organizer motioning to him.

"Yes, I guess I'd better."

She didn't move so he did…away from her and toward the others, his chest feeling heavier with each and every step.

PRIDE, SURE AND STRONG. That's what surged through Geneva as she watched Mace walk center stage in his full uniform, already covered with ribbons and medals, and accept the Navy Cross, the highest Marine honor.

If only he looked happier.

In the time she had known him, she'd never seen his handsome face set in such serious lines. He appeared to want to be anywhere but there. Why? And was that why he hadn't been more communicative about the importance of the day?

Did it have anything to do with his brother?

She didn't know. But she desperately wanted to find out. Not only for his sake, but for his parents and grandparent beaming so proudly next to her.

While she wouldn't ever expect him to jump for joy or boast about the occasion, or the experiences that had led to it…well, humbled would be preferable to grim.

The audience rose to its feet, applauding the day's honorees, the top one going to Mace. As Geneva followed suit, she realized she hadn't heard a single word. She'd been too busy scrutinizing his face, his demeanor, the shadows that clung to him that had nothing to do with the light.

Then she saw her—Janine.

Somehow she continued clapping, even as she met the gaze of Mace's tall, pretty ex-girlfriend back a row and halfway down the length. She looked...smug. Knowing.

The unwanted emotion cut into her, adding to the other uncomfortable feelings she was experiencing—Mace's silence, Dari's rejection, his grandfather's flirting—making it impossible to ignore. One on its own, a simple swallow and deep breath. Two, more concentration. Three...?

Undeniable.

"Geneva?"

Mace's mom was looking at her in concern.

She was unaware of the tear that had streaked down her cheek until she viewed Sharon's questioning gaze.

She quickly picked up her purse. "Tell Mace congratulations for me," she managed to choke out.

"You're not coming to the reception?"

Reception? She hadn't been told of any reception. Which meant she definitely wasn't going.

She was sure Janine would enjoy having Mace all to herself.

"No. I'm sorry," she whispered.

She turned to hurry away.

And ran directly into Mace.

24

MACE STEADIED GENEVA with his hands on her shoulders. Shoulders that seemed to suddenly bear the weight of the world. He feared they might not be equipped to handle it any longer.

He searched her face. Had she been crying?

No. She *was* crying.

The realization was like a blow to the gut, the medal with which he'd just been awarded like a stone he wanted to throw.

Still, she somehow managed to smile. "Congratulations. I'm honored to have been included. And so very proud."

Her voice caught on the last word. Before he could say anything, she threw her arms around him and squeezed tight, her chin resting on his shoulder.

"Thank you."

He squinted at her, barely able to hold her back before she wrenched away and nearly ran toward the aisle.

"Geneva, wait!"

He moved to give chase when a tree trunk placed itself between him and her in the shape of Darius.

"Let her go."

Mace grit his back teeth together. "If you know what's good for you, you'll move. Now."

"This isn't about her, Mace," Dari said quietly, his fingers digging in where he held his shoulder.

Mace was a breath away from decking him when Dari smiled at someone behind him.

"Hello, Mrs. Harrison." He removed his hand and reached around to shake his father's hand. "Congratulations, Mr. Harrison. Our boy done good, didn't he?"

Mace took advantage of the situation to look around, but found that Geneva was long gone, the lingering scent of her perfume where she'd hugged him the only proof that she'd been there at all...

GENEVA WISHED HERSELF one with the darkness when she sat in her apartment much later. She lay on the sofa staring at the ceiling, having cried a million tears and feeling another ten crowding her chest.

Mace...

The autumn wind howled outside, rustling the stubborn leaves that remained on the trees and rattling the windows. The same wind had blown Mace into her life...and now it was blowing him back out.

She didn't want his pity. And she was convinced that's what she'd viewed on his face when he'd caught her by the shoulders earlier.

Pity.

She'd run as fast as her heels could safely carry her, not stopping until she was inside her apartment where she locked herself away from the world...and him.

"...he's going to break your heart..."

Isn't that what Trudy had warned her against?

Isn't that exactly what was happening?

She told herself it had been worth it. The time she'd shared with Mace...

She bit hard on her bottom lip, swallowing the coppery blood that filled her mouth.

Her cell phone screen lit up where she had it laying face-up on her belly but was otherwise silent and still as per her settings. She knew it would be Mace again.

His last message had said he knew she was home since her car was in the lot; that he'd be waiting out there until she let him in.

She hadn't responded.

She also hadn't responded to his other ten voice mails and countless texts telling her he needed to see her, that they needed to talk.

Why? About what?

It was over.

That much was clear.

And while she might have preferred to spend this last night with him, well, that's not the way it had worked out.

She closed her eyes, ignoring the hot tears that seeped through her lashes.

Had she known... Had she guessed...

What?

What would she have done differently?

She didn't so much turn onto her side as she did fold, wrapping her arms around herself. So very much had happened in so brief a time. Was it really only three months ago she'd lost her mother? Wasn't it supposed to get easier?

She'd never missed her mom more than she did that moment.

She blinked at the wall, wondering if her mother was somewhere watching her right now. And if she was, what she made of the entire situation. Would she click her tongue as she'd been known to do, indicating Geneva had been a fool? Or would she merely hug her until she couldn't bear to be hugged any longer?

She didn't know. But, oh boy, she wished she did. She wished for the answers she couldn't seem to find anywhere.

Geneva caught the brightness of her cell phone screen again, the only source of light in the apartment. She blindly reached for where it had slid onto the couch next to her, blinking several times in an effort to clear her vision as she unlocked the phone and saw there were three text messages waiting.

She wiped her nose with the back of her hand and held the phone away from her until she could read the words of the first text.

I should have called you last night...

A sob wrenched from somewhere deep in her chest.

Yes, she silently responded to him. *You should have called last night.*

Perhaps if he had, none of this would have happened. She might be finding hot comfort in his arms instead of trying to hold herself together with her own.

Her eyes burned and her entire body ached. She hadn't eaten or slept since yesterday. This had to get better at some point. Right?

She rode out the wave then mopped her face with a wad of tissues she grabbed from a box near her head.

She accessed the next text message.

I miss you...

The words wended through her and back again.

"I miss you, too," she whispered.

Surely losing a limb wouldn't hurt this much. In that one moment, she'd gladly offer one up if she were promised this fathomless pain would stop.

Somewhere in the back of her mind, she understood that the heartache she was currently experiencing bled together with her grief over her mother's passing, but it was impossible to see where one left off and the other began so it became one massive ball of emotion threatening to suffocate her.

Only her mother was gone; and Mace was still here...

She absently ran the pad of her thumb over the keypad again, keeping the backlight on so she could read the three words.

Tomorrow, he would be on that transport out...

And she could begin healing.

Tonight... Well, tonight, knowing he was so close and wanted to see her...

She accessed the third text message.

I love you.

No fair...

She burst into tears and turned her head into the pillow, wishing the pain away, wishing the next month away, wishing him away...

MACE PACED BACK AND FORTH in front of his parked rental car outside Geneva's apartment building, checking his cell phone every five seconds and staring up at her dark windows. He was still in his dress blues, although he'd taken off the belt and unbuttoned the coat. The night was cold, the wind biting, but he was unaware of both as he moved, his mind on one thing and one thing only—Geneva.

All he could see was the image of her tear-filled eyes the last time he'd seen her.

Damn.

Damn, damn, damn.

The idea he'd hurt her ripped his guts to shreds.

She deserved better. Especially from him.

Still, he'd unwittingly caused her pain he was afraid he'd never be able to ease.

He restlessly checked his cell again. Nothing.

He rounded his car and stared at where hers was parked a few spots up on the opposite side of the lot. Had someone picked her up?

No.

She was there.

He was sure of it.

Then why wasn't she answering him?

He could only imagine what was going through her mind, what she must be thinking. About why he hadn't contacted her last night or this morning...

Still, there was no need for tears.

Was there?

Damn it. He hated not knowing what he'd done.

He hated even more that whatever he had done had caused her one iota of pain.

He rounded his car again and resumed pacing, his steps quick, his black dress shoes clicking against the asphalt.

What was he talking about? He was leaving tomorrow. And the minute he did, their agreement would reach an end.

He stopped. Is that what this was? Was she ending things early? Calling a halt before it went too far?

He thought of his last text.

Damn it all to hell. This had evolved into far more than a simple agreement.

How stupid was he? He should have known he wouldn't be able to keep his emotions out of it. Look how badly Janine had hurt him. And he'd gone into that with his eyes wide open.

And Geneva?

He imagined her tears again and felt like shouting, hitting something, anything to release the pressure threatening to turn him inside out.

Today had been one of the longest of his life. After absolutely no sleep, he'd gotten up and run ten miles before finally showering and attending a ceremony he had zero interest in participating in. Even now, the medal was sitting on his passenger seat, little more than a piece of tin to him.

Marcus…

He tilted his head up and closed his eyes. His brother was the hero—not him.

"Still running after me, little bro?" he could almost hear Marcus say.

The familiar hands—phantom digits that had curiously been missing the past few days—returned to their rightful place around his neck.

He had spent so much of his childhood trying to catch up with his older brother he lost his breath just thinking about it. Marcus was the one everyone looked up to, talked about, while he was the one they patted on the head and told him how lucky he was to have such a great brother.

No one had prepared him for what life would be like when his brother died.

If Marcus had been an ever-evasive shadow in life, in death…well, now he'd never be able to catch up.

He winced at the selfish thought.

Damn it. He hated feeling this way. He hated not being able to think of his brother without a deep sense that he was lacking, would never make the grade. He wanted to remember him with fondness.

It had taken meeting with Janine last night to remind him how deep his feelings went.

And to realize what she'd really been after.

He'd stepped into The Barracks to find the place still packed...and his ex-girlfriend sitting at the end of the bar staring at her cell phone. Waiting for a response from him? He didn't think so. Still, he'd gone and taken the stool next to her.

Her surprised expression had almost been worth the trouble.

Almost.

Janine Johnson had always been an attractive woman. Naturally platinum blond, tall, willowy. Problem was, she knew the value of her good looks...and that devalued them as she used them to push forward whatever objective she put her mind to, whether it was earning a promotion at her job as a sales associate, talking her way out of a speeding ticket...or seducing him out of looking a little too closely at her.

As closely as he was looking at her now.

They'd talked a bit about everything. He'd bought her another drink but had stuck to his one beer limit then asked to pay his tab.

Janine had cleared her throat. "So this medal thing tomorrow..."

He'd grimaced as he peeled off the money to cover his bill.

"What?" she'd said. "Tell me you aren't pleased."

"I'm not pleased."

"Why? It's a great honor. One I'm sure you earned."

He'd stared at her.

"Wait. Don't tell me. This is about Marcus, isn't it? Again."

"I've got to be going."

"Wait." She'd put her hand on his arm.

He'd stiffened, waiting to see what she'd do next.

She'd taken a deep breath and smiled. "I'm sorry. I really don't want to dig up old skeletons." She'd lightly rubbed his arm. "Partly because I have one or two of my own I'd prefer not to see again." She'd dropped her gaze. "Mostly because I'm hoping we can bury them for good and head out for new ground."

She'd blinked up at him.

Mace had found it incredible to think such tactics had worked on him before. But they had, hadn't they? Because he hadn't anything else with which to compare them? The image of Geneva's genuine smile and warmth loomed large in his mind.

Yeah, he was thinking that was the reason.

And now that he did have something, someone fundamentally more meaningful, well, Janine didn't measure up. Not just because of what she'd done, but because of who she was.

"I've got to go," he'd said.

"Come on," she'd said, an angry edge to her voice. "I deserve to be on your arm when you accept that award tomorrow, not that mousy waitress you've been hanging around with..."

He'd known such a moment of blind anger, it had been all he could do to remain speechless as he purposefully removed her hand from his arm, picked up his jacket and turned toward the door.

"You know what, Mace? You're right. You're never going to be as good as your brother. You never really knew what to do with a catch like me. But I bet he would have..."

The door had closed on her words, making them the final ones he ever intended to hear from her.

A car rolled up and a flashlight was focused on him, making him aware that he still stood below Geneva's apartment windows.

Geneva...

He couldn't ever envision her thinking the type of venomous words Janine had uttered—who had done who wrong, anyway?—much less saying them.

However, he did have Janine to thank for one thing: making him realize he was competing against a ghost.

He probably always had been.

"Can I help you?" a male voice asked abruptly.

Mace grimaced and looked back up at Geneva's windows, wondering if she was looking out one of them even as he spoke to the security guard.

"I'm waiting for a friend to let me up."

"And that friend would be...?"

"Geneva Davis."

"Ah. Yes."

The flashlight was removed and then just as quickly, it turned on him again.

"Hey, wait, that makes you Mace Harrison then."

Mace's jaw tightened. "Yeah."

He'd come across his fair share of information seekers in the wake of the Norman incident. Police and security officers tended to be some of the most annoying because they not only wanted details, they wanted to share how they would have handled the situation.

It looked like this guy fell solidly into that category.

And he had neither the time nor the patience for it right now.

He only wanted to talk to Geneva.

He checked his cell phone again.

Nothing.

The security guard was talking about having seen the two attempts on Norman's life on TV when Mace decided to walk to his car. He waved a hand and said, "Sorry, I must be wrong. She's not home. I'll try again later. Good night."

The officer blinked at him then offered a surprised greeting in return, backing up to allow him exit.

Mace took it, trying like hell to figure out what he should do. Or if, in fact, there was anything he could do...

His cell phone rang.

He nearly hit a parked vehicle in his rush to retrieve it from the passenger's seat where he'd tossed it.

"Hello, Geneva?"

"No. It's Dari, Mace. I've got some information you might be interested in knowing..."

25

6:00 A.M.

Geneva's cell alarm went off, loud enough to wake her. But she wasn't asleep. She still lay on the couch, in the dark, dawn still a ways away.

Mace even farther.

Right now he was on his transport out.

She hadn't heard from him after his final text last night. Those last three words would remain with her always. Words she felt and returned with all her heart.

I love you.

He was gone.

She'd expected the knowledge to somehow make her feel better; now the healing could begin. It didn't. Instead she felt oddly…numb. Empty. Not just like a gas tank that could be refilled, but hollow, the space gaping wide and exposed to the elements.

She looked down at where she rubbed her belly, issuing a silent apology to the life growing within her. She'd been impulsive and selfish and was now paying the price. It would have been fine had she been the only one affected. But she wasn't. Not anymore.

She told herself she should get up, eat something, make

an effort to rejoin the land of the living. But she couldn't seem to find the energy to do more than stare at the ceiling and hope the coming sunrise would help her do what she needed to do. Which was go on…

HE HAD HIS MAN…

Mace stood on the other side of the interrogation room watching as Thomas Michael Newsome sat back in the uncomfortable chair, looking a little too comfortable in his handcuffs and leg shackles.

Then again, he should, shouldn't he? Because this wasn't the first time Newsome had found himself in such a situation. And he didn't think it would be the last.

"Attorney," the twenty-nine-year-old with a covert military-op résumé as thick as Mace's penis said.

"9/11," Mace answered, meaning in the wake of the tragic event, local law enforcement could brand a suspect as a possible terrorist and hold him for as long as they wanted.

Despite Dari's recommendation to leave the Norman incidents behind and allow law enforcement to take it from there, he'd acted on the information he recovered from the motel room. Calls had been returned, more specifically, Lazarus partner and old friend Lincoln Williams had contacted Dari with the information he was looking for. Being connected with military intelligence and the FBI, Linc could tap into resources others couldn't.

In this case, the reason why Newsome's prints hadn't turned up on any nationwide criminal database wasn't because he'd never been arrested, but because he was a military gun for hire and some powers-that-be intended to keep his misdeeds covered so they could use him at will.

Only neither Newsome nor his contractors had anticipated he'd shoot the wrong gun at the wrong time.

Even if it had been at the right person.

The familiar phone number Mace had found at the motel had been the private contact number to Norman's head of security.

Meaning Newsome had been directly hired to perform a job. And if Mace was right, and he fully believed he was, Norman's men had arranged for the attempts against Norman. Why? Most likely to boost his national ratings and perhaps put him on the short list of presidential candidates for the next election.

Hell, for all he knew, Norman himself was behind the ruse.

Unfortunately for them, they'd done it under Mace's watch and two men were injured; he wasn't about to let this one slide. While he didn't expect to pin anything on Norman himself, Newsome's capture and the gossip that was sure to leak—he'd see to it—would be enough of a damaging bruise to give him a permanent limp when it came to any future political plans.

And Newsome himself would be out of commission. If not literally, figuratively, because he was now solidly on the radar, no longer operating in the shadows. And Mace intended to keep him that way.

He found himself checking his cell phone. Still nothing from Geneva.

He rubbed his face and nodded at where the police detective who'd allowed him access to the suspect held up three fingers, indicating his time was almost up. He hadn't fooled himself into believing for a second that he'd get Newsome to talk. Men like him were born without tongues. But it was enough for him to know he'd cracked the case, even if he hadn't been under any obligation to do so.

He was nobody's fool.

His cell phone vibrated. He took it out and checked it. He knew a spark of hope when he read he had a text from Geneva.

Take care of yourself...

A part of him stung at the obvious goodbye.

But a bigger part of him knew any contact at all was a good thing.

Even if she believed he was on that transport and couldn't follow up on it.

Especially because she believed he was on that transport.

Without another word, he passed Newsome and rapped on the security door.

He was done here.

THE ART OF MASS DISTRACTION.

Geneva hadn't mastered it. But it was proving to be helpful in at last getting her off the couch and at least appearing to be normal, although she felt anything but.

She'd considered calling in sick for the brunch crowd, but decided engaging in some sort of activity that didn't include a great deal of thinking would help.

Of course, she'd completely forgotten the smiling part.

That combined with her paleness, due to lack of sleep and eating, had garnered her more than a few unwelcome inquiries regarding her health and that of the baby.

But each had been easily avoided...or maybe it was her uncommunicativeness that had kept people at bay, no matter how well-meaning.

Now, nearly twelve hours later after a long, busy day, she felt sufficiently tired enough to sleep. And she'd forced herself to eat at least a little on two occasions.

The best thing was she hadn't cried.

Well, except for that one time when Trudy had shown her the photo of Mace accepting his Navy Cross that was featured in the local news section of the newspaper.

She'd rushed to the bathroom and stayed in a stall for fifteen minutes. After ten, Tiffany had surprised her by sticking a box of tissues under the door and asking if there was anything she could do. The demonstration of human kindness from someone who seemed to operate on a deficit of it had been enough to help her rebalance herself and get back to the diner floor.

Now, however, it was after ten and the last customer had finally departed, leaving her and Trudy and Mel. She bussed the final table then went back into the kitchen, saying something to Mel as she went. Only he wasn't there. And he appeared to have left entirely—his grill jacket hanging neatly on its wall hook—without saying goodbye.

That was odd.

She peered out the window looking for Trudy. "Everything okay with Mel?" she asked.

No answer.

She frowned, not finding Trudy either.

Doubly odd.

She leaned her hands against the counter and closed her eyes. They had probably said goodnight, but she was so out of it, she hadn't registered it.

She reached behind her to untie her apron when she heard the strains of a familiar song: B17.

She left her apron untied and rushed into the other room. "Please, no, don't play that."

Her words trailed off as she found herself staring at the last person in the world she expected to see.

Mace...

"SHOULDN'T THAT BE 'Please, mister, please'?"

Mace's throat was so tight, his mouth so dry at the sight of Geneva looking pale but beautiful, being close enough to touch her again, he was surprised he could think the words much less say them.

She looked like she was caught between fight or flight, a delay likely brought on by her obvious tiredness, which Trudy had mentioned when he'd asked her to empty the place so he could talk to Geneva privately, promising to close up.

"Don't keep her too long. Girl needs some good, solid rest…and not just for herself," Trudy had said.

There had been more in her stern stare, but she'd kept any other advice to herself and agreed to do as he asked. He took that as a further good sign he was doing the right thing.

His gaze went to Geneva's still-flat belly and the way the open apron hung from her, giving the illusion of fullness that hinted at what she might look like in the next few months…which was stunning. In the best possible way.

He was amazed he'd allowed fear to rule his actions, however briefly. But having a child in his life, well, it wasn't a contingency for which he'd ever prepared.

He only wished he could have muddled through it with Geneva rather than let it chase him away from her, cause her the pain he even now viewed as smudges under her unusually bright eyes.

He knew he only had a few more seconds before she fled. But the words he wanted to say to her scrambled like mice into the corner now that he was standing before her.

"I deserve to be taken to the woodshed and given a few good whacks," he said quietly even as the song played.

She remained silent.

The song ended and she looked toward the jukebox. He still had two additional selections to make.

"No," she said quietly. "Both of us are to blame."

Blame?

His stomach pitched five feet below floor level. Was there no hope of her forgiving him? Of grabbing what they were feeling and seeing where it took them?

Was she determined that they were over?

God, he hoped not.

"I prefer to think we're both to credit."

That brought her gaze back to him and he glimpsed a spark of hope in her eyes that nearly knocked him to his knees.

He couldn't resist going to her, enveloping her in his arms, a place he had feared he'd never have her again, a place he wanted to keep her forever.

"I've been so very, very stupid, Geneva," he whispered into her ear, breathing in the scent of her, absorbing her warmth and sweetness and wanting her so completely he ached with it. "I don't know what I was thinking. I'm sorry for ever having hurt you."

He made out her unwitting, soggy reply and drew back, holding her head still in his hands.

"Please, do you think you can ever find a way to forgive me?"

Thankfully she gazed back into his eyes rather than trying to avoid them.

"You…" he began, searching for words. No, he didn't have to search. They were all right there. It was choosing the right ones when there were really no wrong ones.

Damn. Why did this have to be so hard?

"You, Geneva, are incredible." She was that squared. "You're the most amazing woman, no, person I've ever met." He'd never uttered anything truer. "You're smart and funny, beautiful and thoughtful..." He swallowed hard. "And sexier than hell. Not a moment goes by that I don't want to make love with you, bury myself deep inside you..."

She cleared her throat. "That's sex. It'll pass..."

He slowly shook his head. "No, that's not sex. Sex we can get anywhere. This..." He rubbed his thumbs against her soft skin. "This is about so much more. And you know it."

"Do I? I'm not so sure..."

"If it was just about sex, you would have let me into your apartment last night so we could have some."

He glimpsed a shadow of a smile. "Maybe I was tired."

"Maybe you were hurting because of something stupid I said or did, which further demonstrates this is..."

"Shh..." She put her hand over his mouth, effectively hushing him.

When he remained silent, she moved her fingers to trail along his cheek.

"It appears I'm not the only one who got hurt..." she said.

He smiled sadly at that. "Yeah. Call me a coward, but I'd take a full-on assault from an entire enemy battalion over how I've felt the past two days. Any time."

Her eyes softened.

"Tell me, Geneva. Is that just sex?"

She didn't respond immediately. Finally, she shook her head.

He drew her close again and she sighed against him. He couldn't help feeling like the luckiest guy ever born. Not only because she was in his arms, but because she was giving him another chance. And he was determined not to blow it this time.

"Shouldn't you be somewhere in the Middle East right now?" she whispered, her hands trailing up and down his back, her cheek resting on his shoulder.

He took a deep breath. "Probably. But I figured if I had to accept that medal, well, I'd be damned if I didn't cash it in for something important."

She drew back to look at him. "What do you mean?"

He smoothed his hands over her hair then held her still as he leaned in for a kiss. She kissed him back.

"It means I'm not going anywhere. Not today…" He kissed her. "Not tomorrow." He kissed her again. "Not the day after that." He kissed her again. "I'm going to serve out my remaining six months here. Then I'm going to sign on with Darius at Lazarus…"

She looked confused. "I don't understand…"

Holding her gaze, he leaned in again for another kiss. "You will, Geneva. You will." He backed her up toward the jukebox and made his selection while maintaining his hold on her. Elvis's rendition of "Fools Rush In" began playing.

"Now," he whispered into her ear. "Tell me you love me."

He trapped her gasp in her mouth by kissing her.

"Tell me…"

He kissed her again until he felt her shiver and sigh against him.

"I love you…"

Her words were barely audible, but they were enough to make him feel like he'd been propelled into the stratosphere.

He smiled at her and her answering smile caused something monumental to shift within him.

"May I have this dance, Geneva Davis?"

"Yes, Mace Harrison, you may."

As he gently swayed with her close to him, his mind filling with doing much more, he hoped the dance lasted for a long, long time, indeed....

* * * * *

Look what people are saying about this talented author...

"Both the physical and wartime action between the comrades ramp up the excitement in this UNIFORMLY HOT! tale."
—*RT Book Reviews* on *Coming Up for Air*

"A quick pace and easy chemistry make for an engaging read, starring a couple readers will root for."
—*RT Book Reviews* on *No Going Back*

"Sexy characters that you just can't help but fall in love with!"
—*Night Owl Reviews* on *Devil in Dress Blues*

"The romance is intense and sure to please."
—*RT Book Reviews* on *Hot-Blooded*

"Wonderful, sexy characters and an exciting, innovative story make this a winner! 4½ Stars, Top Pick"
—*RT Book Reviews* on *Flyboy*

Dear Reader,

I've always been fascinated by stories about coal miners. Maybe it's because my great-grandfather lost his dad and his four brothers in a coal-mining disaster. Or maybe it's because I'm constantly amazed by the coal miner's indomitable spirit, courage and resilience. And—I'll admit it—there's something incredibly sexy about a guy who's not afraid to get dirty.

Like my heroine, I'm a little claustrophobic and afraid of the dark, so I'm truly in awe of the men and women who willingly descend hundreds of feet below the earth's surface every day, away from the sunlight, in order to support their families. When I decided to write a story about a coal miner, I knew he had to have that same strength and heroic spirit.

Cole MacKinnon is a true hero, willing to put his job, his reputation and his heart on the line for what he believes in. And he believes in Lacey Delaney, the brilliant design engineer who is determined to push him to his breaking point. She's spent most of her life trying to conquer her own fears, but it's not until she meets Cole that she realizes some of the best things happen in the dark...

I hope you enjoy Cole and Lacey's story!

Happy reading,

Karen Foley

A KISS IN THE DARK

BY
KAREN FOLEY

First published in Great Britain 2013
by Mills & Boon, an imprint of Harlequin (UK) Limited,
Eton House, 18-24 Paradise Road, Richmond, Surrey TW9 1SR

© Karen Foley 2012

ISBN: 978 0 263 90295 2
ebook ISBN: 978 1 408 99657 7

14-0213

Harlequin (UK) policy is to use papers that are natural, renewable and recyclable products and made from wood grown in sustainable forests. The logging and manufacturing processes conform to the legal environmental regulations of the country of origin.

Printed and bound in Spain
by Blackprint CPI, Barcelona

Karen Foley is an incurable romantic. When she's not working for the Department of Defense, she's writing sexy romances with strong heroes and happy endings. She lives in Massachusetts with her husband and two daughters, an overgrown puppy and two very spoiled cats. Karen enjoys hearing from her readers. You can find out more about her by visiting www.karenefoley.com.

This book is dedicated to my amazing mother.

1

MORE THAN ANYTHING, Lacey Delaney hated the dark—of being alone in the dark. She wouldn't admit it to anyone, but at twenty-seven years old, she still slept with a bedside light on. It didn't always keep the nightmares at bay, but at least when she woke up, panicked and gasping for breath, she wasn't engulfed in utter blackness. Even now, sitting in the relative safety of her car, she had only to close her eyes to envision her father buried alive in a coal mining disaster so horrific that his body had never been recovered.

Maybe her friend, Julia, was right and she should just find herself a man to keep her so pleasurably occupied at night that she'd be too sated and tired to dream. Unfortunately, both her job as a design engineer for StarPoint Technologies and her overprotective mother kept her too busy to meet many eligible men. Katherine Delaney gave a whole new meaning to the term *helicopter parent*. She didn't just hover; she flew fully armed, ready to obliterate any obstacles in Lacey's path, or to extract her from any danger.

Now here she was…alone, broken down in the middle of nowhere, with darkness pressing in on all sides. If her mother could see her now, she'd have a complete fit. The thought made Lacey smile. Her mother hadn't wanted Lacey to travel to Kentucky; had urged her to give the assignment to somebody else. Of course, the more her mother insisted that Lacey stay home, the more determined she was to go. Sometimes it felt as if the entire course of her life had been dictated by her mother's belief that something would happen to Lacey if she wasn't there to protect her.

Lacey understood the genesis of her mother's anxiety. She'd been just eight years old when her father was killed, and her mother lived in fear that something terrible would happen to Lacey, too. That worry hadn't diminished as Lacey grew older; if anything, it had ballooned into an irrational need to cocoon her against all dangers, real or perceived. And for a long time, Lacey had allowed it. But what had once seemed like parental concern for her welfare now felt like micromanagement of her life. More and more, Lacey found herself resenting her mother's intrusive habits.

She loved her mom, but she wanted to be free, to experience life, and all its pitfalls, on her own terms. She wanted to be taken seriously, and not viewed as someone who needed to be taken care of. Unfortunately, her small stature seemed to bring out a protective instinct in those she worked with, and Lacey was getting a little tired of insisting that she could do things on her own. So when StarPoint Technologies had offered the opportunity to field-test STAR, the new Subterranean Advanced Receiver unit that would become the latest technology in NASA's arsenal of global positioning systems, Lacey had jumped at it.

Her boss had been skeptical, since Lacey's experience was limited to the design lab. She had never before ventured into the field. But Lacey knew if she wanted to be respected as an engineer and a scientist, she needed to be familiar with all aspects of the job, including fieldwork. She just hadn't been prepared for how remote this particular field assignment would be.

The parking lot of the diner, where a short time ago she'd halfheartedly picked at a plate of meatloaf, was completely dark except for one light pole near the entrance. She'd been unable to pick up a signal on her cell phone, and was grateful that the owner of the diner had at least called for a tow truck before he'd snapped off the lights and locked the door, assuring her she'd be fine until Sully—the tow truck driver, she presumed—arrived.

Sighing, she sat behind the wheel of her rental car and left the door open for whatever small breeze might happen by. God, it was hot. Of course, New England could get sticky in the summer as well, but it was only early June and already Kentucky sweltered with heat.

Resting her head against the seat back, Lacey listened to the night bugs in the surrounding trees and watched the tiny blinking lights of the seemingly hundreds of fireflies. Generally, the heat didn't bother her, but tonight was different. Tonight she would have to return to the pathetic little motel she had checked into earlier that evening, knowing she wouldn't sleep a wink. She wasn't a snob by nature, but the only other patrons she had seen were several itinerant coal miners who had been well on their way to getting completely drunk. Knowing a slim length of chain was all that prevented one of them from entering her room would ensure she slept with her clothes on. And to top it off, the room would be about a million degrees since the air-conditioning didn't work.

Her small carry-on bag sat on the passenger seat beside her, and now she dug through the contents, pulling out an emergency pair of panties and bra—courtesy of her mom, just in case the airline lost her luggage—and an eReader as she hunted for the bottled water she had stashed there earlier. Blowing a strand of hair from her face, she took a long swallow of the water and decided it would only be for one night. Tomorrow, she would meet with Sheriff Hathaway, her point of contact while she was in Black Stone Gap, and ask him to recommend somewhere to stay other than the seedy Blackwater Inn. If there *was* any other place, she thought glumly. The motel should have been named the *Back*water Inn, because it was literally in the middle of nowhere. Her own frantic hunt through the phone book she'd found in the bedside table hadn't turned up any other hotels or motels in the area.

She reminded herself again that she wasn't here on vacation. Where she slept didn't matter. She had a job to do, and a dingy motel room wasn't going to deter her. StarPoint Technologies was under contract to NASA to develop a GPS unit that would operate underground, capable of sending and receiving signals through hundreds of feet of rock. Lacey had spent the past three years of her life designing and developing the unit, affectionately dubbed STAR.

Now that the development phase was complete, all that was required before they could turn the unit over to NASA was the final testing. For Lacey, this meant a chance not only to prove herself as a field scientist, but also to get out on her own. She could do whatever she wanted, within limits.

But Lacey was tired of limits.

She'd do her job, but she also intended to have some fun on this trip. Her friend Julia was right; allowing her mother to have so much influence over her life was unhealthy, no matter how good her intentions might be. This was an opportunity to spread her wings a bit and explore her own capabilities.

She'd spend three days with the local search-and-rescue team, demonstrating the use of handheld GPS units designed by her firm, and then one week at the local coal mines, testing STAR. But she'd also have some free time in which to sightsee. She'd spent part of the flight from Boston to Roanoke consulting her tourist book, considering the things she might do while she was in Kentucky. An evening pub crawl with free samples of Kentucky's finest bourbon sounded fun, but so did zip-lining over a forest canopy. Of course, how much free time she had depended on how smoothly the field tests went.

The opportunity to utilize the local coal mines to test STAR had been too good to pass up. Not only would the coal mines that riddled the area around Black Stone Gap provide a perfect test environment, but Lacey owed it to her father to ensure the unit worked deep inside the tunnels, where it could do the most good. If she could prevent even one miner from suffering the same fate as her father, she would be satisfied.

It seemed only minutes had passed when headlights swung toward her through the parking lot. Lifting her head, she peered at a large, beefy tow truck as it turned into the lot where she was stranded. It approached from the side and parked facing her door. The headlights bathed her in a blinding glare as she sat up and shielded her eyes.

She couldn't see who was in the driver's seat, but felt their scrutiny as if it were a palpable thing. She suddenly knew how a deer felt when caught in a car's headlights. Here she was, alone and vulnerable and out in the middle of nowhere, and she could only imagine who watched her from the cab of that tow truck. Lacey had completed a self-defense course in college and she had no doubt that she could take care of herself, but when she heard the opening and closing of the driver's door, it galvanized her into action. Better to be safe than sorry. Swiftly, she pulled her own car door shut and punched the lock down. A figure stepped into the light, silhouetted for a moment in the brightness.

Lacey's breath caught.

His body was lean and powerful, with broad, sloping

shoulders and narrow hips. It was a body that turned a woman's thoughts instantly to sex. The light behind him shadowed his features, but she knew with a certainty they would be as arresting as his body.

He came closer, and as Lacey sat immobile, he leaned down to peer in at her. Her mouth fell open as she stared wordlessly into the bluest eyes she had ever seen. They weren't just your average blue, either. Even in the dim light she could see they were an opulent shade of blue-green that reminded her of tropical waters and warm, secluded beaches.

"Ma'am?" His voice carried low and clear through the car window, and she could see the concern in his eyes. "Are you okay?"

She recognized his voice as the man she had spoken to on the telephone earlier. She would have preferred to roll her window down to talk with him, but with the engine off, the power windows were useless. If she wanted to communicate, she would have to either shout through the glass, or open the door. Already, the air inside the car was suffocatingly hot. She studied him for a moment, and then drawing in a deep breath, pushed her door open but made no move to get out.

He stepped into the opening, bracing one hand on the roof and the other arm along the top of the door frame. He grinned down at her, a lazy this-must-be-my-lucky-night kind of grin. His teeth were white in the darkness of his face. He wore a faded black T-shirt that clung to his muscled torso, and from her vantage point below him, Lacey could see the impressive bulge of his biceps as he leaned into the car.

"You called for a tow truck?" Deep indents flashed in his lean cheeks. His voice was lazy and warm.

Lacey didn't know what was wrong with her. She couldn't seem to find her voice. "Um, yes." She gulped. "I did. My car doesn't seem to want to start."

She wasn't prepared when he suddenly crouched down

beside her. Now he was eye level with her and she could see he had close-cropped, dark hair. Balancing on the balls of his feet, he edged forward and reached toward her legs.

"Mind if I take a peek?" he asked.

A surge of heat coursed through Lacey that had nothing to do with the outside temperature. For one wild, crazy second she was sure he was going to flip back the skirt of her little sundress and, heaven help her, she was going to let him.

But his hand went with unerring skill to the hood release located just under the dash, and only when she heard the popping of the catch did she realize she had been holding her breath. He rose to his feet in one fluid movement and rounded the front of her car to raise the hood, pulling a slim flashlight out of a back pocket.

Lacey sagged back against the seat. If she'd had a fan, it would have been working overtime to try and cool her suddenly flushed skin. He was, without a doubt, the most sinful-looking man she had ever seen, and she thought it had as much to do with the way he looked *at* her as it did with the way he looked.

She struggled to get a grip on her rioting thoughts. What was she thinking? A tow truck driver? She could almost see Julia doing a victory dance. Despite his amazing eyes, he was probably not much better than the leering, beer-swigging coal miners at the Blackwater Inn.

But an image of that leanly muscled physique came back to her, and she knew instinctively she was wrong. He wasn't at all like those men. He was the sort who would take his time with a woman, ensuring her pleasure before reaching his own. He would be assertive, playful and maybe even a little kinky. For one wild instant, her imagination surged. Images of a secluded mountain cabin and fur-strewn floors lingered in her mind. She envisioned him clearly, his tautly muscled body moving softly over her own in the darkness, murmuring husky words of encouragement against her throat, her lips…

He came back around to her door and bent down, interrupting her wayward thoughts. "Ma'am, do you mind if I try to start her up?"

"Oh, of course not!" Unable to meet his eyes, Lacey scooted out of the car to stand out of his way.

She watched as he folded his long frame into the driver's seat and turned the key. Still nothing. He tried again, and then sat back for a moment, considering. Looking up at her, he gave her a lopsided grin.

"Looks like you're going to need my services, after all," he drawled.

Lacey's pulse reacted immediately. *If he only knew.*

Sensing those tropical water eyes on her, Lacey glanced at him. His expression held a heat that made her breath catch, and she knew in that instant that he was interested in her. Then he looked away, his features shuttered.

"Do—do you know what's wrong with the engine?" she asked, clearing her throat against the sudden restriction she felt there.

"Why don't I show you?"

Climbing out of the car, he indicated she should precede him, and her nerves jumped when he placed a hand at the small of her back to guide her. Just that light touch of his fingers seemed to burn through the thin fabric of her cotton dress. A tiny shiver rippled through her. She felt strange, all fluttery and anxious, and her heartbeat pulsed loudly in her ears. She felt shivery, yet flushed with heat. And all because this man had touched her.

He leaned over her engine compartment and flicked his flashlight into its dark interior. He spoke, and she listened to the warm, rich tones of his voice even as she admired the fit of his jeans across his backside. She envisioned those leanly muscled orbs cupped in the palms of her hands.

The next moment she was appalled. What was wrong with her? She was acting like a moonstruck teenager. It wasn't as if she'd never been this close to a gorgeous guy before. She'd had relationships. Okay, so she hadn't been intimate with anyone on any level in several years, and she was probably more than a little sexually frustrated. But between her job and her mother's nearly constant vigilance, she hadn't had an opportunity to develop any relationships, meaningful or otherwise. But here she was, with nobody to tell her what she could or couldn't do. While she didn't think she'd reached the point where she would jump the first attractive stranger she encountered, it was a wonderful feeling to know that she *could,* provided the stranger was also willing.

With a start, she realized the stranger had stopped talking and was watching her, resting one hip against the frame of the car, arms crossed casually over his chest as he waited for her to return to earth.

"Sorry," she mumbled. "You were saying?"

He grinned then, slowly, as if he knew exactly what she had been thinking. "I was saying that it looks like you have an abrasion in the insulation of the wiring harness."

"Oh." Lacey looked at him blankly. "What does that mean?"

The indents in those lean cheeks deepened. "Well, when the wiring isn't seated right, there's too much friction and an abrasion can occur, resulting in a hot spot." He eased himself away from the car and took a step toward Lacey. "When that happens," he said slowly, his voice languid and dark, "the wiring can overheat, melting everything right back to the driveshaft."

Lacey blinked. Her cheeks grew warm. "Really." She slid her gaze away from the sudden heat in those translucent eyes. "A hot spot, huh?"

"Mm-hmm. You're definitely going to need my services."

Turning away, Lacey pressed a palm against her chest and forced herself to breathe normally. "Okay, then. It's a rental car, so whatever's wrong with it, they can fix it. I'll call the rental agency and let them know where they can collect it." She drew in a steadying breath before turning back to face him. "Should I pay you now, or let the rental agency pay you when they come to get the car?"

He shrugged. "Let them pay for it. Here, I'll give you a business card."

She watched as he strode over to the tow truck and began rummaging around inside the cab. He swore softly. "I know they're in here somewhere. Aha!" He came back and handed her a small card. "Give this number to the rental agency."

Lacey glanced at the card. There was the business name, *Sully's Towing Service,* but not his first name. Pushing down her disappointment, she looked back up at him. "Thanks. If you'll wait just a moment, I'll get my things out of the car."

She popped the trunk release and was hauling her presentation materials and the case that contained STAR out, when he leaned in through the driver's door and across the seat. She paused for a moment, peeking around the trunk to admire his ass. When he finally straightened, she realized he was holding her lingerie and carry-on bag in one hand, and her little pocketbook in the other.

"You don't want to forget these."

The delicate satin panties looked ridiculously fragile in his large hand, and she had a sudden image of him sliding them slowly down over her hips. Her eyes flew to his. Those mesmerizing dimples were back again as he handed her belongings to her.

Taking the items wordlessly from him, she struggled to lift the heavy case out of the trunk when he reached in and took it easily from her hands. Then, lifting her presentation case in his other hand, he strode over to the tow truck and tossed them both into the cargo area behind the seats.

"What are you doing?"

He gave her a smile that sent her heart lurching. "I'm taking you home."

Her voice, when she finally found it, came out as no more than a squeak. "You're what?"

"Well, I wouldn't feel right leaving you in a deserted parking lot," he said, running a hand over his crop of short hair and managing to look endearingly concerned. "So unless somebody's already on their way to pick you up, I'll run you wherever you need to go." He gave her a questioning look.

Logically, Lacey knew that what he said made sense. He couldn't leave her here, without a way to get back to the motel. But his words still caused her imagination to surge.

"No," she finally managed. "There's nobody coming to get me. I'm only here for a few days."

"Ah," he said meaningfully. "Well then, why don't you hop into the cab and I'll hook the car up."

Hesitating only briefly, Lacey did as he suggested, sliding past him as he held the door open and taking his proffered hand to hitch herself up onto the bench seat. His skin was warm, his fingers strong and sure as they closed over her own.

She watched him as he came around to the driver's side and pulled himself up behind the wheel. Mere inches away from her, in the confined space of the cab his presence was overwhelming, the sheer maleness of him assailing her senses.

Suddenly, he turned toward her on the bench seat, one arm sliding along the seat back behind her shoulders as he craned to peer through the rear window and align the truck up with her car. Lacey's nostrils flared. *She could smell him.* A clean scent of male sweat and soap. She realized she had only to turn her face and her lips would brush along the smooth bulge of his biceps where they rested on the back of the seat.

Rigid, Lacey clutched her overnight bag with both hands and forced herself to look straight ahead, but found herself staring at his thighs. They were lean and well-muscled beneath the close-fitting blue jeans. She swallowed. His hand on the steering wheel was strong, with long, tapered fingers and neat, clean nails. She noted he wore no rings and felt an unreasonable sense of relief. Sliding a sideways glance at him as he maneuvered the tow truck into position, she couldn't help but wonder what he was thinking about her.

COLE MACKINNON COULD scarcely believe his good fortune as he jumped down from the cab and began the process of hitching the car to the tow truck. He'd been back in Black Stone Gap for less than two days and had stopped by Sully's garage that night on a whim. They'd been kicking back with a cold beer when the call had come in. Sully, his longtime buddy, had been on another line so Cole had automatically picked up the second phone when it began to ring off the hook. He'd helped Sully out before so it was no big deal when he'd offered to tow this one in. He actually enjoyed playing the Good Samaritan. But when the headlights of the truck had first swung over the car, he'd been nearly speechless at the sight of the woman who reclined in the driver's seat.

She was pale and slim, with bare arms and legs, and ginger hair that fell as soft and straight as summer rain to skim her smooth shoulders. In the stifling heat of the Kentucky night, she looked as cool and refreshing as a tall glass of mint tea. When he'd reached under the dash to release the hood, he'd had to fight the urge to skate his palm along the silken length of her leg, fiercely reminding himself that he was there to help her. He had absolutely no intentions of seducing her. No way, not a one.

None.

He finished fastening the coupling on the hitch. As he straightened, he glanced through the rear window of the tow truck in time to see her scoop that silky hair up in both hands and pile it on top of her head, exposing the sweet, vulnerable curve of her neck.

Damn.

He stood transfixed, all his good intentions vanishing, scattering like so many fireflies into the heat of the night.

2

SHE WAS UNEASY. Cole glanced over at her as he eased the truck into gear and slowly maneuvered it out of the parking lot and onto the dark main road. Hell, she should be. If she'd even an inkling of the thoughts that were racing through his head, she'd be a whole lot more nervous. She tried to act casual, but he didn't miss how she stole furtive glances at him, and continually smoothed her fingers over the skirt of her dress.

Everything about her, from her accent to her little designer purse, shouted Northerner. He was betting from somewhere in the Northeast. Which meant she was probably as frigid as a New York winter. She'd no doubt be shocked if she knew of the lustful imaginings he'd just had of her. She'd probably never had a fantasy in her entire life. His eyes slid to the overnight bag that rested on the seat between them. And he remembered what had been spilling out of that bag only moments before.

Scraps of satin and lace.

He felt a smile twitch the corners of his mouth. Okay, so perhaps she did harbor a fantasy or two. He'd give a lot to know what they were. Then do his damnedest to make them all come true.

He'd returned to Black Stone Gap just two days earlier, having been gone for more than five years. Not even Sully knew his real reason for coming back. He'd told his friend that he was looking for work in the coal mines, knowing the word would spread quickly in the small community. A good mining engineer was worth his weight in gold.

But what he hadn't told Sully was that he didn't really need the work; he was undercover for the Department of Labor, investigating an alarming spike in the number of accidents in Black River Mine No. 2, the biggest and most active coal mine in the region. He hadn't wanted to come back; he'd been happy enough in Norfolk, working as a structural engineer for the state of Virginia. Until the night he'd received a call from a friend and former instructor at Virginia Tech.

Cole had studied mining engineering under Stu Zollweg, and had later participated as part of an inspection team led by Zollweg to identify safety issues in several West Virginia mines. He'd found the fieldwork both challenging and satisfying. After obtaining his Master's degree, he'd returned to Black Stone Gap and been hired as an engineer in the Black River Mines. But less than six months into the job, he'd lost a good friend in a tunnel collapse. He'd been consumed with guilt and anger; he should have known about the weak tunnel structure. He should have been able to avert the accident.

Instead of sticking around to help uncover what had gone wrong, he'd bolted. He'd moved to Norfolk the day after his friend's funeral and had gotten a job as a structural engineer, helping to build highway tunnels and bridges.

When Stu Zollweg had called out of the blue, Cole couldn't have been more surprised. But the offer he made was even more surprising. Stu worked part-time for the Department of Labor as a mine safety inspector. The Bureau of Mines had sent safety inspectors into the Black River Mines on several occasions, but had failed to uncover any significant safety infractions. So they couldn't understand why the accident rate in the Black River Mines was higher than other mines in the country. Now the feds wanted someone to go into those mines undercover and find out why the accident rate was climbing. Stu had recommended Cole for the job.

If he could gain access to the tunnels, he could provide evidence of what he had long suspected—that the mines were operating in direct violation of Federal safety codes. He just needed to prove it.

The air-conditioning in the cab was strong enough to softly stir the fabric of her dress, and even by the dim dashboard lights he could see goose bumps raised along her slim arms.

"Cold?" he asked. "I can turn down the air if you'd like."

"No, thanks. It feels good."

She started to say something more when the radio unit on the dash emitted a sudden, loud squawk and a disembodied, static voice filled the cab of the truck.

"Mac, you there? Over."

Cole lifted a handheld mouthpiece from its cradle and pressed a button, speaking into the instrument. "Yeah, I'm here. I'm giving the client a lift home, and then I'll bring the truck and car in. Over."

"Do me a favor, Mac," came the reply. "Can you bring the truck back first? I just got a call that Stu Barlow's boy wrecked his truck out on the gap road and forced another car into the ravine. The kid's fine, but his vehicle's blocking the road. Bobby just headed over there with the other wrecker, so I'll take yours and meet him there. Over."

"Got it. See you in two. Over and out." Cole replaced the mouthpiece and gave his passenger an apologetic smile. "Looks like I need to bring the truck back to Sully first, then I'll give you that lift to wherever it is you're staying." When she didn't immediately answer, he gave her a quick glance. "That is, if it's okay with you."

Her attention had sharpened on him. "You're not Sully?"

Cole grinned. "No, ma'am." Keeping one eye on the dark road, he extended a hand toward her. "Name's Cole Mac-Kinnon."

After a moment, she took his hand. Her fingers were slender and cool. "I'm Lacey Delaney."

Cole thought the name suited her. Soft. Feminine. It conjured up images of delicate lingerie, like the stuff she had in that bag. He slanted her a smile. "Nice to meet you, ma'am." She made no move to withdraw her hand, and Cole's grin broadened as he saw the turnoff to Sully's garage come into view. "Uh, ma'am?" She gave him a questioning look and he dropped his gaze pointedly to their clasped hands. "I'll have to shift in another minute, but in order to do that I'll need—"

She snatched her fingers from his.

LACEY HAD BEEN so busy mooning at the man, she hadn't even realized she was hanging on to his hand. Worse, he was completely aware of her reaction to him. She cleared her throat uncomfortably as the truck turned into a gravel parking lot. There was a large, multibay garage at the far end and she could see lights on in the small office there. A sign over it read Sully's Garage—24 Hour Towing. At the other end of the building were two blue taxicabs, and a smaller sign that read Tara's Taxi Service.

As Cole maneuvered the rental car into a nearby space, the door to the office opened and a huge bear of a man emerged. Sully, she presumed. He had a head of unruly dark hair and half of his face was obscured by a beard and moustache.

Cole glanced over at Lacey. "Wait here where it's cool. I'll unhitch the car first, and then get your things out of the back. No need for you to stand around in this heat."

Without waiting for an answer, he opened his door and jumped down. Lacey watched as the other man approached him. She couldn't hear their words, but she didn't miss when Cole jerked his thumb in the direction of the truck. The bearded man turned his head toward her and Lacey barely resisted the urge to slide down lower in her seat. Sully grinned and said something, and slapped Cole on the back. Lacey heard him laughing as he strode back toward the office.

What had Cole said to him? And why did she suddenly feel like a cheap pickup? But when Cole turned and came alongside the truck to unhitch her car, she could see he wasn't smiling. His face wore an expression of such annoyance that Lacey felt an unexpected rush of gratitude toward him. Clearly he wasn't pleased with whatever conclusion Sully had drawn of his decision to drive her back to the motel.

But when he opened her door, his features were schooled into a mask of politeness. He extended a hand to help her down, and Lacey fumbled for a moment, trying to grasp both her overnight bag and purse. He reached in wordlessly and took the bag from her. As Lacey swung her legs around, her skirt scooted halfway up her thighs, but with one hand firmly clutched around her purse and the other warmly encased in Cole's, she had no chance to tug it down. She heard him suck in his breath, and when she glanced at his face, she saw the heat was back in those translucent eyes.

"C'mon," he muttered. "Let's get out of here before Sully decides to come back out."

She waited as he reached into the back and withdrew her presentation case and STAR, hefting them both in a single grip. "Is he your boss?"

Cole gave a bark of surprised laughter. "Sully? No, he's just a friend. I help him out once in a while, that's all. He's a good guy, but he doesn't have much in the way of manners. Trust me when I say you're better off not getting an introduction. It still amazes me that he actually managed to find himself a wife." He nodded his head toward the opposite side of the parking lot. "This way."

Lacey waited while Cole stowed her gear in an oversize toolbox secured in the bed of a large, black pickup truck. There was no lighting in this area of the lot, and with his dark jeans and T-shirt, the surrounding gloom all but swallowed him up. Lacey hung back, standing just outside the ring of darkness.

She considered herself to be an intelligent woman, but taking a ride from a complete stranger had to be the height of stupidity. It had seemed a perfectly reasonable solution when they were in the tow truck with her rental car hitched to the back. After all, she had been the customer, securing the services of a professional. But discovering he wasn't even affiliated with the towing company, and then accepting a ride in his personal truck seemed somehow...well, personal. Intimate.

"Hey." His voice was quiet, interrupting her thoughts. He had taken a step toward her and now stood watching her. "Having second thoughts?"

The man was perceptive. "No, of course not."

He laughed softly and stepped closer. "Liar."

Lacey barely resisted the urge to step backward as he advanced. His knowing look, combined with a smile that could only be called predatory, should have had her running full-tilt in the opposite direction. Instead, it caused a bolt of awareness to surge through her, rooting her where she stood.

"Why would I be having second thoughts? You don't look like an ax murderer, but if you are, I have witnesses who've seen you with me." She indicated with a nod of her head to where Sully was climbing into the cab of the tow truck. Her voice was light. "You'd never get away with it."

Cole's dimples flashed as he gave her a wolfish grin. "Rest assured, when it comes to pretty women, hurting them is the last thing I have in mind."

Lacey felt her pulse quicken. What, exactly, did he have in mind for her? And how would he react if she indicated, by word or gesture, that she might be a willing participant? The sudden images that swamped her imagination were so vivid and so strong that heat flooded her face, making her grateful for the dim light.

Cole's glance moved beyond Lacey. "If you *are* having second thoughts, now's your chance to say so. Once Sully's gone, it's just you and me."

Lacey turned and watched in silence as the tow truck slowly made its way across the parking lot. She saw Sully raise a hand in brief salute, and then the taillights vanished as the vehicle swung out of the parking lot and onto the main road. Drawing a fortifying breath, she turned back to face Cole with a bright smile. "I guess you have your answer."

He considered her silently for a moment, his expression inscrutable, before stepping back to open the driver's door of the pickup truck. "I guess I do."

He extended a hand toward Lacey, and once more she found her fingers wrapped in the warm strength of his own as he helped her up into the cab. Lacey scooted across the bench seat only to be halted midway by the sight of an enormous animal sprawled on the far side. Its tongue lolled wetly from an open mouth bracketed by long, loose jowls as it regarded her drowsily, and a long tail thumped in greeting against the seat. Her mouth fell open in wordless surprise.

"That's Copper," said Cole, sliding in behind the wheel. "He has a tendency to slobber, so you might not want to get too close." He grinned. "I think he has a thing for redheads."

Lacey recoiled as the dog shook its head, flinging long ropes of saliva against the back of the seat. "Oh, my," she said, laughing in spite of herself, "you weren't kidding. He really does slobber!"

"Sorry," Cole said, sounding anything but apologetic as Lacey drew closer to him in an effort to avoid being splattered. "Once we get going, he'll hang his head out the window, so you'll be safe."

At least from the dog, thought Lacey. With Copper taking up more than his fair share of the seat, it was nearly impossible to maintain a respectable distance from Cole. She could feel the heat that radiated from his lean body, even as he reached over and flipped on the air-conditioning and a blast of lukewarm air billowed her skirt up over her thighs. Lacey pushed it back down and placed her purse over her knees in an effort to keep the fabric firmly where it belonged.

"Here," said Cole, "let me adjust those vents."

He extended one arm across her knees and flipped the louvers upward. His shoulder pressed against hers and his arm brushed against her breast as he pulled back. It was purely accidental, but Lacey was helpless to prevent a swift intake of breath at the intimate contact. If Cole noticed her reaction, he gave no sign, but Lacey thought he reversed with slightly more force than necessary, the tires churning up loose gravel before he changed gears and headed out of the parking lot.

As Cole had predicted, Copper heaved himself to his feet and happily thrust his head out of the open window, his long ears streaming behind him. His hindquarters were dangerously close to Lacey's face, and when his tail started to knock steadily against her chest, she gave a soft exclamation of surprise and gingerly swatted at the offending length.

Cole laughed, the sound sliding over Lacey's senses like warm honey. "That dog," he said ruefully, "has no sense of personal space."

Neither, apparently, did Cole as he leaned suddenly across Lacey's body and with one hand pushed gently but firmly on the dog's rear, forcing it into a sitting position. "There," he said, and his glance slid over Lacey as she pressed herself against the seat. "You okay?"

Lacey met his gaze. Even in the darkened cab, there was no mistaking the expression of taut awareness on his face. In that instant, Lacey knew he wanted her.

The knowledge thrilled her.

Terrified her.

Caused her heart to slam against her rib cage so that she was sure he would hear its betraying rhythm. "I'm fine," she finally managed, hating the way her voice sounded breathless, even to her own ears.

"Where are you staying?" he asked. "Mozelle or Cumberland?"

Lacey looked at him blankly. "Are those hotels? Because I checked and—"

Cole laughed softly again. "No, ma'am, those are towns. The closest ones with decent hotels, at any rate. Unless you're staying with friends here in the Gap?"

Lacey peered at him suspiciously. "Just how close are those two towns?"

Cole shrugged. "Well, they're in opposite directions from here, but I'd guess they're both about an hour away."

Lacey gaped at him. "You'd be willing to drive me all that way?"

He turned to her then, surprise evident on his face. "Yeah. Why wouldn't I?"

Lacey stared at him for a long moment before dragging her gaze away. Of course he was willing to drive her that far. He probably thought he'd be well rewarded for his efforts. After all, she'd done nothing but ogle him since she'd first laid eyes on him. For a moment, Lacey battled with herself, torn between doubt and anticipation, because a part of her wanted him to want her. But she didn't want him to think she was an easy conquest.

His lips tightened before he returned his attention to the road. "I see. You think I'll want some sort of payment in return for the lift."

"No—" Lacey began, ready to deny what she had, in fact, been thinking.

But Cole held up one hand, forestalling any further words. "It's okay," he said. "Because you know what?" He slanted her one long, meaningful look. "You're right. I'd be lying if I said the thought hadn't crossed my mind." He gave a low, self-deprecating laugh. "Hell, it's been the single thing on my mind since I first saw you."

Lacey's breath hitched. His husky confession caused a liquid heat to slip along the underside of her skin, and her pulse began a heavy, languorous thudding. She focused on the dark road, watching as the truck swallowed up the pavement, unable to think of an appropriate response.

"However," he continued easily, "I don't need to use coercion or guilt to get a woman to sleep with me. It's either completely mutual, or it doesn't happen. So you can relax, okay?"

Relax? Was he kidding? Lacey thought she might spontaneously combust. Of course he didn't need to use coercion— he was the kind of guy women fantasized about. Not only gorgeous, but considerate, too. In that moment, she made up her mind. Her friend Julia was right; she'd denied herself for way too long, always putting the needs of others before her own, always conscious of what her mother might think. But out here, there was just her and this man. She was only going to be in Black Stone Gap for ten days. Why shouldn't she do as she pleased? Lord knew when she'd have another opportunity.

She glanced over at Cole. "I'm actually staying here in Black Stone Gap," she ventured, "so you won't need to drive me too far." *To collect your reward.*

He tilted her a questioning look. "Oh, yeah? Where?"

"The Blackwater Inn."

"What?" He bit the word out, his face incredulous.

"There were no other hotels," she said defensively. "The Blackwater Inn is a little grungy, but otherwise it's fine."

He gave a snort of disgust. "Yeah, if you're an itinerant coal miner or a horny barfly."

Lacey looked at him in dismay, recalling the men she'd seen at the motel earlier that night. "I did try to make other arrangements, but there wasn't anything else even close."

Cole ran a hand over his hair. "Hell," he muttered. "If anyone sees you, every guy who's staying there'll be panting at your door. I'll walk you to your room. Once you're inside with the door locked, you should be okay." He shook his head again. "The Blackwater Inn?"

When they pulled into the motel several minutes later, Lacey saw that the bar across the street was doing a brisk business. The parking lot was completely full and the overflow had spilled into the motel's lot. As Cole parked the truck, the door of the bar opened and a man and woman lurched outside, briefly illuminated by the shaft of light from inside the establishment.

Hanging on to each other, they made their way across the darkened street. As they approached the Blackwater Inn, they stopped to exchange a deep kiss. They swayed, stumbled, and then laughingly broke apart to stagger over to one of the guestroom doors. Lacey watched as the woman fitted a key into the lock. The man was groping her from behind. He bent his head and nuzzled her neck even as one hand snaked around to fondle a breast. The woman laughed again and they all but fell through the open door. Lacey caught a glimpse of the two coming together for a passionate embrace before the man kicked the door closed with one booted foot.

Lacey found she couldn't look over at Cole. The raw sexuality she had just witnessed too closely mirrored the fantasy she had briefly entertained about him.

"C'mon," he muttered. "Let's get you to your room."

Opening his door, he slid out and stood back to wait for her. Copper drew his head in from the passenger window and flopped down on the seat once more, staring at them with an expression that stated clearly he was accustomed to being left in the truck. Cole retrieved her gear from his lockbox and indicated she should precede him.

"I'm in the back," she said, aware of his eyes on her as she led him around to the rear of the building. A group of men had pulled several of the plastic patio chairs around a small table on the walkway and were playing cards. Beer cans littered the grass and cigarette smoke hung heavy on the humid air. They paused when they saw Lacey, and the nearest one leered appreciatively at her from over the rim of a beer can.

"Evenin' boys."

Cole's voice was cordial but cool as he hefted Lacey's presentation case over one shoulder and took her elbow with his free hand, propelling her along. Lacey cast a wary look at the men, noting the sullen, almost defiant manner in which they watched her. Despite Cole's casual attitude, she sensed he was on full alert, every muscle in his lean body tightly coiled. He was staring at the men, his eyes challenging them to say something, anything. Two of the men mumbled a greeting and one by one they lowered their eyes beneath Cole's unwavering glare.

"I'm in here," Lacey said when they reached her door. Would he expect her to invite him in? Or would he simply say goodbye? She glanced up at him. He was so close that

one small step back would bring her smack up against that
tautly muscled chest. He was crowding her, his larger physique shielding her from the nearby men.

"Get your key out and open the door." His voice was low
in her ear, brooking no argument.

Turning the knob, she pushed the door open, startled when
he hustled her inside and closed it behind them. In the sudden and complete darkness of the room, her chest constricted
and she couldn't control her suddenly rapid pulse or the per-
spiration that popped out along her hairline. She closed her
eyes and dragged in several deep breaths, telling herself
there was nothing to be afraid of. She heard Cole set her
cases down on the floor. When he flipped on the overhead
light, she blinked and exhaled in relief, and then sank down
on the edge of the bed. Cole opened the door an inch or so
and examined the broken deadbolt, testing it. Then he fingered the dangling chain.

"This lock is broken." He slanted her a questioning look.
"Did you realize that?"

Lacey swallowed, momentarily unable to form a response.
She thought she'd gotten a good look at him in the truck.
She'd thought him gorgeous then, but by the glaring light of
the overhead fixture she realized she had been wrong. The
man wasn't just gorgeous.

He was magnificent.

His face was a masterpiece of lean, chiseled features
paired with a sensuous mouth. For an instant, Lacey imagined feasting on those lips with her own. His blue eyes were
fringed with thick, dark lashes and his short hair was a deep,
rich brown. His skin was bronzed by the sun and his arms
were an incredible mix of bulging muscles and lean sinews.
Her hands would probably be incapable of spanning those
impressive biceps. When he wasn't smiling, like now, he had
a decidedly dangerous aura. In the confines of the room,

he seemed inordinately large. Lacey should have been nervous, but she wasn't. She'd been an apt self-defense pupil, and if things began to turn sour, she was more than capable of defending herself.

"Yes." She nodded. "I notified the front desk, but apparently there aren't any other rooms available."

Cole closed the door with a click and took several steps into the room. His gaze swept over the gaudy bedspread and stained carpeting, missing nothing. "It's hot as hell in here."

He was right. Fine beads of moisture had gathered on Lacey's skin and her sundress clung damply to her. In the confined room, the heat was suffocating. "It's just for one night. I'll find something else in the morning."

Cole looked doubtfully at her as he fiddled with the thermostat. "I doubt you'll survive a night in this furnace." He flicked the wall thermometer in disgust. "Looks like the air-conditioning is on the blink." He moved to the window and Lacey watched with renewed interest when the muscles in his arms and shoulders bunched with effort as he tried unsuccessfully to raise the sash. After a moment, he stepped back. "Unbelievable. I think they've permanently nailed it shut."

He turned to look down at her, his expression inscrutable. Lacey smoothed her skirt down over her knees and tried not to think about the fact that she was alone in a motel room with an absolutely mouthwatering man. Any fantasy she might have harbored about him had been completely dashed the moment he stepped through the door. He was obviously disgusted by the seediness of the room, and the temperature alone was enough to wilt any blossoming desire. She steeled herself for his departure, unwilling to examine why she felt so depressed at the prospect of his leaving.

She'd been ready to take the plunge with this guy, to step out of her comfort zone and do something thrilling and naughty. The realization that she'd be spending the night alone in this tawdry motel room was a complete letdown. But she could at least accept the inevitable with good grace. There was no way she would let him see her disappointment.

"Well." She pushed to her feet and stood by the door, her hand on the latch. Outside, she could hear raised voices as an argument broke out among the men playing cards. She forced a brisk, businesslike tone to her voice, but found she couldn't meet his eyes. "Thank you so much for your help. I really appreciate everything you've done for me."

There was silence, and when Lacey finally looked up, it was to find Cole standing with his hands braced on his hips, watching her with a bemused expression. He dominated the small room. Lacey's eyes traveled slowly up the length of his body, noting how the black T-shirt emphasized the taut flatness of his stomach and the muscled planes of his chest. There was a light sheen of sweat on the strong column of his throat and she imagined tracing her tongue along that slick skin.

"You don't actually think I'm going to leave you here, do you?" he asked.

Now it was her turn to look bemused, even as her pulse quickened. "What do you mean?"

Her eyes widened when he turned and scooped her discarded pantsuit from the back of a chair where she had tossed it. He folded it neatly in half, dropped it into her open suitcase and flipped the case shut.

"There's really only one thing to do." His mouth curved in a rueful grin. "I'm taking you home with me."

3

LACEY WAS CERTAIN he had to be kidding, but there was nothing humorous in his manner as he zipped her case shut, hefted it neatly in one hand, and stepped toward the door.

"Wait a minute." Lacey threw up a hand to forestall him. "You can't be serious."

"Yeah, you're probably right." Cole's voice was low. "You're definitely better off staying here. I'm sure those men out there will be more than happy to take care of you tonight." He stabbed a finger toward the commotion outside. "From the sound of things, they're well on their way to getting completely messed up. If I leave you here, how long do you think it'll take for them to decide you're fair game? Hmm? Do you really think you're safe in this room?"

Lacey was silent. He had verbalized what she had been thinking. But to go home with Cole? Did she dare? Because she'd be lying to herself if she believed nothing would happen between them. Even now, the tension in the room was almost palpable.

"Look," he said, interrupting her thoughts. "I know what you're thinking." Reaching into his back pocket, he produced a slim wallet, flipped it open and extended it toward her. "Here's my I.D. If you want to take a look and then call somebody to let them know who you're with, go ahead."

Glancing at him, Lacey took the proffered wallet and looked down at the I.D. beneath the plastic protector. It was a Virginia driver's license with a Norfolk address. The photograph had captured the incredible blueness of his eyes. She tried not to stare.

"You're not even from around here," she said, handing him the wallet. "Were you planning on driving back to Norfolk? That's what—five hundred miles from here?"

Cole pocketed the wallet, frustration evident in his expression. "I grew up here in the Gap, but I moved to Norfolk after I got out of school. My family has a place not too far from here, and everyone in town knows who I am. You're safer with me than you are here."

Lacey didn't know about that. Her intentions where Cole was concerned could be classified as anything but *safe*.

He looked expectantly at her. "Okay? Are we good? Now can we please get the hell out of here before we both suffocate?"

He was right. The heat in the room was oppressive. Still, Lacey hesitated. Once she committed to going with him, there would be no turning back.

Seeing her misgivings, Cole sighed, put the suitcase down and spread his hands out in a supplicating gesture. "Look, you're going to have to trust me on this one, okay? I promise, you're absolutely safe with me. I'm staying just a couple of miles from here and there's a separate guest suite so you'll be completely private." He gave a small snort of laughter and muttered an expletive beneath his breath. "I'll even go spend the night at Sully's if it'll make you feel better. But there is no way in hell you're staying here tonight, okay?"

Lacey had the distinct impression that if she refused to go with him, he'd throw her over one broad shoulder and haul her bodily out of the room. She knew instinctively he wouldn't hurt her, would even put himself in harm's way to protect her. It was herself she didn't trust. Just the thought of being alone with this man for an entire night caused her body to react in a way she was unfamiliar with. Her knees felt shaky when she looked at him. There was a fluttering sensation in the pit of her stomach. She'd never been so acutely aware of her own body before.

"Okay," she said, before she could change her mind. "I'll stay at your place, but just for tonight."

"Good." There was no mistaking the satisfaction in his voice.

Lacey followed him outside, unwilling to look at the men as they passed, aware they had ceased arguing the moment she and Cole had emerged from the room. But when one of the men abruptly stood up, shoving the flimsy chair back and nearly upsetting the makeshift card table, Lacey understood why Cole had deliberately positioned himself between her and them.

"Hey, baby," the man crooned, "why you want to go with him, eh?"

"Yeah, stay wi' us," slurred a second man. "We'll show you a good time…a *real* good time."

Lacey edged closer to Cole's protective bulk.

"Don't worry," he said in a low voice, "they're not coming near you."

Lacey looked at the men and knew it was true. While they might muster enough courage to throw comments at hers and Cole's retreating backs, they didn't have the guts to confront the hard-eyed man who propelled her along with one hand at the base of her spine.

Copper lay panting on the seat where they had left him, and now he thumped his tail lazily in greeting. After stowing her gear in the back, Cole started the truck and swung out onto the road. The dog made no move to clamber to its feet and hang its head out the window, as if the heat had finally sapped what remained of his energy. Instead, he gave a jaw-splitting yawn and dropped his head onto Lacey's thighs with a contented huff of breath.

Lacey snatched her hands from her lap and looked down in consternation at the animal. "Well, he certainly isn't shy," she remarked with a laugh. Her hands hovered uncertainly over the dog. "Will he mind if I pet him?"

Cole gave a laugh that was half groan, and eyed the dog with something like envy. "Are you kidding? He thinks he just died and went to heaven."

Smiling in spite of herself, she tentatively stroked the animal's head and ran her fingers over his long ears. "He's so soft," she murmured. "What kind of dog is he?"

"He's a bloodhound."

"Like the kind you see in movies, tracking escaped criminals?"

Cole laughed. "Yeah, except Copper's never had that particular honor. He's retired now, but when he was younger he had no problem tracking down kids and hikers who'd gone missing in the hills around here."

"Really!" Lacey was impressed, and gave Copper a generous scratching behind his ears to show it. "What a good boy. I hope you got an extra treat and a nice, long tummy rub for that."

Cole laughed, a warm sound that caused Lacey to smile back at him. "What's so funny?"

He hesitated, then impaled her with the full heat of his aquamarine eyes. They locked gazes briefly before he returned his attention to the road. "I was just thinking," he murmured, "what an incentive that would be for the local search-and-rescue team. Coming from you, that is."

"What would be?"

Cole slanted her a swift glance. "An extra treat and a tummy rub. Their success rate for rescues would be about a million percent."

Lacey's breath hitched. She stared at his profile, unable to rid her mind of the images his words evoked. Images of her hands stroking over the taut hardness of his stomach, and lower.

She cleared her throat. "Do you happen to know the team?"

"Yeah. But forget about getting an introduction." His mouth tilted in a small smile. "They'd eat you alive."

Lacey laughed softly. They could try.

"So," Cole said, changing the subject, "where are you from and what brings you to Black Stone Gap?"

Lacey couldn't keep the amusement out of her voice. She was born in West Virginia, less than three hundred miles from Black Stone Gap, but she and her mother had moved to New England after her father's death.

"I'm from New Hampshire," she answered, "and part of the reason I'm here is to work with the Black Mountain Search and Rescue Team."

There was a momentary stunned silence, and then Cole laughed ruefully. "You're kidding, right?"

"Nope."

"Don't tell me—you're here to demonstrate the GPS units."

"Right. But how did you know that?"

Cole looked at her. "Sully mentioned something about it earlier tonight. Bringing the rescue team into the twenty-first century is big news around here. Their equipment is all but obsolete, and I understand they're pretty excited about the new devices. But I thought the company was sending a man." His gaze skimmed briefly over her, missing nothing. "And, sweetheart, you're a far cry from that."

Lacey felt herself go warm beneath his regard. "There was initially some talk about sending one of our sales reps out to demonstrate the GPS units, but I volunteered." She sensed his curiosity. "I'm here on other business, in addition to showing the rescue team the benefits of the handheld units."

"I see." There was a pause. "Does Cyrus know about this?"

"Who?"

"Forget it. If he did, he'd never have allowed you to stay at the Blackwater Inn. He'd have insisted on putting you up at his place."

"Oh, you mean Sheriff Hathaway. I was planning to talk with him in the morning and see if he could recommend somewhere else to stay."

Cole gave a short laugh and his voice was like rough sandpaper. "There is no other place to stay, unless you don't mind driving an hour or so each way. Even Cyrus lives a good ten miles outside of Black Stone Gap."

Lacey digested this in silence. She didn't want to stay an hour away, didn't want to traverse the winding mountain roads each day. She'd stay with Cole tonight, but even if they ended up in bed together, she couldn't assume that he'd want her living with him for the entire time she was in Black Stone Gap. That would just be awkward.

Cole swung off the main route, and they made their way up a steeply winding road, pressed close on both sides by dark forest. Twice, the headlights of the truck reflected the glowing eyes of some woodland creature before it darted into the dense underbrush.

Suddenly, they emerged into a clearing and Cole drew the pickup truck alongside a large log cabin. Lacey had envisioned him in a mountain cabin with fur-strewn floors, but even her imagination couldn't have created this charming structure, perched on the mountain crest and bathed in moonlight.

She peered through the windshield, taking in the sweeping porch that surrounded the house, the soaring stone chimney and dramatic windows. It may have been constructed of logs, but the architecture was pure elegance.

"This is your home?" Lacey couldn't keep the surprise out of her voice.

"Well, it's more like the family retreat. I share ownership with my siblings." He opened his door and looked over at her. "Don't worry—they're not here now. We sort of take turns coming out here. C'mon in and make yourself comfortable."

Before she could respond, Lacey's cell phone rang. By the time she fished it out of her bag, the ringing had stopped. "Wow," she commented, reading the signal bar, "you get really good reception up here."

"One of the many benefits to living on top of a mountain." He smiled. "I'll wait outside for you."

Lacey scrolled through her missed calls and saw that her mother had tried calling her eleven times. She sighed. The last thing she wanted to do was to talk to her right now, but she knew her mother would fret until she called. She answered on the first ring.

"Lacey? Is everything okay?"

"Everything is great, Mom. Really."

"I've been trying to call you for hours. Why haven't you answered?" Her mother's tone was reproachful.

"The cell phone reception is terrible, Mom. But I made it here safely and I'll be meeting with Sheriff Hathaway in the morning. Please don't worry about me. I'm *fine*."

"Give me the name of your hotel so I can reach you on their phone."

Lacey hesitated. There was no way she could tell her mother the truth about where she was staying. "It's called the Blackwater Inn, in Black Stone Gap. But I'll hardly be there, Mom. Why don't we just agree that I'll call you each evening?"

"But what if I need to reach you? I need to be able to reach you, Lacey."

She suppressed a frustrated sigh. "Then by all means try my cell phone, but I can't guarantee that you'll always be able to get through, or that I'll answer." She glanced out the window to where Cole sat on the bottom step of his porch, scratching Copper behind his ears. "Look, I have to go. I'll call you tomorrow, okay? Good night, I love you!"

She closed the phone, pushing down the guilt she invariably felt after talking with her mother. Then, just in case her mom decided they hadn't finished their conversation, she turned the cell phone off. Sliding out of the truck, she walked toward Cole, watching as he stood and gathered up her cases. Copper stretched lazily before plodding his way up the steps to the porch.

"Did you grow up here?" Lacey asked. "I mean, in this house?"

Cole snorted. "Not likely. My folks had a ramshackle house at the bottom of the hill, on the main road. My younger brother owns a timber-frame company. After Dad retired, we pitched in and had this place built for him and my mom."

"Are your parents…?"

"Passed away, yeah. They had a few good years here, though."

He spoke matter-of-factly, but Lacey thought she detected a note of regret in his voice. "You said you don't live here year-round." She turned to stare at him in bemusement. "Why not?"

Cole gave a shrug as he preceded her up the steps. "I couldn't wait to get out of Black Stone Gap. I found work in Virginia, and I didn't look back."

Lacey followed him onto the wide porch, waiting while he opened the door. "So what brings you back now? Are you on vacation?"

"Actually, I came back because I got laid off from my job over in Norfolk, but was fortunate enough to find work here in the Gap."

Something in his voice caused Lacey to glance sharply at him, but his expression was carefully blank. She didn't know Cole at all, but she guessed it must be difficult for him to admit that he had been laid off.

"What kind of work?" she asked, but she suspected that she already knew.

"I got a job at the Black River coal mine."

Lacey shouldn't have been surprised, since the coal mines were probably the largest employer in the region, but she hadn't envisioned him as a miner. Although, she acknowledged reluctantly, beggars couldn't always be choosers. He probably knew people who worked in the mines; may even have asked them to pull a few strings in order to get him a job. But she couldn't stop her imagination from conjuring up images of Cole, buried beneath hundreds of feet of earth. She shivered.

Leaning forward, he thrust the door open, leaned in to flip on a light switch, and then stood back to allow her to enter.

Lacey stepped past, unable to prevent herself from brushing against him in the confines of the door frame. She glanced up at him, and with the interior light slanting across his face, his eyes glowed with an intensity that caused a primal awareness to surge through her.

As she stepped inside she had a general impression of soaring ceilings crisscrossed with massive beams, a stone fireplace that dominated one wall, and casually comfortable furnishings strewn with throw pillows and the odd quilt. The coffee table still bore the remnants of his morning coffee, and newspapers, books and paperwork littered the end tables. The natural wood of the floor and walls lent a warm, golden glow to the entire room and Lacey gave a soft exclamation of pleasure.

"Wow," she said. "This is nice."

"Thanks." Striding to the coffee table, he began gathering up the loose papers and stuffing them into a folder. He glanced at her as he shoved the entire packet into a leather attaché case. "It's probably a little rougher than you're accustomed to, but it's comfortable."

"Why would you say that?" she asked, genuinely surprised by his comment.

Cole looked embarrassed. "I don't know," he admitted. "I guess I just picture you in one of those expensive old brownstones in the city."

Lacey made a noncommittal sound, neither denying nor confirming his words. She didn't want him to know the truth; that she still lived with her mother. After her father died— she made a mental correction—*after the state declared her father dead,* she and her mom had moved to New Hampshire and bought a small house near the coast. Right after college, Lacey had moved into an apartment with two other girls, and she'd loved the freedom. But her mother would frequently drop in unannounced, and then spend hours redecorating the small space, cleaning, or cooking enough food to keep them fed for a week.

At first, her visits had been welcome, but it wasn't long before Lacey's roommates began to view them as intrusive. When Lacey had tried to talk to her mother about it, to insist that she really was okay on her own, her mother would become emotional, leaving Lacey racked with guilt for even suggesting that she not visit so often. Eventually, Lacey had acknowledged that living on her own wasn't working, and she had moved back home.

But now here she was, alone with a guy whom she found incredibly sexy, with nothing to prevent her from doing whatever she wanted. Knowing that he found her attractive, too, gave her added courage. The fact that he was a coal miner was a little disconcerting, but it wasn't as if she was going to marry the guy, right? After what had happened to her father, and what she'd seen her mother go through following his death, she'd made a promise to herself never to get involved with a miner.

She reminded herself again that she was only here for a few days. She would deliver the handheld GPS units to the search-and-rescue team, and then work with the owner of the local mines to test STAR. And then she would return to New England. End of story. So whatever developed between her and Cole would be limited to the time she was here.

She allowed her gaze to drift over him, taking in the wide shoulders and lean hips. With her overnight bag and laptop slung over one shoulder, his T-shirt was pulled taut across a chest that was unmistakably muscular.

"I like your house." She gave him a meaningful look. "And everything in it."

The response was instantaneous as the heat smoldering in his eyes flared to life. A muscle worked in one lean cheek as he took a step toward her. His eyes raked her features.

Lacey stopped breathing. He was going to touch her. This was it. The moment when she would either cross the line or step back.

He stopped just short of her and his gaze held hers for a long moment. He was close enough that she could see the amazing striation of blues and greens in his irises, see the individual stubble of whiskers that shadowed his lean jaw and the small scar that bisected his upper lip and made her ache to trace her fingertip across it. His mouth fascinated her. It was a hedonistic mouth, capable of doing wicked things.

She stared at it, mesmerized. As if time itself had slowed, he bent his head fractionally toward hers. Lacey's eyes drifted closed and her lips parted slightly in anticipation.

"I'll show you to your room."

The words were like a dash of cold water, and her eyes flew open. He had stepped abruptly away from her and was now striding across the room.

Lacey almost sagged in disappointment. She had been so certain he was going to kiss her; couldn't believe she had misread him so completely. With a small huff of laughter, she turned to follow Cole.

He made his way up a wide, open staircase to a loft area that overlooked the living room. There was a cozy sitting area complete with armchair, floor lamp and television. Cole pushed open an adjoining door to a darkened bedroom. She stood in the doorway and watched as he set her gear down, moved to a bedside table and switched on a small lamp, bathing the room in a soft glow. A large bed dominated the room. The vaulted ceiling was angled overhead, and through two enormous skylights, Lacey could see the stars against the velvet backdrop of the night sky.

Cole turned to look at her, and there was a taut awareness about him that was almost palpable. She hovered in the doorway, unwilling to be deceived by what she was now certain was her own cranked up libido.

"Thanks," she said, forcing herself to smile. "It's perfect, and just like you said—completely private."

"Yeah, well, the bathroom's next door and you should find everything you need. Help yourself to whatever's there."

"Okay, thanks." Lacey stood back to let him pass, but he continued to stand there, watching her.

COLE KNEW HE should leave. He should go back downstairs and leave her alone, but man, oh, man, all he could think about was this woman in his bathroom. Standing naked in his shower with water sluicing down that gorgeous body.

It had taken every vestige of willpower and restraint he had not to kiss her earlier. He knew she had wanted him to, had seen the spark of heat in her eyes that said she would welcome the feel of his lips against hers. She had all but invited him free rein to that sweet, tempting mouth. He knew the attraction that smoldered between them wasn't just in his imagination. He could practically feel her need and everything in him longed to satisfy it, but he had promised that she would be safe with him.

But there was no denying the fact he wanted her. Wanted her with a fierce urgency he couldn't recall feeling for another woman in a long time. It was with extreme difficulty that he managed to get a grip on his rampant imagination.

"How about something cold to drink? A beer, maybe?"

To his relief, she smiled. "That sounds great. But do you have anything nonalcoholic? I have to get up early tomorrow morning."

"No problem. How about some lemonade?"

"Sounds good."

He indicated she should precede him back down the stairs, and he could have sworn that was a look of longing and regret she flicked between him and the bed before she turned away. With an inward groan, Cole followed her.

In the kitchen, he watched her covertly as he mixed up a pitcher of lemonade and poured two glasses, taking a long swallow from his own. She was standing and looking at a display of framed photos on the nearby wall.

"Is this your father, here?" She indicated a photo of him standing next to an older man, dangling a pair of freshly caught trout from a fishing line.

"Yeah."

She slanted him a sidelong look and a quick smile. "I can see where you get your good looks."

Cole laughed softly. *Oh, baby, flattery will get you everything.* He came around the corner of the island to hand her a chilled glass of lemonade. "Thanks."

She took the proffered glass and turned back to the collage of photos. She sipped at the drink, and as Cole watched, a bead of condensation slid slowly down the length of the glass, hung suspended for a brief instant, and then plopped wetly onto the fragile line of her collarbone. She made no move to wipe it away, but continued to study the photos. Mesmerized, Cole followed the droplet's path down over the smooth plane of her upper chest until it slid slowly from sight beneath the edge of her sundress.

"Are these your siblings?"

Cole dragged his gaze upward. "Huh?"

"It looks like you come from a large family."

Cole leaned over her shoulder to inspect the picture she was pointing to. Damn, she even smelled delicious. He tried not to inhale as he peered at the photograph. "Yeah, that's me with my brothers and sisters, taken a few years ago."

"There are so many of you!" She gave an amazed laugh. "That must have been fun, growing up in such a big family."

"Fun? I don't know if that's the word I would've necessarily chosen. *Interesting,* maybe. *Chaotic,* definitely."

He didn't want to talk about himself or his upbringing. What would a woman like her know about the hardships of living in a small coal-mining town, with barely enough money to scrape by? Or that he and his six siblings had pretty much raised themselves while their mother worked double shifts at a hospital nearly an hour from Black Stone Gap? Nope. Definitely not stimulating conversation. And not nearly as exciting as standing directly behind her.

He couldn't help himself. He bent his head fractionally and allowed himself to breathe deeply. There was the clean fragrance of her hair and the subtle scent of a light perfume. Beneath that was the delicate fragrance that was hers alone. The combination was intoxicating.

She turned her head and he heard her suck her breath in sharply, as if she was suddenly aware of just how close he was. He knew he should back off, but was momentarily transfixed by the small pulse that beat frantically along the side of her neck. Just that tiny disturbance beneath her smooth skin completely distracted him. Made him ditch every good intention he had of maintaining a respectable distance.

She turned slowly, and his eyes skimmed over her face. God, she was pretty. Gray-green eyes, clear skin combined with a faint dusting of freckles across the bridge of her nose, and a pair of lips so pink and lush he ached to caress them with his own. This time, he knew he wouldn't resist.

She was staring at him with a mixture of cautious awareness, as if she were half-afraid he might kiss her and more afraid that he wouldn't. Slowly, he reached out and took the glass of lemonade from her, leaning over to place it on the countertop without ever taking his eyes from hers. He told himself to go slowly. Be ready to back off if she gave the slightest indication this wasn't her game.

He slid his hands beneath her hair and gently massaged the soft skin behind her ears with his fingertips. His thumbs smoothed over her cheekbones.

Lacey's breath hitched audibly, and as he watched, her eyelashes fluttered and then closed, and her breath escaped on a soft sigh of pleasure. He felt his own desire kick up a notch. She swayed slightly, a barely perceptible movement toward him, and with a groan, Cole bent his head and covered her mouth with his own.

She tasted every bit as good as he knew she would. Her lips were unbelievably soft, and when she made a small, incoherent sound in the back of her throat and pressed closer to him, he nearly groaned aloud in satisfaction. He deepened the kiss. He buried his fingers in the silken mass of her hair and tipped her face up to more thoroughly explore the sweet recesses of her mouth.

Her breasts thrust softly against his chest and her hands had crept up to rest against his rib cage. His senses were filled with the taste, smell and feel of her. He was intoxicated by it. And so completely aroused that he knew she must be aware of it.

With supreme effort, he dragged his mouth from hers and stared down at her. Her face was flushed. And right now her eyes were definitely green and glazed with pleasure.

"Damn." His voice was husky, filled with awe. He traced his thumb over her swollen, damp lips. "Lady, if that's what your kisses are like, then we'd better stop right now because anything more is going to kill me."

To his utter amazement, she turned her head and followed his finger, taking it moistly into her mouth and biting down gently on the pad with her white teeth.

Sweet mercy.

The sensation was like a bolt of hot liquid shooting straight down to his groin, where he was already straining against the denim fabric.

His hand cupped her cheek, and she covered it with her own, her skin cool and soft. She raised luminous eyes to his. "What if I don't want to stop?"

He ceased breathing. Damn near ceased existing except to try and formulate some coherent response to that statement.

She didn't want to stop.

The heat that was already coursing through him turned molten.

"Then, baby," he whispered, dipping his head to taste the corner of her mouth, "I'm going to die a happy man."

4

WHATEVER LACEY EXPECTED, it wasn't to be swept completely up into those rugged arms. She gave a little cry of surprise and instinctively clutched him around the neck as he strode from the kitchen and through the living room to a separate wing beneath the loft.

"I want you so badly," he growled low in her ear, "but I don't want our first time to be on the kitchen counter."

Our first time. He spoke as though there was absolutely no question about there being a second time, and even a third. And maybe, if she was very lucky, it would be on the counter. Lacey shivered with anticipation.

He shouldered a door open and they were in a bedroom, dark but for an enormous wall of windows that allowed the moonlit sky to illuminate the room. Cole set her on her feet beside a low, wide bed, but didn't release her. He slid his hands up over the bare skin of her arms to her shoulders and drew her into his warmth.

"Lacey." His voice was low, husky. He threaded his fingers through her hair, cradling her scalp and tilting her face up to receive his kiss.

The intensity of his lips on hers seared through her, fanning the flames of her desire until she moaned softly and wound her arms around his neck, pressing wantonly against his hard frame. His tongue tangled with hers and she welcomed it, drew his head down and slanted her mouth against his to allow him better access. His own mouth was hot and sweet and tasted faintly of lemonade. She was being consumed, lost in a kiss so molten she felt she might actually melt. And all she could think was that she wanted more.

Lacey dragged her lips from his, gasping. Even in the indistinct light, he looked like he was going to devour her. And didn't that sound good? She searched his eyes, seeing her own need reflected there. She knew it was crazy, this overwhelming urge she had to be in his arms, to be crushed against that solid chest and surrounded by his heat and strength.

This man had the ability to send her pulse rate off the charts with no more than a heated glance. She didn't want to wait another minute to discover just what he could do when he *really* put his mind to it.

Silently, without taking her eyes from his, Lacey grasped a handful of his T-shirt in each hand and slowly began to tug it free from the waistband of his jeans. She pushed the fabric up and slid her palms over the lean, muscled contours of his waist. God, he was hard everywhere. There wasn't an ounce of extra flesh to be had, at least from what she could feel. His skin was like hot silk.

"You're incredible," she breathed, and she wasn't exaggerating.

She pushed the fabric up higher until she could feel the hard thrust of his pecs. She smoothed her palms over his muscles until her fingertips encountered the small nubs of his nipples. She heard him suck in his breath, felt his body tighten beneath her questing hands. Barely pausing, she continued to slide the material upward, and he helped her by raising his arms and dragging the shirt over his head.

Oh. My. God.

Lacey gaped at the man standing before her. Moonlight slanted in through the window behind him, gilding his body in silver. He was astonishingly beautiful. Breathtaking. All rigid muscles and lean contours, from the hard thrust of his powerful shoulders down to the sculpted ridges of his stomach.

Lacey's mouth went dry and a liquid heat pooled at her core. Even her overly active imagination could never have created the perfection that was Cole MacKinnon. And she hadn't even seen the rest of him, which she was definitely going to have to do something about.

"Okay." Cole's voice was warm and husky in the darkness. "My turn."

Lacey's insides turned to jelly at the implicit promise in his softly spoken words. She stood in boneless anticipation as he reached out and drew her slowly forward, until an inhale of breath was all that prevented the tips of her breasts from brushing against his chest. He cupped the nape of her neck and tipped her head to the side to allow him unrestricted access to the sensitive skin of her throat. His lips trailed a path along her jaw as his other hand swept down her back, smoothing over the arch of her spine and taking her zipper with it.

Then he was sliding the fabric from her shoulders, easing it down over her arms until it settled around her waist. Lacey shivered, despite the warmth of the evening. He stepped back slightly and switched on a small bedside lamp. She could feel the heat of Cole's gaze like a lick of flame along her flesh.

Holding her gaze, he took her hands in his own and intertwined their fingers as he slowly drew her arms away from her body. Only when they were stretched outward did he allow his stare to drift downward. The hot, raw masculine desire she saw in his eyes was unmistakable, and the sweep of his gaze across her body was like a physical caress. Her nipples tightened and her skin warmed beneath his intimate regard.

"You're perfect," he said on a husky note, and with her fingers still tangled warmly in his, drew her hands up until they encircled his neck. He dipped his head briefly to capture her lips with his own, caressing them.

Lacey closed her eyes, giving herself up to his expertise. His body began a slow, rhythmic swaying against hers as he slid his hands down the length of her arms. Hardly aware of doing so, she pressed closer and then gasped softly into his mouth as he deftly unhooked the back of her bra and eased the straps down.

"I want to see you," he rasped. "All of you."

Setting her slightly away from him, he lowered her arms until the bra slid from her body to the carpet. He made a low growling sound of approval and filled his hands with her breasts. He cupped them, lifted them and squeezed them gently until the nipples thrust upward, practically begging for more. Lacey felt weak, and when Cole dipped his head and swirled his tongue around one engorged peak, she thought she would collapse from sheer pleasure.

"Ohmigod," she gasped, uncertain whether it was the sensation of his mouth, hot and wet, against her sensitive flesh or the sight of his dark head against her breast that caused every rational part of her brain to completely shut down.

She clutched at his head, running her fingers over the rough velvet of his hair and urging him silently to continue. He rolled one nipple between his teeth and then drew sharply on it, his hands sliding down over her hips and back up again, this time beneath the fabric of her sundress. He cupped her bottom as he suckled her, his fingers scant inches from that part of her that was pulsating and damp with need.

Lacey arched her back, wanting to be closer still. She slid her hands over the muscled contours of his arms and up over his shoulders, reveling in his hardness and his heat.

Releasing her breast, he captured her face between his hands and claimed her mouth in a kiss that was completely off the charts. It was a no-holds-barred kind of kiss that was all-consuming and said without words how desirable he found her. She made no protest when he reached down and pushed the sundress from her hips to pool on the floor. Without breaking the kiss, he slid his hands into the back of her panties and cupped the soft mounds of her cheeks, squeezing gently while he fitted himself against her hips. Through the material of her panties and his jeans, his arousal was unmistakable.

"Tell me what you like," he demanded hoarsely, pulling back and searching her face. "I want to make this right, to make it good…"

Lacey laughed unevenly. Was he kidding? Five minutes of his mouth against hers was better than anything she'd ever experienced. From here on, anything else he did was just an added bonus.

"Okay, then," she whispered. "Why don't you start where you are and, um, work your way down?"

"Sweetheart, nothing has ever sounded so good," Cole assured her, and eased her back until her legs came up against the edge of the bed.

With a soft murmur of assent, Lacey lay back across the coverlet and drew him down with her, but he scooped her up and hefted her more fully into the center of the bed, settling himself alongside her. True to his word, he started at her ear, circling it with his tongue, his warm breath sending shivers of anticipation through Lacey. He kissed her briefly, intensely, his tongue sweeping against hers before he began to work his way down her body. He filled his palms with her breasts, kneading them and rolling the distended tips between his fingers before laving each one with his tongue.

Lacey drew her breath in sharply at the exquisite sensation

and arched upward against his questing mouth, her hands exploring the ridges and valleys of his back and shoulders. Too soon, he released her breasts and trailed his lips across her stomach, sliding his hands beneath her.

When he reached the edge of her panties, he kissed the delicate skin just above the fabric and looked up at her. Lacey's breath was coming unevenly. It was almost embarrassing how intensely aroused she was. She wanted nothing more than for him to settle himself on top of her so she could rotate her hips against his hardness.

"Open your legs," he whispered, and cupped her knee with one hand, urging her legs apart.

His soft command was so sexy that Lacey was helpless to prevent her legs from falling open. He bent his head and kissed her through the silky fabric of her panties. The heat of his mouth on her was almost her undoing and her hips jerked in response. "Oh, please, please..."

"Soon, baby, soon," he murmured and reared up to kneel between her splayed thighs. And just like she had imagined, he began to slide her panties slowly down over her hips. She lifted her bottom to help him, raising one leg so he could tug them off completely, and then she was lying there with absolutely nothing to shield her from his molten gaze.

"You're so damned gorgeous," he whispered hoarsely, and cupped her lightly with one hand. "And hot. So hot."

Watching him as he looked at her through half-closed eyes was an incredible turn-on. His expression made Lacey feel as if she was the sexiest woman on earth. She was practically purring.

He bent forward, and Lacey wrapped her arms around him, seeking his mouth and drawing on his tongue. God, he tasted so good. But as wonderful as he felt beneath her hands, she wanted more. She reached between them and began to work at his belt, frustrated when it wouldn't release for her.

He laughed softly, the warm sound curling along her senses. "Easy, sweetheart. We have all night." But he obliged her by pushing her hands aside and releasing both his belt and the button on his jeans in a few deft movements.

"Finally," Lacey panted, and scarcely believing her own boldness, she reached down and cupped him through the denim, watching his eyes darken with desire. He was large, that much she could tell. Leaning forward, she slid his zipper down and began to ease the fabric over his lean hips. "My turn," she whispered. "Now I want to see *you*. All of you."

Cole sat up and swiftly removed his boots and socks. With an urgency that was almost comical, he shoved his jeans down over his knees and kicked his legs free.

He was wearing a pair of black boxer briefs. They were snug and hugged the taut curves of his backside. His thighs were lean and corded with muscle. He could have been a cover model for men's underwear. And when he turned toward her once more, Lacey saw the impressive bulge that strained against the fabric.

Reaching out, she slipped her fingers into the waistband of the briefs and tugged him closer. With a laugh that was half groan, he tumbled onto her, scooping her into his arms at the last minute and rolling across the bed so that they ended up, breathless and laughing, with Lacey half-sprawled across his chest, their legs intertwined.

With her hair hanging like a curtain around their faces, they stared at each other for a wordless moment, until Cole slid one hand to the back of her head and drew her down for his kiss. Their tongues tangled and his other hand cupped and kneaded her bottom.

Lacey moaned softly into his mouth, feeling his hardness pressed against her. She gasped when he dipped his hand between her thighs and stroked her intimately with his finger.

"God, you're so wet," he groaned, and his kiss deepened, his tongue spearing into her mouth even as he caressed her damp, swollen flesh. Lacey's legs straddled his, and she arched her back to grant him better access.

"Cole," she gasped, "I want you inside me."

"Say that again," he growled.

"I want you."

He laughed huskily. "Oh, yeah. I love hearing you say that." He stroked his lips across hers again. "But you said my name. I want to hear you say my name again."

"Cole," she breathed.

In one smooth, fluid movement he flipped her onto her back and then he was over her, kissing her mouth, her jaw, her throat, and working his way lower.

"Wait," she panted when he reached the apex of her thighs and cupped her with his hand, sliding one finger into her while he stroked and teased her breasts with his other hand. An orgasm teetered just out of reach and she knew that if he put his mouth on her sensitized flesh, she would explode. And she didn't want this to end too soon. "Cole, stop."

He glanced up at her, a wicked grin tilting his luscious mouth. "Is there a problem?"

He inserted a second finger and Lacey's hips bucked. "Oh, God, Cole, you have to stop." She gasped when he stroked his thumb over her, a shudder of pleasure racking her body. "Please."

Cole withdrew his hand, but made no move to scoot back up the length of her body. "Well, jeez," he said huskily, "that's a shame, considering I was just getting to know you so well." He smoothed his hands over her hips and then beneath them, raising her up slightly. "Maybe this will change your mind..."

Before Lacey could form a coherent thought, he lowered his head and her entire existence was reduced to this one man and the unbelievable, overwhelming sensation of his mouth on her. And when he flicked his hot, velvet tongue against her, she gave a strangled cry and thrust her hips upward, convulsing in an orgasm so powerful she thought she might actually die.

Only when she stopped shivering did Cole raise himself over her. She wound her arms around his neck and kissed him, tasting her own delicate essence on his lips. He groaned softly against her mouth.

"Oh, man," he rasped with a soft laugh, "that was amazing. Truly, unbelievably amazing."

Lacey had to agree with him.

"I've never felt anything quite so—so powerful before," she admitted, stretching languidly beneath him. "I'd almost forgotten how good this could be."

Cole cocked his head and gave her a quizzical look. "What do you mean?"

Lacey looped her arms around his neck and pressed a kiss against his mouth. "Let's just say it's been a while since I've done this. But I'm glad that you're the one who ended my dry spell."

Cole gave her a tender smile that did odd things to her equilibrium. "Well, I'm glad, too. Can I ask just how long it's been?"

"A couple of years."

Cole drew away slightly, his face registering surprise. "Are you serious? Are the guys up north blind?"

Lacey laughed. "Thanks, but it's by choice. My job is pretty demanding and I don't have a lot of free time."

It was a partial truth, at least.

"I get it, but a couple of *years?*"

"You'll have to help me make up for lost time," she said, and moved suggestively beneath him.

"Oh, yeah? Well, I'm all for that."

Lacey liquefied under his tender expression and the implicit promise in his words. She could feel the hard thrust of him against her hips and, reaching down, tugged at his briefs. "Maybe you want to start by taking these off."

He helped her, sliding them off and kicking them free. And there he was, rising thick and heavy against the tautness of his abdomen. Lacey's mouth went dry.

Unable to prevent herself, Lacey wrapped her fingers around him. He jerked reflexively in her hand. He was hot. And hard. And as smooth as satin beneath her fingertips. She slid her hand down the length of him and felt a surge of feminine pride when he sucked his breath in sharply and buried his face against her neck. Lacey continued to stroke him, tentatively at first and then with growing confidence as he groaned softly and bent his head to her breast, capturing a nipple in his mouth and drawing deeply on it.

And there it was again. The slow, throbbing ache that made her long to wrap her legs around him and bring him completely inside her.

"Cole," she whispered against his hair.

He raised his head from her breast and his eyes were startlingly blue. "Yeah?"

"I want you. Now."

"I almost forgot." He slanted her a crooked grin and then leaned over to open a drawer in the bedside table and drew forth a small foil package.

A condom! God, she hadn't even thought about protection.

She watched as he expertly covered himself, then positioned himself above her. Reaching down, he lifted one of her legs and laid it across his hip, opening her for him. He stroked a finger along her damp cleft and Lacey gasped at the exquisite sensation. But when she felt the fullness of his erection pressing against her, a liquid heat gathered at her core and she lifted her hips in invitation. His breathing was ragged as he gazed down at her and, in one smooth movement, surged forward and buried himself inside her.

Lacey groaned as he filled her and clutched at his shoulders. He captured her mouth with his, sweeping his tongue against hers as he began to move, his hands cupping her buttocks and lifting her to better meet the bone-melting thrusts of his hips. Lacey arched against him and raised both legs to wrap them around his lean hips.

"That's it," he rasped huskily against her mouth.

Lacey had never felt anything so all-consuming. She was being swept upward in a vortex of sensations, clinging with mindless abandon to this amazing man who seemed to understand what it was she needed before she did. He was as attuned to her body as if it were an extension of his own, as if he was somehow hardwired into her. He thrust again, slowly, moving his body sensuously against hers, and she barely suppressed a huff of laughter as she realized he *was* hardwired into her. And she was about to experience a total system overload.

"Ohmigod," she breathed raggedly, as pulsating pressure built once more and threatened to undo her. "Cole..."

He smoothed the damp tendrils of her hair back from her face. "I'm here," he breathed huskily. "I'm right here with you, baby." He ground his hips against hers, thrusting deeper, until he filled her completely.

"Oh, oh," Lacey gasped, and Cole caught her small, frantic cries with his mouth, spearing his tongue against hers as he moved faster, deeper. Reaching a hand between their bodies, he stroked a finger over her, and the simple contact was enough to push her completely over the edge.

Lacey climaxed in a blinding white-hot rush of pleasure, even as Cole gave a harsh cry and she felt him stiffen and then shudder inside her. As she drifted slowly back to reality, she stroked her hands over his back, slick with sweat, and reveled in the feel of his body, heavy and replete against hers.

Cole kissed her, slowly and languorously, but made no move to withdraw from the warmth of her body.

"Hey," he murmured, "you okay?"

Lacey gazed at him and nodded mutely. She couldn't have articulated what she felt at that moment if her life depended on it. Her body still shuddered with small aftershocks. In the indistinct light, his eyes were filled with a tenderness that made her chest constrict.

Rolling away from her, he quickly cleaned up and then returned to the bed, pulling her against his chest and drawing the sheet over them. His hand stroked a lazy pattern over her arm.

"I have a feeling that neither of us is going to get much sleep tonight," he murmured against her hair.

His voice held infinite promise, and outside the night sky was still brilliant with stars. And for tonight, at least, it was enough. She wouldn't think about tomorrow, or all the tomorrows after that.

5

COLE HAD BEEN AWAKE for hours. He bent his arms behind his head, careful not to disturb the woman who lay curled against him like a contented kitten, one hand resting over his heart. Her hair spilled over his shoulder like a skein of pale red-gold silk and her skin was almost translucent against the suntanned brown of his own. One slim leg was thrown across his thighs, and she was pressed against him from his neck all the way down to his ankles.

He groaned softly and tried not to think of how incredibly soft her skin felt, or how good she smelled, or how he had only to turn his hips slightly to gain access to the sweetest, most intimate part of her.

It was almost six-thirty, but he was reluctant to wake her. Reluctant to end a night filled with some of the most amazing moments of his life. He didn't typically go in for one-night stands, and on the rare occasion that he did, he acted in true insensitive-jerk style and made sure he was gone long before the sun rose. He'd never spent a full night with a woman he'd only just met. And he'd never brought a strange woman back to his place.

Until now.

His gaze drifted over Lacey, lingering on the soft fullness of her lips, watching the rhythmic rise and fall of her chest in utter fascination. Her breasts were small, the nipples pale and pink, but they fit perfectly in the palms of his hands.

He closed his eyes and groaned inwardly, knowing he was in real danger here. She aroused every protective male instinct he had. Hell, she just plain aroused him. They hadn't slept more than an hour all night. And in between the mind-blowing sex, they'd talked and nestled together until their bodies recovered and clamored for yet more. She hadn't been kidding when she'd said she was making up for lost time. Yeah, it was definitely a night he was going to remember for the rest of his life.

But right now, all he could think about was how she would react when she woke up in his bed, still wrapped around him. Would she be warm and welcoming, or self-conscious and uncomfortable, wanting only to be gone from his life? He'd been there, done that, and even if *he* had been the one wanting to be gone, it wasn't exactly a fun-fest for either party.

As if on cue, she murmured something incoherent, her eyelashes fluttered, and then he was gazing down into the luminous gray-green of her eyes. Sleepy and bemused, she stared up at him for a moment, and then smiled.

"I'm still dreaming."

"Not unless I'm having the same dream, baby," Cole said softly, and stroked a hand over her hair.

She continued to stare up at him, and the sleepy confusion was slowly replaced with an expression of dawning awareness as she came fully awake.

"What time is it?" She sat up, withdrawing her limbs from his body and curling them inward, dragging the sheet over her nakedness.

So that's how it was going to be. Damn.

"It's barely six-thirty," he answered.

He couldn't help himself. He cupped the nape of her neck and drew her head down, intent on sampling her mouth. She gave him a chaste, closemouthed kiss before pulling away.

"I should take a quick shower and then get going," she said apologetically.

Cole pushed down his own disappointment and opted instead for a light tone. Maybe she was just being typically female, uncomfortable at being seen with bed-head and no cosmetics. Although, hell, he'd never seen a woman look as desirable as she did first thing in the morning.

"Well, as long as you're taking a shower," he said huskily, "can I offer to scrub your back?"

She cast him a swift glance and Cole could have sworn she was considering it. Her gaze slid over him, and he was helpless to prevent the instant reaction of his body. But if she was tempted, she did a great job resisting. She dragged the sheet around her and stood up.

"Thanks, but I really am going to be quick. I have some calls to make, and I'm sure you have things you need to do."

What would she say if he told her the only thing he wanted to do—needed to do—was her?

"Yeah. Okay. Take a shower, and I'll make some coffee. Then I'll run you over to the sheriff's office."

"Thanks." As if on impulse, she leaned down and pressed a swift kiss against his mouth. "And thanks, too, for last night. It was great."

Her words had a ring of finality, and Cole watched as she walked across the room, the sheet trailing behind her. He heard the bathroom door shut, and then there was the unmistakable sound of the lock clicking into place.

Yep. That had gone real well. He flung himself back against the pillows and threw an arm across his eyes.

She was so gone from his life.

But what did it really matter, anyway? He would only be in Black Stone Gap long enough to obtain the evidence he needed to prove the coal mines were operating illegally, and then he'd return to his home on Virginia Beach, just outside of Norfolk. He'd agreed to go undercover for the

Feds, but he hadn't counted on how hard it would be to lie to his friends and family about why he'd returned. If anyone knew his real reasons for wanting to work in the mines, they'd despise him. The local coal mines were the biggest employer in the region, and if they shut down, hundreds of people would lose their jobs. But that was preferable to losing their lives, wasn't it?

Even if he'd been inclined to pursue some kind of relationship with Lacey, it wasn't like she lived locally. Christ, she was from Boston. He could just picture where she lived, in one of those elegant old brownstones on a cobbled backstreet of the city, where the rents went for about a zillion bucks a month and the number of piano bars per capita was exceeded only by the number of young investment brokers.

He snorted. It was no wonder she was anxious to leave. Hell, she'd been slumming last night. No doubt she and her girlfriends would have a good laugh over martinis about how she once did it redneck-style.

But then he recalled her confession that she hadn't been with anyone in a long time, and he knew instinctively he was wrong. This was a woman who apparently didn't share much of herself with others. He suspected she was more than a little self-conscious by her passionate response to him last night. She'd probably never had a one-night stand in her whole life.

All things considered, he was beginning to feel a little better about the situation. He'd almost forgotten that she was from New England, home of the original Puritan. But hell, he wished she wouldn't feel embarrassment over the things they'd done. Because if he had anything to say about it, they'd be doing a whole lot more of those things.

WHEN LACEY CAME out of the bathroom, she smelled the tantalizing aroma of bacon cooking, and heard Cole whistling softly in tune to the radio as he prepared breakfast.

"Smells good!" she called as she scooted down the hallway and up the stairs, wearing nothing but a towel.

"Hey, we don't dress up for breakfast around here," he shouted after her. "Come as you are!"

Lacey smiled, but didn't answer. She could easily envision what would happen if she came to the table wearing only a towel. Not that those images weren't appealing, but Lacey knew she had to get away while she still could; Cole Mac-Kinnon was too irresistible. If she wasn't careful, she could easily be tempted to scrap her work and spend all her time with him, instead. She blushed every time she thought about the previous night. Which was, like, every second since she had woken up plastered against his hard body.

Had that really been her doing those things with a virtual stranger? The entire night was like some surreal fantasy, as if some alien sex goddess had temporarily taken control of her body. That uninhibited, wanton creature surely hadn't been her. And while she didn't regret a single second of the previous night, neither did she want Cole to become a distraction to her real purpose for being in Kentucky. This was her first field assignment and she didn't want to screw it up. She needed to stay focused.

In the guest bedroom, she retrieved her cell phone, turned it on, and saw she had several text messages from her mother, mostly chiding her for turning her phone off. There was another message from her office, and she punched in the number as she changed. Her friend Julia, who worked in the customer service department, answered on the first ring.

"Good morning, StarPoint Technologies. How may I direct your call?"

"Julia, it's me...Lacey."

"Lacey, where are you? I tried calling you last night and you didn't answer."

"I know. I had my phone on avoidance mode. Sorry."

Julia made a sympathetic noise. "Your mom? I understand. As long as you made it there safely, no worries. But please give her a call today or she'll start calling the office, and you know how Sam hates that."

Sam Caldwell was their boss, and although he understood that Lacey had her hands full with her mother, there were limits to his patience.

"I'll call her. Yes, I made it here safely, but…" Her voice trailed off as she wondered just how much she should share with her friend.

"But what?" Julia asked. "Spit it out, Delaney, or I'll start imagining the worst."

Lacey sat down on the edge of the bed. "I met a guy last night and stayed at his place."

"*What?* Oh, come on. You're pulling my leg."

"No, I'm not kidding." Lacey quickly told Julia about the previous night, leaving out only the most intimate details. On the other end of the phone, Julia made little gasping noises, as if she couldn't quite believe what Lacey was telling her.

"When I said you should cut loose and live a little, I didn't exactly mean with the first guy you meet!" Julia said, once Lacey had finished. "Oh, man…your mother is going to kill me! I know she thinks I'm a bad influence on you."

"She can't know, and you can't tell her. I gave her the number of the motel where I initially checked in, but I don't plan on going back there. If she calls the office, just tell her that I can't be reached because of the poor reception in this area, but you'll get a message to me through Sheriff Hathaway. That will calm her down a little. I hope."

"Don't you think you should just tell your mom that it's your life? I mean, c'mon. You're twenty-seven, old enough to do what you want."

Lacey sighed. "You're right. I'll talk with her when I get home. I promise."

They talked for a few minutes longer, and although Lacey would have liked to speak with Sam, he was in a meeting and unavailable. After she hung up, Lacey donned underwear and bra, pulled on a pair of jeans and was just shoving her arms into a pale green top when a voice from the doorway startled her.

"I brought you up a cup of coffee."

Lacey whirled, her fingers pausing over the buttons of her blouse. Cole leaned negligently against the door frame, wearing a pair of jeans and a crisp white T-shirt that only served to emphasize the sun-browned hue of his skin and the startling blue of his eyes. With the morning light slanting through the skylights, she could see the faint shadow of whiskers on his lean jaw. He looked altogether edible.

"I'm almost ready," she said, swiftly fastening the last buttons.

"Hey." He came to stand directly in front of her. "Are you okay?"

She smiled brightly at him. "Of course. Why wouldn't I be?"

He looked at her with a mixture of tenderness and resignation that caused her chest to constrict. "I'm getting the distinct impression that you're either avoiding me, or keeping me at arms' length. What happened between last night and this morning? I mean, did I miss something?"

He made no move to touch her, just stood cradling a mug of hot coffee between his hands as he watched her. She tucked a damp tendril of hair behind her ear and bit her lip to stop herself from blurting the truth. What had happened between last night and this morning was phenomenal, and it scared the hell out of her. She wasn't prepared for her own emotional response to him.

She cleared her throat. "Last night was amazing." She raised her eyes and met his gaze fully, letting him see the truth in her words. "Really amazing. But for obvious reasons, it can't ever be more than what it was. You know…a one-night stand."

"Oh, yeah?" His gaze was intense, the heat in his eyes causing a now familiar flutter in her midsection. He took a step closer and pressed the mug of coffee into her hands, wrapping his own hands around hers so that she was encased in heat. "What if I told you that I want to see you again? No matter what?"

Lacey stared at him and her stomach did an odd flip-flop at the expression of fierce determination on his face. She couldn't breathe. Couldn't speak. Couldn't form a single coherent thought.

He stepped away from her, raked a hand over his hair and swore softly. "Christ, I'm losing my mind." He turned abruptly back to her, his hands raised as if to stop her from speaking. "Listen, I know you're here on business, but I'd really like to spend some time with you. Okay? Even if it's only for a day or so. After that…well, maybe we can work something out."

"Do you think that's a good idea? I mean, we hardly know each other."

To her surprise, he laughed, a rich sound that slid along her senses like a warm caress. "My point exactly." He grasped her gently by the shoulders and pulled her toward him. "We've been as physically intimate as two people can be, yet we hardly know each other. There isn't an inch of your body that I'm not familiar with, and I'm not going to lie and tell you that I wouldn't love to have a repeat of last night." He gave a self-deprecating laugh. "Hell, I live in hopeful anticipation of just such an event."

Lacey's body reacted instantly beneath his heated regard, warming and growing pliant, until she found herself swaying fractionally toward him.

"But it's not enough, Lacey." He stroked a thumb across her cheek. "I'd like more."

"I really like you." She smiled ruefully. "Obviously. But I don't have time for a relationship, you know? Especially not a long-distance one."

"No, I *don't* know." He tipped her face up, forcing her to meet his gaze. "But I do know one thing, and that is we're good together. Better than good. Let's start with that."

He wanted to see her again. Even if it was only for the short time she was going to be in Black Stone Gap. She desperately wanted to see him again, too. That was the problem. Even after just one night, he'd managed to get under her skin.

"I'm leaving in just a few days," she hedged. "And I'll be working most of the time. I don't know how much free time I'll have."

"Okay, so we'll make adjustments based on your schedule. But you need to eat dinner, right? And who better to show you around the area than me?" He dipped his head to stare directly into her eyes. "Will you at least consider it?"

Looking into his blue eyes, Lacey found her resistance slipping. She nodded. "Okay."

"Okay. Great." He gave her a lopsided grin. "When you've finished getting dressed, come downstairs and have some breakfast."

After he left, she shoved her belongings into her overnight bag and slipped on a pair of soft leather flats. She swiftly ran a brush through her hair and then carefully applied a light coat of mascara and lip gloss before examining herself critically in the full-length mirror. Deciding that she looked presentable, she gathered up her bags and made her way downstairs. Dropping her suitcase and overnight bag near the door, she entered into the kitchen. Cole was just scooping some crispy bacon onto a plate, and Lacey's mouth began to water when she spied the omelet and sliced fruit on the table.

Cole looked up and his gaze turned hungry as he watched her. "You look great."

Selecting a wedge of melon from the plate, Lacey smiled at him. "Thanks," she said, and took a bite of the juicy fruit.

Cole's eyes fastened on her mouth. "In fact, you look good enough to eat."

Her mind was immediately swamped with vivid memories of the previous night. She pushed them unwillingly aside. "You've just gone too long without food," she teased. "You're a guy—at this point, anything probably looks good enough to eat."

He grinned unrepentantly and held a chair out for her. "In that case, we'd better eat quickly and satisfy my appetite, or I'll start looking around for something else to do it."

Lacey sat down in the chair he held out for her. His words both thrilled and alarmed her, and a part of her was tempted to sweep the breakfast aside and offer herself up instead. She'd had relationships before, but she couldn't recall any guy who'd made her feel as sexy as Cole did. If her job here in Kentucky wasn't so important, she could easily envision herself and Cole holed up in his bedroom for the next month.

They ate in silence, but Lacey was acutely aware of Cole's eyes on her. He was a difficult man to ignore, and she wondered if she would have the resolve to leave him when her time in Kentucky ended. She wondered if she even wanted to.

6

As Cole drove Lacey to the sheriff's office, she couldn't help but be amazed at the beauty of the surrounding landscape. Lush green mountains sheltered deep valleys, where tiny towns nestled alongside winding rivers. She had spent the first eight years of her life not far from Black Stone Gap, but she had few memories of those days, aside from her father's death.

"I didn't expect Kentucky to be so unspoiled," she finally admitted, turning her gaze from the window to the man beside her.

Cole glanced over at her, one dark eyebrow raised. "What were you expecting?"

"I know this is a coal-mining region, so...I don't know. I guess I was expecting to see strip-mined hillsides and some kind of processing plants spewing black smog." She saw the amusement that curved his lips, before he gave her a tolerant look. "Okay," she admitted ruefully, "so I was wrong. You don't have to look at me like that."

Cole grinned. "Sorry. You're not entirely wrong. Most of the mining is done belowground, so you don't see it. But sometimes it's a battle to keep the rivers and streams clean of the runoff."

"You must know a lot about mining, having grown up here. I mean, even your name says it all."

Cole smiled as he negotiated a sharp turn on the steep road. "Yep. My old man was a coal miner. When he was young, he was injured in a mining accident and my mother was the nurse who cared for him in the hospital. They got married and I was born. They named me Cole for obvious reasons."

Lacey gave him a wan smile. *His father had been a miner.* Now Cole also worked in the mines. "What a romantic story."

He shrugged. "Yeah, well, I wouldn't call their life romantic, but my mom never complained. Mining is in our blood."

"Were you a coal miner before you got laid off?"

"I got my degree in mining engineering, but I only worked in the coal mines for about six months, right after I graduated. I left mining about five years ago and went to work for the State of Virginia as a structural engineer."

"Until you got laid off," Lacey clarified.

"Right."

"Do you think you'll stay here? Or will you try to get back to Virginia?"

He was silent for a long moment, as if struggling with a response. "This is just temporary," he finally said. "My goal is to return to Virginia as soon as I can."

The news should have made her feel relieved, but all she could think was that he would spend time in the coal mines. It didn't matter if he was an engineer; he could still die in those tunnels.

"Well, I hope that works out for you," Lacey said, meaning it sincerely. She fixed her attention on the passing landscape, telling herself that as an engineer, he would naturally take precautions and pay close attention to the conditions inside the mines. Nothing would happen to him, and she wouldn't let her imagination conjure up any horrific images of all the things that could go wrong. She refused to let her fears control her life, the way her mother's fears controlled hers.

They turned down a dirt road near a sign that read Rod and Gun Club. Lacey gave Cole a questioning look. "Where are we going?"

"This is where the rescue team meets, since the sheriff's office isn't much more than a broom closet in the town hall." His gave her a reassuring smile. "I'll get you settled with the team, and then come back when you're finished."

"You don't need to do that," she said quickly. "I'll ask Sheriff Hathaway to give me a ride back when we're through."

They hadn't talked about where she would stay after today, but when she'd tried to carry her suitcase out of Cole's house that morning, he'd set it firmly back inside, telling her they would figure it out later.

"Here we are," he said, ignoring her comment.

They pulled alongside several other pickup trucks beside a low, sprawling structure. It looked to Lacey to be a recreation center of sorts, with picnic tables and barbecue grills scattered beneath tall trees. Beyond the picnic area, she could make out a shooting range. But it wasn't this that caused her words to fade.

The entire area was swarming with men. There were about fifteen of them, and at first glance, they looked remarkably similar, each of them wearing blue jeans, black baseball caps, and bright orange T-shirts with the words *Black Mountain Search and Rescue* emblazoned across the back. For a moment, Lacey wondered if they'd stumbled across some crime scene investigation in progress. There was an assortment of electronic equipment, ropes and climbing gear strewn across the grass, and the men were painstakingly examining and packing each piece.

"They must have just returned from a call," Cole commented as he thrust the truck into Park and turned off the engine.

Lacey glanced at her watch. It was barely nine o'clock. As they climbed out of the cab, one of the men looked up, spoke briefly with the others, and walked over to greet them. He was too young to be Sheriff Hathaway. In fact, he looked to be about Cole's age, and was just as good-looking in his own right, with chocolate-brown eyes and a shock of tawny hair.

"Cole," he said with a grin. "Good to see you, man." He thrust a hand out to Cole, who shook it warmly. "I heard you were back in town. What brings you out here?"

"Carr, I'd like you to meet Lacey Delaney. She's come from Boston to demonstrate the GPS units." He took Lacey's elbow in one hand and drew her forward. "Lacey, this is Carr Hamilton. He heads up the search-and-rescue team."

Carr's eyebrows shot up briefly in surprise before he swiftly composed his features, but Lacey didn't miss the sharply questioning look he gave Cole. "Ma'am." He inclined his head toward Lacey and extended a hand in greeting. "How'd you manage to hook up with Cole?"

Lacey wondered at his choice of words, but was spared from having to answer by Cole.

"I came across her broken down in Mel's parking lot last night. She was staying at the Blackwater Inn, but they're having problems with their air-conditioning, so I persuaded her to spend the night with me." He turned away to retrieve Lacey's presentation materials from the bed of his truck, but not before she saw a telltale dimple flash briefly in one lean cheek.

She bit the inside of her cheek. Not "stay at my place," but "spend the night with me." There was no way anyone could miss the blatant message in those words. He'd just stamped her with his own seal of ownership as surely as if he'd said, "Hands off—she's mine."

To his credit, Carr's expression never wavered from one of polite interest. "Well, you couldn't have been in better hands."

Lacey's face turned warm at the unintended double meaning. "I agree," she murmured in acknowledgment, and didn't dare look at Cole as he set her equipment down on the grass beside the truck.

Unaware of her discomfort, Carr continued blithely on. "Cole used to be part of the rescue team. He was the best damn tracker we ever had. It was a real loss to the team—and the community—when he left." He turned to Cole and stared at him directly, as if challenging him to dispute his words.

Beside her, Cole smiled, but Lacey could almost feel the tension in him. But when he spoke, his voice was friendly. "I signed on as the new engineer at the Black River Mines, but I have no interest in rejoining the team," he said. "And I'm sure the entire community drew a collective sigh of relief the day I left Black Stone Gap."

Carr gave him a quizzical look before clapping him on the back. "Absolutely not so. The team would welcome you back, you know that. Nobody ever blamed you for what happened, except yourself."

"Carr." Cole's voice held a soft warning. Lacey risked a curious glance at him. He turned back to his truck and made a show of rearranging the tools he carried in the back.

Carr considered him for a long moment, and then focused his attention on Lacey, making a visible effort to steer the conversation back to less dangerous ground.

"So, you're actually checked into the Blackwater Inn? That place doesn't have a great reputation. You're smart to stay at Cole's place while you're here."

"It's only a temporary situation." She didn't dare look

over at Cole. "I intend to ask Sheriff Hathaway to recommend another place just as soon as I see him."

Carr's eyebrows drew together and his brown eyes turned somber. "Well, that may not be anytime soon. His wife was involved in a car wreck and she's in the hospital."

Cole turned sharply from the truck. "What? When did this happen?"

Carr removed his hat and ran his fingers distractedly through his hair. "Last night. Seems she was run off the road by Stu Barlow's boy on the way home from her weekly bridge game. She suffered a massive heart attack."

"Christ." Cole stared at Lacey. "That was the wreck that Sully was heading out to last night."

Lacey recalled the radio conversation Cole had had with Sully on their way back to the garage. "You're right."

"He didn't mention that it was Dot Hathaway in the other car. I'd have headed out there myself if I'd known."

Carr's face was sympathetic. "You couldn't have done anything. She's in the cardiac care unit over at County Hospital, but I think Cyrus is going to take at least the next week or so off to be with her."

"Will she be okay?"

"Yeah, I think so. She'll need to stay in the hospital for the time being, though."

Cole turned slowly back to Lacey, and although he said nothing, she could read the expression in his eyes clearly enough. He intended to extend his hospitality to her for a while longer. And heaven help her, she was going to accept.

"So," Carr was saying, as Lacey tried to ignore the promise in Cole's eyes, "I'll be taking over for Sheriff Hathaway while you're here, Lacey. If there's anything you need—day or night—just let me know." He winked at her. "Even if it's a place to stay."

"Lacey has a place to stay." Cole's voice was firm.

Carr gave him an amused glance. "Okay. Just trying to be friendly."

The look Cole gave him was more expressive than words would have been, but Carr only laughed before turning back to Lacey. "Why don't you come with me, and I'll introduce you to the rest of the team."

Giving Cole a tolerant look, Lacey followed Carr over to the grassy picnic area, where the men were rolling up lengths of nylon rope and examining the assorted metal clasps and hooks before stowing them in duffel bags.

"Okay, boys, listen up!" Carr clapped his hands together to get their attention. "This is Miss Lacey Delaney, and she's come all the way from New England to outfit us with her GPS units. But before I trust you morons with expensive equipment like that, you're going to need some training. So finish packing up and we'll reconvene in fifteen minutes in the recreation room."

There was some laughter and a few crudely humorous remarks, but the men seemed friendly enough.

"Don't mind them." Carr jerked his head in the direction of the group. "They're a good bunch of guys, just a little rough around the edges. But they're the best damned search-and-rescue team in the state. We're comprised entirely of volunteers, and we specialize in wilderness, swift water, high angle and cave rescues."

"Just get back from a call?" asked Cole, as he joined them.

"Yeah. Two hikers didn't return to the trailhead last night. We found them a couple of hours ago, about a mile north of Hawkins Ridge. One of them had taken a tumble off a pretty steep cliff, and his buddy was stranded on a ledge trying to reach him."

Lacey couldn't prevent her small intake of breath. "Are they okay?"

Carr shrugged. "The first guy is busted up pretty good, but he'll pull through."

She frowned. "How long were you out looking for them?"

"We headed out just before dawn. Didn't take us more than a couple of hours to locate them, though."

"Your men must be exhausted. Would they rather I come back tomorrow?"

Carr laughed in genuine amusement. "Are you kidding? These guys aren't about to miss this training op. But I think I should warn you they'll probably be very slow to catch on. You might need to extend your stay by, oh, a month or so before they finally figure out how to use the GPS units."

Lacey laughed. "Well, let's hope it doesn't take that long." She slid her gaze to Cole. "I'd hate to outstay my welcome."

Cole grinned, but Lacey didn't miss the heat that flared in his eyes. "No chance."

Before she could think to protest, he caught her against him and claimed her lips in a kiss that was swift and hard. Cole set her gently away from him, and Lacey felt herself sway slightly without his support.

"You're dangerous." He moved away to open the driver's door of the truck. "I'll be back to collect you around 4:30."

Lacey nodded and strove for composure. Cole grinned, fully aware of his effect on her, before climbing into the cab and driving away.

Lacey turned back to Carr, prepared for a snide comment or a knowing smile, but he only looked good-naturedly disappointed. "I always thought MacKinnon was a lucky S.O.B., and now I'm sure of it."

"He's incredibly charming," she admitted. "Shall we get started?"

"Sure thing." He scooped up her gear, and as Lacey followed him over to the building, he pointed out the various members of the team. "That one there is Sam, but everyone calls him Skeeter."

Lacey looked over at the tall, rangy man. "Why do they call him that?"

"Because he looks just like a mosquito—you know, a 'skeeter.'"

Lacey gave the man a closer look. When he glanced up at her and grinned, she saw he had the longest, pointiest nose she had ever seen. "Oh!" She barely suppressed the laughter that threatened to bubble forth. "I see now where he gets the name."

Carr chuckled. "That fella there is Poke, and the one over by the table is Harlan. The two boys over by the shooting range are the Armstrong twins, Bill and Bob. We just call them Blob for short."

Lacey had never heard such an odd assortment of names in her entire life, and she was certain she would not be able to keep them all straight. She suspected it was going to be a very long day.

7

LACEY WAS SO INTENT on her discussion with Carr, she failed to immediately notice Cole's truck when it pulled into the gravel parking lot. It was only when Carr tapped on her arm, interrupting her enthusiastic spiel about the various applications of the GPS units, that she followed his gaze to where the truck was parked. The sight of Cole striding easily across the grass toward her caused her breath to catch.

He smiled as he came closer. "So, how'd it go?"

Lacey could scarcely form a coherent thought. Late-afternoon sunlight slanted through the overhead trees and played across his features as he made his way toward her. A light breeze molded his T-shirt briefly against the smooth muscles beneath and then fluttered it away again. His eyes gleamed with warmth and pleasure, and Lacey found herself wondering if he would kiss her, the way he had when he'd left her that morning. Instead, he stopped just short of her and rested his hands easily on his hips. He made no move to touch her.

She and Carr were standing near the entrance to the Rod and Gun Club, having wrapped up the last segment of the training just minutes earlier. It had taken nearly twice as long as she had estimated to get through the first phase, but it wasn't because the rescue team was slow in comprehending the mechanics of the GPS units. Rather, they were intensely interested in how the units worked and how they might be used to improve their rescue operations. Lacey had found herself bombarded with questions and what-ifs and she'd been pleasantly surprised and flattered by the team's obvious interest. The day had flown by.

Carr was holding her GPS unit in his hands. "It went better than I had hoped, although I still think Lacey might need to extend her visit." He grinned at her and gave her a friendly wink.

"Actually," she said quickly, "the team has done a great job getting the hang of the units. We even went out and did a couple of practical demonstrations. I think, overall, it went really well."

At Carr's request, she'd called Julia and had ordered a unit for each team member and agreed to conduct some field exercises with them. But with Sheriff Hathaway at the hospital, she still had not made firm plans on where she would test STAR. Since Carr was filling in for the sheriff, Lacey hoped to spend some time with him, outlining her requirements.

"I came by around 4:30," Cole was saying, "but you were still pretty well involved." He glanced at his watch. "It's almost six now. Hungry?"

Before she could answer, Carr's pager started to beep. He yanked it from his belt and glanced at the display, and then punched a number into his cell phone. As Lacey listened, she realized he was receiving an emergency call.

He flipped the phone closed and glanced at Lacey. "Looks like I've gotta run. Three kids have gone missing in the hills, and a fourth kid thinks they went down an abandoned mine shaft."

Without waiting for a reply, he ducked into the building and Lacey could hear him barking commands to the team members still inside.

"C'mon," muttered Cole, hefting her presentation materials in one hand, "let's get out of here."

Lacey turned to him. "Shouldn't we stay?"

"Trust me," he said grimly, "the best thing we can do now is keep out of their way."

As if on cue, the doors of the club burst open and Skeeter and Harlan came through at a jog, rescue equipment thrown over their shoulders. The Armstrong twins were right behind them, and then Poke and Carr. Lacey watched as they loaded the gear into several trucks. She couldn't help but be impressed with the efficiency they demonstrated. There was no confusion about what needed to be done. They had everything stowed and ready to go in less than two minutes.

"Hey, Mac," called Carr. "How about coming along? We could use another hand."

Beside her, Cole raised both palms. "No, thanks."

Carr shrugged and then climbed into one of the trucks. He plunked an emergency light onto the roof and waved farewell before following the other vehicles out of the parking lot.

Lacey turned to Cole. He was walking toward his own truck, his steps long and purposeful. She caught up with him and waited while he secured her belongings in the bed of his truck.

"I hope you didn't refuse because of me," she ventured.

He glanced at her. "My refusal had nothing to do with you."

Lacey frowned. "Then why wouldn't you go with them? They're looking for a bunch of *kids,* Cole. I'd think that would be enough for most people to want to get involved."

He sighed and then turned to her, and Lacey saw something in his expression that made her chest constrict.

Regret. Resignation.

"It's not as easy as that, Lacey." He passed a hand over his face. "There are things you don't understand. Things I'd rather not talk about."

Before she could prevent herself, she put a hand on his arm. He angled his head to look at her, and his lips curved in a small smile.

"I don't do mine rescues," he said in explanation. "The last time I got involved in one of those, it was a complete disaster. I swore I'd never do it again."

Lacey knew her face went pale, but she couldn't prevent her thoughts from returning to the day that the rescue efforts for her father had been suspended. Amidst the chaos of emergency crews, the dozens of media personnel and the throngs of townspeople, she hadn't fully understood what was happening. But she would never forget the faces of the rescue workers as they had murmured words of regret and sympathy to her mother while Lacey had clung to her hand, unable to comprehend that her father wouldn't be coming home. Had something like that happened to Cole?

"Carr said they could use an extra hand," she persisted. "Maybe you could just, you know, help them track where the kids went into the shaft, and then leave the actual rescue to the team."

"Trust me," he said, with a laugh that sounded bitter, "they don't want me on the team any more than I want to be on it. Carr was just being polite."

Privately, Lacey disagreed. Carr had sounded pretty sincere to her and she sensed just from being in his company for one day that he wasn't the type of person who said something unless he meant it.

She watched as he shoved her gear into his stow box, not looking at her. "About my staying with you," she began. "Are you sure—"

Cole smiled then, a rueful smile that revealed the indents in his lean cheeks. Lacey felt her stomach do a slow, backward roll.

"I'm absolutely sure. I want you to stay at my place while you're here." He held up his hands. "No strings attached. If something happens between us...well then, it'll be because you want it to happen, okay?" He dipped his head to look into her eyes. "But I can't leave you at the Blackwater Inn. It's not safe. Is that fair enough?"

He was completely sincere. It was there in his eyes and his earnest expression. God, she was weak. She had absolutely no willpower to resist him. Especially not when he looked at her like that.

She was prevented from answering by the sound of a truck engine rumbling closer. Turning, she saw Carr's pickup truck making its way toward them down the gravel road, followed by the other two vehicles that had headed out at the same time.

They watched as the men got out. Carr threw a bundle of gear over his shoulder. "What, still here?" he called with a roguish grin. "I thought for sure you two would be—well, never mind what I thought."

"False alarm?"

"Yeah, we got a call about a mile out that the kids were found. They're fine. Didn't go down a shaft at all. They were just pulling a prank on one of their friends, and about scared the poor kid to death."

Harlan came around from the side of his pickup, hefting a bag that must have weighed a ton as if it were no more than a briefcase. He was a big man of few words, but Lacey sensed that very little escaped his notice. While the members of the rescue team took great enjoyment in teasing Poke and the Armstrong twins, they took no such liberties with Harlan. Lacey admitted to herself she was more than a little intimidated by the man. Now he nodded in her direction and disappeared inside the club to put away the equipment.

"Well," said Lacey, "I'm glad the kids are safe."

Carr grinned. "We all are, trust me." He shoved his hat back on his head. "Listen, we're heading into town for a drink and a bite to eat. Why don't you join us?"

Cole hesitated. "Thanks anyway."

"C'mon, man. Bring the lady out and show her a good time."

"Maybe another time."

Carr turned to Lacey. "You know, you really hooked up with the wrong guy, ma'am. Now if it had been *me,* I wouldn't be such a cheapskate. I'd be wining and dining you—"

"Okay. Fine. We'll join you." Cole gave the other man a friendly glower. "Just don't feed her that line when we all know how *you* treat the ladies."

Carr looked chagrined. "Well, I *would* at least feed her."

Cole looked over at Lacey. "Does that sound okay to you?"

"Sure. Why not? It sounds like fun." She gave Cole a bright smile.

He gave her a tolerant look. "You know," he said several minutes later, when they were in the truck and following Carr out of the parking lot, "we don't have to do this. We could go somewhere else, just the two of us."

"Why? Aren't you and Carr friends?"

Cole shrugged. "We've been good friends since we were kids. He was pretty upset with me when I left Black Stone Gap, and now that I'm back he likes to give me a hard time."

"Well, he speaks highly of you," she said. "I wouldn't mind having dinner with him and the other guys. It really does sound like fun."

Lacey realized she was hungry, and she'd enjoyed spending time with the rescue team. But when they pulled into the congested parking lot of a club called *The Bootlegger,* with country music blaring through the humid air courtesy of exterior-mounted speakers, Lacey realized they weren't just going out for a bite to eat. This place looked like a true boot-scootin', country-Western club. Lacey leaned forward in anticipation. She wondered if she could persuade Cole to teach her how to country dance.

The atmosphere inside the club was loud, smoky and festive. Lacey was surprised and a little dismayed by how crowded it was. Even at this hour, the place was nearly packed.

Country music filled the low-ceilinged room and throngs of people milled around an enormous bar, or crammed tables that ringed a large dance floor. Somebody—one of the Armstrong twins, although she couldn't tell which one—waved them over to an area at the far end of the bar. Cole took her arm and steered her expertly through the crowd.

"This place is insane!" she shouted to him, although her voice was nearly inaudible above the din.

Cole grinned and bent his head to her ear. "This is nothing. Wait until the live band kicks up around nine o'clock. Then you'll know what crazy is."

Cole procured a stool for her at the bar with Carr, Skeeter and the Armstrong twins on either side of her, then took up position directly behind her. Even without looking at him, Lacey was acutely conscious of him standing close to her, his large frame acting as a shield when the other patrons squeezed by. Within minutes, she found herself with a glass of iced tea in her hands as Cole took a long swallow from a bottle of beer.

He leaned down to speak directly into her ear, and Lacey caught the tantalizing scent that was his alone. Her pulse quickened. She had a nearly overwhelming desire to turn her face and trace her lips along the strong line of his jaw. Memories from the preceding night came flooding back, and she was helpless to prevent the warmth that slid along her veins.

"I ordered us a couple of sandwiches," he was saying, oblivious to the effect he was having on her. "We'll stay long enough to eat, then we can get out of here."

Lacey looked up to tell him she wanted to dance first, but something had caught Cole's attention farther down the bar. One moment his expression was warm and relaxed. The next instant, his features were taut and Lacey caught a glimpse of steel in their depths before he quickly averted his gaze.

Curious, she looked to see a man leaning negligently against the far end of the bar. He was well-dressed in a sports jacket and slacks, in striking contrast to the other men in the club, who wore blue jeans and boots. He smiled as he chatted with the bartender. Lacey guessed him to be in his early forties. He had a little bit of a paunch, and his hairline was receding, but she decided he had a nice face. As if sensing her scrutiny, he glanced in her direction and for a moment, their gazes met. He smiled and raised his bottle toward her in a friendly toast, and Lacey found herself smiling back at him.

"Who is that?" she asked Cole.

"My new boss, Buck Rogan," he said curtly, and nodded in the man's direction.

As they watched, the man pushed away from the bar and threaded his way toward them. Beside her, Cole stiffened, but when she glanced at his face his expression seemed cordial enough.

"Evening, ma'am." The man named Buck stood just outside their small circle. Up close, Lacey could see he was older than she'd originally thought, maybe in his early fifties. "Hello, MacKinnon. My foreman tells me he hired you on as our new engineer. Welcome aboard."

Cole nodded. "Thank you, sir. I'm looking forward to working with you."

"Really." The word was laced with mild sarcasm and even a touch of amusement. "I seem to recall you once told me that you'd see me in hell before you ever worked for me again."

To Lacey's surprise, Cole laughed, although it didn't sound genuine to her. "Well, I said a lot of things back then, I guess. I was young, and it was an emotional time." He thrust his hand out to Buck. "I hope we can let bygones be bygones."

Buck's eyes narrowed briefly, as if he also wondered at Cole's sincerity. Finally, he smiled and took Cole's hand, pumping it firmly. "Of course we can. Your daddy was the best foreman that ever worked for me. I heard about your troubles in Virginia and I'm glad that I can help you out, the economy being what it is. I always have room on my payroll for a good engineer."

"Thank you. I appreciate that."

Buck turned to Lacey. "And who is this pretty lady? I don't recall seeing you in town before."

Before Cole could answer, Lacey thrust out her hand. "I'm Lacey Delaney. I'm here from Boston, working with the search-and-rescue team."

Buck clasped her hand warmly. "Buck Rogan. Very pleased to meet you. I recall Sheriff Hathaway did tell me that you would be in town. He also mentioned that you were interested in doing some work in the mines."

Lacey couldn't believe how easy this was working out for her. "Yes, that's right. I work for a GPS company called StarPoint Technologies. I'm here to perform a field test on a prototype GPS unit that we developed for NASA. I was hoping to bring it into the mines and run it through a series of tests."

Cole turned sharply toward her. "*What?* You didn't tell me you needed access to the mines."

"You didn't ask," she replied lightly. "So Mr. Rogan, is that something you would be willing to let me do? If it's a liability issue, I understand, but I'm willing to sign a waiver."

"No." Cole bit the word out.

Both Lacey and Buck looked at him in surprise. His expression was tense, and Lacey sensed that he forced himself to relax and smile. "I only meant that the mines are no place for someone without experience," he explained lamely.

"I'll make sure that Miss Delaney is well taken care of," Buck said smoothly. Reaching inside his jacket, he pulled out a slim card holder and withdrew a business card. "Call my office and we can make the arrangements." He gave Cole a shrewd look. "Why don't you come over to the mine and see me in the morning? We'll have a cup of coffee and chat, and then I'll show you your new office."

A muscle worked in Cole's cheek, and finally he gave a curt nod. "Fine."

"Good." Buck tipped an imaginary hat at Lacey. "Nice meeting you, ma'am, and I'm looking forward to talking with you about your project."

He turned and made his way through the crowd toward the exit, and Lacey turned to Cole. "Considering that man just gave you a job, you could have been a little friendlier to him."

"I was friendly," Cole protested.

Lacey snorted. "Oh, okay."

"Why didn't you tell me you intend to go into the mines?" The words sounded like an accusation, and Lacey bristled.

"I didn't know that I was supposed to," she retorted. "Do you have a problem with that?"

"Damned straight I do."

Lacey was taken aback by his vehemence, but before she could say anything more, Carr interrupted, smoothly stepping between them. Until then, Lacey had forgotten he was even there. As she glanced at the other members of the rescue team, she saw they all looked uncomfortable, and none of them would make eye contact with Cole. What had just happened?

"How about you and I take a whirl around the dance floor?" Carr asked.

"I'd like that," she said hurriedly, grateful for the interruption.

"I'll watch your drink for you," Cole said stiffly.

Lacey gave Carr a brilliant smile as she slid her hand into his and allowed him to pull her out onto the dance floor. Once there, however, she wondered what she'd gotten herself into.

The small dance floor was crowded with couples who were expertly negotiating the steps to a complicated country dance; one that involved twirling and holding hands, and moving your feet in a precise manner that otherwise might have you tripping up your partner and losing your balance.

Carr was doing his best to guide her through the steps, and Lacey was laughing in spite of herself, embarrassed by her own clumsiness as she stumbled along beside him. The other couples gave them a wide berth as she twirled in the wrong direction, away from Carr, and came up hard against the solid chest of another man.

Cole.

He caught her by the upper arms and before she could protest, tucked her against his side. He nodded briefly to Carr, who gave Lacey a rueful smile and shrugged regretfully before he made his way from the dance floor.

"Looked to me like you could use some help." He smiled. "I figured I should step in before somebody got hurt."

The country song came to an end, but before Lacey could protest that she'd rather not dance, after all, another song started and Cole pulled her firmly into his arms. It was a slow ballad, with a man's heart-wrenchingly velvet voice singing about how shameless he was when it came to loving his woman.

Cole intertwined his fingers with hers, curling her hand against his chest as he pulled her close, and his other hand at the small of her back. Lacey resisted for about a second, her body stiff against his. But when he started swaying softly in time to the music, it was all she could do not to melt against him. God, he smelled so incredibly good, and she could feel the warmth from his body through the layers of their clothing. Her free hand rested on his upper arm, and, seemingly of its own free will, crept upward until it encountered the nape of his neck. His short hair felt like rough velvet beneath her fingertips.

He sighed and pulled her fractionally closer. "I'm sorry. I don't want to fight with you."

"Me either," she murmured. Tipping her head back, she looked up at him. "What was that all about, anyway? Why don't you want me in the mines?"

"Let's save it for another time. It's probably nothing anyway, just me being overly cautious."

"Well don't." Lacey's voice came out sharper than she intended, but she was so tired of having people think that she needed protection. She softened her tone and moved closer to his warmth. "I can take care of myself, okay?"

He made a noise that could have been disbelief or assent, but his big hand slid along the curve of her spine, and she found she no longer cared about anything but the feel of his body against hers.

"I thought about this all day," he murmured into her ear. His warm breath feathered against her neck and caused goose bumps to shiver their way down her spine.

"About dancing with me?" Her voice sounded slightly strangled.

He laughed, his voice husky. "Yeah, that, too."

"Maybe you didn't notice, but I'm not much of a dancer."

"The only thing I noticed," he breathed, "is how damned pretty you are and how much I'd like to kiss you."

Lacey's breath caught. She was trapped in the intensity of his stare. His eyes were fathomless; bottomless pools of translucent blue in the dim light of the dance floor, and she thought she finally knew what it meant to drown in somebody's gaze. She didn't resist when he released her hand from where he held it against his chest and instead pulled her fully into the warmth of his body. The dance floor was crowded, but he apparently didn't care. His hands slid over her back and he pressed her against his solid bulk even as his lips nuzzled her neck.

But it wasn't enough.

As they swayed in time to the music, Lacey wound her arms around his neck, reveling in the feel of him beneath her fingers. "Then kiss me," she whispered, surprised by how much she wanted him to kiss her, right here, right now.

Cole pulled back and searched her eyes. He groaned, and swept his mouth across her lips in a kiss that was hotly sweet and much too short. Before she could protest, he stepped back, grabbed her hand in his and began pulling her behind him as he strode off the dance floor. They were outside in the humid darkness of the parking lot before she fully realized what he was doing.

She laughed. "What about our sandwiches?"

"To hell with them. I'll make us something to eat." His look was filled with promise. "Later."

When they reached his truck, instead of handing her up into the cab, he held her against the side of the vehicle, imprisoning her with his own body. "I'm sorry, baby," he growled softly, "but I can't wait another second…"

He cupped her face in his large palms and slanted his lips across hers in a kiss that rocked her all the way down to her toes. She sighed into his mouth and arched against him, all thoughts of maintaining any distance from him completely gone. If she had her way, there would be absolutely nothing between them. Desire curled through her as he deepened the kiss, spearing his tongue against hers and feasting on her lips.

Oh, God. If he didn't stop, she was going to haul him into the truck and beg him to make love to her right then and there. She dragged her mouth from his, breathless.

"Wait," she panted.

He cupped her face and his fingers massaged the tender skin behind her ears. His eyes glowed as he gazed down at her. "What's wrong?" His voice was husky.

Lacey's gaze slid to where several young men made their way across the parking lot toward the club. "We're in a public place."

He dropped his forehead to hers. "See what you do to me? I think I have a blanket or two in the back—I know of a meadow about two minutes from here where the stargazing is phenomenal." His voice was languid and full of promise.

Lacey's body responded instantly, liquid heat pooling at her center. Her breasts ached where they were pressed against his chest. She wondered briefly if it was possible to become addicted to someone's touch. She didn't want to wait to reach a meadow, or even his cabin. She wanted him, and she wanted him now.

"Let's just drive," she whispered, pulling his head down, "and see where we end up." Her eyes fluttered closed, and then his tongue was in her mouth as he flattened her against the side of the truck and devoured her. The kiss was long and deep, and Lacey felt herself turning to mush in his arms.

He tore his mouth from hers. "Let's get out of here."

He handed her into the cab and flipped the radio dial to a soft country station as he maneuvered the truck out of the parking lot and back onto the main road. He glanced over at her. "We'll be at my place in less than ten minutes."

Lacey was only vaguely aware of the dark forest, interspersed with the occasional light from a home, flying past the windows. She knew she should tell him to slow down, but she wanted him to go faster; didn't want to wait a second longer than she had to to feel him inside her.

"Hurry," she murmured, and laid one hand over the hard muscle of his thigh.

COLE LEANED HARDER on the accelerator, and then, thank God, there was the turnoff to the steep incline that led to his cabin. The truck barely skidded to a stop before he leaped out. He told himself to go slowly and not rush things, but when he opened Lacey's door he had to restrain himself from carrying her bodily into the house. She didn't speak as she preceded him inside, but as soon as he closed the door, she moved into his arms and skated her mouth along the line of his jaw.

Cole nearly groaned at the sensation of her moist lips on his skin. She flattened him against the door with the weight of her body, sliding sensuously against him even as she cupped him through the denim of his jeans. He'd been hard since they left the club, but he felt himself grow beneath her fingers. Meanwhile, she dragged her mouth along his jaw, planting soft bites on his throat and chin, before licking at his mouth.

"So good," she muttered. "I want to taste you everywhere."

Cole groaned. *Oh, yeah.*

Bending his head, he covered her mouth in a kiss that he knew was neither gentle nor seductive, but a testimony to the raw need that raged through him. He wanted to consume her, to take her right there and then, without any preliminaries. His hands slid down to cup her rear and pull her against him so that she couldn't help but feel his arousal. She made a purring sound of approval and wound her arms around his neck, pushing her fingers into his hair. He lifted her, gratified when she hitched her legs around his hips and clung to him.

With their mouths still fused together, he carried her across the room and deposited her on the sofa, shoving aside pillows and swiftly lowering himself onto the cushions beside her.

"Can you turn on a light?" She sounded breathless.

Oh, man, a woman who wasn't afraid to be seen. Could things get any better? Reaching over her head, he switched on a small table lamp.

"Better," she said breathlessly. "I want to see you."

With a small groan, he slanted his mouth across hers. Her tongue slipped past his teeth, the texture and taste of her fueling his own rising need. He felt her working the snap on her jeans, and then she was shimmying out of them, pushing them down over her legs until she could kick them free. Then she pulled him on top of her and hooked her heels against the back of his thighs, settling him into the soft cradle of her hips. She rocked against him, rubbing herself along the length of his erection, and Cole had to grit his teeth against the sensation.

Bracing his weight on one arm, he reached down and skated his palm along the length of her leg until he encountered the edge of her panties. When he eased his hand beneath the silky fabric to cup one smooth buttock, Lacey kissed him and drew hungrily on his tongue. Her hands were everywhere, pulling his shirt up, smoothing over his back, gripping his backside and urging him closer.

"Take these off," she gasped against his mouth. "Hurry."

Cole didn't need any further encouragement. Sitting up, he quickly shucked his boots and then stood up to unfasten his belt. He pushed his jeans and his briefs off in one movement, and then dragged his shirt over his head before lowering himself onto the couch beside her and gathering her into his arms. She was soft and supple and welcoming, and when she slid one leg over his, he nearly groaned aloud.

"I want to see you," he muttered. Raising himself on one arm, he unfastened the buttons on her blouse and pushed the fabric aside. Beneath the fragile cups of her bra, her breasts rose and fell quickly. Cole pressed his hand against her skin, feeling the rapid beat of her heart beneath his fingers. He pushed the lacey material aside, releasing one breast. Her nipple strained toward him, and he bent his head to draw it into his mouth. He heard Lacey's indrawn hiss of breath, but was unprepared when she reached down and curled her fingers around his straining erection. He groaned against her breasts, and she responded by stroking his length and then swirling one finger over the blunt head of his penis.

"I want you inside me," she breathed into his ear, and raised a leg across his hips to emphasize her meaning.

Cole lifted his head. Her skin had flushed and her breathing was unsteady. She moistened her lips and squeezed her hand around him, and Cole was a goner.

"A condom," he managed to mutter. "I don't have a condom."

"I'm on the Pill," she said quickly, and when he sharpened his attention on her, she gave him a smile. "I've been on it since college. I'm safe, in all the ways that matter."

"I'm safe, too," he finally said. "So if you're sure…"

"I am." As if to prove her point, she shifted so that he lay nestled between her thighs, his erection flush against her.

With a rough sound of need, he reached down and grasped her buttocks. All he could think about was being inside her—

being part of her. She'd occupied his thoughts every moment of the day. It was like he'd discovered a secret treasure he wanted to keep to himself for as long as possible, while at the same time he wanted to climb to the tallest rooftop and shout it out to the world. She groaned deeply as he pressed, hard and hot, against the most intimate part of her, and then he was pushing himself into her welcoming moistness.

She gasped in pleasure and raised her legs higher, wrapping them around his hips even as she met the thrusts of his tongue against hers with equal fervor. God, she felt incredible, all slick heat and pulsating tightness. He grasped her silken buttocks in his hands and drove himself into her, knowing he wasn't being gentle, but beyond the point where he could restrain himself. She rode him just as fiercely, moving beneath him with equal urgency. Her fingers speared through his hair and she was moaning into his mouth, making small sounds of pleasure.

He dragged his lips from hers and slid one hand between their straining bodies. "I want you to come," he growled softly. "With me inside you."

"You feel so good," she gasped against his neck.

Cole stroked her hard and she cried out, arching her back. He stroked her again and a shudder went through her body. He felt her tightening around him, gripping and squeezing him until, with a harsh cry, he climaxed in a powerful rush of exquisite pleasure, heat surging up from his balls to explode inside her.

Her arms came around him as he collapsed against her, and the only sound in the room was their harsh breathing. Her fingers stroked his hair, and Cole turned his face and pressed a kiss against the juncture of her neck and shoulder, where her skin was damp with exertion. She smelled wonderful and she felt good in his arms. She'd said she was safe in all the ways that mattered, but in that instant, he knew she was wrong.

She was a danger to him in more ways than she realized.

8

COLE OPENED THE fridge and grabbed two bottles of water, tucking them beneath one arm before picking up both plates of sandwiches. "C'mon. It's a gorgeous night. Let's eat outside."

He and Lacey had showered, and while she dressed, he made them both some food. Now he led the way to the porch at the back of the house and settled himself on a swinging settee, indicating that Lacey should sit next to him.

"Here." He handed her a plate and tucked the bottles of water between them. He nodded toward the horizon. "Take a look."

Lacey gazed out over the panorama that lay before them, and Cole saw her eyes widen in awed pleasure. It made him feel ridiculously pleased. The cabin had been carefully situated to take advantage of the sweeping vista of valley and mountains, bathed tonight in the soft glow of moonlight.

"It's beautiful," she breathed.

Cole hadn't taken his gaze from Lacey, and now he let it drift down over her profile, over the smooth forehead and gentle slope of cheek and nose, past the softly parted lips to the chin that bore the slightest trace of a cleft.

"Yeah," he agreed, "it sure is."

She shot him a swift look and then gave him a soft smile of pleasure. "This is nice," she said. "Really nice. I'd forgotten how much I love the mountains."

Cole gave her a warmly quizzical look. "Don't they have mountains in New England?"

"Of course, but not like this, And I live about five minutes from the ocean, so a trip to the mountains means having to drive for at least a couple of hours."

"How do you like being on the coast?"

Lacey took a sip of her water and nodded. "I love it. I'm not sure I could be landlocked. Although this would be very hard to give up."

"Leaving Black Stone Gap was the hardest thing I ever did," he acknowledged. "But I understand why you love living near the water. My place in Virginia is right on the beach and I fall asleep to the sound of the surf."

"Wow. That sounds amazing. My house isn't quite that close to the water."

"I'll bring you to Virginia. We can fall asleep together."

Lacey didn't say anything. Instead, she slipped her arm through his and put her head against his shoulder. But he knew what she was thinking; that once she returned to New England, whatever it was they had would be over.

He brought her hand up to his mouth and pressed a kiss against her palm. *Baby,* he thought, *you have no idea how wrong you are.*

BY THE LIGHT of the bedside lamp, Lacey stared at her own reflection in the overhead skylights. She looked small and alone in the generous bed. She *felt* small and alone. The windows were black, and because she had the bedside light on, she couldn't even see the billions of stars that she knew blanketed the sky.

How had her entire life changed in the space of two days?
She'd never before met a man like Cole MacKinnon. She
couldn't stop thinking about him. She'd insisted on sleeping in the guestroom despite Cole's objections. Somehow, it
had seemed presumptuous of her to assume that Cole would
want her to move into his room for the remainder of her stay,
and she hadn't given him the opportunity to try and change
her mind. To his credit, he'd apparently meant what he said
when he'd told her that any relationship they had would be
on her terms.

Now she wished she hadn't been so insistent on sleeping
alone. Once she got home, she'd be alone every night. But
Cole was meeting with Buck Rogan in the morning, and she
wanted him to be well rested. Neither of them had gotten any
sleep the previous night, and he needed to be sharp and alert.

With a groan, she rolled over and buried her face in her
pillow, scrunching the soft mound in her hands. Even now,
her body craved his touch. She thought of how she'd left him
earlier, standing in the middle of the kitchen, watching her
through heated eyes as she practically bolted for the stairs
that led to the guestroom. She hadn't given him the chance
to pull her into his arms, knowing if he did, she'd be lost.
She had no willpower where he was concerned; if he kissed
her, she'd be toast.

She flopped onto her back, restless. She didn't know how
long she'd been lying awake, thinking about him. About
them. Hours, it seemed. Memories of their lovemaking
haunted her. God, she'd been so desperate for him. The only
thing that had mattered was him, hot and hard inside her.
He'd been so powerfully masculine, surging into her, his
face taut with desire.

For her.

Her skin felt flushed and overheated. Just thinking about
it made her want him again. Thanks to him, she was becom-

ing familiar with the needs of her body, recognizing the slow, throbbing pulse that signaled her desire. Even her breasts ached, her nipples tight and erect.

With a despairing huff of breath, Lacey threw aside the sheet that covered her and swung her legs over the side of the bed. The room suddenly felt overly warm; suffocating. Even the circulating ceiling fan did little to cool her heated flesh. She thought longingly of the swinging bench on the front porch of the cabin. It had to be cooler out there than in here, and the idea of lounging on the cushioned swing with a bottle of chilled water seemed the perfect antidote to her current ailment.

She crept carefully down the stairs, alert to any sign Cole might not be sleeping. Given her current state, she'd probably attack *him*. She retrieved water from the fridge and headed for the porch. As soon as she stepped outside, she drew in a grateful breath. The humidity had dissipated and the temperature was, thankfully, cooler than it had been in her bedroom. She leaned on the railing, drinking in the cool night air as she tried to push away the thoughts of Cole that still threatened to invade her peace.

The night was far from quiet, however. The sound of crickets was everywhere, interspersed with the occasional hoot of a night owl, and the distant scream of something Lacey didn't want to think about. Fireflies dotted the lawn below the deck, their blinking lights like a reflection of the overhead stars. Tilting her head back, Lacey studied them. She had never seen stars like this in the city. They were brilliant, and so abundant it was as if some careless hand had strewn billions of diamonds across the sky.

A masculine voice cleared itself behind her. With a small cry of surprise, she jerked upright and dropped the bottle of water that dangled from her fingers. Cole lounged back on the swinging settee, much as she had imagined herself doing.

Copper lay sprawled at his feet, and now his tail thumped lazily in greeting. Cole wore a pair of boxer briefs and nothing else. His face, however, was cast in shadow and she was unable to discern his expression.

"I didn't realize you were out here," she said. "I couldn't sleep. It must be the heat."

Cole sat up and swung his legs to the porch floor. "I didn't mean to startle you. Come join me."

Lacey hesitated. She couldn't be blamed for keeping him awake if he was already up. She was so tempted.

"Come here," he said gruffly, reading her thoughts. "You just said it was hot up there—stay until you've cooled down."

It *was* much cooler out here than indoors. Surely it wouldn't hurt just to sit with him for a bit. Picking up her bottle of water from where she had dropped it, she crossed the porch and settled on the swing, tucking her bare legs beneath her. Cole's arm rested along the cushion behind her head, and he used one long, muscled leg to push them into a gentle swing.

"So what's up for you tomorrow?"

Lacey fingered her bottled water. "Well, if it's not too much to ask, I need a ride back out to the Rod and Gun Club in the morning. I'm going to run through several more demonstrations of the GPS units with the team."

In the darkness, she heard his small grunt of exasperation. "It's not too much to ask, Lacey. I'm happy to drive you wherever you need to go. You know that."

She slanted him a rueful smile. "Thanks. I appreciate that."

"There's a county fair over in Pikesville this weekend. I could pick you up early and we could head over there." He continued to push the swing gently with his toe. "You might enjoy it."

Lacey hesitated. Images of cotton candy, Ferris wheels, and strolling hand in hand with this man through the arcades was more tempting than she cared to admit. "Aren't you meeting with Buck Rogan in the morning?"

"That's just an informal meeting. I'm not officially on the clock until Monday morning. It's supposed to be a gorgeous day tomorrow. It'd be a shame to spend it working."

The gentle rocking motion of the swing was almost hypnotic. Lacey looked over at Cole; at all that lean, hard muscle gleaming softly in the moonlight. He'd said his meeting with Buck wasn't formal and he wouldn't actually begin working in the mines for a few more days. Acknowledging that it was useless for her to even try to resist him, Lacey uncurled her legs and stretched out until she reclined back against his solid frame. His arms came around her, and Lacey sighed in pleasure, admitting that this was what she had been missing, alone in that bed.

"I don't know," she mused now, teasing him just a little. "I'm not sure I can spare the time. I have a lot of work to do while I'm here."

She thought he would tease her a little in return, maybe even use some physical persuasion to get her to agree to go with him. Instead, he was oddly quiet as he continued to push them with his foot.

"What is it?" she asked, twisting to look at him. "What's wrong?"

"At the club tonight, when I said I didn't want you to go into the mines, I meant it. I don't want you near those tunnels."

"Why?"

Cole hesitated. "Call it intuition. I have a bad vibe about them and I'd feel a lot better if you just stayed away."

Lacey stared at him, wondering where this had come from. "Cole, nothing is going to happen. I'm not afraid to go into the mines, and you shouldn't be afraid to let me go."

"What's so important about this GPS unit that you need to field-test it inside the tunnels? You won't be able to pick up a signal."

"No, that's where you're wrong. You see, it's a prototype that we designed for NASA. It can operate beneath the earth's surface. The coal mines are the perfect environment to test its functionality. NASA wants us to start full production right away. This contract is huge for StarPoint Technologies, and could really put the company on the map. My boss is depending on me to get this done."

Untangling himself from her, Cole stood abruptly up, causing Lacey to hang on tight as the swing lurched into unsteady motion. He raked a hand over his hair, seemingly oblivious to the fact he was wearing no more than a pair of boxer briefs.

But Lacey was aware. He was all satiny skin over sculpted muscles that layered their way down his stomach. She could see the faintest trace of dark hair that ran downward from his navel and disappeared beneath the waistband of his boxers. The briefs hugged his lean hips and molded themselves over the tops of his powerful thighs. They clung lovingly to the impressive bulge of his...

With a half groan, Lacey tore her gaze from where it was riveted, closed her eyes and took a healthy swig of the water, but the chilled liquid did little to cool her overheated senses. Swiping the moisture from her mouth with the back of her hand, she looked helplessly up at him.

"You need to trust me on this," he said. "My best friend died in those tunnels. I won't let you take that risk."

Lacey felt her heart tighten with compassion and something else; a recognition of sorts. Setting the water bottle down, she stood up and slid her arms around Cole's waist. He hugged her fiercely.

"Nothing is going to happen to me, Cole, I promise."

"You don't know that. Devon was an experienced miner who always put safety first. If it could happen to him, it could happen to anyone."

"Listen to me," Lacey said, using the calm, rational tone that she had perfected when talking with her mother. "I understand your concern, I really do. Don't you think that I worry about you working in those mines? But I would never try to talk you out of doing your job. And this is my job, Cole. This means so much to me. If I can demonstrate that STAR is operational, the potential for saving lives is limitless."

"It's more complicated than that."

"How so? You're the engineer—is there something you know about the mines that you're not saying?"

He sharpened his gaze on her. "What? No. I told you, it's just a feeling I have. But I do know that the number of mining accidents has increased over the past few years."

An image of her father lying trapped beneath hundreds of feet of rock flashed through Lacey's imagination. "Is it just one mine, or all the mines in the area?"

Cole rolled his shoulders and turned abruptly to stare out into the darkness. "I don't know. Like I said, I just get a bad feeling about it."

Lacey understood. She dreaded going into those dank tunnels, but her father's death compelled her to do just that. She'd never rest until she'd assured herself that STAR worked as intended. She wouldn't be able to think of her father at peace until she found some way to ensure that another miner didn't die the way he had. So even though Cole might have reservations about her going into the mines, Lacey knew she had no other choice.

"I'll be the first to admit that I'm not crazy about the idea," she confessed. "But I have a job to do. Maybe if you talked to Buck Rogan, he'd agree to let you come with me."

After a moment, he blew out a hard breath. "If this is something you absolutely have to do, I'd prefer that. Would you mind if I came with you?"

Lacey couldn't help it. Her entire body flushed with heat at his words. Her only excuse was that she'd been consumed with thought about him all night, and now here he was, almost naked and too tempting for her to resist. The empty aching sensation that had plagued her earlier became an insistent throbbing and her nipples tightened instantly. She wanted him again.

Badly.

"I'd like for you to come with me," she said suggestively. "Over and over."

"Lacey." The word was no more than a husky whisper that caused a molten thread of desire to lick its way through her body. Bending his head, he kissed her neck, just below her ear. Lacey shivered as his lips teased the delicate skin. When he caught her earlobe between his teeth, she gasped softly.

"I want you." His husky admission caused a tightening in her body and with a helpless exhalation, she sagged against him, tilting her head to allow him better access.

Her small surrender seemed to spark an answering surge of need in him. He made a sound that was half laugh, half groan, and swept her up into his arms. Lacey didn't protest. Instead, she wound her arms around his neck and clung to him, burying her face against his neck. This was, after all, what she had been longing for since she had gone to bed, hours earlier, alone.

He strode swiftly through the house until they reached his bedroom. Lacey was breathless with anticipation by the time he shouldered the door to his room open and deposited her in an unruly heap on top of the bed.

"The light," she urged softly. "Turn on the light."

As he had their first night, Cole turned on the small lamp before dropping onto the bed beside her and gathering her close against his hardness.

"God, I've been dying to do this," he growled. "I couldn't get to sleep for thinking about you. About touching you... tasting you." He laughed ruefully. "If you hadn't shown up on the porch tonight, I probably would have come upstairs and begged you to have mercy on me." His hands were everywhere, sliding over her back and down over the curve of her hips, while he buried his face in her neck and pressed his lips along the sensitive length of her neck. "God. It's like I can't get enough of you."

His words were like an aphrodisiac. Throbbing with need, Lacey twined her legs around his and pressed her hips against him, telling him with her body how much she wanted him.

The man didn't let her down. In one movement, he swept her nightshirt over her head and slid his hands beneath her bottom, lifting her so that she was pressed fully against him.

"Oh, yeah," he breathed, his voice warm in her ear. "You make me crazy for you." Turning his face, he captured her lips in a kiss that was searingly hot. Lacey moaned softly and wound her arms around him, pulling him closer.

This was what she had been longing for; this man in her arms, driving her wild with the things he did to her. She ran her hands down the length of his back, tracing her fingers over all that bare skin and reveling in his hardness. His lips slanted across hers and she welcomed the intrusion of his tongue, wanting to be closer still.

She was hardly aware of him tugging her panties off, and then there was nothing between them. Lacey dragged her mouth from his, her breathing fast and uneven. He pulled back slightly, keeping his weight on his elbows, and dipped his head to capture a nipple between his lips, drawing it into his mouth. She gasped in pleasure and instinctively arched against him, feeling him hot and hard, poised at the juncture of her thighs.

Lacey knew that at the slightest indication from her, he would take her to heaven. But suddenly, she wanted to be the one to take him there; to do things to him that would make him lose control. She pushed at his shoulders and with a bemused smile he rolled away from her. But Lacey didn't give him a chance to question her, covering him swiftly with her own body.

"What? Hey—" He laughed uncertainly, but when Lacey dipped her head and traced the whorl of his ear with her tongue, he groaned and collapsed back against the pillows. She pushed his hands up above his head, and slid her own hands down the undersides of his arms, silently admiring the impressive bulge of his muscles. Her fingers continued downward, and she scooted backward until she straddled his thighs.

Sitting up, she looked down at him. Her breath caught at the sight he made. He was the embodiment of every fantasy she'd ever had. He lay still beneath her, but there was nothing remotely relaxed about him. His entire body was rigid and his eyes glittered as he watched her through half-closed lids.

"Now it's my turn," she whispered. "You see, I couldn't sleep either because I've been wanting to do *this* all night." She leaned forward until her breasts brushed against his chest and she traced her lips across his. He cupped the back of her head and drew her down for a more thorough, satisfying kiss. Lacey had intended to tease him, to maintain control of their love play until he begged her to release him. But when he smoothed his free hand along her flank and then reached between them to touch her intimately, she knew she was lost. He used his hands to splay her thighs even wider where she straddled him. Then there he was, hot and thick, moving into her little bit by little bit, until Lacey made an incoherent sound of need and pushed back, thrusting him fully inside her.

"Oh, man," he groaned. "That almost feels too good."

Lacey silently agreed, and slowly raised herself up until he was nearly free of her body, before pushing down once more, burying him to the hilt. The hot, throbbing sensation increased as she moved on top of him, gripping him tightly. His hands were on her hips, guiding her, and she watched his face go taut with pleasure. When he slid his hands upward to cup and knead her breasts, Lacey closed her eyes in mindless bliss.

"Yes," she breathed.

"Look at me."

The words were soft but insistent. She opened her eyes and stared down at Cole, seeing the raw, masculine desire on his face.

"I want you to look at me when you come," he rasped. His expression had tightened, and seeing his desire mount just served to fuel her own. She knew he was close to losing control, but when he reached down and slid a finger over her swollen clitoris, Lacey was right there with him. With a soft cry, she began to orgasm. She might have closed her eyes but for his soft command.

"Look at me."

And when he reached his own climax, their gazes were locked on one another in raw intimacy, until with a last shudder of pleasure, he smiled into her eyes and tugged her down until she lay replete against his chest.

He pressed his lips against her hair, and his hands stroked soothingly down her body. When she turned her face up to his, he kissed her sweetly and she could see the tenderness of his expression. If they had been characters in a romantic movie, this would be the scene where he'd confess that he'd fallen in love with her.

"Christ," he said ruefully, "maybe now I can get some sleep."

She mentally rolled her eyes, laughing at her own fanciful daydreams. He was only hers for ten short days, and she told herself that she was okay with that. She'd wanted this. Wanted him. They still had another week to be together, and Lacey intended to enjoy every minute of it.

He tucked her closer against his side, and one hand traced lazy patterns on her shoulder and arm. "Are you okay? I don't think you've said more than five words since we came inside."

A reluctant smile tugged at her lips. "The words *yes, yes, oh, yes* don't count?"

He chuckled. "Maybe if you added, 'Please, Cole, make love to me again,' I'd feel better."

Lacey laughed softly and didn't object when he drew her closer. "Cut me some slack. I'm not as comfortable with all of this as you are."

"Comfortable? Hell, lady, I've been in a serious state of *discomfort* since I first met you. All I can think about is you," he murmured into her ear, his breath warm on her cheek.

Lacey understood exactly what he meant, because it was the same for her. Rolling toward him, she rose up on an elbow to look at him. "When I came down here, I fully intended to step out of my comfort zone and live a little, but I never expected you. Or this."

"Any regrets?" he asked softly.

Only that she had to leave, eventually. She traced a fingertip along his jaw. "Not yet."

His mouth tilted in a half smile, but his expression was serious. "I think about that first night a lot. What if I hadn't been hanging out at Sully's? What if I hadn't volunteered to answer your call for a tow?"

"Then we never would have met."

"I'm not so sure," he mused. "Sometimes, things are just meant to be."

Lacey smiled. "I think you're a romantic. It's one of the things I like best about you. You're so honest about your feelings. About everything."

Cole didn't answer. Instead, he pulled her down until she lay with her head on his shoulder, mostly because he couldn't meet her eyes.

COLE WAITED UNTIL Lacey fell asleep before he slipped out of bed and pulled on a pair of loose pajama bottoms. Moving silently into the family room, he pulled out his laptop case and the thick sheath of paperwork that he had brought with him from Norfolk. He sat down and began to thumb through the dozens of accident reports that had been filed by the Black River Mines. Many of them were vehicle accidents that had occurred inside the tunnels, but several involved injuries sustained from falling debris. By the time the accident reports had been filled out and a safety inspection team had been sent in to investigate, the area had been cleaned up and the risks mitigated.

Cole pored through the reports, wondering how Buck Rogan could have addressed each deficiency and corrected it so quickly. Unless the reports had been falsified, there was no way he could have.

Withdrawing a set of blueprints from a document holder, he rolled them out on the coffee table and studied them. They detailed each level of tunnels within the Black River Mines. Cole had put a small mark near where each accident had occurred. Or, he amended silently, where Buck and his foreman *claimed* each accident had occurred.

He traced his finger along the length of one tunnel, to where it abruptly ended deep inside the mountain. Fifty feet of rock and shale separated that main tunnel from an older network of tunnels that had been abandoned years earlier for safety reasons. The tunnels that made up Rogan's Run Mine No. 5 weren't shown on the blueprint. As far as Cole knew, they weren't on any current blueprints. The Bureau of Mine Safety had deemed Rogan's Run Mine No 5 too unstable to mine, despite the rich veins of ore that existed.

What if Buck had found a way to access those tunnels without anyone knowing? He would have to pay the workers a substantial fee in order to guarantee their silence. Cole knew how tempting that could be to a man with a family to support.

If Buck Rogan really was capable of that kind of duplicity, there was no telling what else he could do. Cole glanced back toward the bedroom. He wanted to come clean with Lacey about his real purpose for being in Black Stone Gap, but he couldn't risk that information leaking out and getting back to Buck. But he promised himself one thing: Lacey would never enter those tunnels, not if there was the smallest chance that something could go wrong.

9

LACEY COLLAPSED GRATEFULLY onto the picnic table bench. The heat and humidity of the day had completely sapped her of whatever energy she had left, which, considering how much she'd expended the previous night, wasn't a whole lot.

In the end, she'd agreed to spend the morning with the rescue team, and the afternoon with Cole at the Pikesville County Fair. It was a small event by any standards, but as far as Lacey was concerned, that only added to its country charm.

Cole had been amused by her fascination with the quilt displays. She had lingered so long over one particular quilt that he'd finally offered to buy it for her. Lacey had adamantly refused, and had let it fall back onto the display rack.

He'd just shrugged. "If it would make you happy, then I'd like to get it for you."

She couldn't explain to him that it wasn't so much the quilt itself, although it was beautiful, as the bittersweet memories it evoked. She'd had one almost like it when she was a little girl. She remembered her parents tucking it securely around her at bedtime, and how safe it had made her feel. The quilt had been lost when she and her mother had moved to New Hampshire.

"Thanks anyway," she had told Cole. "It's just that I had one sort of like this when I was a kid." She smiled, embarrassed. "It brought back memories, that's all."

Cole had looked at her quizzically, but hadn't pressed her. And he hadn't bought the quilt. She glanced up at him now from the picnic table, grateful for the overhead canopy that gave some relief from the sun.

"I'll go grab us a couple of cold drinks," he said. "Will you be okay?"

Lacey smiled at him. "I'm fine, just a little tired."

He braced his hands on the picnic table and leaned down to plant a warm, hard kiss against her lips. "That's my fault," he murmured. "But when the options are sleep or make love to you, it's a total no-brainer. I just wasn't thinking about the fact that you'd be exhausted."

Lacey couldn't help it. She reached up and drew him down for another kiss. "Hey," she responded softly, "you don't hear me complaining."

He pulled back, his eyes warm. "I'll go grab those drinks and be right back."

Lacey watched him go, and then stretched out sideways on the bench, lifting her feet up and smoothing the skirt of her sundress down over her legs. She closed her eyes and tipped her head from side to side, stretching her tired muscles.

"Looks like you could use a good massage."

Her eyes flew open, and for a moment she couldn't focus on the tall figure standing in front of her. When she did, she sat upright, shoving her feet back under the table and smoothing her skirt over her knees. It was Buck Rogan.

He extended a hand to her now. "It's a pleasure to see you again, Ms. Delaney."

Lacey accepted his outstretched hand. "Hello, Mr. Rogan."

"Oh, please," he said, laughing as he released her hand.

"Call me Buck. When I hear *Mr. Rogan* I look around for my old man."

"Okay, but only if you call me Lacey."

He chuckled. "Agreed."

He was well dressed in a pair of lightweight chinos and a blazer. Despite the heat, he looked cool and distinguished.

He indicated the bench opposite her. "Do you mind if I sit down for a moment?"

"Of course not," she said. "I was going to give you a call tomorrow to talk about my project."

He frowned, clearly puzzled. "Really? Cole spoke to me about that this morning, and I understood those plans had been scrapped."

Lacey frowned. She knew that Cole had spent the morning in Buck's office, but when he'd come back to the house just before lunch, he'd only said that the meeting had gone well. If he and Buck had discussed her project, he hadn't mentioned it to her.

"I'm sorry, I don't follow. Cole told you that my plans to test the prototype had been scrapped?"

"Yes, ma'am. He didn't say why, but I got the impression that you had found another testing site."

Lacey bit back the denial that sprang to her lips. Her gaze slid away from him and she searched the surrounding crowds for Cole, but there was no sign of him. She had no idea why Cole would have told Buck such a thing when it was blatantly untrue. But she didn't want to expose Cole as a liar to the man who was now his boss. She knew how much he needed this job, and she wouldn't do anything to jeopardize that.

"Hmm," she said instead, pretending to consider his words. "I think I know why he said that, but it was definitely just a misunderstanding." She actually had no idea why he would have said that, and her mind scrambled furiously for an adequate reason for Cole's statement. "He knows that I'm terrified of being underground, and probably thought he was doing me a favor."

That, at least, was a partial truth and for all she knew, Cole might have thought he *was* doing her a favor.

Buck sat down. He put one arm on the picnic table, drummed his fingers and considered her thoughtfully. "I assure you that you would be perfectly safe in my mines. I don't go into them much myself anymore, but I have a foreman who I would trust with my life. You would have nothing to worry about."

"Thank you. I appreciate that."

They spent the next few minutes talking about STAR and what Lacey was looking for in terms of a testing environment. Buck was attentive and cordial.

"Based on the parameters you've described, I think I know exactly which mine would work best for you," he said when she had finished explaining about the field test. "Now that Cole is my lead engineer, I need to take care of his girl."

Cole's girl.

Before she could protest that she wasn't Cole's girl—not really—Buck continued.

"You know what they say...*happy wife, happy life*. Oh, I know you're not married, but I've seen that boy's face when he talks about you. Same way his daddy looked when he talked about Cole's mama."

"You knew Cole's parents?" she asked, curious in spite of herself.

"Shoot, I grew up with Cole's father. When I took over the mines, he was the foreman." His face grew pensive. "Best damned foreman I've ever seen. He had a real way with people, and he couldn't have been prouder of Cole than that first day I hired him as an engineer, straight out of college and still wet behind the ears. A damned shame what happened."

He grew quiet, remembering. Lacey knew she shouldn't ask, but she was dying to know. "What happened?"

"You don't know? Well, I guess it's natural that Cole wouldn't want to talk about it. In fact, it's why he high-tailed it out of here five years ago."

It took all of Lacey's self control not to reach over and shake the man. *What had happened?* She sat patiently and waited.

"Cole left the Gap after a rescue mission went bad." He paused, gauging her reaction. "His friend was trapped in one of the vertical shafts, and Cole had this plan on how he was going to get him out." Buck snorted. "It went so foul it still stinks to this day. Not that anyone ever blamed Cole, mind you."

Lacey stared at him. In her mind, she could see the scene clearly and a shiver went through her.

"The shaft collapsed, and three miners died, including his friend," Buck elaborated, reading the unspoken question in her eyes.

Lacey's chest constricted. She thought of her father and how his death still haunted her, nearly twenty years later. Did Cole have nightmares about his friend? She now understood his reluctance to rejoin the rescue team.

"I'm sure it wasn't Cole's fault," Lacey said. "Mine rescues can be a tricky business. There are no guarantees." She was repeating the very words that she and her mother had been told all those years ago; words she hadn't wanted to believe then, because she'd needed to blame someone for what had happened to her father. But she didn't want Cole to take the blame for what had happened to his friend.

"You're right," Buck said. "Coal mine rescues can be unpredictable, but—" He broke off abruptly and waved a dismissive hand. "That's all in the past, and as far as I'm concerned, Cole's come back to town with a clean slate. I was surprised to see him, though, but I guess the need for redemption can be a powerful thing."

The implication was clear to Lacey—Buck thought that Cole was to blame for his friend's tragic death. Lacey decided that she'd heard enough.

"Well, it's been nice talking with you. I will definitely give you a call tomorrow to set up a time for the testing."

Buck took the hint and rose to his feet. "It was my pleasure, ma'am. Enjoy the rest of your day." He tipped an imaginary hat to her, before he turned and strolled away.

Lacey sank back down onto the bench, her mind whirling. Why had Cole told Buck that she wouldn't be using the Black River mines to test STAR? And why did Buck insinuate that the accident had been Cole's fault? If she didn't know better, she'd think there was some bad blood there, but he'd had nothing but good things to say about Cole's father.

She found that she didn't want to ask any favors of Buck Rogan, but she'd do it in order to test STAR. The prototype represented years of hard work and sacrifice. But it also represented hope. Hope that no other miner would have to die the way her father had died. The way Cole's friend had died. Testing STAR was her single most important mission right now. There was no way she'd go home without accomplishing that.

"Was that Buck Rogan I saw you talking with?"

Lacey dropped her hands away from her eyes and stared up at Cole. He stood by the table holding two glasses of lemonade in his hands and staring after Buck with an expression of concern.

"Yes."

"What did he want?"

Lacey accepted the proffered lemonade and took a long swallow. "Nothing, really," she fibbed. "He was just being friendly. You were gone an awfully long time. What kept you?"

"I ran into someone," he said, and swung his leg over the bench and sat down facing her. "So what did the two of you talk about?"

Lacey put the lemonade down and carefully swiped a fingertip across her lips before looking at him directly. "He was under the impression that I no longer wanted to use the mines as a testing environment for STAR. I told him there had been a misunderstanding, and that I very much wanted to bring STAR into the mines."

For a moment he just stared at her, and then he blew out a hard breath. When he finally spoke, his voice was low.

"I wish you wouldn't do this."

"Look, Cole, I'm sorry to be blunt, but this has nothing to do with you." Lacey didn't know why she suddenly felt the need to defend her decision. "I need to get into the mines to test STAR. You know how important this is to me. It's why I came here. My company is depending on me to do this. I *have* to do it." Aware that people were beginning to look at them, she lowered her voice. "You had no right to interfere."

Cole leaned forward and tried to take her hands in his, but Lacey pulled them away and looked expectantly at him, waiting for his response.

"There are things you don't know," he finally said, his voice rough.

"Then tell me!"

"I can't."

"Oh, for God's sake." Lacey threw up her hands. "You have to give me something. And not just that you have a bad feeling."

Cole set his drink down on the table. He looked around, taking in the fair-goers at the surrounding tables and seemed to come to a decision. "C'mon," he said. "Let's get out of here."

Before she could protest, Lacey found herself hauled to her feet and practically dragged alongside him as he steered her through the crowds.

His features were set in grim lines and a small muscle worked in his lean jaw as they made their way through the congested fairgrounds to where the truck was parked at the back of a field. There was no one else around, and the air was redolent with the scent of freshly cut grass. Once there, he turned to her.

"I can't let you do it, Lacey."

Lacey tugged her arm free of his grasp. "We've been over this already."

"Let me bring you to a mine where safety won't be an issue."

Lacey narrowed her eyes at him. "Where? West Virginia?"

"What does it matter, so long as you have a safe environment in which to perform your tests?"

"But why drive hours, when I could do it right here in Black Stone Gap?"

Cole stared at her and a muscle worked in one lean cheek. "I'm trying to protect you, damn it."

Lacey tamped down her rising annoyance. Maybe she should have felt appreciation, but she'd heard the same message for nearly her entire life from her mother. She didn't want Cole to see her as fragile or needing to be saved.

"This is part of my job, Cole." She gave him an encouraging smile. "I've dedicated the past several years to developing this unit. I want to help make the mines safe for people like you. I want all miners to come home to their families when their shift is over. I'm sure that's what you want, too, isn't it?"

"That's exactly what I want." He opened the door to the truck and indicated she should climb in. "C'mon, let's go home. There's something I want to show you."

Home. He said it so casually, as if they had been together for years and not just days.

"Cole," she said wearily. "Why won't you let me just do my job?"

He searched her face. "This is important, and it has everything to do with your job. Just hear me out on this, okay? I'm being sincere when I say that I only want you to be safe."

Lacey found her irritation evaporating. She trusted him. If he didn't want her to go into the mines, then there had to be a good reason why. She climbed into the cab of the truck, but when Cole would have turned away, she caught his hand.

He looked over at her, his expression questioning.

"What—"

She pressed a fingertip against his mouth, and then put her other hand at the back of his head, drawing him down. She loved the rough velvet of his hair, and speared her fingers through it, reveling in the feel of his scalp. "Kiss me."

Cole stared at her, and even with the sunlight full in his eyes, she saw his pupils dilate. "Lacey..."

She leaned forward and pressed her lips sweetly against his, tasting him ever so lightly with the tip of her tongue. At the same time, she placed his hand on her knee and slid it upward beneath the hem of her sundress. She felt him go still as his warm palm came into contact with the satin edge of her underwear. But when she lifted her hips, he didn't pretend to misunderstand her, and swiftly drew her panties down her legs until she kicked them free.

"What are you doing?" he rasped softly against her mouth, but his hand was firm and warm against her heated flesh.

"Seducing you," she whispered back. "Is it working?"

"Here?" His voice sounded slightly strangled.

In answer, she shifted to give him better access and nearly came off the seat as he stroked her once. She'd never done anything so bold before. This man made her do things that she'd never thought herself capable of.

"No," she murmured against his mouth. "Let's go home."

10

COLE GRIPPED THE steering wheel of the truck and tried to control his growing concern. After they had returned from the fair, they'd spent several long, memorable hours in his bed. Then he'd shown Lacey the blueprints of the mine. He'd explained his suspicions to her without revealing that he was working undercover for the Department of Labor. When she'd asked how he had obtained such detailed plans of the mine, he'd fibbed and told her they were from five years earlier, when he had first worked for Buck as a new engineer.

He'd shown her where each of the accidents had supposedly occurred, and how they all taken place near the old, vacated mines. She'd been skeptical about his theory that Buck was working the closed sections, but had been willing to consider the possibility. In the end, they had agreed that she would meet with Buck and talk about the field test, but she would not utilize any tunnels that Cole considered to be dangerous.

Cole would spend the day at Black River Mine No. 2 with a team of engineers, inspecting the internal support structures of the tunnels. He hoped that as the lead engineer, he would have access to the blueprints for all the Black River mines, including Rogan's Run No. 5, which had been closed for more than fifty years. He was convinced those closed portions, deemed unsafe by any standards, were being secretly but actively worked. He was certain Buck was paying the miners an exorbitant hourly wage in order for them to work those areas and keep their mouths shut.

Now he just needed proof.

But it would take time to gain the trust of the miners, especially since many of them still remembered the horrible rescue effort that had taken the life of his friend five years earlier. No doubt there were those who still associated his name with that disaster, and maybe even blamed him for it.

"Are you sure about this?" he asked now. "I could bring you to any number of mines over in West Virginia. You don't need to meet with Buck Rogan."

Lacey looked over at him and he could see that she wasn't nearly as confident about this as she pretended to be. But she tipped her chin up and gave him a smile.

"It'll be fine," she assured him. "The only thing that has me a little nervous is the fact that I'm showing up unannounced. He's not expecting me until tomorrow."

"Just say that you have a conflict tomorrow. He's not going to tell you to come back some other time. If nothing else, Buck Rogan is a gentleman. You're only going to talk about the test parameters and look at the blueprints." He cast her a stern glance. "Under no conditions are you to let him take you into the mines."

Lacey smiled. "I've got it, Cole. Relax. I'm not going into any mines today. I didn't even bring STAR with me, so there would be no point to it anyway, okay? Don't worry about me."

But he did. He knew she was stronger than she appeared, and yet he still worried about her. He didn't want her to meet with Buck Rogan, but he also knew how important testing her GPS unit was to her. He wouldn't stop her, as much as he might want to.

"Okay, fine. You have my cell phone number. I'll be on the other side of the complex, so call me if you need me."

They were emerging from the thick, impenetrable woods that enclosed the road for most of the twenty-minute drive, and turned onto a wide, gravel lane. Tall wire fences lined the perimeter, marked with No Trespassing signs and directions to the mine entrance.

The route wound upward until they entered a large parking lot ringed with work trailers and wooden structures. Cole drew the truck to a stop in front of a large, concrete building and switched off the engine. He turned to face Lacey. "This is Buck's office." He indicated a work trailer on the far side of the parking lot. "I'll be over there. Call me when you're through, and I'll drive you home."

She gave him a grateful look before she slid out of the cab and closed the door to the truck. As she climbed the steps to the office, the door opened and Buck's massive bulk filled the door frame. He exchanged a few words with Lacey but they were too far away for Cole to hear them. Buck stepped back and Lacey brushed past him into the house. Buck raised a hand in greeting to Cole, and he gave a brief nod in return. Buck stood in the doorway for a scant second longer, before he stepped back and closed the door.

Cole checked his cell phone to ensure he would hear any incoming calls, before he thrust the truck into gear and punched the gas pedal down with his foot, gaining no satisfaction from the sound of the tires as they squealed in protest.

LACEY WAITED AS BUCK closed the door and then turned to face her. As always, he wore a well-cut sports jacket over a crisp, white dress shirt. He looked every inch a successful executive.

"I wasn't expecting you until tomorrow. But no matter. Come into my office," he invited, and indicated she should precede him down a short corridor. They passed an older woman sitting at a desk, who Lacey guessed was his secretary. "Patty, could you bring us some coffee, please?"

"Of course, Mr. Rogan."

Buck opened the door to his office, and Lacey saw it was richly appointed with mahogany furniture, including a desk and a large conference table, and a wall of deep filing cabinets. The desk itself was covered with papers and blueprints, and one wall of shelves contained what looked like more rolls of drawings. He had samples of coal and other minerals displayed in glass boxes on one shelf, and framed photos of miners covered two walls. A window at the rear of the office overlooked the entrance to the mine itself, and Lacey could see a group of workers preparing to go down into the tunnels.

"Have a seat," he invited, indicating the conference table. "So what, exactly, are you looking for?"

Lacey opened her presentation case and withdrew the specifications for STAR and spread them out on the surface of the table. "Here are the specs for the unit I'd like to test. If you look here, you'll see the optimum conditions that we need to achieve in order to perform a successful test."

Buck studied the sheets for several moments. "You need to be at least five hundred feet below the surface, and at least one quarter mile into the tunnels."

Lacey nodded. "Yes, that's right."

Moving away from the table, Buck opened a drawer in one of the file cabinets and withdrew several blueprints. When he spread them out on the table, Lacey saw they were similar to the ones that Cole had shown her.

"These blueprints show the Black River Mines No. 2," he

said indicating one set of tunnels. "I think they would suit your needs perfectly."

Before Lacey could respond, there was a light knock on the door, and Patty came in with a small tray of coffee and muffins. She set them down on the conference table near Lacey.

"Here you are," she said brightly. "Let me know if you need anything else."

Buck thanked her, and as Lacey prepared her cup of coffee, she listened to Buck explain the various attributes of the mine, and had to agree that the conditions sounded perfect in which to test STAR. She wished now that she hadn't been so quick to promise Cole that she wouldn't go into the mines.

"Does this mine have a good safety record?" she asked.

Buck sharpened his gaze on her. "Why would you ask that?"

Lacey decided that honesty was the best policy. "My father died in a mining accident when I was a little girl. I helped to design STAR for NASA, but there is a huge commercial potential for the unit, as well. These could be utilized in the mining community to accurately pinpoint the location of miners in the event of an accident." She gave him a wry smile. "I wouldn't want to jeopardize the project by getting killed during the testing phase."

Buck's face was somber. "I'm sorry for your loss. I won't lie and tell you that we haven't had our share of accidents over the years, but I can promise you that the No. 2 mines are absolutely safe."

Lacey also knew they were located miles away from Rogan's Run Mine No. 5, where Cole thought Buck might be mining illegally. There would be no chance of her seeing anything down there that she shouldn't see. At that moment, there was another knock on the door, and then it was thrust open to reveal a man wearing an agitated expression.

"I'm sorry for interrupting," he said, speaking directly to Buck. "But I need to speak to you." His gaze flicked to Lacey and then back to Buck. "It's, um, urgent."

As Lacey watched, Buck's gaze flew to something on his desk. Lacey looked, too, but saw only rolls of blueprints. For a moment, Buck hesitated, as if he would snatch them up. In the next instant, he nodded at the man.

"Excuse us for just a moment," he said to Lacey.

Lacey murmured her assent, but she didn't miss the deep concern and something else in Buck's eyes, before he left the office, leaving the door open a few inches. But Lacey recognized that expression.

Fear.

She listened as the two men moved away from the door, and then quickly walked over to his desk, her eyes scanning the blueprints that lay scattered across the top. Technical drawings were very familiar to her, and blueprints were not much different. Keeping an eye on the door, she thumbed swiftly through the documents, wondering which one Buck had wanted. Then she found it.

A blueprint of Rogan's Run Mine No. 5, and the date at the bottom was current, from less than a year earlier. He obviously hadn't been prepared for her visit. If he'd known she was going to show up unexpectedly this morning, he never would have left these documents out in the open. Lacey quickly scanned the blueprint and saw that access to the closed tunnels could be gained through the Black River Mine No. 6. Quickly, her heart thudding, she folded the blueprint in half, and then in half again. Walking back to the conference table, she had just shoved the document deep into a zippered pocket on her presentation case when the door opened and Buck came in. He schooled his features into a polite smile, but Lacey could see the anxiety etched onto his features.

"You'll have to forgive me, but I need to excuse myself. Perhaps we can continue our conversation at another time?"

Lacey gathered up her specifications and replaced them in her presentation case. "Please, there's nothing to forgive. You weren't even expecting me this morning, so I appreciate the time you were able to spend with me. I'll let you get back to work."

"Thank you. I'll see you out. Can one of my men give you a ride somewhere?"

Lacey followed him back through the office to the front door. "No, thanks. I'm all set."

After he closed the door, she stood for a moment, acutely aware of the pilfered document in her case. What if he returned to his office and realized it was missing? He would know she had stolen it. She made her way quickly across the compound toward Cole's trailer, expecting to hear Buck Rogan coming after her at any second.

Cole opened the door immediately when she knocked. He took one look at her face and dragged her inside the trailer, closing the door quickly behind her.

"What is it?" he asked. "Are you okay?"

"You were right," she said without preamble. "I think he's working inside the closed section of the mines." She unzipped her presentation case and pulled out the folded document. "Here. I found this on his desk. There were other blueprints, too, but I didn't get a good look at all of them."

Cole took the paper from her and unfolded it, before swiftly scanning it. He gave Lacey one astonished look and then quickly refolded it and shoved it into the back of his jeans, pulling his jacket on to conceal it. He glanced through the window toward Buck's office.

"C'mon," he said, taking her elbow. "Buck is leaving. Let's get out of here before he figures out what you've done."

"I'm sorry," she said as she followed him to the truck. "I don't know what made me take it. I should have just left it there, but I thought you would want to see that your suspicions are correct. "

"No, you did the right thing," he assured her, handing her into the cab. "Did Buck say where they were going?"

Lacey shook her head. "No. A man came into the office to talk with him, and I got the sense it was urgent. Buck seemed pretty anxious to get rid of me."

"That was his foreman. There must have been an accident in one of the tunnels." Cole thrust the truck into gear and accelerated out of the compound. Behind them, a group of workers were jogging toward the entrance to the mine. "Yeah, something is definitely up. Listen, I'm going to drop you off at the house, okay?"

"Where are you going?"

"I have something I need to do. There's food in the refrigerator. I may not be back until late, but don't wait up for me."

There was something in his expression—something calculated—that kept Lacey from asking any questions. Reaching over, she covered his hand with her own.

"Be careful."

11

As COLE HAD PREDICTED, it was late by the time he returned to the cabin, but not so late that Lacey would be in bed. He noted with satisfaction that the porch lights were on, as well as the living room lights. He parked the truck and bent to greet Copper, who bounded down the steps, tail wagging.

Cole had met with two Department of Labor agents in Roanoke, a drive that had taken him nearly three hours each way. But before that, he'd headed over to the entrance of Rogan's Run Mine No. 5, but there had been no telltale activity outside the long abandoned entrance. On a hunch, he'd also driven past the entrance to the Black River Mine No. 6, where the pilfered blueprint indicated there was access to the closed mine. As he'd suspected, there was a flurry of activity at the entrance to the mine, but there hadn't been any rescue crews or ambulances.

He'd returned to his work trailer and had made some discreet inquiries, but his questions had been met with blank stares. Nobody had heard of any accidents occurring that morning. So he'd left word that he needed to take the rest of the day off, and had headed to Roanoke with Lacey's blueprint in his pocket. But the diagram alone wasn't proof that Buck was using the mines, and after a lengthy discussion with the agents, Cole had returned home with instructions to continue with his undercover surveillance.

He found Lacey curled up on the sofa in the living room, reading a book, wrapped in his terry bathrobe. She looked relieved when he crossed the room and dropped a light kiss against her mouth.

"You look tired," she commented as he crossed to a small wet bar and poured two glasses of bourbon. "Where have you been?"

He handed her a glass and lowered himself onto the cushions beside her. "I had to drive out to Roanoke today."

She stared at him. "Roanoke? But that's hours from here. What was so urgent that you needed to go all the way out there?"

"Business," he said, and tipped back his bourbon and drained the glass.

"Want to talk about it?"

Cole shrugged. "I gave the blueprints to the Bureau of Mine Safety, thinking they would be sufficient evidence for them to send a team of safety inspectors into the abandoned mines, but I was wrong. They won't go in without more substantial proof. Having updated blueprints of an abandoned mine isn't an indication that those mines are being worked. In fact, the Bureau was impressed that Buck had the good sense to have the mines properly documented."

"Aren't you afraid that Buck will find out? I don't want you to lose your job over this." She pulled a face. "What if he realizes that I took the blueprint? He won't let me into the mines. Now I'll have to come up with another plan to test STAR."

"Hey," he murmured, and pulled her into his arms. "Everything will work out. I told you I would take you to another mine, and I meant it. Whenever you're finished with the search-and-rescue team, we'll drive over to West Virginia and I'll take you into one of the coal mines there."

She let him hold her for a minute before she pulled away. "What about you? Will Buck be upset that you took off like that today?"

"He probably doesn't even know."

"What if he finds out that you gave the blueprint to the Bureau of Mine Safety?"

"Don't worry about me."

He didn't want to tell her that his job with the Black River Mines was just a cover. Or that until today, he hadn't been able to figure out how Buck could be accessing the mines without anyone knowing. But thanks to Lacey, he finally knew.

Buck had done a good job concealing whatever illegal mining he was doing. The tunnels extended through the mountains for miles. Only someone involved in the scheme could pinpoint the precise location of the illegal activity. He wanted to tell Lacey the truth, but he'd maintain his secret until he had the irrefutable proof he needed.

DESPITE THE WARMTH of the evening, Lacey leaned into Cole and savored the heat and strength of his body. His fingers absently stroked her upper arm. Lacey thought she could easily spend every night just like this. But she knew that couldn't happen.

Too soon, she would return home and Cole would remain in Black Stone Gap. Despite telling herself it was for the best, she found the thought left her feeling depressed. But she couldn't stay in Kentucky. Even if she had the fortitude to accept what he did for a living, she had her own career to think about back in New England. She loved her job, and she was pretty sure she wouldn't find anything similar in Kentucky.

"So what happens tomorrow?" she asked carefully. "You've just started a new job, and I still need to test STAR. How are you going to drive me to West Virginia if you're working?"

He blew out a hard breath. "I'll take care of it. Why don't we plan on heading out on Wednesday morning?"

"I'm not sure. I'll finish up with Carr and the others tomorrow, and then give my boss a call and see what he wants me to do. He has the final say." She gave a soft laugh, and then groaned and covered her face with her hands. "I still can't believe I stole that blueprint. You should have seen me—I felt like a spy stealing top secret documents. What if he had caught me in the act?"

Cole hugged her briefly. "He didn't. He may still have no idea that the document is missing, and even when he does realize, I doubt he'll suspect you." He hesitated as if debating his next words. "I hope I'm wrong about the closed mines, but I don't think I am. But I want you to know that not all mining operations are corrupt. Your GPS unit could still make a difference."

"I know it will make a difference. What if I told you that I first became involved with StarPoint Technologies because of a miner?"

"I'd say that I'm trying very hard to suppress my jealousy."

"There's no need to be jealous. He died a long time ago."

Cole sobered instantly. "I'm sorry. Tell me about him, and how you got involved in the GPS business."

Lacey swallowed and looked down at her hands, wondering how much to share with him. She hadn't talked about her father to anyone in years. Even her mother never spoke about him, as if the memories were still too painful. But a man like Cole would understand. She took a deep breath.

"My father was killed in a coal mining accident when I was eight years old. His body was never recovered."

There was a shocked silence. "You're kidding."

"I wish I was."

"Which mine was it?"

"The Spruce River mine in West Virginia. They lost eight men in a tunnel collapse. They survived the initial event and at first the owners were optimistic that they could rescue all the men. But after a week, when two more cave-ins occurred, they discontinued the rescue effort and sealed the mine. I can still remember…" She gave herself a mental shake, unwilling to dredge up those old memories. "Anyway, after that, my mom and I moved to New Hampshire and we've been there ever since."

Cole shook his head, his expression one of dismay. "Wow. I can't believe you lost your dad in that accident. I remember studying that disaster in school."

"I still have nightmares sometimes," she confessed. "About him being alive in the pitch-dark, knowing that nobody would be coming to save him."

Cole's arm tightened around her. "That's why you prefer to keep the lights on."

Lacey nodded. "Logically, I know that he couldn't have survived, and that he was already gone when they stopped the rescue efforts, but sometimes at night…I wonder."

"So you devoted your life to developing a tool that would prevent another tragedy."

"Well, maybe not my life," Lacey replied, "but the last five years, anyway. I was really hoping to field-test STAR while I was here in Black Stone Gap. Even though we're developing the unit for NASA, I can't help but think of all the other applications it could be used for."

"I'll make sure you get your unit tested," Cole promised. "It won't be here in Black Stone Gap, but you'll have your test results."

"I feel like my whole life has led to this," she said. "If STAR can save even one miner's life, then all the years of research and lab work will have been worth it." She raised her eyes to his. "Maybe I'll even be able to sleep without the light on."

"Speaking of which, it's been a long day." Without giving her time to object, he stood up and pulled her to her feet. "Time for bed."

The combination of cool sheets and warm, hard Cole sounded like the perfect antidote to the long day she'd spent worrying about him. She wanted nothing more than to feel his arms around her. She followed him to the loft area. Her room was only dimly lit from the hallway until Cole flipped on the small bedside lamp. In the soft light, his expression was inscrutable. Lacey stood by the bed and waited for him to touch her, to pull her close and slide his hands beneath the edge of her bathrobe and over her bare skin.

Instead, he leaned over the bed and held the blankets up. "C'mon," he said. "In you go."

Lacey was too surprised to protest. She didn't even remove the robe. Obediently, she slid beneath the covers and watched as he pulled them over her, tucking them neatly at her sides.

"Aren't you—"

"Try and get some sleep. I'll see you in the morning." He turned toward the door.

"Cole..."

"I'll be downstairs if you need me. Get some rest."

He left. He pulled the door almost completely shut behind him, leaving a crack of light to spill in from the hallway. Lacey lay still for a moment and wondered what had just happened. She had been so sure he was going to make love to her, or at the very least spend the night in the same bed with her, even if it was just to sleep.

With a small sigh, she shifted onto her side and bunched the pillow beneath her cheek and thought about the events of the day. Cole had driven all the way to Roanoke, Virginia and back. Of course he was exhausted. The man hadn't gotten much sleep since he'd met her.

Tomorrow she would wrap up with the search-and-rescue team. They had their GPS units, and although she suspected they knew perfectly well how to use them, she'd agreed to spend one more day with them. On Wednesday, she and Cole would drive to West Virginia to test STAR. Lacey expected she would need two days to conduct the field test. She would stay in the area long enough to do the follow-up analysis, and then she would return home.

Home.

She thought about how, in the space of just a few short days, she'd begun to think of Cole's house as home. He hadn't actually asked her to stay in Kentucky, and she wasn't sure what she would do even if he did. She'd never intended to stay. So why did she feel so let down because Cole had opted to sleep in a different room? And if she couldn't get through one night without him, how in the world was she going to get through all the nights to come?

COLE STOOD IN the doorway of Lacey's bedroom and watched her sleep. Her hair fanned out on the pillow behind her, and she slept with her hands tucked beneath her cheek, like a child.

With a sigh, he looked down at the small glass he held in his hand, and then tossed back the remnants of the bourbon he'd been nursing. He told himself he should just go back downstairs and go to bed.

It had taken all his willpower not to climb into bed with her earlier that night. He'd just wanted to hold her; to reassure both her and himself that she was safe. But he knew from experience there was no such thing as just holding Lacey Delaney. It seemed whenever they touched something flared, hot and urgent. He had no illusions that if he climbed into that bed with her, he'd have to make love to her. He was incapable of keeping his hands off her. But at some point during the past several days, what he felt for Lacey Delaney had changed. Maybe in the beginning it had been about sex, but not anymore. He was falling for her, and falling hard. When she'd told him about her father, he'd been floored. He still had trouble getting his head around the fact that she came from a coal mining family. That her father had died in the tunnels. No wonder she was so determined to test the prototype.

He'd been shocked by the revelation of her background. Given her innate elegance and conservative nature, he'd been certain she came from wealth and privilege. At least, he amended silently, she was conservative outside the bedroom. The things she did to him when they were alone together completely blew his mind. She'd rocked his world in ways he couldn't even comprehend. But she'd also forced him to face some hard truths of his own.

He'd come back to Black Stone Gap for just one reason—to shut down Buck's mining operations. He held Buck personally responsible for the accident that had killed his friend, Drake Wilson, some five years earlier. He wanted answers. He needed to know why Drake had been working a part of the mines that should have been closed. Buck insisted that Drake had gone into the closed area without permission, but Cole had his doubts. And, of course, there was the part he himself had played in Drake's death.

He rubbed a hand across his eyes, recalling the events of that day. Drake had been trapped in a small cavern as a result of a cave-in. Cole had been so certain his plan to drill a vertical shaft alongside the cavern, and then tunnel horizontally to where Drake was trapped, would work. Instead, the drilling had triggered another cave-in, and Drake had been killed.

After the initial investigations were over and Buck had been cleared of any wrongdoing, Cole had left Black Stone Gap. He hadn't planned on coming back until he'd received a phone call from his former professor Stu Zollweg.

But meeting Lacey Delaney had never been part of the plan. As he watched her sleep, she murmured incoherently and then turned onto her stomach and kicked the blanket aside with one leg. At some point, she'd removed his bathrobe and it lay crumpled on the floor. By the light from the bedside lamp he could see her perfect rear, smooth and round beneath a pair of pale blue panties.

"Jesus," he muttered, all thoughts of maintaining his distance completely gone. He turned to leave before he could act on his desire to join her, but was stopped short when he heard his name.

At first he thought he had imagined it. He looked back at the bed. Lacey had raised herself up on one elbow. Now she pushed her hair back from her face and peered sleepily at him.

"Cole?" Her voice was husky.

"Yeah, it's me. I didn't mean to wake you. Go back to sleep."

"I was dreaming. Cole…" She sank back down against the pillows and extended a hand to him. "Come here."

There was no mistaking her meaning, and Cole made a swift rationalization. He was, after all, just a man. No one could blame him for succumbing to such a sweet invitation. And it didn't have to be about sex. He would just hold her. He could do that. Couldn't he?

With a soft groan, he swiftly crossed the room, setting his empty glass down on the bedside table. He stood beside her, suddenly hesitant. She was all smooth, bare skin and tempting softness.

"Lacey…"

"Come here."

He gave a soft, self-deprecating laugh. "I am so toast." He wore a pair of loose pajama bottoms and nothing else, and the thin material tented over his arousal. He slid in beside her, gratified when she wrapped her arms around him and entwined her legs with his own. Her skin was warm and silky against his.

"I'm just going to hold you, okay?" His voice sounded gravelly with the effort it took to keep his rampant desire under control.

"Okay," she agreed breathlessly, skating her lips along his collarbone, "just so long as you're inside me while you're doing that."

"Lacey…" Her name came out on an agonized groan. "I'm trying to do the right thing here, and you're killing me."

She pulled back enough to search his face in the darkness. "Then do the right thing and make love to me." She traced a finger around the whorl of his ear. "I wanted you to earlier. Why did you leave?"

Cole blew out his breath. "Trust me, it wasn't easy. But you need to get some sleep, and I don't want you to think that I'm only interested in sex." Unable to help himself, he splayed his fingers against her back, feeling the thrust of her shoulder blades and the smooth bumps of her spine. She was both supple and soft, her skin like satin beneath his questing hand.

She made a soft murmuring sound of pleasure and arched against him, rubbing herself sensuously against his bare chest. "Mmm. You feel so good." Her hands roamed across his back and traced a random path over bone and muscle until they encountered the fabric of his pants. The elastic waistband stretched easily beneath her questing fingers, and then her hands were inside, smoothing over his buttocks and grasping them, urging him closer. "You feel *really* good."

Cole gave a laugh that sounded more like a groan. "Lacey, sweetheart, I'm not sure—"

"I am." The words were whispered on a husky note, even as she slid one hand over his hip and around to the front, where his erection strained upward. She grasped him lightly, her fingers exploring the thick rise of his flesh. "Please, Cole…"

With a soft groan of defeat, he bent his head and pressed his lips to the tender skin beneath her ear. He slid his hand down her back to the sweet curve of her bottom, and cupped one cheek, kneading gently. "Okay," he whispered, "but only because you insist and it would be rude for me to refuse."

"Spoken like a true Southern gentleman."

"I aim to please."

"Then prove it." Her voice was warm with laughter.

"With pleasure." It became harder to speak as her hand began to stroke him, and his breathing grew more rapid. "Easy, baby. I've got something to prove, remember?"

She gave a soft laugh, and then her hands were pushing his pants down over his hips, freeing his arousal to bump enticingly against her stomach. She gasped when he kicked the fabric free of his legs and rose over her, pushing her gently back against the mattress.

"God, I want you," he rasped. He searched her face, seeing desire and something else reflected in her eyes. Something he didn't dare to identify. Hope flared inside him once more. He hesitated, wondering if he dared risk another rejection. He'd already told her he wanted more than just a temporary relationship. Maybe he'd do better to just take what she was willing to give him and bide his time.

She parted her legs beneath him and arched her hips, rubbing herself against him. He groaned and lowered his head to press searing kisses along her jaw and down the slender length of her throat. "It was all I could do not to come up here after you'd gone to bed. I want you so much, Lacey."

Her arms drew him down closer and she rained soft, moist kisses over his face. "I want you, too."

He lowered his head and nibbled gently at the corner of her mouth, then traced his tongue lightly along its contours. When she murmured her assent, he dipped his head lower and blazed a trail of molten kisses along the column of her neck and lower still to the fragile line of her collarbone.

He slid a finger beneath the slender strap of her bra and drew it down over her shoulder, pulling the lacy cup with it. He lifted his head and watched in utter fascination as her nipple contracted into a tight bud.

Glancing up at her face, he saw she was watching him through heavy-lidded eyes. Her lips were parted and her breath came unevenly. He smiled and then dipped his head, swirling his tongue around the hard nub, reveling in its texture. She gasped when he drew it into his mouth and suckled her. He cupped her other breast through the thin fabric of her bra, pinching the nipple until it stood tightly erect.

She was rolling her hips now, arching restlessly against him, and it was all he could do not to tear her panties from her and claim her; to plunge himself into her slick heat and make her his own. He slid a hand beneath the silky fabric. She was wet. He inserted first one finger into her tight depths, and then another, gratified when she moaned and thrust her hips against his palm.

"Oh, man," he breathed against her breast, "I don't think I can wait..." He reared back and dragged her panties down the length of her legs. "Here, roll over."

"What?" Her voice was thick with pleasure.

"Roll over."

"Okay." She turned onto her stomach and gave him a seductive look. "Like this?"

"Well, actually more like this..." He raised her hips upward and shoved the pillows beneath her. "Yeah, just like that."

He leaned back on his heels to admire her perfect rear in the moonlight, unable to resist smoothing his hands over her buttocks. She lay with her face against the mattress, and her hands curled into the sheets. He loved the way her slender back flared into the womanly curves of her hips, loved the way she responded when he nudged her thighs apart, affording him a clear view of her feminine center.

He stroked her from behind, first with his hand and then with the tip of his engorged shaft, while she clutched at the sheets and writhed against him. When she rose up on her elbows and looked back at him, he thought he'd never seen anything as erotic or beautiful.

"Cole, please...you're making me crazy..."

He grasped her hips and positioned himself, then in one fluid movement, thrust himself home. She cried out in pleasure and pushed herself back against him. Cole bent forward, covering her with his body. He swept her hair away from her neck and caught an earlobe gently between his teeth before he teased the delicate whorl of her ear with his tongue.

She was moaning now, making sexy sounds deep in her throat as she rocked back against him, her body fisted around him. Cole thrust deeply, and reached around to cup her breast and toy with her nipple.

"Oh, God," she gasped. "you feel so good..."

Cole felt himself swell even more at her husky words, and knew he wasn't going to last. Reaching down, he slid his fingers through her damp curls until he found the slick nub of her clitoris. He swirled his finger over it, trying to give her the friction that their position wouldn't allow, gratified when he felt her stiffen beneath him. Her breath came in short, shallow pants. When she cried out and convulsed around him, he gritted his teeth, willing himself not to lose control.

Grasping her hips with both hands, he raised himself up and slowly withdrew before thrusting himself back into her, his eyes fastened on the point where her body gripped him. But the combination of her flesh squeezing him and the erotic sight of himself sliding into her was too much, and with a strangled cry he climaxed, the force causing his back to arch before he collapsed, completely drained.

He rolled onto his side, pulling her with him, until she lay with her back against his chest. She was still breathing unevenly. He smoothed her hair back from her face and planted a warm, lingering kiss against her jaw.

"That was amazing," she breathed. "The sensations…"

"Yeah," Cole admitted huskily, "pretty incredible." And he wasn't just referring to the sex, although it was without doubt the most amazing he'd ever had in his life. He would never tire of coaxing those sweet sounds of pleasure from her.

He pulled her closer against his chest and tucked his knees behind hers so that he was spooning her. She yawned convulsively and then sighed in contentment. He could hear her breathing gradually become deeper and more even as sleep claimed her. He tightened his arms around her, knowing he had to say it.

"I'm falling in love with you, Lacey Delaney." His voice was no more than a whisper.

Beside him, she gave a soft snore.

12

COLE WAS GONE when Lacey woke up the following morning, but she could hear him moving around on the first floor, and smelled fresh coffee brewing. Glancing at the bedside clock, she saw it was already eight o'clock. Throwing back the sheets, she crossed the room to the adjoining bathroom and turned the shower as hot as she could stand it. She stood under the pulsing water, her thoughts going back to the previous night.

He was falling in love with her.

His words had caused her chest to constrict in a way she was unfamiliar with, and a suspicious lump had formed in her throat. She'd wanted to turn in his arms and see the truth of his words in his eyes, but had been immobilized by sudden panic. Instead, she'd closed her eyes and pretended to be asleep.

She couldn't let him know she'd heard him. What would she say? That she was falling in love with him, too? That despite their differences and despite the fact they'd only known each other a short time, she was already coming to depend on his strength and support?

She didn't want to depend on him; didn't want to entrust her heart to someone when they might break it, even if they didn't mean to. There was no way she could let herself fall for someone who worked in the coal mines, no matter how perfect he might be. She'd never stop worrying, and eventually she would come to resent his job. But she knew Cole well enough to realize that he wouldn't give up his job as a mining engineer, not even for her. Buck may fire him, but he'd find another position in another mine. Nope, better to pretend she hadn't heard those softly impassioned words and save what was left of her heart.

She turned her face into the spray of water and let it sluice down her body, recalling the tender passion of their lovemaking. The truth of his words had been there in his touch. In his kiss. In the reverent way in which he'd held her afterward.

The knowledge both thrilled her and terrified her.

Oh, God, what was she going to do? As she turned the shower faucet off and reached for a towel, she realized it was already too late. Because she was falling for him, too.

Downstairs, she expected to find Cole in the kitchen, but he was nowhere in sight. She was pouring herself a mug of coffee when she heard his voice from outside. Moving to a window, she saw him standing on the porch, talking on his cell phone. His voice drifted toward her.

"Give me another week and I can prove he's operating in the closed section of the mines." He paused, listening. "Lacey? I've told her what I suspect is happening, but that's it. She doesn't know my real purpose for being in Black Stone Gap. Don't worry—she won't be a problem. She's on our side. In fact, she's the one who gave me the blueprint." Another long pause. "I said not to worry. I'll take care of her."

Lacey backed away from the window. Who was he talking to? And what did he mean *she doesn't know my real purpose?*

She watched as he shut off his phone and turned to enter the kitchen. His expression registered warm pleasure when he spotted her, but then he frowned when he saw her expression. "What's wrong?"

"Who were you talking to?" she asked.

"A former professor of mine from grad school. Why?"

Lacey swallowed hard. "Because I heard you. What did you mean when you said I was on your side, or that I won't be a problem? What's going on, Cole?"

He smiled at her, but Lacey thought it looked a little strained. "Nothing. At least, nothing you need to worry about. Are you hungry? I thought I'd make breakfast."

Lacey waved a dismissive hand. "I'm not hungry. Tell me what you meant when you said I don't know your real purpose for being here. What does that mean? I thought you were an engineer."

"I am," he said simply.

"Then why—?"

He took a deep breath and braced his hands on the counter, before angling his head to look at her. "I'm working undercover for the Department of Labor."

Lacey frowned. "What?"

"They asked me to help," he explained. "And I agreed." He scrubbed a hand over his face, looking frustrated and tired.

Realization dawned. "You're investigating Buck Rogan. You want to shut him down."

Cole raised his hands in self-defense. "That's up to the Bureau of Mine Safety, and only if I find evidence that he's operating in violation of safety laws. Buck Rogan runs a mining operation that borders on illegal. In fact, I'm pretty sure it is illegal."

"Why didn't you tell me?" she asked. "All this time, I've been thinking you were a mining engineer and you're actually some kind of undercover agent?"

Cole's voice grew terse. "I *am* an engineer. I just also happen to be working this investigation. I couldn't tell you the truth without jeopardizing the entire operation. What difference would it have made, anyway?"

Lacey stared at him in disbelief. "You could have told me. I wouldn't have said anything to anyone."

He made a sound of exasperation. "I told you as much as I was able, except for the part about working undercover. That's why they call it undercover work, Lacey, because nobody is supposed to know about it."

"Buck said that you blame him for your friend's death. Is that why you're so determined to expose him? As revenge?"

Cole stared at her for a moment, and a dark flush shadowed his lean jaw. "If you believe that, then you don't know me at all. But for the record, I do blame Buck for Drake's death. But not as much as I blame myself."

Lacey considered everything he had told her. She was shocked to find out that he was working undercover, and although there was a part of her that resented the fact he hadn't told her, she also understood why he hadn't. What he'd said was true; they were on the same side. He wanted to save lives as much as she did.

"Okay," she finally said. "So what's your plan? How are we going to prove he's operating in the closed sections of the mine? Is there any access to those tunnels?"

Cole looked at her in disbelief. "First of all, there is no *we* in this operation. I won't have you involved. It's enough that you took that blueprint. No, you just spend the day with Carr and the boys, and let me figure this out."

"But I can help you," she insisted. "I could tell Buck that I need access to the mines right away, and that I need an engineer to come with me. He's seen the test parameters, and he knows that would be the truth. Once we're in the mine, we can work our way over to where you think the access to the closed section is."

"Absolutely not. Out of the question, so you can just forget it."

"Why? I can help you with this."

"I won't risk you getting hurt," he clipped. "And that's the end of it, Lacey. If you're not hungry, then I'll drive you over to the Rod and Gun Club."

Lacey compressed her lips and nodded. She knew he was right, but that didn't mean she had to like it.

"Lacey—" His cell phone rang, interrupting his sentence. He glanced at it, his face reflecting sudden tension. "I need to take this call, and then we'll talk, okay?"

She watched as he stepped outside, keeping his voice low enough that she couldn't make out his conversation. He returned less than two minutes later, his expression grim.

"That was Buck," he said. "He wants to see me in his office right away."

A frisson of alarm shot through Lacey. Had he discovered the missing blueprint? Or had he discovered that Cole was working with the federal agents?

"I'll come with you," she said quickly. "I'll explain about the blueprint."

To her surprise, Cole stepped forward and caught her face between his hands. "No, I want you to stay here. It may very well be nothing, but whatever it is, I can handle it."

"But Cole—"

"I'm serious." As if to punctuate his words, he pressed a warm, firm kiss against her mouth. "Stay here, fix yourself something to eat, and I'll be back as soon as I can."

THIRTY MINUTES LATER, Lacey was pacing the kitchen when the sound of a car engine in the driveway alerted her. Peeking out the window, she spotted a taxi, and frowned. Then she saw Sam Caldwell, her boss, climb out of the back and speak to the driver.

Alarm shot through her. What in the world was her boss doing here? She strode through the house and pulled open the front door. Sam was just climbing the steps and his face was set in grim lines. When she opened the door, he looked up and his features sagged in relief.

Sam was in his early forties and had started StarPoint Technologies right out of grad school. Lacey had worked for him while she was in college, and had been thrilled when he'd hired her as a full-time member of his development team. He treated her like a favorite kid sister, and now she felt a pang of guilt that she hadn't called him since she'd arrived in Black Stone Gap.

"Sam, what are you doing here?"

"Jesus, Lacey, thank Christ you're okay."

Stepping back, she opened the door wider and gestured for him to come in. "Of course I'm okay. Why wouldn't I be?"

Sam stepped into the living room, his gaze sweeping around the spacious living room in appreciation. But when he turned to Lacey, she could see he was annoyed. With her.

"You've been down here for five days, and I haven't heard from you once. *Not once,* Lacey. You literally vanished into the wilds of Kentucky with a piece of equipment valued at more than two million dollars, and you ask me why I look upset? *Jesus!*"

Lacey's mouth fell open. Had she really not contacted him since she'd arrived in Kentucky? Her mind flew back over the past several days, and she realized he was right. She'd turned her phone off in order to avoid having to talk with her mother. "I spoke with Julia," she said lamely.

Sam thrust a hand through his hair, making it stick up wildly. "Once. You talked to her once. How do you think

I felt when I called the motel and discovered that you'd checked in, but that you left with a man that first night and hadn't been seen again since? Hmm?"

Lacey felt her face go hot with embarrassment. "My car broke down, and then I met this guy—"

To her astonishment, he grasped her by the upper arms and shook her lightly. "I was ready to call that search-and-rescue team to go look for you! Your mother is frantic, Lacey. She's been calling me incessantly and I couldn't even tell her with any certainty that you were okay. I finally reached Sheriff Hathaway, and he told me he hasn't even met you yet. Do you know what went through my head?"

Lacey shook him free. "Okay, I get it. I'm sorry if I worried you. I should have called, but everything is fine, Sam. You had nothing to worry about."

"I realize that now. I tracked down Carr Hamilton this morning, and he told me that you did a fantastic job demonstrating the handheld GPS units."

Lacey glanced at her watch. It was barely eight-thirty. "You've already seen Carr? When did you get here?"

"Last night. I'm actually staying at the Blackwater Inn, probably in the same room you were originally checked into." Finally, he gave her a crooked smile. "I don't blame you for leaving—that place is a dump."

Sensing that forgiveness was within her reach, Lacey stepped toward him and gave him a brief, hard hug. "I'm so sorry, Sam. I should have called. I turned my phone off because my mother wouldn't stop calling me."

Sam laughed and stepped back. "Trust me, I understand." He looked questioningly around the room. "So where is this guy you've hooked up with? Carr assured me he's decent, and that you were never in any danger. I already knew that, but I'd like to meet him for myself."

"Cole isn't here. He's actually over at the Black River Mines, talking with the owner. But he should be back soon." She paused. "Wait. What do you mean, *you already knew that?*"

Sam sighed. "Cole MacKinnon called me the other day and expressed his concern about testing STAR in the Black River Mines. He thinks they're dangerous, and after talking with him, I'm inclined to agree. I want you to pack up your gear and come home with me."

What? Lacey stared at him, dumbfounded. "Cole actually called you?"

"He did, yesterday. He thought I should know that the Black River Mines are part of a federal investigation, and that he considers those tunnels to be a danger."

"I don't believe this," Lacey murmured in disbelief. It was one thing to ask her to conduct her testing elsewhere, but why did he have to call her boss? "I haven't even begun to field-test STAR. We can't leave yet, Sam. Even if the Black River Mines are off-limits, Cole is going to bring me to one of the mines in West Virginia tomorrow."

Sam shook his head. "That's not necessary. We'll do the testing in New Hampshire, in the caves near Plymouth."

"The Polar Caves?" she asked in disbelief. "Sam, they're not deep enough. They won't give you an accurate reading. I thought we agreed that the coal mines would be perfect."

Sam's face grew serious. "That was before I knew about the accident rate in these mines. Cole is right—it's too risky." He glanced at his watch. "I'll give you ten minutes to grab your things."

As Lacey packed her belongings, her mind worked furiously. Because of Cole, her first field test was a failure. More than that, he'd made her look incompetent. As if she couldn't be trusted to do anything on her own. She still couldn't believe he'd had the audacity to call her boss!

In the next instant, she sat down on the edge of the bed, acknowledging that Cole hadn't made her look incompetent; she'd done that all on her own. She should have maintained communication with her office while she'd been here. But she'd been so determined to do this on her own that she hadn't considered how it would look when she didn't call in each day. The fact that Sam had flown all the way here to make sure she was okay was mortifying. And now he wanted her to return to New England with him, and she couldn't very well refuse.

She sat on the bed for several long moments, trying to control the tight, panicky feeling in her chest at the thought of leaving Cole. It was the same way she felt when she found herself alone in the dark. As if she might suffocate. As if she, too, might die alone in the utter blackness. With effort, she picked up her suitcase and her overnight bag and made her way downstairs to where Sam waited.

"All set?" Sam asked, as she entered the living room.

Lacey nodded. "Yes, I just need to get STAR. Sam, do you think we could stop by the mine before we head out? I don't want to leave without saying goodbye to Cole. He wouldn't understand."

Before Sam could respond, there was the sound of tires crunching on the gravel driveway outside. Lacey looked out the window to see Cole's truck skid to a stop behind the taxicab. He wrenched open the door and jumped out, leaving Copper in the cab. He cast a quick glance at the taxi before he took the steps two at a time. The door burst open and he was there, filling up the space with his energy.

Lacey's glance flew guiltily to her suitcase and presentation cases, lined up neatly by the door. She braced herself.

"Cole—" Whatever words she had been about to say died on her lips as she took in his tight expression.

"Lacey, I'll explain on the way. Grab that thing you call STUD or STAR, or whatever it is. I think you're finally going to get your chance to field-test it."

"What are you talking about?"

She was forced to step back as he shouldered his way into the living room. "I put it in the back closet." He stopped when he saw Sam standing in the middle of the room. Then he looked at her gear lined up neatly beside the door, and went completely still. When he finally turned around to face her, Lacey caught her breath at his expression.

"What's going on?" His voice was dangerously soft.

"Cole, I want you to meet Sam Caldwell, the owner and founder of StarPoint Technologies. My boss."

Sam extended his hand, and Cole shook it. "We talked the other day on the phone," Sam said. "I appreciate your confiding in me about the conditions of the mine. I wouldn't want to jeopardize her safety."

Cole nodded, and then turned to Lacey. Seeing her expression, he gave an apologetic shrug. "I did what I thought was right. You're strong-willed and quite frankly, I wasn't sure I'd be able to say no to you if you insisted on going into the Black River Mines."

"So you called my boss."

"I did what I thought was right. You did tell me that he had the final say." He gave Sam a resigned look. "I just didn't think he'd come down here to bring you back."

Sam glanced at his watch. "We should get going. If we leave now, we'll just get to the airport in time."

Lacey nodded, unable to believe that this was it; that she would be leaving Kentucky. There was so much she wanted to say, but not in front of Sam. Not like this, with Cole looking distracted and off balance. She recalled again how he had looked when he first came through the door, as if he was on a mission.

"What did you mean when you said I was going to get a chance to field-test STAR?" she asked. "Did something happen?"

"It doesn't matter." He gestured toward her bags. "You need to go if you're going to catch your flight."

"Just tell me what's going on, Cole."

He hesitated, then blew out a hard breath. "Three boys went into an abandoned mine. They triggered a cave-in and now they're trapped."

Lacey felt the blood drain from her face. "When did this happen? Are they alive? Can you get them out?"

Cole shook his head. "I don't know. It happened about an hour ago and we believe they're still alive. Look, I should get back." He extended his hand toward Sam. "It was good to meet you."

Without looking at Lacey, he turned and strode swiftly out the door. Lacey followed him, unable to believe he was going to just leave when there was so much they needed to say.

"Cole, wait."

He stopped halfway down the steps and turned to face her. His expression was bleak.

"Did you know that Sam was going to come down here? Did you know I'd be leaving this morning?"

He shrugged. "I didn't know for sure, but I had a hunch he would. I told him that I would take you to West Virginia, but he seemed uncomfortable with the idea. He cares a lot about you, Lacey."

"And what about you? Do you care a lot about me?"

He came back up the steps and caught her face in his hands. He searched her eyes. "You know I do. That's why I called Sam in the first place. I am curious, though. Were you going to leave without saying goodbye?"

She covered his hands with her own. "No, I was going to come by the mines to see you. I hate this, Cole. I'm not ready to leave."

"Then don't. Stay here." His eyes burned into hers.

"I can't. Not after Sam came all this way to get me."

"He came to make sure you're okay, and to protect his investment," Cole said drily. "Tell him you want to take some time off. He'll understand. Stay a little longer."

The words hung in the air between them, and it took all of Lacey's control not to break down and throw herself at him and tell him that of course she would stay. She stared at him, then let her gaze drift beyond him to the rolling mountains that extended for as far as the eye could see. She loved the rugged beauty of the land and the simplicity of life here. She hadn't expected to love the area—or Cole.

She took a step back, acutely conscious of Sam watching them from inside the open door. "I can't. Now's not the right time. I need to go back to New England and perform the field test for STAR."

Cole considered her for a moment, and then looked past her to Sam. He sighed deeply. "Okay. I understand. Look, I need to get back to the mines. I came here to bring you and the prototype to the rescue site. If you're leaving, then I guess using it is out of the question. I'd better get back and help the team. They'll need to figure out where those boys are by using more conventional methods."

"Like what?"

Cole smiled humorlessly. "A good old-fashioned wild-assed guess."

Lacey's eyes widened. "Are you—?"

"Going in? You bet."

"But you said you'd never do another mine rescue," she protested, knowing it was hypocritical for her to care, when even now Sam waited to take her to the airport. But she couldn't think about Cole going into the mine without her heart clenching in terror.

"I'll be fine. You'd better get going."

Lacey drew in a deep breath and ignored the sharp pain that caused her chest to constrict. "I'll call you when I get to Boston. To find out how the rescue went."

"Just tune in to your local news channel. Once you get back to Boston, that is. I'm sure every major network will be carrying the story."

"You think it will take as long as that?" Lacey frowned.

"Rogan's Run No. 5 mine has been abandoned for about fifty years. It'll take most of the day just to pinpoint where the boys are and then determine the best extraction method."

"Of course." Lacey didn't know what else to say. She knew what was involved in a mine rescue, and how quickly it could all go terribly wrong. There was no way she wanted to witness any of that.

"Well, I guess this is it, then," Cole said grimly, watching her.

Lacey blinked furiously, and looked away from him. "Yes. I guess so."

He gripped her by the upper arms. The fierceness of his gaze penetrated her, making her feel as if he could see all the way to her soul. "Take care of yourself."

He pressed a hard kiss against her mouth. Without another word, he turned and strode to his truck. He didn't look at her as he turned the ignition and thrust the vehicle into gear.

Lacey watched with blurred vision until his taillights disappeared down the wooded road. Then she swiped her eyes and turned determinedly away.

13

LACEY SAT IN the back of the blue taxi and watched Black Stone Gap rush past. There was the diner where she'd broken down that first night when Cole had come to her rescue. Her hand tightened on the purse she held on her lap.

"Everything will work out," Sam said quietly beside her. "You'll see. Things happen for a reason."

She nodded. "I know."

"We'll find another test site for STAR."

Lacey suppressed a small laugh. She thought he'd been referring to herself and Cole. Of course he'd been talking about STAR. While Sam might genuinely care for her, his first concern was for his investment.

"You sure you don't want to test STAR right now? The entire community is scrambling to rescue three boys who are trapped in an abandoned mine."

Sam's expression was grim. "I can understand why you want to bring STAR to the rescue site, but the prototype is untried. What if it fails?" He sighed deeply. "I wouldn't want to give anyone false hope."

Lacey stared at him. "But what if it operates exactly the way we designed it to? What if we're able to pinpoint the boys' location and help the rescue team? This is why we developed STAR." She hesitated, her mind working rapidly. "You said that things happen for a reason. What if the reason we're here is because this community needs us? What if we're here to help with the rescue? Imagine how amazing it would be to have the owner and developer of the unit right on-site."

Sam was quiet for several long moments. "I don't know. Cole indicated the mines—and this one in particular—are dangerous."

"But what if we don't need to go into the mines?" Lacey asked in growing enthusiasm. "I've been thinking about this a lot, since Cole was adamant that I not go into the tunnels. We could equip one of the rescue workers with the remote camera and you and I could control the operations from aboveground. It's what I had intended to do anyway."

Sam looked at her. "That might work."

Something broke free in her chest, and she impulsively hugged him. "It will work, I know it will."

She would see Cole again. He had touched her life and her heart in ways she hadn't thought possible. She couldn't leave without letting him know. She leaned forward to speak to the taxi driver.

"Do you know where Rogan's Run No. 5 is?"

"I guess I do. It's only the entire community of Black Stone Gap that's out there right now, trying to rescue those boys. We can be there in about twenty minutes."

Lacey smiled. "Think you can make it in ten?"

The driver grinned. "No problem."

THEY TURNED OFF the main road onto what looked like a logging road. It wound steeply upward into the trees, and the land on either side was roped off with barbed wire and strung with signs that read Private. No Trespassing.

The road ended at a derelict mining facility. A gravel lot butted up against a wall of shale and rock, and punched into the center was the portal to the mine itself. It looked like a gaping black mouth. Lacey could see it had once been sealed off with timbers, which now lay in a dusty heap next to the entrance. A rusted sign with the words *Danger! Stay Out!*, hung askew from one of the discarded boards.

The taxi driver hadn't exaggerated about the entire community being present for the rescue attempt. It seemed there were fifty or more cars and trucks in the weed-choked lot, and dozens of residents milled around outside the entrance to the mine, which had been cordoned off with yellow tape. Two police officers stood on the other side of the tape and kept people from entering the mine itself. Beyond the small crowd, Lacey counted three police cruisers, a fire truck, and two ambulances parked alongside the other cars. She strained unsuccessfully for a glimpse of Cole's pickup truck.

At the entrance to the parking area, they were stopped by a police officer wearing a khaki-and-green uniform. He leaned down to peer in at them. He was an older man, with a seamed face and a graying mustache, but his eyes were shrewd.

"Morning, Tara," he said to the driver, and his gaze swept past her to where Lacey leaned forward in the backseat, desperately searching the crowd for any sign of Cole. "I'm guessing you're here to lend a hand. Right now, there's not much you can do, but they're organizing food and whatnot for the rescue team down at the church. I'm sure they could use an extra hand."

"Actually, Sheriff, we're here to assist with the rescue." Sam leaned forward and extended his hand through the window. "I'm Sam Caldwell from StarPoint Technologies, and this is my lead engineer, Lacey Delaney."

The sheriff turned a sharp eye on Lacey, and a slow smile

transformed his grizzled features. "So you're the gal that Carr and the boys have been telling me about." He thrust a broad, blunt-fingered hand in through the window to Sam, and then Lacey. "I'm Cyrus Hathaway. I'm sorry I wasn't here when you arrived, but I guess you heard about what happened to my wife."

Lacey took his leathery hand in her own. "Yes, I did. I hope she's doing better."

"She'll be home in a week or so. I hope Cole's been taking real good care of you."

Lacey couldn't be certain, but she thought she detected a glimmer of amusement in his eyes. She blushed and released his hand. "Yes, sir, he has. Actually, I need to see Cole. I have a prototype GPS unit with me that I think he'll be able to use in the rescue."

"Oh, yes. Cole told me a little about it. Let's see if it lives up to its potential." He indicated a parking spot near the entrance to the mine. "Tara, drop them off over there. I'll radio Harlan and have him come out to meet them."

"Thank you, Sheriff Hathaway." So it wouldn't be Cole who met her. Lacey pushed down her disappointment. Tara pulled up near the entrance to the mine, and got out to open the trunk for her.

Sam hefted STAR out of the trunk. "Let's hope we're doing the right thing," he said quietly.

"I know we are."

"Ma'am?"

Lacey turned and saw Harlan striding toward them. He wore a hard hat, and his rawboned face was streaked with coal dust. He carried two extra hard hats and safety goggles for her and Sam.

She quickly made introductions. "Where is Cole?"

"I'll bring you over to where the command center has been set up," Harlan replied.

Lacey glanced quickly toward the small crowd of people who were gathered behind the tape. Some of the women were weeping, causing Lacey to wonder if they were the boys' mothers. She had little idea what had happened beyond what Cole had told her, but fervently hoped she could help.

"Here we go," she murmured to Sam as they followed Harlan.

"Is Cole at the command center?" she asked.

"He's already gone in."

"In? As in, *into the mine?*" She hurried after Harlan as he skirted the crowd of people and the rescue vehicles and strode toward a dilapidated building made of concrete and steel that was almost falling down from neglect.

"That mine is a maze of tunnels, and the kid that escaped the cave-in couldn't remember which ones they'd explored. Cole's the best tracker we've got. Besides, he has Carr and the other guys with him. They'll track the boys to where the cave-in occurred, and then we'll figure out how to get 'em out."

Lacey stopped in her tracks as a wave of fear washed over her, making her dizzy. Cole was in those mines. Her imagination conjured up images of dark, twisting tunnels with unstable walls and roofs that might fall and crush him to death without warning.

Sam paused beside her, watching her through concerned eyes.

"Hey." Harlan's voice cut through her lurid imaginings. "Don't you worry about Cole. He knows the dangers and he'll be careful. C'mon."

He thrust the steel door of the building open. Inside, at least a dozen men were closely studying a series of maps that were spread across the surface of a long table, crudely constructed out of wooden sawhorses and sheets of plywood. Cole's dog, Copper, lay under one of the tables, but surged to his feet when he saw Lacey, his tail wagging furiously. Lacey bent to pet him, and then stood up to survey her surroundings. More maps were tacked onto the nearby wall. As they approached, Lacey could see they were topographical maps and a series of blueprints of what might have been the mines.

They looked up as she and Harlan approached. "This is Lacey Delaney and Sam Caldwell," Harlan said in an expressionless tone. "They brought the GPS unit Cole was talking about."

One of the men detached himself from the group and approached Lacey. She recognized him as the man who had interrupted her meeting with Buck on the day she had stolen the blueprint.

"I'm Wendall Riggs. I'm a foreman in the Black River Mines." He gestured to the men behind him. "We all have experience with mine rescues. Cole said he thought you might be able to help us pinpoint where the boys are."

Lacey forced herself to shift gears, to drag her thoughts away from Cole and the danger he might be in, and concentrate instead on how to help him. She indicated the case that Sam still carried. "This is STAR, our Subterranean Advanced Receiver unit. It can pick up and transmit signals through hundreds of feet of rock."

The men continued to stare at her. Finally, one of them gave a snort of disgust. "How's that going to help us?"

Aware of Sam watching her, Lacey grabbed the case out of his hand and hefted it up onto the table. She snapped open the locks and carefully opened the case, gratified when the men gathered for a closer look. She could almost feel their awe at the display of high-tech equipment inside.

She freed a series of metal poles from where they were secured inside the case and swiftly snapped them together until the entire unit stood about seven feet high. Then she attached a small satellite receiver dish to the top. A GPS unit, not unlike the handheld ones she had supplied to the rescue team, snapped onto the pole.

She carefully removed a small black box from where it was secured inside the case, and slipped it into what looked like a tiny harness. She flipped a switch on the back of it and gestured for Harlan to come closer.

"This is the transmitter," she said briskly. "It has a small camera and sound recorder built into it. I can attach it to Harlan's hard hat, or hang it around his neck, like so."

Harlan obediently bent down so she could slip it over his head. A small red light blinked steadily above a tiny lens on the front of the unit.

"This," she continued, indicating the metal case, "is the control center." Built into the case was a small computer monitor and a sturdy headset. She flipped the power on, and a series of lights flashed alongside the monitor. "If I bring my receiver unit outside so that it can relay with the satellite—" Lacey indicated the pole with the satellite dish "—the transmitter will begin sending signals, which are then displayed on the GPS unit, providing the operator with the precise location of the transmitter, including distance from the earth's surface."

Lacey glanced at the faces around her. They were mesmerized. "If Harlan were to wear the transmitter and go into the mines, Sam and I could sit up here and it'd be just like we were with him. By watching this monitor, and wearing these headphones, we can see and hear everything he sees and hears. Additionally, I can track his precise location on the GPS display. Once he reaches the site of the cave-in, I can tell you the precise location. Then you can make the decision about how best to reach that location to get the boys out."

"Christ," breathed Wendall, "it's exactly what we need." He turned to the other men. "Walt and Ed, take Miss Delaney and Mr. Caldwell outside and help them get the equipment set up. Harlan, can you and Poke catch up with Cole and the rest of the team?"

"Of course." His expression didn't change as he drew the transmitter over his head. "I think we should mount the transmitter to my hard hat, though. That way, if I need to crawl, or if I encounter pooled water, I'm less likely to damage it."

Lacey tried to squelch the lurid images she had of Cole, trapped in a narrow tunnel as it filled with torrents of water, struggling to escape. It was just her overactive imagination, she knew, but part of her wondered if she had the strength to watch Cole on the monitor as he made his way through the mines. In the next instant, she knew she had no choice.

Outside the entrance to the mine, volunteers were setting up canopies and tables for the food and water being brought in from town. Several reporters had also arrived and were talking to the police and the bystanders about what was happening.

"We'll set you up over here," Harlan said, indicating a table and chair on a patch of grass away from the mine's entrance and away from the distraction of the rescue personnel and townspeople. "I'll have a canopy brought over so you can sit in the shade."

"Thanks." Lacey set up the receiver and the satellite dish, and hooked everything to the central monitor. Copper flopped down at her feet and put his head on his paws. Sam watched, but let her control the process. It took her several more minutes to key in her location, but she was rewarded when an image of herself seated at the table popped up on the monitor.

"Hey, that's pretty neat," Harlan enthused, bending closer. Immediately, her image filled the small screen and became distorted.

Lacey laughed in spite of herself, and glanced up at the small unit that had been fastened to his helmet, directly beside the headlamp. "I guess the transmitter is working. Here, don't stand so close." She waved Harlan back from where she was sitting, and the image on the monitor shifted into focus again. "Okay, let's just run a few preliminary tests to ensure the unit is working, and then we can get started."

Ten minutes later, when Lacey had verified the equipment was in working order, she turned to Harlan. "We're all set. The battery in your unit is good for twenty-four hours. After that, I'll still be able to track your location on the GPS receiver, but I won't be able to pick up images or recordings."

"Okay. Can I hear you if you want to talk with me?"

Lacey shook her head. "No. It was never designed to be a two-way communication system."

"I'll make a note," Sam said. "Lacey, I want you to start working on that as soon as we get back."

Lacey nodded. She wouldn't tell Sam that she wasn't going back to Boston. She'd made a decision in the past hour. If Cole wanted her to stay, then she would.

"Harlan, wait."

Harlan turned back to her.

"When you find Cole, tell him...tell him I'm not going anywhere. And tell him to be careful."

She was aware of Sam's arched eyebrows, but Harlan grinned then, revealing a row of strong, white teeth. Lacey couldn't recall him ever smiling before, and for a moment she was taken aback at the way it completely transformed his stern features. "Don't you worry, ma'am. We'll bring those boys—and your man—out of there safely."

He spoke with such easy confidence that Lacey almost believed he could do it. She watched as Poke joined him. Their leather belts were saddled with canisters of water and oxygen, and they each carried a small bag of tools on their hip. Together they disappeared into the black maw of the mine's entrance.

14

SAM PULLED A chair up next to Lacey as she sat down at the table and placed the headphones over her ears. She watched the monitor as the small camera on Harlan's hat adjusted to the darkness of the mine, and the image slowly came into focus. Despite sitting outside in the sunshine, with a warm breeze buffeting her skin, she felt chilled by the utter blackness that surrounded the men.

She watched, enthralled, as they filed into a steel-walled elevator. "Ms. Delaney, if you can hear me, this is what we call 'the cage.'" Harlan's voice sounded hollow and disembodied over the speakers. Through the tiny camera mounted on Harlan's hard hat, Lacey watched as Poke clutched the hand chains over his head. The picture on the monitor lurched sideways as the cage began to descend.

"Seems like the power was never shut off in these mines, but it's anyone's guess as to what kind of condition the equipment is in." Harlan tipped his head down and on the small television screen, Lacey looked past the toes of his worn boots to the grated floor he was standing on. Even on the monitor, the black abyss they were descending into made her feel slightly ill. The fact that the picture was in black-and-white only added to the creepiness of the scene.

She glanced at the GPS, noting their rapid rate of descent. Two minutes later, when the cage came to a grinding halt, they had descended nearly five hundred feet beneath the earth's surface.

"How's it going?"

Lacey looked up into Sheriff Hathaway's face. She quickly removed her headphones. "They just reached the bottom of the shaft. Harlan is going to meet up with Cole and the rescue team, and we should be able to see everything they see from up here." She indicated the monitor, which showed Poke exiting the cage, and then Harlan's hand as he closed the grated door of the elevator behind them.

"Well, I'll be damned," the sheriff muttered. "The miracles of modern technology never cease to amaze me." He tapped a finger against the monitor. "You'll be able to watch them the entire time?"

"Well, provided the camera isn't damaged or the batteries don't die."

As Harlan made a complete sweep of the area they stood in, Lacey could see the two men had come out of the cage into a cathedral of chiseled rock. The walls and high ceilings glowed eerily white in the darkness.

"What is that?" Lacey murmured.

"They coat the walls with fire-retardant limestone powder," Sheriff Hathaway answered. He dragged a chair over to the table and sat down, his eyes glued to the monitor.

Lacey could see ancient, truck-sized power generators covered in dust. Rail-car tracks disappeared into dark portals, and a dizzying network of tunnels twisted outward from where they stood.

She put the headphones back on, wishing she could communicate with Harlan. They had already determined that the ancient telephone system installed in the mines was no longer operational.

"See this mark on the wall?" Harlan's headlamp swept over the entrance to one of the tunnels. "That was put there by the rescue team to indicate which way they went. We'll be able to move fast by following these signs."

Lacey peered at the encircled arrow that had been drawn on the wall. But despite Harlan's predictions that it wouldn't take long to catch up with Cole, she spent nearly two hours watching Poke's back as he negotiated the maze of intersecting tunnels, before he gave a whooping shout.

"Ms. Delaney, if you can still hear me, we've found the rest of the team."

Lacey leaned forward, only vaguely aware of the small crowd of people who had gathered around her equipment and watched with equal fascination. In the distance, barely visible on the monitor, she could see a series of bobbing lights. As Harlan drew closer, she realized they were the headlamps of the rescue team.

"Hey, Carr! That you?" Harlan's voice echoed eerily through the headphones as he shouted down the length of the tunnel. "It's Harlan and Poke and Ms. Delaney!"

Lacey heard the amusement in Harlan's voice as he called out to the others, and she smiled. Then there was Cole, sprinting out of the darkness of the tunnel into the light of Harlan's headlamp, his eyes searching the darkness beyond the two men.

Lacey's heart constricted and she felt weak with relief. He was safe. His face was so close to Harlan's that she could see the coal dust streaking his lean features, see the brilliance of his eyes as he glared at the other man.

"Goddammit, I told her not to come into these mines." He looked furious. "Where the hell is she? I swear, if you left her back there—"

"Easy, man. She's right here." Lacey saw Harlan's hand as he reached up and tapped the small transmitter. "She's safe aboveground, watching and listening to every dumb-ass thing you do and say." Harlan laughed aloud as Cole narrowed his eyes, and then looked directly into the camera.

Directly at her.

Lacey's breath caught. She couldn't help herself. She reached out and traced his image with her fingertips, uncaring of who watched. "Tell him what I said," she whispered urgently.

"She said to tell you she wasn't going anywhere," Harlan added, as if he could hear her talking to him. "Oh, yeah, and to be careful."

Right then, as she watched, Cole's face twisted and he swiftly looked away for a moment. When he finally turned back to the camera, he was smiling, but Lacey could have sworn there was a suspicious sheen to his eyes.

"Sweetheart," he said, "I know we have a lot to work out, but we'll get there. I'm going to help get these boys back home, and then you and I are going to figure this thing out, okay?"

Lacey pressed a hand against her mouth to prevent a small sob from escaping, but she couldn't stop the swift flow of tears that his words caused.

"Oh, Christ, this is embarrassing," she heard Harlan mutter. "Very touching, of course, but completely embarrassing."

Lacey gave a snort of laughter, even as she swiped at her damp cheeks, her gaze clinging to Cole's.

Beside her, Sheriff Hathaway chuckled. "He's a good boy, that MacKinnon. Like his daddy. Recognized true love as soon as it looked him in the eye, I guess."

Lacey nodded, sniffling. "Thank goodness he recognized it. I was too blinded by my own prejudices."

"Well, we all got our faults, I suppose. I just wonder how your boss feels about the fact that you're not going back."

He shot her a sharply questioning look. "You *are* staying, aren't you?"

She nodded mutely, still watching the monitor.

Sam gave an exaggerated sigh. "Damn it. I guess I'm going to have start looking for a new design engineer." But he was smiling, and Lacey knew he approved.

"Okay. Lacey, darlin', I'll see you on top." Cole grinned at her in the camera, and then turned away.

Harlan and Poke followed him along the tunnel to where the rest of the rescue team were standing at the intersection of a bisecting tunnel, staring at something. Lacey tensed.

Harlan's headlamp swept into the adjoining tunnel, and Lacey frowned, peering at the image. For a moment, she wasn't certain what she was looking at, then realized the connecting tunnel was illuminated by a series of overhead industrial lights. In the middle of the tunnel was an enormous piece of machinery that even to Lacey's inexperienced eye didn't appear to be a relic from five decades earlier.

"Son of a bitch," she heard Harlan mutter. "You were right, MacKinnon."

"Yep. Looks like somebody has broken through from the Black River Mine No. 6 into Rogan's Run Mine No. 5."

Lacey watched as the rescue team continued to make their way down the tunnel. It was supported along the sides by evenly spaced old timbers. Cole looked at the ceiling, and when Harlan tipped his own head back, she could see a series of bolts embedded in the overhead rock.

"No question about it," Cole said grimly. "Somebody is mining where they have no business mining. These tunnels have been closed for fifty years, but here I see ceiling bolts that look brand-new. Although——" he took several more steps, still staring upward "——it appears he's cut corners here. Even if this mine were in any condition to be worked—which it's not—I count one roof bolt for an area that should have a minimum of three." He angled his gaze at the camera, looking directly at Lacey. His expression was somber. "I'll give you one guess as to who it could be."

Lacey risked a peek at Sheriff Hathaway, whose own expression was darkening with each passing minute as he peered over Lacey's shoulder at the monitor.

He yanked out his radio and pressed the button. "I want Buck Rogan up here just as soon as you can find him. He has some answering to do. And tell Wendall Riggs to get his ass out here." He glanced down at Lacey. "This ain't going to be pretty. MacKinnon suspected this was going on, he just couldn't prove it."

Lacey recalled her own doubtful reaction to Cole's suspicions. She saw Wendall Riggs approach them, and from the expression of weary resignation on his face, she knew Cole was right. Wendall was one of the foremen in the Black River Mines. If anyone knew anything about Buck's illegal mining practices, it would be him.

Sheriff Hathaway gave a long-suffering sigh and pushed himself to his feet. He laid a friendly hand on Lacey's shoulder. "You keep up the good work, and let me know as soon as they find those boys. I got to take care of some unpleasant business."

Lacey watched him go, and then turned back to the monitor, adjusting the volume upward in order not to overhear the sheriff's conversation with Riggs.

"Hey, Ms. Delaney." Harlan's voice was sharp. "We found something up ahead. Looks like a rockfall."

Lacey's heart hitched as Harlan approached what looked to be a dead end. As he got closer, however, she saw it was actually a jumbled pile of rock and debris that effectively sealed off the tunnel and prevented them from going any farther.

"Okay, I think we've found our cave-in."

Lacey tore the headphones off and shouted to Sheriff Hathaway. She was immediately surrounded by a dozen or more people, all of them clamoring for a view of the monitor and demanding to know the precise location of the cave-in. She checked their position on the GPS unit, and swiftly gave the coordinates to Sheriff Hathaway. "If the boys are, in fact, on the other side of that cave-in, they're about 550 feet below the surface."

"Okay, let's see what Carr's team wants to do," the sheriff said, gesturing for silence.

Lacey sat down again and replaced the headphones, wishing fervently that the system was equipped with a two-way speaker.

"Okay, folks," Carr said, "we'll need to drag some timbers over here to shore up the roof, but I think we can get to the boys from this side." Carr was examining the rockfall and the roof above it with a critical eye. "It doesn't look like a major fall—more debris than anything else. I don't see any slabs that've come down. We should be able to get through."

Lacey repeated what Carr had said to the people who were crowded around her chair, and a jubilant cheer went up.

"I want five more men in that mine helping move that rock," shouted Sheriff Hathaway. "I want three stretchers and four paramedics down there with them."

He hadn't even finished talking before men were scrambling to obey. If she'd been impressed with the speed and efficiency of the search-and-rescue team, Lacey was equally impressed by the determination and fearlessness exhibited by these people as they hastened to help.

On the monitor, she watched as the rescue team in the tunnel shored up the exposed portions of the roof, and began methodically removing the rock and debris that blocked the tunnel. It was backbreaking work and the process was agonizingly slow. Sheriff Hathaway sat beside her as she watched the monitor, occasionally stepping away to update the townspeople and the increasing number of reporters on the progress they were making.

Two hours later, Lacey was beginning to wonder if the rockfall might not be more extensive than they originally realized. The team continued to work tirelessly to remove the debris, but even she could see they were beginning to flag.

She was massaging her aching eyes when a loud cheer came through the headphones. Lacey's eyes snapped open and she stared at the monitor, expecting to see they had finally broken through the barrier. Instead, she realized that the reinforcements sent in by Sheriff Hathaway had succeeded in reaching the first teams.

Lacey sighed in relief, and turned to announce the news to those gathered nearby. They smiled and embraced each other, cautiously optimistic. During the past several hours, the townspeople had moved away from the entrance of the mine and had instead congregated around Lacey and Sam, taking turns peering over their shoulders at the small screen. Sympathizing with their hunger for news, Lacey kept up a steady narrative of what was happening down in those dark depths. Now, with nearly a dozen additional men, Carr and his crew set back to work with renewed vigor.

"Lacey, we're through," called Harlan.

At first, Lacey didn't understand. They were through? As in done? But when she peered at the activity on the monitor, she realized they had actually succeeded in breaking through the obstruction.

"They're through!" she cried. Hardly aware of her actions, she leaped to her feet and snatched the headphones off. Wheeling around, she grabbed the portly sheriff in an exuberant hug. "They're through!"

Sheriff Hathaway grinned, and then gently disentangled himself from her arms. "That's fine news. Now let's see if the boys are okay."

Replacing the headphones, Lacey watched as a small opening appeared at the top of the rockfall. Carr and Skeeter worked to enlarge the hole until finally it was wide enough for Carr to poke his head and shoulders through.

"I can see two boys," he called back to the rescue team. "They're not moving."

Lacey bit her lip, and looked over at the sheriff.

"Well, what is it?"

"They can see two of the boys," she said quietly, "but they're not moving."

He leaned back in his chair and blew out a breath. "Okay. They could be knocked out from the rockfall, or unconscious as a result of the air quality. Not much oxygen down there. Guess we'll have to wait and see."

"Do you want to tell the others?"

The sheriff sighed. "Guess I better get them prepared." He heaved himself to his feet, and Lacey watched, her heart in her throat, as he slowly gathered the family members away from the rest of the crowd.

"Ms. Delaney." Harlan's voice echoed through the headphones. "Carr and Cole and the medics are going in to check on the boys. I'll go in so you can see for yourself what's happening."

Mesmerized, Lacey watched as Carr wormed his way into the small hole until only his lower legs and boots were visible. Then he was gone.

Cole and Skeeter carefully picked their way up the incline of loose rubble until they reached the small opening near the top. Cole glanced back at Harlan, and before he vanished through the small opening, he looked directly into the camera and winked. Two of the four paramedics went next, but the hole wasn't large enough to permit the stretchers to go through.

"Okay, we'll have to work on opening this up a little more," Harlan said. He directed his gaze back toward the rockfall, and on the monitor, Lacey saw Cole poke his head back through.

"We found all three boys, and they're all alive," he called down to Harlan. "One of them is trapped beneath the rock, and the other two are injured, but if we can get them out quickly, I think they'll pull through."

Lacey tore the headphones off and leaped up. "They found them and they're all alive!"

She found herself grabbed in an enormous bear hug as those nearby simultaneously cheered and cried. Lacey didn't know the woman embracing her, but she hugged her back with equal enthusiasm.

When she was finally freed, she turned back to the monitor and put the headphones on, unable to contain her foolish grin. They had done it. They had found the boys. Even Sam was being embraced by complete strangers, and he looked as happy as Lacey felt. *Now, please, God, let them all come out quickly and safely.* She wanted Cole back aboveground; wanted to touch him and reassure herself of his safety. But more than anything, she wanted to tell him she had been wrong in thinking she could walk away from him. She knew now she didn't want to live without him.

As if to mock her silent prayer, she heard Harlan swear.

"Goddamn it, MacKinnon! Let's move! It's coming down!"

He turned his head, and Lacey saw the timber posts along the side of the tunnel begin to bow under the tremendous burden of earth. At the same time, she became aware of an odd noise, like a deep groaning. In dismay, she realized it was the walls of the tunnel beginning to creak and pop.

"Oh, my God," she breathed. "The mine is collapsing."

She was hardly aware of the press of people around her as they stared in horrified fascination at the small screen, or that she was gripping Sam's hand so tightly that her knuckles were white. When Harlan tilted his head back and looked up, Lacey saw the steel roofing bolts begin to snap and shoot to the floor with a metallic *ping*. The groaning noise was louder now, and Harlan was shouting at the other men, telling them to run.

"Get out! Get out!" Lacey was only distantly aware of somebody yelling to the team, and then realized it was her.

Harlan started to run toward the pile of rubble and the opening where Cole and the boys were, but then the camera angle altered sharply, as if he had abruptly changed direction, or somebody had grabbed him and spun him around.

She caught a glimpse of the other rescue workers fleeing back down the tunnel. There was a tremendous roaring noise, like a locomotive, and a swift blur of movement on the monitor.

Before Lacey's horrified eyes, the small screen went black, and the headphones grew silent.

15

Rocks rained down on him. Choking dust filled his nostrils and mouth. The pitch-black cave was filled with suffocating silt, but at least the terrible roaring noise of the cave-in had subsided. Dust filled his lungs. He coughed, spat and coughed again.

Beneath him, the boy whose body he protected with his own shifted and groaned. Cautiously, Cole lifted his head. Swirling clouds of dust made visibility nonexistent, but he thought he heard a voice to his left. He'd heard the telltale sounds of the impending collapse and had only precious seconds to warn the others and corral them into the far corner of the small cavern where they'd discovered the boys before the roof had let go.

"You okay, son?" He pushed himself away from the boy, shaking the loose rock and debris from his body. His headlamp was broken, and now he groped in the darkness for the boy, his hands moving swiftly over him, checking for injury.

"I—I'm okay," the boy croaked.

Cole knew the kid had suffered a broken arm and possibly several broken ribs from the previous rockfall, but it seemed this one had at least spared him further injury.

"What's your name?" he asked the boy.

"Devin."

"Okay, Devin, I'm going to leave you here for just a minute while I go and check on your buddies. Can you tell me their names?"

"Jack and Ryan."

Cole patted the child's face. "You'll be fine, okay? You'll still be able to hear me, because we're going to keep on talking. Can you do that?"

"Sure. My arm really hurts."

"I know it does, and you're going to have a real impressive cast once you get out of here." Cole had already moved away from Devin toward the spot where he'd heard the voices. "The girls will love it."

"Ew, gross."

"Not into girls, huh?" Cole groped his way across the rock and rubble that littered the floor, gratified when he touched a denim-clad leg. "That'll change. Who's this?"

"Hey, Cole." It was Skeeter. "I've got one of the boys here with me. He's breathing, but still unconscious from when we found him."

Cole dropped his head and breathed a silent thank-you for their safety. "Okay, what about Carr and the paramedics and the third kid?"

"Dunno."

"I'm over here," called a disembodied voice. "It's Joe Green. I've got the third boy over here."

"I'm coming," Cole called to him.

The dust had begun to subside, and Cole saw Skeeter's headlamp glowing dimly in the darkness. It was as if a thick, black fog had descended over them.

"Hey, Devin, how're you doing over there? Can you still hear me?" Cole called to the first boy.

"Yes, sir."

"Good boy. Stay where you are. I'll be back in a minute."

He patted Skeeter's leg. "Let me borrow your headlamp. I'm going to check out the rockfall and try to locate the others."

They exchanged hard hats, and Cole made his way gingerly over the uneven floor of the cavern. The boys had worked their way through the tunnels until they had come up against a dead end, the result of a previous cave-in. Cole knew that sometimes it took no more than the vibration of a raised voice to cause a rockfall in an area already compromised. In this case, the boys had been lucky that they'd been trapped in a small area between the two cave-ins. They could have been crushed. His headlamp picked out a boot and then a leg, and he realized it was one of the paramedics.

"Joe Green?" he called.

"I'm still here." The voice was close, but it didn't come from the body in front of him.

"I think I found your partner." The man's body was almost completely buried beneath rubble. Working quickly, Cole cleared the debris away and was rewarded when the man rolled to his side and began coughing.

Cole sat back and wiped the sweat from his face. The dust had settled to the point where he could more or less see the entire cavern. Swiftly, he scanned the small chamber, looking for Carr. He could just make out Skeeter and the boy who lay limp in his arms on the far side. Several feet away, Devin had pushed himself to a sitting position and sat huddled, cradling his injured arm.

Joe Green was several feet behind him, still working to free the boy who had been trapped by the first rockfall.

"What's your name, son?" Joe asked.

"Ryan." The boy groaned softly as Joe tried to work his foot free from where it was pinned beneath a slab of shale.

"Where the hell is Carr?" Cole muttered, and then froze. Protruding from the pile of rubble was a man's head, shoulders and arm. He was so completely covered with dust and small rocks that Cole had missed him at first glance. "Skeeter, give me a hand over here."

They scrambled over to where Carr was half-buried under the rocks, finally managing to pull him free. He was unconscious.

"His pulse is thready," Skeeter said. "No telling what kind of internal injuries he might have."

"Okay, let's make him comfortable, and then let's get that boy dug out."

It took them more than an hour before they were able to free Ryan's foot. It was badly broken. They moved him over to join the other two boys. Carr and the injured paramedic lay side by side. Skeeter, Joe and Cole sat with their backs against the cold sable wall, each lost in their own thoughts.

They were all alive, which was a miracle in itself, to Cole's thinking. He fervently hoped Harlan and the rescue team had fared as well on the other side of the rockfall.

"I'm going to see how bad the cave-in was," he told the others, and clambered over to where the opening had been. It didn't take long for him to realize the new rockfall had completely buried the opening to the tunnel. There wasn't the slightest hint of air movement, light or noise where the hole had once been. He had a bad feeling about the fate of Harlan and the others. He didn't believe they could have moved away in time to avoid being crushed beneath the falling torrent of shale and rock. As he surveyed their small cavern, he realized it might very well become a tomb. It could take rescue workers hours, maybe days, to dig through the new rockfall to reach them. He suspected they would run out of oxygen long before then. He thought of Lacey's father, who had died under similar circumstances. The last thing he wanted was for her to endure another tragedy.

"Okay, let's take an inventory of our supplies," he said, picking his way back down into the chamber. "If we're conservative and keep only one headlamp on at a time, and ration our water and oxygen, I think we can make it until a rescue team arrives."

"Can we dig ourselves out?" Skeeter asked.

"I don't think so. We're pretty well buried, and exerting ourselves would only deplete our air and water. I think our best bet is to sit tight and wait for help."

"You don't sound too nervous," observed Joe.

Cole looked at the other men. "I'm not. You see, I happen to know there's a lady up there with a very sophisticated piece of equipment, who can pinpoint our exact location. They'll be down here to pull us out before you know it." He ruffled Devin's hair. "You wait and see. In a few hours, you'll be safe at home."

They fell silent once more.

Hours slipped by, and both Devin and Ryan fell into a fitful sleep. Cole and Skeeter monitored the two injured men and the unconscious boy, and rationed out sips of the water they had with them. The air quality was poor, and Cole knew the sleepiness he felt was a direct result of the dwindling oxygen. Despite what he had said about Lacey and her equipment, inwardly he was scared to death—scared the rescue team he knew was on its way might not reach them in time. He didn't want to think about that; didn't want to think about never seeing Lacey again, of not being able to tell her how much he loved her.

With a deep sigh, he tilted his head back against the wall and closed his eyes. He could see her in his mind's eye, with her ginger hair and luminous eyes, smiling at him. God, he wanted to be with her. He knew she must be terrified, wondering if he was alive or dead. She wasn't as tough as she liked to pretend. She was soft and vulnerable, and completely head over heels in love with him, even if she couldn't admit it.

Which was why he intended to survive.

"Hey, Cole," murmured Skeeter, "you feel that?"

Cole stilled. It was a deep, distant rumble that caused the wall at his back to vibrate.

"Come here, son," he commanded softly, and dragged the nearest boy closer, keeping his eyes on the overhead ceiling. He hunkered over the child, using his body as a shield against this new menace.

A shower of small rocks rained down on them. The vibration increased to a rumble.

"Jesus," Cole whispered, watching the shower of dust and debris continue to fall.

Suddenly, even his headlamp failed to penetrate the thick, choking dust that blossomed around them as overhead the roof exploded inward.

16

DAWN WAS STILL several hours away. The first fingers of light hadn't yet begun to filter over the distant horizon. Lacey could scarcely believe it had been more than forty hours since Cole had first disappeared into the mines. Of course, you'd hardly know it was dark outside with all the floodlights that had been brought to the site.

They had moved the rescue operation to a spot in an open field, directly over the cavern where Cole and the boys were believed to be trapped. Even now, an enormous machine was drilling down through five hundred feet of earth to reach them. If the coordinates on Lacey's equipment were correct, they had penetrated the roof of the cavern more than ten hours ago. Warm air was being pumped through a pipe to keep any survivors comfortable. They were working on enlarging the shaft enough to lift them out.

When they had first broken through to the cavern, they had heard what they believed were the survivors tapping on the pipes. But that had been more than eight hours ago. Sheriff Hathaway had suggested the noise from the drilling might have drowned out attempts at communication. Lacey wanted to believe him, but she couldn't shake the fear that overrode every rational argument presented, and lingered despite the sheriff's assurances. She knew the feeling wouldn't subside until Cole was safe in her arms. Her stomach felt hollow. She was restless with anxiety.

The sheriff had sent an additional dozen men into the mines to determine the extent of this new cave-in, and to determine if Harlan and the others had survived. Bitterly, Lacey wondered how many more men would be sacrificed to the greedy belly of the mines. Even now, law enforcement officials and rescue teams continued to arrive from neighboring communities to help bring the victims out.

"How are you holding up?"

Lacey turned to see Sam and the sheriff standing beside her. The rescue effort was taking its toll on Sam, as well. His face was haggard and his eyes were red-rimmed and weary. She shrugged and tried to smile.

"As well as can be expected, I guess. I just wish—I just wish I knew if he was okay." Her voice broke. She turned swiftly away and pressed her fingers against her eyes, willing herself not to cry. She felt the sheriff's hand, large and comforting, on her shoulder.

"It'll be okay, gal. You're sure about the coordinates for their location, eh?"

Lacey blinked back the tears that threatened to spill, and turned back to the sheriff, smiling. "Yes. It's the only thing I am sure of. I went over those coordinates a dozen times."

"You know if you're wrong..."

"She's not wrong," Sam asserted. "This unit is operating beautifully."

"But if she is..." the sheriff persisted.

"I know. A miscalculation of even a few feet, and we waste precious time by drilling in the wrong spot." She met the sheriff's narrowed gaze. "But I'm not wrong. I trust my equipment, and I trust what I saw in those last seconds before I lost visual contact. Harlan was running away from the

cave-in. Whether he was…killed, or if he just lost his hard
hat, the GPS indicates the transmitter is just outside the spot
where Cole was last seen. I've adjusted the coordinates to
take that into account. I'm certain we've got the right spot."

A thirty-inch-diameter drill had arrived from West Virginia before nightfall to drill a shaft wide enough to drop a
rescue cage down and pull the victims to the surface. Drilling was expected to last at least twelve hours. Lacey didn't
think she could stand the suspense. She'd go crazy.

Her gaze drifted over the people who had gathered to
wait. Sheriff Hathaway and the rest of the rescue team had
thought of everything. Ambulances waited to bring the victims to the nearest hospitals. Several helicopters stood ready
in case the severity of the injuries required the victims to
be air-lifted out. The family members of those who were
trapped or missing had been notified, and although most of
them had gathered at the local school, there were still others
who insisted on remaining at the rescue site. The only person
who was conspicuously absent was Buck Rogan.

Lacey had recognized Cole's siblings, distinctive because
of their blue eyes. Her heart had nearly exploded out of
her chest when she caught her first glimpse of his younger
brother Garrick. She had been just steps away from flying
into his arms before she realized it wasn't Cole. Garrick
had been amused. Apparently it wasn't the first time he had
been mistaken for his older brother. He had introduced her
to his siblings, but Lacey found herself consumed by a sudden shyness. Cole's family had regarded her with cautious
politeness, but Lacey could see they were curious as to her
relationship with their brother.

"You should go back to Cole's place and try to get some
rest," Sam advised her. "I'll be here, and I'll call you if there
are any new developments."

Lacey smiled wanly. "I wouldn't be able to sleep, know-ing he's down there. Thanks, but I'll stay."

She sat down at the table where she had set up STAR. The blank monitor stared dully back at her. She picked up the headphones for what seemed like the hundredth time and put them on, but there was only silence. She checked the GPS display, but the blinking light that indicated the location of the transmitter hadn't moved.

"Please, God," she prayed silently, "let Cole and the oth-ers be okay. Let them all be okay."

She removed the headphones and set them aside, and then laid her head down on her forearms. Behind her, the noise of the enormous drill was deafening. She would close her eyes, just for a moment. Maybe, if she was lucky, she would open them to find it had all been no more than a terrible dream.

"LACEY, GAL, WAKE UP!" A hand shook her shoulder.

Lacey raised her head, feeling bemused and bleary-eyed. Her back and neck were stiff from having slept half-sprawled across the table. Her mouth was cottony and her eyes felt swollen.

"What? What is it?" She pushed the hair back from her face, and looked up at Sheriff Hathaway. It was still dark, but Lacey could see the barest shimmer of red-gold on the distant horizon, heralding the arrival of morning.

"How long did I sleep? Why didn't you wake me? What if Cole needs me?"

"Hush, gal. Harlan and the others just came out of the mine on the elevator."

"What? Harlan? Oh, thank goodness." Lacey ran her hands over her face. "Is he okay?"

"He and the others are a little banged up, but otherwise they're fine. They managed to dodge the cave-in, but Harlan lost his hard-hat. That's what the transmitter was attached to, so that's what we've been tracking on the GPS unit."

"Where are they now? Can I speak to Harlan? Maybe he knows something."

"They've been taken to the hospital for a checkup." He indicated the machinery behind them. An enormous crane was positioned directly over the hole that had been drilled overnight. "But I didn't think you'd want to miss this. They're getting ready to lower the cage to bring the boys up."

Lacey leaped to her feet, but was prevented from sprinting forward by Sheriff Hathaway's strong arm.

"Best stay back here. We'll know soon enough how your young man is."

Lacey searched the crowd that surrounded the area. Sam stood with several of the rescue crew, but as if sensing her scrutiny, he turned and met her gaze. He gave her a subtle thumbs-up. She spotted Cole's family standing together, their attention riveted on the hole. Throngs of rescue workers swarmed across the site. Pulsating beams of red, yellow and blue strobe lights from the nearby emergency vehicles flashed across the faces of the crowd, lending an eeriness to the already tense atmosphere. Her eyes narrowed when she spotted Buck Rogan on the edge of the crowd. He was flanked by two sheriff's deputies.

Then, as she watched in utter fascination, the cage slowly rose out of the hole. A small figure was strapped securely inside, and before the cage had completely cleared the hole, eager hands reached for it and pulled it to safety. The crowd erupted into jubilant cheers. Lacey watched, her heart in her throat, as the first of the injured boys was rushed to a waiting ambulance. His mother clung to his stretcher, her face streaming with grateful tears.

It was another twenty minutes before the next boy was lifted out of the hole, and then the next. Lacey's heart beat hard against her ribs as the fourth trip brought up a man. He was so covered in dust she couldn't determine his identity. She surged forward with the rest of the crowd, and this time the sheriff didn't try to stop her.

It was Carr, barely conscious. Lacey had no opportunity to get near him before he was transferred to a stretcher, and then to a waiting ambulance.

The cage was lowered once more into the shaft.

The two paramedics came out next, then Skeeter. Lacey's throat constricted with happiness as he stepped nimbly out of the cage and waved to the cheering crowd.

The cage descended for the last time. It seemed an eternity passed before the hydraulic winch began raising the cage to the earth's surface. Lacey clutched Sheriff Hathaway's arm in a near death-grip. She could hardly breathe. Her chest felt tight with dread and anticipation. The cage slowly rose into view, and Lacey would have recognized the lean, hard body inside anywhere.

She released the sheriff's arm and moved forward through the crowd, pushing past the throngs of rescue workers and reporters, nearly blinded by the glaring lights that had been set up around the perimeter. The cage opened, and Cole stepped out. He was immediately surrounded by emergency personnel and well-wishers, and for a moment, Lacey lost sight of him.

In the next instant, he pushed free of the surrounding crowd. Lacey saw him search the crowd of people. His face was completely black with coal dust, making the brilliance of his eyes all the more startling. His clothes were torn and filthy. But when he finally found her, he grinned, his teeth white against the blackness of his face.

She saw his lips form her name, and then she was running toward him as the crowd parted. He opened his arms, and she flung herself at him, hardly aware of the cheers of approval that roared around them. She was in Cole's arms, crushed against his hard body as he held her fiercely. She could hear him laughing.

"I love you," she said raggedly, choking on tears of happiness. "I couldn't stand that I didn't tell you, and now you have to know. I love you so much."

"I know, baby, I know." His hands buried themselves in her hair as he tipped her face back, and then his lips claimed hers in a kiss that was both fiercely possessive and heartwrenchingly tender.

"Oh, Cole," she gasped, when he finally lifted his head. "I've been so scared...not knowing if you were okay. Don't ever do that to me again!"

"Sweetheart," he murmured against her lips, "that was nothing compared to the scare I had not knowing if I'd ever see you again."

She stroked a hand along one lean, dusty cheek. "I want to stay here with you. Is your offer still open?"

"Well, I'm going to look like one hell of an idiot if I don't, seeing as how the entire town seems to know that I'm crazy about you." His eyes crinkled in tender amusement. Copper had squirmed his way through the crowd and now he pushed at Cole's legs, demanding his attention. Bending down, Cole gave the dog a hug, and laughed as Copper lapped his face.

Lacey couldn't help it. She began to cry. She thought she'd lost everything, and now it seemed she was being given a second chance. She didn't deserve to be so happy.

"Hey now, don't do that," Cole admonished, and pulled her into his arms.

Lacey laughed through her tears, and pressed the palm of his hand against her cheek. "They're happy tears. I'm happy."

Cole hooked an arm around her shoulders and tucked her against his side. "In a few minutes," he murmured against her temple, as he began to make his way through the crowd to his siblings, "we're going home, and you're going to come into the shower and help me wash this coal dust off, and then I'm going to make you happier still." He slanted a mischievous glance down at her. "Deal?"

Lacey smiled, her heart accelerating at the implicit promise in his voice. "Deal." On the outer perimeter of the crowd, she saw Buck Rogan being led to one of the police cruisers. "What's going to happen to him?"

"There'll be an investigation, and he'll be cited for illegal mining practices and a whole slew of safety violations. They'll close all the Black River mines temporarily until they're up to standards, and then they'll reopen again."

"Will Buck still be the operator?"

"Well, not if I have anything to say about it, but I guess that's up to the Feds. Quite frankly, I just don't care what happens to him."

"Me, either. I have you, and that's all I care about."

She kissed him, uncaring of the cameras and lights and onlookers.

She was home.

Epilogue

One Year Later

COLE PAUSED ON the threshold of the back porch and drank in the scene that greeted him. He wondered if he would ever get used to the fact she was his.

Lacey sat on the swinging bench wearing a nightgown that made her look incredibly sexy. Copper lay contentedly at her feet. She lounged against the cushions and stared up at the stars. As he stepped onto the porch, he kept the package he had for her hidden behind his back.

Lacey looked at him as he walked toward her, and her eyes glowed with pleasure. "There you are." Her eyes narrowed, and she smiled. "What are you hiding?"

Cole grinned and sat down next to her, drawing the package out to lay it gently across her thighs. "I have something for you. An anniversary gift, if you'd like. It's been a year since you first came to Black Stone Gap, and I think the occasion warrants an acknowledgment."

They had traveled from his house in Norfolk to Black Stone Gap just the day before. Since the dramatic deep-mine rescue a year earlier, StarPoint Technologies had been overwhelmed with requests for STAR. With Sam's support,

Lacey had developed a commercial version of the prototype, and equipped it with a two-way communication system. In the end, StarPoint Technologies had opened an office in Norfolk.

She had wanted to work through the summer, but Sam had been adamant that she take at least two weeks of vacation. She and Cole had decided to spend that time in Black Stone Gap. The Black River mines had reopened under new management, and although Buck Rogan hadn't actually served any jail time, he was prohibited from having any involvement in the actual operation of the mines. From now on, he would sit on the board, more a figurehead than anything else.

They had invited Lacey's mother to join them for one of the two weeks but to their surprise, she had declined. It seemed she had met someone through her volunteer work at the hospital, and things were going so well that she didn't want to leave, even for a week.

Now Lacey stared at the pretty package on her lap and her mouth fell open. She turned to Cole with a stricken expression. "I didn't know we were celebrating an anniversary. I didn't get you anything."

Cole laughed gently. "Sweetheart, you've already given me everything I've ever wanted." Leaning forward, he pressed his mouth against hers. It was a slow, restive searching of her lips, and Cole was gratified when she leaned into him and sighed her pleasure.

"Open it," he coaxed.

Lacey pulled back and stared at him. He could see the childish anticipation on her face before she ripped the ribbon free and tore away the bright wrapping.

"Oh...Cole." She lifted the quilt free of the tissue paper and held it up to admire the intricate pattern that had been stitched with such care. "I didn't know...you never said..."

She raised her face to his, and Cole could see her eyes were damp. "It's so beautiful."

Cole kissed her, enjoying her pleasure.

"It's the same quilt from that day we spent at the county fair," she breathed, tracing her fingertips along the stitching. When she looked up at him, her eyes were misty. "You never told me you bought it."

Cole shrugged. "There never seemed to be the right time. But you said the quilt brought back some nice memories of your childhood." He grew serious. "I'm glad that you have some good memories."

Lacey smiled, and shook the quilt open, then covered them both with it as she stretched out and drew Cole down beside her. "I do. I have some very good memories. In fact, I haven't had any nightmares in months. I'm looking forward to sleeping under this quilt every night."

"Speaking of which, it's pretty dark out here tonight. Do you want me to turn on the porch light?"

"No." Lacey slid her arms around his neck and nuzzled him. "I enjoy the dark, especially when you're kissing me."

With a soft groan, Cole slid his hands beneath the hem of her nightgown, smoothing his palms along her thighs until he encountered the silken skin of her buttocks. He raised his head. "You're not wearing any panties," he growled in delight.

She arched against him. "Nope," she agreed wickedly, and unsnapped his jeans. "Maybe we can make some memories of our own under this quilt."

"With pleasure," Cole rasped, and captured her mouth in a soft kiss.

* * * * *

Or fill in the form below and post it back to us

THE MILLS & BOON® BOOK CLUB™—HERE'S HOW IT WORKS: Accepting your free books places you under no obligation to buy anything. You may keep the books and return the despatch note marked 'Cancel'. If we do not hear from you, about a month later we'll send you 4 brand-new stories from the Blaze® series, including a 2-in-1 book priced at £5.49 and two single books priced at £3.49* each. There is no extra charge for post and packaging. You may cancel at any time, otherwise we will send you 4 stories a month which you may purchase or return to us—the choice is yours. *Terms and prices subject to change without notice. Offer valid in UK only. Applicants must be 18 or over. Offer expires 31st July 2013. **For full terms and conditions, please go to www.millsandboon.co.uk/freebookoffer**

Mrs/Miss/Ms/Mr (please circle)
_____

First Name
_____

Surname
_____

Address
_____

_____

                                                        Postcode
_____

E-mail

Send this completed page to: Mills & Boon Book Club, Free Book Offer, FREEPOST NAT 10298, Richmond, Surrey, TW9 1BR

Find out more at
www.millsandboon.co.uk/freebookoffer

Visit us Online

0113/K3XEb